ELEKTRA

ALSO BY JENNIFER SAINT

Ariadne

ELEKTRA

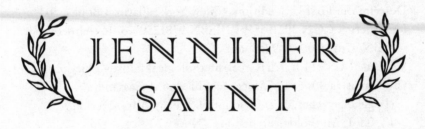

JENNIFER SAINT

FLATIRON
BOOKS
NEW YORK

This is a work of fiction. All of the characters, organizations, and events
portrayed in this novel are either products of the author's imagination
or are used fictitiously.

ELEKTRA. Copyright © 2022 by Jennifer Saint. All rights reserved.
Printed in the United States of America. For information,
address Flatiron Books, 120 Broadway, New York, NY 10271.

www.flatironbooks.com

Designed by Devan Norman

Library of Congress Cataloging-in-Publication Data

Names: Saint, Jennifer, author.
Title: Elektra / Jennifer Saint.
Description: First U.S. edition. | New York : Flatiron Books, 2022.
Identifiers: LCCN 2021055593 | ISBN 9781250773616 (hardcover) |
    ISBN 9781250773609 (ebook)
Subjects: LCSH: Electra (Greek mythological figure)—Fiction. |
Clytemnestra, Queen of Mycenae—Fiction. | Cassandra
    (Legendary character)—Fiction. | Trojan War—Fiction. |
    LCGFT: Mythological fiction. | Novels.
Classification: LCC PR6119.A359 E44 2022 | DDC 823/.92—dc23/
    eng/20211119
LC record available at https://lccn.loc.gov/2021055593

Our books may be purchased in bulk for promotional, educational, or busi-
ness use. Please contact your local bookseller or the Macmillan Corporate and
Premium Sales Department at 1-800-221-7945, extension 5442, or by email at
MacmillanSpecialMarkets@macmillan.com.

First U.S. Edition: 2022

10 9 8 7 6 5 4 3 2 1

For Alex

I know my own passion, it escapes me not . . . But never will I cease from sore lament, while I look on the trembling rays of the bright stars, or on this light of day . . . For if the hapless dead is to lie in dust and nothingness, while the slayers pay not with blood for blood, all regard for man, all fear of heaven, will vanish from the earth.

—"ELEKTRA,"
THE TRAGEDIES OF SOPHOCLES, TRANSLATED
BY RICHARD CLAVERHOUSE JEBB, 1904

PROLOGUE

Elektra

Mycenae is silent, but I can't sleep tonight. Down the corridor, I know that my brother will have kicked away his blankets. Every morning when I go in to rouse him, he has them in a wild tangle about his legs as though he has been running a race in his sleep. Maybe he runs after our father, the man he has never met.

When I was born, it was our father who named me. He named me for the sun: fiery and incandescent. He'd told me that when I was a little girl: that I was the light of our family. "Your aunt's beauty is famed, but you're far more radiant than her already. You'll bring more glory to the House of Atreus, my daughter." And then he'd kiss me on my forehead before he set me down. I didn't mind the tickle of his beard. I believed what he said.

Now, I don't care about the lack of suitors clamoring in our throne room for me. I've heard the stories about my aunt Helen, and have never felt envy. Look at where her beauty led her. All the way to a foreign city that has held our men for ten years. Ten years that I have lived without my father, clinging to every victory related to us by messengers who pass through Mycenae. News of each triumph gives me a surge of pride, of elation, that it is my father, Agamemnon, who has fought for so long, and who rallies his men to fight on until the towering walls of Troy crumble into rubble before them.

I see it all the time, in my mind's eye. How he will storm the gates of the city; how they will fall cowering at his feet at last. And after it all, he will come home to me. His loyal daughter, waiting here for him as year after year passes.

I know that some people will say he never loved his children, that he couldn't have, given what he did. But I remember the feel of his arms around me and the steady beat of his heart against my ear, and I know there will never be a safer place in this world for me than that.

I have always wanted to grow up to be the woman he thought I would become, the woman I could have been, if only he had been able to stay. To live up to the name he gave me.

More than anything else, I want to make him proud.

Somewhere in this palace, I have no doubt that my mother will be wandering, staring out into the distant dark. She is always noiseless, her soft feet cushioned in delicate sandals, her hair bound back with crimson ribbons, scented with crushed petals and perfumed oils, her polished skin gleaming in the moonlight. I won't leave my chamber and risk encountering her. Instead, I rise and walk toward the narrow window cut into the stone. I expect to see nothing when I rest my elbows on the sill and lean out: nothing, except perhaps a smattering of stars. But as I watch, I see a beacon burst into flame up on a distant mountaintop, and, in answer, another light, and then another, in a chain of fire that leaps toward Mycenae. My heart pounds in my chest. Someone out there is sending us a signal. And there is only one thing that all of us are united in waiting to hear.

A flutter of orange sparks spirals into the sky as another beacon lights, closer still. Tears start in my eyes. As I watch the beacons in disbelief, I feel a spark ignite within me, the dazzling realization of what this means.

Troy has fallen.

My father is coming home.

PART
I

CHAPTER ONE

Clytemnestra

The House of Atreus carried a curse. A particularly gruesome one, even by the standards of divine torment. The history of the family was full of brutal murder, adultery, monstrous ambition, and rather more cannibalism than one would expect. Everyone knew of it, but when the Atreidae, Agamemnon and Menelaus, stood before me and my twin sister in Sparta a lifetime ago, well, the silly stories of infants cooked and served up to their parents seemed to shimmer and crumble like dust motes in sunlight.

The two brothers were full of vitality and vigor—not handsome, exactly, but compelling, nonetheless. Menelaus' beard glinted with a reddish tint, while Agamemnon's was dark, like the curls that clustered tightly around his head. Far more handsome suitors stood before my sister—indeed, the great hall in which they gathered seemed to swell and groan with the sheer volume of sculpted cheekbones and fine shoulders, jutting jawbones and flashing eyes. She had her pick of the finest men in Greece, but Helen had eyes only for the awkward Menelaus, who shifted his powerful bulk uncomfortably and stared mutely back at her.

Daughter of Zeus, that's what the stories said of Helen. While I was born red-faced and squalling from the commonplace indignity of childbirth, my sister supposedly tapped her way delicately through a pure white eggshell and hatched whole and beautiful. The legend was adorned with fanciful details—it was well known that Zeus could adopt many forms, and on this particular occasion he had appeared to our mother feathered and snowy white, gliding down the river toward her with unmistakable purpose.

To be blessed by Zeus in such a way was a thing of glory. That's what everyone said. If Leda, our mother, had been deemed lovely enough by the ruler of the gods himself, it was a great honor to our family. It was not a disgrace to our father to raise the product of such a union himself.

And Helen's beauty was legendary indeed.

They had gathered at our home in their dozens, these suitors of Helen. How they jostled one another, surging forward, peering at her fluttering veil, eager for a glimpse of the woman named the most beautiful in the world. As the mood shifted, became restive, I noticed how their hands hovered closer to the swords at their hips. Helen noticed it too and turned to me briefly, just long enough for our eyes to meet and a moment of concern to dart between us.

At the edges of the hall, our guards stood straighter and gripped their spears a little tighter. I wondered, though, how quickly the boiling heart of the crowd might spill toward us, and how long it would take the guards to fight their way through the tumult.

Our father, Tyndareus, wrung his hands. The day had started out so promisingly for him; our storerooms overflowed with the rich gifts each young man had brought to support his own cause. I had seen him gloat over the loot and the status this glorious day had brought him. Blithely, he had placed all of his confidence in the ability of our brawny brothers to protect us as they had always done, but I had to doubt even their proficiency against the number of men who had come here to win my sister today.

I looked at Penelope. Our quiet, gray-eyed cousin could always be relied upon to keep a cool head. But Penelope did not return my frantic stare, for she was intent upon Odysseus. The two of them gazed into each other's eyes as though they wandered alone across a fragrant meadow, rather than being trapped in a hall with a hundred fraying tempers and the spark about to be struck to light them all into flame.

I rolled my eyes. Odysseus was here as one of Helen's suitors just like the rest of them, but of course nothing that man did was as it seemed. *We could rather do with his famous wits in this situation*, I thought, frustrated that he instead preferred to lose himself in some romantic daydream.

But what I had mistaken for a dreamy exchange of glances between my cousin and her lover was actually the silent formation of a plan, for Odysseus bounded up onto the platform where we sat and shouted for order. Although he was short and bandy-legged, his was a commanding presence, and the hall fell silent at once.

"Before the lady Helen makes her choice," he boomed, "we will all swear an oath."

They listened to him. He had a gift for bending the will of others to his own purpose. Even my clever cousin was enthralled by him, and I had thought no man's intellect could ever be a match for hers.

"We have all come here today for the same purpose," he continued. "We all wish to wed the beautiful Helen, and we all have good reason to think that we are a worthy husband to such a woman. She is a prize beyond any that we can imagine, and the man who can call her his own will have to go to great lengths to protect her from those who would seek to seize her away from him."

I could see that every man in the room was imagining it. They had all envisaged being the one to have her, but Odysseus had soured the dream. They gazed up at him, enrapt, waiting for him to reveal the solution to the conundrum he had presented.

"So, I propose that we all swear that, no matter whom she chooses, we will all join him in protecting her. We will all make a most solemn vow that we shall defend his right to have her—and keep her—with our own lives."

Our father leaped up, overjoyed that Odysseus had saved his triumphant day from almost certain disaster. "I will sacrifice my finest horse!" he declared. "And you shall all make your promise to the gods upon its blood."

And so it was done, and all our father lost that day was a horse. Well, a horse and his daughter, I should say, and a niece as well, to make it quite the bargain. All were taken off his hands in one fell swoop, for Helen had only to breathe the name "Menelaus" before he was up, clasping her hand in his and stammering out his gratitude and devotion; Odysseus offered for Penelope in almost the next breath; but my eye was caught by the dark-haired brother, whose surly gaze stayed fixed upon the stone tiles. Agamemnon.

⸙⸙⸙⸙⸙

"Why did you choose Menelaus?" I asked Helen later. A flurry of handmaidens encircled her, draping her dress, braiding her hair into elaborate swirls, and making countless tiny adornments that were entirely unnecessary.

Helen considered my question before she answered. People only ever spoke of her dazzling radiance, sometimes moved to poetry or song in praise of it. No one ever mentioned that she was thoughtful or that she was kind. I could not deny the odd pang of envy that had reared up inside me, cold and poisonous, growing up alongside a twin whose magnificence would always throw me into shadow. But Helen had never been cruel to me or tormented me. She had never boasted about her beauty or mocked her inferior sister. She could not help that heads would swivel to gaze wherever she walked any more than she could turn the tides of the sea. I had made my peace with it, and, to be truthful, I didn't yearn to bear the weight of her legendary allure.

"Menelaus . . ." Helen said meditatively, lingering over the syllables of his name. She shrugged, twisting a smooth curl of hair around her fingers, to the visible annoyance of one of the handmaidens, whose fussing ministrations had produced nothing like the bounce and gleam that Helen's effortless coiffing did. "Perhaps there were others richer or more handsome," she said. "Bolder, certainly." She curled her lip slightly, maybe thinking of the undercurrent of violence that had throbbed invisibly around the hall as the suitors eyed one another. "But Menelaus . . . he seemed different."

She did not need treasure; Sparta was wealthy enough as it was. She did not need good looks; she could provide all the beauty in any partnership. Any man was eager to be her husband, as we had seen. So, what was it that my sister had been looking for? I wondered how she knew, what magic had sparked between them, what it was that made a woman sure that a particular man was the right one. I sat up straighter, waiting to be enlightened.

"I suppose . . ." she breathed out as a girl handed her an ivory-handled mirror, the back of which was ornately carved with a tiny figure of Aphrodite emerging from her great shell. She flicked her eyes over her reflection, tossed back her hair, and adjusted the gold circlet that rested atop her curls. I heard a faint sigh go up from the clustered girls who awaited her judgment on their unnecessary efforts. "I suppose," she continued as she bestowed a smile upon them, "that he was simply so very *grateful*."

I paused, the words I had sought evaporating on the air.

Helen noticed my silence, perhaps read some reproval in it, for she straightened her shoulders and fixed me directly in her gaze. "You know that our mother was singled out by Zeus," she said. "A mortal woman beautiful enough to catch his eye from the peak of Mount Olympus. If our father were not of a quiet and uncomplaining disposition . . . who knows how he may have felt? If he were more like Agamemnon than Menelaus, for example."

I stiffened a little. What did that mean?

"A man like that doesn't look like he would take any affront without protest," she continued. "Would he see the honor in his wife being chosen, or would he see it differently? I don't know what my destiny might be, but I know that I was not born to do nothing. I don't know what the Fates have planned for me, but it seemed"—she searched for the right word—"*prudent* to make my choice carefully."

I thought of Menelaus, the adoration in his eyes when he looked at Helen. I wondered if she was right, if he'd be able to see things the way our father had done. If winning the contest in our halls really would be victory enough, whatever might happen later.

"And of course, this way I can stay in Sparta," she added.

For this, I really was thankful. "So, is it agreed? You will live here together?"

"Menelaus can help Father with the ruling of Sparta," Helen said. "And, of course, Father can help him in return."

"How?"

"How much do you know about him and Agamemnon?" Helen asked. "And Mycenae?"

I shook my head. "I've heard stories about the family. The same ones as you. The curse of their ancestors, fathers killing their sons and brothers turning on each other. It's all in the past, though, isn't it?"

"Not entirely." Helen waved away the girls around her and leaned in confidentially. I felt a little thrill. "They came here from Calydon, you know."

I nodded.

"But that's not their home; they've stayed there with the king. He gave them hospitality, but he couldn't give them what they really need—what Father can."

"What's that?"

She smiled, delighted to be the one to impart something exciting. "An army."

"Really? What for?"

"To take back Mycenae." Helen tossed her head. "They're taking what's theirs. Their uncle killed their father and exiled them when they were children. Now they're men, and they have the support of Sparta."

I knew that much of the story. Menelaus and Agamemnon were sons of Atreus, whose brother, Thyestes, had murdered him for the throne and cast them out. I suppose he had just enough mercy not to want the blood of children on his hands. That was the crime for which their family had been cursed by the gods generations before: the crime of Tantalus.

Perhaps it isn't surprising that Helen is intrigued by Menelaus, I thought. The old legend of the family was one we'd heard before, a grisly story that chilled the blood but seemed so distant from reality. Now it was a step closer—two brothers seeking justice, healing the wounds of a tortured family with one final act.

"Won't Menelaus want to go back to Mycenae, then?" I asked.

"No, Agamemnon will take Mycenae," Helen said. "Menelaus is happy to be here."

So, Menelaus would get the prize of Helen and Agamemnon would have the city. No doubt that seemed a fair bargain to them both.

"It's just a question of what they do about the boy."

"Which boy?"

"Aegisthus," Helen said. "The son of Thyestes—just a boy, like they were when Thyestes killed their father."

"Won't they exile him too?"

Helen raised an eyebrow. "And let him grow up like they did? Nurturing the same dreams that they did? Agamemnon won't want to risk it."

I shuddered. "He won't want to kill a little boy, though, surely?" I could understand the brutal logic of it, but I couldn't bring myself to picture the young men I'd seen in that hall plunging a sword into a weeping child.

"Maybe not." Helen stood up, smoothing out her dress. "But let's not talk about war any longer. It's my wedding day, after all."

⁓⁓⁓

Later, I slipped away from the celebrations. They would go on all night, I was sure, hours still to come of feasting and drinking, but I was tired and felt strangely flat. I wasn't in the mood to dodge the increasingly drunken nobility of Sparta; the usually stern and severe military generals becoming red-faced and loose-tongued, their clumsy hands groping out like the tentacles of an octopus. All were puffed up with self-congratulation at the alliance and the oath sworn by all the important men of Greece to defend Menelaus' prize. Their loyalty was bound to Sparta.

I walked to the riverbank. Wide and lazy, the Eurotas wound its way through our city to the distant southern harbor, which was the only way any foreign invaders could reach us. To the other sides, the great mountains of Taygetus and Parnon towered west and east, while the northern uplands were equally impenetrable to any army. We were snug in our valley, protected and fortified against any who might come intent on sacking us for the wealth and lovely women that gave us our fame. And now the loveliest of them all had a waiting army ready to rise up in her honor against any possible enemy. No wonder the men relaxed and drank deeply tonight.

Beacons burned across the valley, bright flames in the darkness proclaiming the momentous importance of the day. Smoke would be rising from every shrine, carrying the savor of the pure white bullocks whose throats had been slit, taking it up to the Olympians through the black skies.

I had noticed that Agamemnon alone held himself apart from the celebrations. No doubt he was preoccupied by the impending invasion of Mycenae. And Helen's new husband would be gone within days, off to fight alongside his brother. They had an army, and I knew that Spartan soldiers were renowned for their skill and ferocity. There was little to worry about. But it was there, in the back of my mind, the sneaking, treacherous worm of a thought. If the battle didn't go in favor of the brothers, if they didn't come back, then nothing would have to change. Helen and I could go on a little longer, as we'd always been.

I shook my head, as though I could dislodge the idea altogether. It would all change, even more so. A hundred men had come to marry her; the next one would take Menelaus' place in an instant.

And then I saw him, half hidden in the shadows.

His head turned at the same moment, and our eyes met. I saw his surprise and confusion, a mirror of mine.

"I didn't realize anyone else was out here," he said, making to withdraw.

"Why aren't you inside?" I asked. I hadn't spoken a word to Agamemnon so far, and I certainly shouldn't be starting a private conversation with him, unseen in the darkness, away from everyone else. But something about the stillness of the night, the shouts of laughter drifting over from within the palace, the feeling I had that everything we'd known so far was about to come to an end, one way or another, made me reckless.

He hesitated.

"Don't you want to celebrate with your brother?"

His heavy brows were drawn together. He looked wary and unwilling to speak.

I sighed, suddenly impatient. "Or will you wait until after you've conquered Mycenae?"

"What do you know about that?"

I felt a little victory in having prompted him to reply. A breeze rippled across the water, and I felt a yearning all at once for something I couldn't name. So much was happening—weddings and war—and none of it involved me. "I know what Thyestes did," I answered, "to your father and to you. How he stole your kingdom."

He nodded curtly. I could see he was about to walk away, go back inside.

"But what will you do about the boy?" I asked.

Agamemnon looked at me incredulously. "The boy?"

"Thyestes' son," I said. "Will you let him go?"

"What does it have to do with you?"

I wondered if I'd gone too far, if I'd genuinely shocked him. Everything about this conversation was wrong. But I'd started it now. "It's a Spartan army that you're taking with you. Whatever you do, it's in Sparta's name too."

"Your father's army. Menelaus' army."

"It just seems wrong."

"To you. It can be dangerous, though, to let a son grow up with vengeance in his heart." He was looking out over the river, his whole stance radiating discomfort, but he glanced back at me briefly. "There is a curse on my family; it has to be ended."

"Can it be ended like that? What if it angers the gods more?"

He shook his head, dismissing my words. "You want to be merciful," he said. "You're a woman. But war is the business of men."

I bristled at that. "You have Sparta," I said. "You'll take Mycenae. And all those men in the hall, all the fighters and rulers and princes who came for my sister, they all just swore loyalty to your brother. You have a chance to unite so many kingdoms together behind you. The power will belong to you—so how could one boy be a threat, however vengeful he grows up to be? What could he do to you? With so many at your command, surely you could be the greatest of all the Greeks."

That caught his attention. "An interesting point," he mused. "The greatest of all the Greeks. Thank you, Clytemnestra."

And then I saw it, just before he stepped back between the columns, back toward the sounds of revelry from within the palace. Just the flicker of a smile, curving his stern mouth at last.

CHAPTER TWO

Cassandra

Every word I speak is unwelcome. My throat is raw from the words that are torn from me when I touch someone, when I look into their eyes and see the blinding white truth. My prophecies rip out my insides, but still they come, unbidden, even as I quake at the consequences. My listeners curse me, they chase me away, they say I am mad, and they laugh.

But when I was a child, I could not tell the future. I was preoccupied only with the concerns of the now; with my most treasured doll and how best to adorn her—for even she could be swathed in the richest of fabrics and bedecked with tiny jewels. My parents were Priam and Hecabe, king and queen of Troy, and our luxuries were legendary.

My mother, however, had visions. A blinding flash of knowledge, bestowed no doubt by one of the many gods who smiled upon us and helped us avert misfortune. Perhaps even Apollo himself, for he was said to love my mother as one of his chosen favorites. She bore my father many children, and he was granted many more by his concubines. When her belly swelled with yet another, we readied ourselves for a familiar joy. When the time came for the baby to be born, my mother settled herself to sleep, anticipating as usual pleasant dreams of what this new child would be.

Not this time. A child of seven, I was roused by shrieks that tore apart the night and chilled my small bones to their marrow. I rushed in to where she crouched, her midwives hurtling down the corridors in fear that something was horribly awry.

Although the sweat plastered her hair to her forehead and she panted like a hunted animal, it was not the pains of labor that tormented her. Pushing away the helpful hands that sought to soothe her through the birth that was not upon her after all, she cried with a hollow desolation, the like of which I had never heard in my cosseted little life.

I shrank back. The room was busy, confused with the chaos of women, and I hovered uncertainly in the shadows cast by the thin torches that the women lit. The narrow orange flames flickered and twisted, and, on the stone walls, monstrous dark shapes cavorted grotesquely with their snaking rhythm.

"The baby," my mother was gasping, and the violence of the passion that had seized her initially seemed to be ebbing away. She allowed the women's ministrations, but as they eased her back onto her couch, softly assuring her that the baby was not coming and that all was well, she shook her head and tears streaked across her face. The dark hollows below her eyes and the stringy tendrils of hair made her look not like my mother.

"I saw him—saw him born," she was rasping, but as the women murmured that it was only a dream and nothing to cause concern, I saw her imperial dignity returning. She silenced them all with a wave of her arm. "My dreams," she went on, "are not just dreams. It is known."

A hush fell over the chamber. I did not move. The stone wall at my back chilled my flesh, but I stayed frozen against it. At the firelit center of this eerie circle, my mother spoke again.

"I pushed him into the world like the babies I have borne before him. I felt the burning of my flesh once more, and I knew this pain and that I could bear it again, like I have done before. Only it was different this time—the burning, it felt . . ." She paused, and I saw her knuckles tighten as she twisted her fingers together. "The blaze of his birth, it burned longer and more fiercely than any I could imagine. I felt the blistering of my skin and I smelled my own flesh charred and blackened." She swallowed, a harsh sound in the silence. "He was no baby; he was a torch like one that you hold, his head a roaring flame, and all about me was smoke, consuming everything."

I felt the tension, the growing tide of anxiety in the chamber. The women's eyes flickered to the mound of my mother's belly.

"Perhaps it was only a dream," one of them ventured. "Many women fear the birth; bad dreams are not uncommon at this time—"

"I have borne a dozen babies," my mother snapped. Her dark eyes fixed on the unfortunate speaker. "I have no fear of the birth of another. But this . . . I cannot know if it is a baby at all."

Horror seeped into the room. The women's eyes flicked one to the other, searching for an answer.

"Aesacus!" One of the women spoke decisively, her voice reverberating sharp and sudden off the stone. "The seer. We will ask the seer to interpret your dream, Queen Hecabe. Perhaps, in such a time as this, the true meaning of your dream is hidden even from you. We will ask Aesacus, and he will tell us what it signifies."

Nodding; murmurs of agreement around the room. Anything, it seemed, the women wanted anything that would leach the blank shock from their queen's eyes. Any chance that the seer could change what she had seen in her vision.

He was summoned to the throne room. The women draped a dress about my mother's swollen body and guided her from her chambers. No one paid any mind to me, so I followed them there in time to watch as she took her throne beside my father, who had been roused from his bed, his face creased with anguished concern. He held my mother's hand in his as Aesacus came forward.

The seer's face was smooth and blank. His age should have carved his skin with wrinkles, but instead it stretched across his skull, thin and papery. His eyes were milky, a film obscuring what color they had once had. I wondered how he saw through the murk, but perhaps it did not matter to him if the physical world was blurred, for he saw the world beyond it with crystal clarity.

My mother explained the dream to him again. She had mastered herself, and there was scarcely a crack in her voice to give away her strain.

The seer listened. When she fell silent, he did not speak. All eyes were fixed upon him as he crossed the great hall. From a stone shelf, he took down one of the bronze bowls of fire that lit the cavernous room and placed it on the ground. Resinous wood burned within it, casting a flickering glow across the painted scenes on the wall behind, turning the wolves that adorned the fresco into prowling monsters. Aesacus prodded the flames with his staff, pushing the wood over the leaping mouth of the fire until it hissed out, a wisp of gray smoke pluming from the dying embers. His face was shadowed. As I watched him, a breeze whispered through the stone columns and stirred the ashes in the bottom of the bowl.

The ashes settled. I thought of my mother's dream: the baby with a burning head of fire. The seer's expressionless face as he suffocated the flames.

"This prince will destroy the city," he said. His voice was soft, like an echo spiraling from the depths of a cave, but so very cold. "If he is allowed to grow up, I see Troy consumed by fire, a fire he is destined to start. The child must not live."

No one questioned him. It seemed that he confirmed what Hecabe knew already; the reason she had woken screaming from the nightmare. And after all, this baby would be one of many sons born to Priam, with plenty of daughters besides. To lose one of so many children and save his city from ruin might seem to be a price worth paying.

Neither my father nor my mother could bring themselves to pay it, though. When my brother Paris was born, they could not bear to fling that tiny baby from the high walls of Troy, or to smother him with a fine piece of cloth, or even to lay him down on the empty mountainside and walk away. They gave him to a shepherd instead; told him to leave the child to be taken by the cold night air or the ravening teeth and claws of whatever wild animal might be passing.

I wonder if they told the shepherd why he was to do it. If he knew the future of Troy depended on the hardening of his heart to that mewling, pitiful cry. I wonder if he tried; if he set the baby down on the scrubby hillside, if he took a step and then another before he turned around. Did he look at Paris' tiny nose, his bald head, his soft arms reaching out for comfort, and dismiss the words of the seer as superstition and nonsense? How could a baby bring down a city, he might have wondered. Perhaps his wife was barren, their home never blessed with children. Perhaps he thought that if he kept Paris outside the city walls and raised him as nothing more than a herder of goats, Troy would be safe. Its great stone towers, its mighty oak gates bolted with iron, its wealth and power must have seemed impervious to harm.

My brother lived in secret. He grew from defenseless infant to young man and none of us dreamed of his existence on the mountains outside Troy. No one spoke again of Hecabe's nightmare, and that whole night would have taken on the quality of a dream itself, except that I remembered the scrape of stone against my back as I edged away from Aesacus. I could not forget the milky film that streaked his eyes, and the scent of smoke. The pity I felt for that soft little bundle that days later I saw carried from Hecabe's chamber by a weeping slave, mixed with the relief that my mother had dreamed no such dreams about me.

I did try to talk to her about it once, long after it had happened. My voice was timid, and I could see that my hesitancy irritated her. I was curious about her dream, what quality it had to make her trust the seer so readily, what magic it had to make her know it was the truth. I suppose it was insensitive, looking back, but I was wrapped in the selfishness of youth, and I wanted to know.

"You weren't there, Cassandra," she snapped. The instant dismissal wounded me, and a flush bloomed in my cheeks. I only felt the recoil of my own pain, not a thought for what I was asking her to remember as I pushed on, eager to understand.

"I was," I protested. "I remember Aesacus and the fire—I remember what he said."

"What? Speak up, girl," she commanded. She hated how quiet my voice was. As a child, I rarely made it through a sentence without being told to start it again and say it more loudly, more clearly.

No one ever asks me to repeat myself now.

I tried, haltingly, to describe the room and the rituals of the seer, but she shook her head sharply. "Nonsense, Cassandra, another of your imaginings," she said. Her tone stung. I think she noticed the hurt stamped across my face because she softened then, put her arm around my shoulders and squeezed me briefly. She spoke more gently. "It was not like that at all. Aesacus took my dream to the oracle, and he heard the prophecy there. Your mind has run away with you again. You must learn to hold back the wilder excesses of your imagination. Perhaps if you spent less time alone . . ."

"Apollo only comes to you when you're alone, doesn't he?"

She drew back and looked hard at me.

I squirmed a little, unused to such scrutiny.

"Is that what you want?" she asked.

The note of doubt in her voice rattled me. Why would anyone not want it? If you could see into the future, know what was going to happen, if you could protect yourself against it—why did she make it sound as though it would be absurd to want such a gift? "It's just— I'm your daughter, if the gods send visions to you, I wondered if they might—if I might . . ." I trailed off, thrown by the worry writ across her face.

"The gods act as they do according to reasons we cannot know," she said. "Apollo loves Troy, I am the queen—any vision that comes from the god is for the good of the city. It isn't a gift to me; it isn't something I sought out. It isn't for us to ask for such a thing."

I felt shame spread through me. She was the queen of Troy; I would never be. I had older brothers who would rule our city and the wife of whichever of them became king would take my mother's place. Perhaps this woman would receive the queen's visions then, the dreams Apollo sent for the greater good of Troy. I felt so small and so stupid that I wished I could disappear. "I didn't mean—" I began, but my mother was shaking her head. The conversation was over without me knowing how to say what I'd meant in the first place.

"Go and play, Cassandra," she said firmly, and I went.

But no one wanted me near, not really. All the other girls seemed so sure, so certain of themselves. I felt like a reed swaying in the wind, never daring to say what I thought aloud, not wanting to face scorn or laughter. Hecabe's dream, though, and the seer—that I was certain of. Perhaps she preferred to remember it differently, but I would never forget that night; it was seared into my very bones.

I could never make myself understood, even then, and my mother was a busy woman. She had no time to try to understand me. If she had seen what I was to become, seen a vision of me and not just Paris, I feel sure she would have hurled my infant form onto the rocks herself. But no one peered into ashes to divine my future. No one intervened to try to stop me from becoming what I became.

CHAPTER THREE

Clytemnestra

While the Atreidae were gone, I was consumed with restlessness. The days, which had always been so easy to fill, now seemed to drag, especially the afternoons.

Penelope was gone already to the rocks and goats of Ithaca with Odysseus. But Helen remained, and we had passed the previous sixteen years together companionably enough. I couldn't see what had changed. I supposed it was the flurry of excitement there had been for a time: the arrival of the Atreidae at our shores to seek our hospitality, then the gathering of Helen's suitors, and, of course, the weddings of both my cousin and my twin. Perhaps things were bound to feel a little flat after all that was done.

Becoming a wife hadn't changed my sister. She seemed remarkably unperturbed by her husband's absence, and it frustrated me that it was I who seemed to fret the most with the brothers on their way to Mycenae to topple their usurping uncle.

"Sparta's finest men are at their back," Helen said, dismissing my worries as she lay in the sunshine by the river, shading her eyes from the white glare of light reflected on the water. "They will return victorious soon enough."

"Don't you worry for Menelaus, though?" I propped myself up on my elbow to look at her. "Thyestes has soldiers; he took the throne from Atreus. He will try to defend it. What if Menelaus is killed?"

I wanted to see the smooth skin of her forehead wrinkle, to see consternation in her laughing eyes. I loved my sister more than anything, and had she come to me to say she feared for Menelaus' life, I would have gone to any lengths to reassure her. But her serenity annoyed me, especially in comparison to my own rumpled state of mind, and I was desperate all at once to see her crack.

She only smiled. "He will return," she said. "I have no doubt."

I slumped back down. The sun shone too brightly and the mountains that ringed us on three sides seemed suddenly to press too close. I shut my eyes. I longed for it to be evening, for the endless afternoon to finally be over. Once night fell, I knew I would yearn for dawn.

"And when the brothers do come back," she said, a teasing note in her voice, "do you know that Father has plans for you and Agamemnon?"

She had no fear in asking her questions directly. Her charm was in her openness, her daring, and nothing she said ever seemed too impertinent or shocking. Perhaps it was the laughter that always bubbled in the back of her voice and the sparkle in her eyes that made everything she said seem light and airy. She never feared a rebuff or a sharp word. She certainly never minded prodding me.

I picked up a pebble from the riverbank. Its smooth curves fitted neatly into my palm, and I turned it over and over. "I hope he and Menelaus right the injustice that has been done to them." I hadn't told her about the odd, abrupt conversation I'd had with Agamemnon out by the river on the night of her wedding. There had never been a topic of conversation off-limits between us, but she was a married woman, and I was still a girl. I felt an unaccustomed shyness.

"Go on," she coaxed. "What do you think of him?"

With Penelope and Helen wed in such quick succession, I knew it was only a matter of time before Tyndareus found a husband for me. He was a benevolent father, happy to let Helen have her choice, and I had never feared the day in my future when he would speak of my marriage. My sister and my cousin seemed satisfied with their lot, and I had always expected to feel the same. But now, when I thought of a visiting prince arriving in our halls for me, I no longer felt that pleasant fizz of anticipation. What if I were to be taken to a far-off land, somewhere strange and removed from everything I had known? What if this man did not care about what I thought and said, only about my birth and blood and the wealth my father could give him?

Agamemnon and his brother had a glamour about them, I couldn't deny it, arriving from their unjust exile and heading off bravely to take back what belonged to them.

Also, Helen had chosen Menelaus from a hundred men. If she were happy with him, perhaps I could trust that I might find the same with his brother. It would be better than pinning my faith on the kindness of an unknown stranger, surely?

"Just think," she went on, "how nice it would be if we sisters were married to brothers."

I watched the river flowing on, out to sea. I didn't have Helen's confidence that the future would always be as sunny as the past.

But what if Father's plans didn't come to anything? I pictured my future then. Would every afternoon stretch on like this one, a monotonous roll of days until a different suitor stepped off a ship and offered for me?

Helen had unleashed a flood of questions in my mind. I scanned the winding sweep of the river down to the distant southern harbor every day, waiting for the sight of the brothers' ship.

The weeks rolled by, until at last, one morning, the shout went up and echoed the length of the river as the watchmen called out from post to post. "The Atreidae have returned!"

Helen and I exchanged a quick, panicked glance, my self-possessed sister unbalanced for a moment. We hurried to the palace gates to wait for them, and she caught my hand in hers.

And then there they were, striding along the river toward us. The sun glinted off the reddish tints of Menelaus' hair, and I was reminded of the first time we had met. Except that now, Agamemnon did not glower at the floor, but looked up toward us, his face open and clear.

The reunion of Helen and Menelaus was a joyous one and I stood back from their embrace. Our father was close behind us, taking Agamemnon's hand, a flurry of words and welcome and congratulations abounding.

Agamemnon's face was transformed. No seriousness, no scowling. It was quite the difference to see him with the weight shrugged from his shoulders. "Thyestes is dead," he said, a note of quiet exultation running through his words. "But his son, Aegisthus, lives." He glanced at me as he spoke. "The gods can be pleased that no innocent blood was spilled."

Perhaps that was it. The curse that plagued his family, lifted at last. Perhaps that explained the difference in him.

My imagination had been given free rein while he had been away. Now he stood before me in the flesh. Perhaps a trifle shorter than I had remembered, the set of his features a little heavier. Still, the lightening of his spirits had worked wonders. He didn't have the fine nose and jawline that a sculptor would long to carve in marble, but he put me in mind of a bearskin my brother had brought back once from hunting. He'd borne it home as testament to his prowess with its head intact, its face still frozen in a snarl, before it was cut into furs for Helen and me to nestle in through the chill of winter nights. Something about Agamemnon's bristled brows reminded me of it. Helen had been afraid of it, but I had been intrigued by the thought that it had so recently been roaming the mountains, wild and savage, and I could reach out a hand and stroke its fur.

Agamemnon's eyes flickered to mine again before my father moved between us, slinging his arm about Agamemnon's shoulder, urging him to come inside, promising fine wine and celebrations. Agamemnon's face stretched into a smile.

The men walked ahead—Menelaus reluctant to drop his wife's hand, but pulled along by my exuberant father—and Helen and I turned to follow. She pulled me close as we walked together, the perfume of her hair sweet and soft against my face, my uncertainties forgotten for the moment, obliterated by the triumph of their successful homecoming.

I suppose he was emboldened by victory, for he did not hesitate in finding me later that evening as the celebrations roared on. This time, he wasn't hiding in the shadows, but instead caught my arm with a lightness that felt almost playful as he invited me to walk out into the courtyard, away from the heat of the great hall.

I paused, not sure how best to demur. It was one thing to meet him alone outside by chance as we had before, but quite another to go with him to some secluded place on purpose. He saw my reluctance and leaned close. "Your father permits it."

I accompanied him. I supposed this was the moment, and I still did not know entirely what to say. Outside in the courtyard, the moon shone full and bright against the painted pillars.

"I will return to Mycenae tomorrow," he said.

I waited for him to go on. I had watched him through the evening as he drank and cheered with the rest of them, and I had wondered if there was anything different about him after all. I found that I quite missed his solemnity, the burden he had carried before. Maybe I didn't want a conquering hero shouting about his victory; I had rather preferred the tormented anguish of the exile.

"I hope." He cleared his throat. "I hope that if I send for you, you will come."

"To Mycenae?" I asked. "For what reason?"

The tips of his ears reddened beneath his thick, dark curls. "I said before I left that I could not look for a wife before I had reclaimed my throne," he said. "But now that I have—I've asked your father, and he is happy for us to marry."

I felt oddly calm, standing in the cool night air. I looked at this man standing before me, a king of his own city, born of an intriguing family, the brother of my sister's choice, and the man my father had chosen for me. *It could be worse*, I thought.

My father was eager to cement his alliances, and I felt all of Sparta hum with a contented buzz as the preparations for my departure to Mycenae got underway. I could see that Agamemnon and my father were in accord that their influence and power could only be strengthened by the friendship between Mycenae and Sparta; that the rest of Greece would surely bow to their combined might. It felt like the spread of the Peloponnese would belong to us.

"We will see each other again soon," Helen vowed as we held each other tightly on the creaking wooden deck.

Though I knew she sought to soothe herself, I could not help feeling the unlikelihood of her words. The distance was not far, but I knew our visits would be sparse. The great sprawling Arcadian mountains would tower between us. Besides, we had never been separated for as much as a day. Even if it were only months before we saw each other again, it was an unimaginable length of time.

The air was cool against my damp face as the sails flapped and bulged behind me. It would be speedy sailing, Agamemnon had assured me, for the winds were fair and on our side. I twisted my hands together, feeling the absence of Helen's fingers twined through mine as the cries of the oarsmen went up and the ship slowly set forth upon the white-tipped waves. I could read triumph in my father's face as he stood, stately and regal at the harbor, watching us go. Helen's face was hidden in Menelaus' shoulder, but as the oars sliced cleanly through the foam, she looked up at me and I saw her face shining, radiant and proud. I had grown so used to her beauty that I hardly noticed it anymore, until a moment like this when she would sweep away my breath in a heartbeat. Her smile was the last thing I saw as I hung over the wooden rails, waving frantically, undignified, in half laughter, half tears.

CHAPTER FOUR

Cassandra

I shifted uncomfortably from foot to foot as I waited, the rising steam from the hot water making my dress cling to my skin. My sister Laodice reclined luxuriously in her bath, her hair piled in curls on top of her head, her eyes dreamy, while the slaves darted about, intent on the preparations. My eyelids were heavy; I was tired from the late feast the night before and I longed to close them. We had been up at sunrise: our father had offered a pure white lamb for sacrifice to Hera, seeking her blessings for Laodice's marriage. There was still so much of the day to be done and already I longed for the quiet comfort of my own bed.

A tugging at my dress startled me. There was my sister, little Polyxena, her round cheeks flushed from the warmth, her big eyes fixed on the bath, intrigued by the novelty of the day. "What will the wedding be like?" she asked again, for at least the dozenth time.

I sighed, not wanting to explain it all again. "I don't know."

She pursed her lips, annoyed not to be indulged. "Why do people get married?" she tried.

"I definitely don't know."

My mother swept past, tutting as she went. "You'll know in good time, Cassandra," she said. "It'll be your turn soon."

I reddened. There was an abundance of princes and princesses of

Troy, and my parents had no need for me to provide any more grand-children, but still the prospect of a husband shadowed my future. My elder sister Ilione had married the year before. Now it was Laodice's turn, and I worried that her disappointed suitors might turn their attentions to me. Helicaon, Laodice's intended, seemed inoffensive, but that was the best I could say of him. The idea of spending a moment alone with him or any other man filled me with nothing but dread. I had none of my sisters' ease in conversation or charm. I was considered odd in general—quiet and awkward, and prone to striking a conversation dead.

A great bustle of activity commenced in getting Laodice out of her bath, dried, dressed, and veiled. I hung back, hoping I wouldn't be called on to offer any opinion.

I wasn't. I hovered at the fringes all day, watching the guests mingling freely, Laodice resplendent and beautiful, my mother and father proudly accepting congratulations. I felt sick picturing myself at the center of such a scene. The only peace I had felt all day was in the temple at dawn, scattering barley before the priest took up his knife.

I still coveted the hidden secret of my mother's dreams, even though the memory of that long-ago night repelled me. That was what I wanted; not a wedding, not a husband or children. And then it struck me. Apollo had the gift of prophecy; he might yet choose to bestow it on his most devoted followers. The service of Apollo was a noble calling. It would be a convenient route for an inconvenient daughter.

I made it known to Hecabe and Priam the very next day. They made no objection to my choice. The mighty sun-god's glorious, golden light made our city shimmer, for the city of Troy was as beloved by Apollo as he was by us. But it was not his radiance or his healing powers or even the melodious music of his lyre that I longed for when I burned the incense at his statue's feet or slit the throat of the sacrificial animals that bled in his honor. When I made my oath to become his priestess, I did not fear that terrible divine privilege of seeing what was to come. As a priestess, I would have no children of my own, no baby that

I might be forced to consign to a desolate mountainside, so I was not afraid of what he might show me. If I was gifted by him to see the kind of things that my mother saw—perhaps even more than her—then I might not hang my head and mumble; my voice would be, at last, clear and brave. If I could speak the will of the gods and see the very fabric of fate, I could command attention and respect. With all my heart, that was what I wanted. To be something other than myself; to speak in someone else's words instead of my own.

I was dutiful, I was devoted. I knew that Apollo would see me, his dedicated servant, at his temple every day, and I trusted I would be rewarded for my piety.

The day that it happened began like any other. I had no inkling of what was to come. I walked on the shore before dawn and then I came to the temple as I always did. I sang at his altar and hung flowers about the neck of the statue in its center, my head clouded by the fragranced oils burning in dishes and the rich aroma of the wine I poured to him. The silent peace of the dim interior was a sanctuary for me, a place of respite. The place I belonged more than anywhere else in Troy.

Light trickled through the soft smoke, melting into it like liquid, streams of gold that suffused the shadows, brightening the air wherever it touched. I couldn't see where it was coming from. I paused, my hand hovering above the petals I was about to sprinkle. And, as I looked around, I felt something stir: a breeze in the empty room, whispering over the nape of my neck.

The golden light steadily intensified, coalescing around a burning glow in the center of the room, so bright that I couldn't see anything else. Panic began rising in my chest and I put up my hand to shield my eyes, stepping back, groping for the doorway that should have been somewhere behind me.

And then, out of the light, he stepped forward. My hands dropped, hanging useless at my sides. There was nothing but his presence—his true, real presence—suffocating, overwhelming, dizzying in its intensity. It was impossible that he was truly there, but he was. Apollo, an Olympian god made flesh, beautiful and terrifying at once.

The burning light dissipated and there was only him, standing before me. The air was as fresh as a summer meadow, as warm as sunshine. "Cassandra," he said, and his voice was like the soft plucking of mellow strings, humming with poetry; nothing like a human voice.

I'd imagined that he would come to me in a dream, that he'd send me a message to interpret, something vague and cryptic. I had never thought he would come like this. I couldn't find my voice to speak. But then, why would I need to? He could see into my soul. He knew what I longed for; I'd prayed to his statue a hundred times.

He stepped closer. I was fixed in the center of his gaze, held fast as he moved, sinuous and snakelike, toward me. I shrank back, afraid that his touch would sear my skin, that he would turn my bones to ashes with the brush of his fingertips. He smiled. And then he seized my face between his hands and pressed his immortal lips to mine.

A chaos of images and a roar of indistinguishable sounds tumbled through my head, too fast, too loud to make sense. I couldn't stand, only his hands held me upright, but then he released his grip on me, and I staggered away, falling against the wall.

"You have it. My gift to you."

The stone was solid against my back; I clung to it, nauseated by the dizzying rush inside my mind. Faces, distorted and unrecognizable, pleading and grimacing, begging for answers, for knowledge. Radiant flashes flickering over them: a baby squinting in the sunlight; oars splashing in moonlit waters; flames leaping into the sky. I felt that my skull would shatter, that it would rain down in fragments. He had breathed it into me; a gift I was sure I would not survive. Prophecy, the prize my mother had warned me never to ask for.

And then his face was against mine again and I wanted to scream, but I couldn't make a sound. His fingers moved to unfasten the ribbons that held my hair, to slide down the bare skin of my arms, to the bronze clasp at my shoulder that held my robes, the sacred robes of Apollo's virgin priestess. His gift was not free. I realized the price he wanted to take.

I was frozen, confused and terrified. Only one thought was coherent in my mind. That in becoming a priestess of his temple, I had given myself, pure and untouched. I knew what would happen to me if I broke the oath of virginity, even if it was to lie with Apollo himself. I would be cast out from the temple, the only place in my city that felt like home.

Frantically, I jerked my head, side to side, searching for escape. "No," I croaked. "Please, no."

His great brows drew together, his golden eyes darkening. His hands tightened like iron bracelets around my arms; his face was so close to mine I could feel the impossible softness of his perfect skin and the sweetness of his breath in my mouth. I thought he would force me down, but he did not kiss me.

I heard the hiss of it, felt the droplets in my throat as he spat. The burn of his saliva in my mouth; the ragged traces of it dripping down my tongue, seeming to writhe and twist as he clamped my lips together with his hand. The heat of his eyes driving into mine; the inflexible power of his divine will.

I swallowed. It was like molten fire. And then he was gone, as suddenly as he had appeared.

I sank to the floor, my legs as useless as the seaweed I had seen rippling in the foamy water when I had walked the shore that morning, a whole lifetime ago. I knew he was truly gone; the air felt empty around me. I did not know why he had left me unhurt.

It wasn't until the other priestesses came that I realized. I told them the truth, and, when they didn't believe me, I told them everything I could see, the visions coming in a flurry. Their lives, their hopes, their fates all opened up to me and I clutched at their arms, at their robes identical to mine, and I told them all of it in my frenzy.

Apollo had blessed me with his gift, and the truth of the world belonged to me. But the other girls, who loved him just as ardently as I did, did not recognize the words I spoke. Their eyes slid across me, met each other's doubtful stares; they shook their heads almost imperceptibly, and when I saw what he had done, I howled and howled, and I tore at my own flesh until others came and stronger hands restrained me, carried me to my chamber and locked the door on my screams.

I truly had the gift of prophecy, breathed into my mouth by Apollo himself. But no one would ever believe another word I said.

CHAPTER FIVE

Clytemnestra

My farewell to Sparta was emblazoned on my memory; an image burned against the darkness when I shut my eyes. I built it over and over in my head through the first nights at Mycenae, conjuring the details I had not known I noticed at the time: the tang of salt in the air and the screeching of the gulls overhead; the way the sun struck against the surface of the water, making rainbows in the spray; the white of Menelaus' knuckles as he clung so tightly to Helen's arm, as though she might fall and be swept away by the ocean tides if he did not hold her fast.

My arrival at Mycenae, in contrast, was a tumultuous blur of sights and sounds and confusion. I remembered the huge blocks of stone built into a mighty wall around the palace, so vast they could not have been moved by mortal men. Cyclopes had built it, Agamemnon assured me: that brutal and half-wild race of one-eyed giants to whom the lifting of an enormous boulder was no more effort than shifting a sack of barley. He glowed with pride, clasping my hand tightly in his. Beneath his stern demeanor, I could see his delight. I thought it was for me; his joy in showing his newly won kingdom to his newly won bride.

In Sparta, we had lived in the valley with mountains rising to three sides, like friendly guardians overlooking us. Here, the palace was built on high ground, towering above the neighboring hills, and it felt as though the whole world lay at our feet.

Past the thick stone walls, we entered through a monumental gateway and into the palace itself.

I did not exult in the deep-painted columns, the vivid colors of the frescoes, and the gleam of gold, ivory, and jeweled adornments everywhere I looked. I could not relish the warm sunlight that poured through the light well in the roof above us, illuminating the great megaron, the throne room from which Agamemnon would rule. In those early days, I felt little but a hollow sickness in my stomach as I yearned for the familiar simplicity of Sparta.

When I had been back at home, just a girl laughing with my sister, I had dismissed the legendary curse upon the house of Atreus. Now, shaken from my roots, I could not stop the thought rustling in the back of my mind, like the stirring of dry leaves swept up in the first chill of autumn. Cursed or not, this was a palace where father had murdered son, where brothers had drawn swords against one another, where Agamemnon had drawn his dagger across his uncle's throat and let the blood drain across the fragmented tile of the mosaic floor. I knew the slaves had scrubbed it clean, but if you looked closely, you could trace the bloom of the stain where it had spread. Now that I knew where it lay, I could not prevent my eyes from being drawn to it, could not keep myself from picturing Agamemnon in the full blaze of his avenging fury. I could not quite reconcile that image with the man who shared my bed.

It felt almost as though I had two husbands, one whom I had never seen before. I had felt his nerves when he stood in our great hall in Sparta. I would not let him see that it was me who felt shy and overwhelmed by the change in my circumstance. I remembered how Helen would behave, cool and imperious, with mischief bubbling in her eyes, and how the strongest of men would be like liquid before her. I might not have the golden blood of Zeus in my veins, but I had learned from my sister, and I assumed her loftiness like a cloak, pulling it around me every day. I tried to make my voice arch and knowing like hers, to pretend that I knew the world's secrets and that nothing could perturb me. I wanted Agamemnon to find me a challenge and a mystery, not a sniveling, homesick child. I pretended to myself that I was Helen until it felt natural to me; until the control I feigned to wield was truly mine indeed.

And I found, to my surprise, that I was not so insignificant as I might have thought myself here. The attitude of the slaves was reverential, respectful, as I would have expected, though they were less timid than those in Sparta. Here, I felt their eyes upon me, and I had been taken aback by their direct and often friendly gazes. I was even more startled when the slave-woman fastening the rope of glittering gems at my neck stopped for a moment and breathed out, "Thank you," so softly I barely heard it.

"For what?" I asked, twisting my head around to see her more clearly.

She dropped her eyes. She was not young, and her face was lined heavily from a lifetime of slavery.

"We know that you saved the boy, Aegisthus," she murmured. "We were glad of the mercy Agamemnon showed him. We know that it came from you."

"How do you know that?"

She looked at me directly then. Her palm was warm and dry against my neck. "He said it was in your name that he spared the child. He said it when he—when he killed Thyestes."

I wanted to know more, but it felt too indecorous to probe for details. "Were you fond of the boy?" I asked instead.

She nodded. "We all were," she said.

I felt the unspoken words burn between us. I wondered what she thought of Agamemnon; how the inhabitants of the palace had felt seeing their former master slain, and whether they celebrated or mourned the return of the rightful king. Would anyone here remember further back, before the usurping Thyestes? Were there aged slaves somewhere who had silently cheered the sparing of Agamemnon and Menelaus when they fled as boys? I felt dizzy, assembling the pieces in my head. It was too much to think of. But what I could be sure about was that my advice to Agamemnon had been sound.

I exulted in telling him as quickly as I could how right he had been to let Aegisthus go, but I was surprised to see his lowering brows draw together.

"Why would I be pleased to hear the prattling of slaves?" he grumbled.

I felt wrong-footed, confused by his reaction. "You have won their loyalty with your generosity—" I started, but he cut me off.

"What does their loyalty matter? I have the throne. I don't care for the opinion of slaves."

These were the first words we had spoken at odds since our marriage, and I found myself all at once floundering. "It was the wise thing to do," I said carefully. "No one doubts your power, but when the strong show kindness, people speak their admiration and—"

He swept away my words with an imperious wave. "If I had killed the boy, they wouldn't dare to speak at all."

I wanted to turn, to walk away from him altogether, so horrified was I by this, but curiosity held me to the spot. "Is that what you would prefer?" I asked.

He brooded for a moment. I feared what he might say next. But in a moment, the storm clouds on his face parted and he looked again like the man I had married. "It doesn't matter what anyone thinks," he said. "It is done."

I took what he said for truth, though I had cause to remember that first sharp exchange later.

⁘

Before I had lived a year in Mycenae, our first child was born. I had felt relief when I had known myself with child; this baby would extinguish the last flickers I had of insecurity here, for I would be mother to the heir of Mycenae. As well, I felt a powerful surge of gratitude that I would have blood of my blood with me at last. With no sister at my side, I had felt adrift and alone, but with my baby in my arms, I would have my place in the world again.

She was born as dawn broke across the city, as though Eos herself proclaimed my daughter's existence to the world. I had thought a new baby would be such a fragile, breakable thing, but her soft solidity felt more like an anchor, as though it was she who held me safe in the world, instead of the other way around.

Agamemnon deferred to me for the naming of her, and I knew it at once. "*Strong-born*," I said to him, in those precious first hours of her life. "That's what it means." He was pleased, thinking I meant that she was a healthy child, pink and full of vitality from the start. But it was the strength I derived from her that I was thinking of when I gave her the name.

He had been proud, benevolent. "What is the name?"

I drew in my breath, sore and exhausted but bathed in contentment, so commonplace and magical all at once, and I spoke her name aloud for the first time.

"*Iphigenia*."

At first, Agamemnon was a generous, joyful ruler of Mycenae, his project of uniting all the Greeks a long-held ambition that he was grateful to be realizing. But, slowly, a peevishness began to settle over him and I saw him fretting from time to time. His imperious dismissal of what the slaves might think had been bluster. He couldn't help letting slip his worries that perhaps he had not stamped out all lingering loyalty to Thyestes in his kingdom. Further afield, the Greeks were scattered across their islands, each with their own king and their own laws. Agamemnon worried that, even with the strength of Sparta and Mycenae together, the other lesser kings of Greece did not always recognize his superiority.

"Do they think of Odysseus as the wisest?" he would say. "Or Ajax the strongest? Who will they follow if it comes to a choice?"

I wondered what would be enough for him, what would soothe the broken boy within who had been chased from his home as his father's blood spread across the marble floors of his own palace.

I had my own concerns. From the moment my baby daughter was born, the world seemed an altogether more alarming place, full of dangers I had never noticed before. This was love, I realized, looking at her tiny face, and with it came a swarming cloud of brand-new fears. An upturned pot of scalding water, a startled snake rearing from the grass, the rattling breath of disease—there seemed at once such a host of threats to her plump, perfect flesh. And it suddenly struck me as careless, arrogant even, to bring a defenseless infant into a place so haunted by grief and violence and the condemnation of the gods themselves. I could not ignore the fragments of the story that I knew any longer.

I sought out the slave-woman again. She had known Thyestes; what else could she tell me about the family that I had borne my little girl into?

"You want to know about Atreus?" She sounded disbelieving.

I wondered what she thought of me. Why had I not sought to find out more before I even married him? "I have heard some stories," I began guardedly. "But . . . I know there are other stories, too. Older stories."

The slave-woman sucked in her breath. "No one in Mycenae would tell those stories," she said. "No one who valued their own skin."

I paused. The fire burning at the hearth was the only light. Through the window, an oblong of starless sky was visible, flat and dark and empty. "Only the Queen of Mycenae listens to you here," I said. "There is no danger in any story you tell."

Her eyes flickered to the sleeping Iphigenia in my arms. "The King of Mycenae might disagree."

"He doesn't need to know."

She smiled without mirth.

"Please trust me," I said. "I want to know anything that might threaten my daughter. Any way that I can keep her safe." Speaking it aloud made me feel foolish. In Sparta, I could laugh this off. But here, it felt different.

She gave me a long, measuring look. I wondered what I was asking of her, if telling me the secrets of Mycenae might really put her at risk. I thought she wasn't going to answer at all, but she glanced around at the closed door and, reassured that we were alone, she spoke. "It began with Tantalus," she said. "He was the first. Do you know what he did?"

"He offended the gods." I shuddered, thinking of it. "He tried to trick them—he invited them to a banquet and . . ." I swallowed. Motherhood was still new and raw to me. I couldn't treat this as I had before, as a sensational tale consigned to a darker, more savage past. I was here, in the very palace where it had happened, where it felt as though the grisly specters could reach out across the years, as though they could claw through the earth itself to clutch at me. At my daughter.

The slave-woman nodded. "He was a powerful, wealthy man, and the gods had favored him with their friendship." Her words began to gather pace; although she had told me that no one would speak of this in Mycenae, now that she had my permission, the story flowed like one well practiced. I wondered how many times these legends had been passed on here. "Despite the nobility of his blood, he was betrayed by the wretchedness of his nature. His cruelty and ambition tormented him, buzzing in his brain like a trapped mosquito, never giving him respite. He yearned for glory beyond the reaches of any mortal. He longed to see the gods humbled, to be the one to humiliate them. He imagined the sting of their shame and it warmed him better than the fire burning in his hearth. He could taste its rich sweetness like ambrosia flooding his mouth."

I couldn't tear my eyes away from her.

"The foulness of his plot only made it more delicious to him. The more depraved his ideas, the more delightful they became, until no stirring of conscience or pity could restrain him. Overcome with the worst of his hideous fantasies, he seized his own infant son, slit the child's throat, carved his flesh, and boiled him up to serve as meat to test the gods' omniscience when they visited his table."

Instinctively, I clutched my baby a little tighter to me, trying to shake the image from my mind. "Surely they must have known." The gods couldn't be fooled.

"In an instant! All except for Demeter. She was so distracted by her grief for her daughter, Persephone, that she took a bite. But the other gods saw at once what Tantalus had done, and they were horrified. They restored the boy to life, Hephaestus himself carving a shoulder from ivory to replace what Demeter had eaten. In punishment, they hurled Tantalus into the deepest cavern of Tartarus, where he stands to this day, suffering an eternity of thirst in a lake from which he can never drink, a thirst that will never abate for even a moment's relief."

I had heard of the fate of Tantalus, but it had seemed fantastical and far away. Now, the stories she was telling felt like a web she wove around me, as though she was a spider, hunched and malevolent, spinning the words that would hold me fast. In the stifling gloom of the chamber, the ancient tale felt so close that I could almost hear Tantalus' howls of agony echoing from the abyss. "And the boy?" I whispered.

"The boy grew up," she went on. "But he was tainted by his father's blood."

"Pelops," I said, the memory of it resurfacing. I wondered why I hadn't paid more attention back in Sparta. "That was his name—I know he killed a servant in a quarrel."

She was shaking her head. "Worse than a quarrel. Pelops sought a bride, and plotted sabotage and murder to win her from a rival suitor. He bribed the other man's servant, a man named Myrtilus, to be his accomplice and to replace the pins in the would-be husband's chariot with wax. The chariot crashed and the suitor died, but Pelops had yet more treachery in his heart. Rather than reward the servant, as he had sworn to do, Pelops pushed Myrtilus from the cliff edge, onto the jagged rocks below. As he fell, the betrayed servant shrieked out a curse of vengeance, imploring the gods to punish Pelops and all his line who followed thereafter."

"But they were *both* murderers!" I couldn't contain myself, my voice louder than I intended. Iphigenia stirred and whimpered, and I jumped to my feet, patting her and rocking her, soothing myself as much as her. More softly, I went on. "Why would the gods punish Pelops' innocent children?"

The woman raised an eyebrow at me. "The children of Pelops were far from innocent."

I sat back down, baby in my arms, a feeling of defeat swamping me.

"Untroubled by remorse, Pelops married the girl, and she bore him three sons: Chrysippus, Atreus, and Thyestes. But the younger brothers were as brutal and faithless as their father, and his father before him. They nurtured a resentment against Chrysippus and, together, they conspired to kill him and take the throne. But they couldn't be satisfied with that, and it wasn't long before they turned upon each other. Thyestes seduced Atreus' wife and tried to take Mycenae for his own."

Atreus was Agamemnon's father. My baby's grandfather. I wanted to stop her, to hear no more, but I was transfixed by the relentless rhythm of her tales, and I had to know. "What was Atreus' revenge?"

The fire flickered, shadows jumping about the room, casting her face into darkness. "He drove them out of Mycenae, but it was not enough. For years, Atreus brooded on the punishment he owed his brother. He invited him back, pretended to hold a feast in reconciliation. And Thyestes was foolish enough to forget the banquet his grandfather had once held, and did not realize what was in Atreus' heart."

A monstrous circle; a hideous repetition.

"Atreus butchered his brother's sons himself and roasted their tender bodies. Thyestes never suspected what he had done, until the terrible moment after he swallowed the last bite, when Atreus whipped away the dome of the final serving dish to reveal his children's heads, staring blankly up at him from the table."

I had married this man's son. The horror of it was dizzying.

"Stunned by grief and devastation, Thyestes fled the city. But in his exile, he planned his revenge. He came back and murdered his brother, though some pity stirred his heart enough to spare the young Agamemnon and Menelaus. For a time, there was peace. Atreus was dead and Thyestes ruled. Another son was born to him, a boy he named Aegisthus, a comfort to his father, who still wept for the sons he had lost."

But far away, I thought, the two banished sons of Atreus had grown to manhood, dreaming of the revenge they would one day return to take upon their uncle. The Atreidae, who came marching back with a Spartan army at their heels. I had been so confident that Agamemnon had closed this terrible cycle, that his victory had ended the bloodshed.

I could not vanquish the treacherous thought wriggling in my mind. What if he had simply given the wheel another spin? Somewhere out there, was Aegisthus growing up, nurturing a vision of his own revenge? A struggle for power was one thing—common enough, perhaps—but the history of this family I had joined was a gnarled and warped tangle, like the twisted roots of an ancient tree. Could I really believe that Agamemnon had severed the knot? That the death of Thyestes would sate the ravenous maw of the House of Atreus at last?

I watched my daughter sleep, blameless and innocent, in my arms. I thought of the babies born at Mycenae before, of their crumpled faces and the sweet softness of their flesh.

"These stories are in the past," I whispered. I looked the slave-woman in the eye. "Thank you for telling me. I won't breathe a word of it, not to anyone." I could feel her eyes still steady upon me as I stood up, careful not to disturb Iphigenia. "Don't speak of it again," I said as I opened the door. I was grateful to breathe the cool air of the corridor, to be out of that room, away from the claustrophobic darkness and the hideous legends.

I was Queen of Mycenae now. My Spartan blood ran in my daughter's veins just as much as the cursed blood of Atreus. Our fortifications were strong, and our army was powerful. She would be protected from anything that could threaten her from the outside.

But her father, my husband, was the son of Atreus. The descendant of killers more wicked than I could have dreamed. There was no crime more terrible than slaying your own kin; no greater evil imaginable.

And however fast our defenses against the world beyond our kingdom, I didn't know how I could keep her safe if the enemy was already inside our walls.

CHAPTER SIX

Elektra

My first memory is illness. A fever that racked my body, bathing me in sweat as I shivered from head to foot. My eyes burning in the darkened room. Weird shapes twisting and blooming in front of me, and bursts of livid color. A nightmarish landscape that swelled up and shrank again, leaving me panting and bewildered. Monstrous creatures rising from the floor that I screamed and shrank away from. Snaking coils shifting around me, brushing my face. I clawed at them, trying to tear them away, and I heard my mother's voice telling me to be still, to be quiet, to rest and it would all stop.

When the fever abated, it burned away all my energy with it, and I lay in bed too weak to move. Food sickened me and even the effort of lifting my head to drink seemed too great. I slept in long, heavy stretches of blankness, never knowing if it was day or night when I woke. They summoned a healer. I remember her in flashes: a dark silhouette in the dim light, her muttered incantations, the sharp stink of the herbs, bitter liquid swirling in a cup. Once, I woke to hear my parents talking in hushed voices in the doorway.

"But could she die?" I heard my mother say. I felt my body go rigid, my breath halting in my chest as my eyes widened and I strained to make out the answer.

"We've made offerings to the gods." I shrank back from the sound of the healer's voice. "We can only wait."

My father's voice was clear, no mumbling or softness. "They'll spare her. There's no need for worry."

I breathed out, reassured by his ring of confidence, his authority. My mother carried on talking, rapid and shrill, making my head ache more. I shifted in my blankets, my throat so dry I felt like the insides of it would stick together.

Alerted by the sound of my feeble movement, she was at my side at once. Her hand slid behind my head, raising it up, her other hand holding a cup to my lips. Water, just water this time, clear and sweet and pure. I sipped at it gratefully. My father was already gone. Already I wanted to go back to sleep, but what she'd said before had scared me. What if I fell asleep and died?

Her hands were on my face, smoothing my hair back, her touch soft and gentle as she settled me into the soft cushions. I clung on to my father's words as sleep pulled me back under.

A bright morning, the surface of the long oak table shining in the sunlight that streamed through the window. My mother trying to persuade me to eat. I pursed up my mouth and shook my head, shoving the bowl away, sending it clattering down the table. I remember the noise it made as it crashed to the floor, how she stared at the broken shards on the stone tiles. For a moment, she looked as though she would be angry, but then she laughed and kissed me on the forehead. "You must have your strength back, to send the bowl flying so far" was all she said before she summoned a slave to clear away the mess.

The happiest memory: outside in a courtyard, my father lifting me up in his arms. I was fascinated by the golden clasp at his shoulder that held the fine woolen edges of his purple cloak together; how it glinted in the sun. A little gem sunk into the center, with two tiny figures embossed upon its surface: warriors in combat.

He had a pair of daggers made of bronze that I loved to look at. The blades were inlaid with gold and silver. One was decorated with sea creatures, shining tentacles looping across the surface. The other, my favorite, was a scene of men hunting lions. I loved to trace the tiny bright gold spears, the silver shields, the snarling faces of the lions. He laughed, pleased at my interest.

An evening when I couldn't sleep. The distant sound of my parents arguing somewhere in the palace, my mother storming from a room. The only word I heard distinctly was Helen's name.

CHAPTER SEVEN

Cassandra

In Troy, I had grown used to walking out of step with everyone else. But I had never known what it was to be shunned. The other priestesses pitied me at first for my madness, but they soon grew impatient with my wild claims to have been visited by the god himself. I saw how their faces pinched when they looked at me, the sympathy draining from their eyes. It was replaced by suspicion, exasperation, and, finally, a cold disinterest. I suppose they thought I lied for the attention, and they grew tired of hearing me.

They had brought me to the palace after it had happened, my hair wild around my face.

"Who has done this?" I heard Priam ask. "What's happened to her?" He was poised, alert, ready to command his guards, to hunt down any perpetrator. The image of it was ridiculous; I thought of his armed men marching up the sides of Mount Olympus and laughter erupted from me.

"She's hysterical," Hecabe said, wringing her hands together. "Take her to rest, summon a healer for her."

I pushed at the women around me, shoving their solicitous hands away before they could bear me off. "It was Apollo." I stood as straight as I could, trying to stop my legs from buckling under me. A murmur of disquiet rippled through the women, a note of irritation that I was still clinging to this nonsensical story. "It was. He came to me, in the temple. He was there." I knew what I looked like—a madwoman—and I couldn't force my tongue to shape the words that would make them believe me. Everything sounded absurd and impossible; I could hear it myself, and the more I tried to make the truth sound believable, the more preposterous it became. "He kissed me," I said. "And then—"

My mother drew her breath in sharply, her face frozen as she stared at me.

"He gave me his power," I continued. "I saw so many things, all at once."

"What things?" Priam asked.

"I—I don't know, exactly. It was a blur; I couldn't see it clearly."

Already, his eyes were sliding away. "Perhaps the seer could interpret?" he asked my mother doubtfully, but she shook her head.

"The god doesn't visit us," she said. "His messages don't come like that. What is there for a seer to interpret in what she's saying? If it was a dream, then perhaps—but this, this is a fantasy. It's an insult to Apollo to say this. We risk his anger in even hearing it spoken."

Panic flared in my chest. "I know he comes to you in dreams, but it doesn't mean he wouldn't come to me in another way," I cried.

"No!" She stood, a quick and convulsive movement. "Don't say it; don't repeat it!" She smoothed down her dress, breathed deeply, and closed her eyes for a moment, gathering her calm. "I told you once before, Cassandra, it is not a gift. I serve the god. Perhaps he has chosen me sometimes to be the vessel for his message, for a seer to interpret and understand what he wants us to know, but I would never dare to say that he comes to me, that he would show himself to me."

The answer thickened in my throat. How could I tell them why he had shown himself to me and not to her? I looked around the room, from one doubting face to the next, and then back to my parents. It pained me to see the mingling of love and frustration in their eyes. The powerful desire they had for me to go away, to keep my wild stories to myself. I let them tend to me, to bring the healers to try to calm me, to cure the madness they were sure must have overtaken me. Lying in the dark solace of my bedchamber, I wondered if the memory would recede, if it would become shaky, if the herbs they crushed for me and made me drink would dull the chaos of visions in my brain.

It didn't happen. I knew as surely as anything I had ever known that Apollo was there that day. I had felt the grip of his immortal hands on me. I had felt the burn of his venom in my mouth. The memory of it flowed in my bloodstream; the echo of his touch imprinted on my skin; the visions he had given me flickered and twisted in my head, all of them fighting for supremacy, never settling into one clear picture. But for the sake of my anxious parents, I tried to push down the memories and to master my words, to hold in the tide of unwelcome prophecy that I knew no one wished to hear, that would only be taken as evidence of, at best, my madness and, at worst, my impiety.

But when a powerful vision came, it would split my mind with a roaring chasm of light and there was no way of holding myself in one piece. When Apollo's gift set my senses aflame and blinded me to everything but the revelations he showed me, I rolled on the floor and screamed with the agony of it. It was better to keep myself alone as much as I could.

Even in my own bedchamber, there was no peace for me, no safety. There was no escape from Apollo's invasions into my head. I had no sanctuary in the city; not even my mind felt like my own. Even in the respites between his attacks, I felt afraid, never knowing when the visions would seize me again.

In an hour of calm, I lay awake in the soft silver moonlight. My eyes ached and my body was exhausted, but everything was quiet. A tray of food lay untouched on the table, where the slave-girl had left it earlier, her eyes lowered as she backed out, desperate to be away from me. A pile of olives gleaming in brine, the rich tang mingling with the salty scent of the crumbled cheese, made me think of the dark tangle of seaweed down at the shore where I used to walk. The sweetness wafting from the jug of wine carried the memory of the temple, the silent hours I had spent there in dedication. The only place in the city that had ever really felt like it was mine.

I was still his priestess. I'd sworn my oaths. I was bound to serve him for the rest of my life. The idea of going back there made my heart quicken in fear, but I couldn't banish the thought that perhaps that was the only hope I had of ending my suffering. In the peace of that night, I could reason with myself. If I returned, if I showed him my loyalty and my obedience, then maybe he would grant me his mercy. Maybe he would end this punishment for my defiance and quell the visions. I quaked at the prospect of setting foot on those stones again, of kneeling before his statue. But he had inflicted this curse upon me, and only he could take it away.

No prophetic agony split my head apart that night, and by the morning, I could see no other choice but to return to the temple. It made my parents relieved to see me dress once more in my sacred robes, to put on the semblance of the girl I had been before. If the others didn't want me back there, they didn't dare say it to the king's daughter. I took up my duties again. I laid offerings at the feet of Apollo's statue, as I had always done. He remained impassive: silent, motionless stone.

When I was not in the temple, I fled to the shore, leaving the walled city behind me. It was better to have nothing but the waves as company, to mutter my truths to the empty wind and the water, where the clusters of seaweed would wave in the froth as though in agreement with me.

I was used to being misheard and misunderstood. I had been a timid child and an awkward young woman, always striving to make my voice clear and brave. I was no stranger to struggling with my words, feeling them die in my throat when people looked at me. And I could see with bitter clarity that everyone thought this new manifestation of madness that had come upon me was just another part of my oddness; that I had always lived in a dreamworld, and it had only got worse. While the world saw my encounter with Apollo as further proof of my strange mind, I saw that the day he had come to me in the temple was like a lightning bolt shattering the center of my life, the cracks in the earth spiraling from it in every direction. I knew that the madness within me had not been building to that moment, but rather that the echoes of his devastation had rung back through my years as well as forward. Such was the power of Apollo: he could shatter my existence from beginning to end.

∽∽∽∽

The night before Paris came back to Troy, I slept even more fitfully than usual. The next morning, I could feel the tenderness around my eyes, the gritty soreness that told of the hours I had spent awake in the bowels of the night. Everything that day seemed like an illusion, as though the city itself was made of rippling cloth; as though the ancient foundations of the mighty walls could sink at any moment into quicksand and disappear. I longed for the fresh salt of the air outside the walls, for the quiet murmuring of the breeze and the soft surge of the seawater staining the sand dark. But my duties at the temple took so much longer than usual, my fingers fumbling as I tried to light the incense and melt the scented wax to oil, to crush the flowers and create sweet fragrances to please the god who tormented me. If I could appease him, perhaps he would let me use what he had given me to help my fellow Trojans, since he loved us so dearly. I felt the stifling darkness of the room close in about me at Apollo's altar; the eyes of his statue narrowed in silent contempt, making me drop the blooms across the stone floor.

I could tell by the blaze of the sun on the flagstones that it burned at its zenith, and I knew I was expected at the palace, but I could not turn my feet toward it. I felt that pull, stronger than ever, drowning out my sense of duty, drawing me from the city toward the shore.

I wanted the solitude, the peace, of that quiet expanse of sand, the gleam of the water in the distance while the city broiled behind me full of chatter and bustle and noise. But as I peered down from the high city walls, I could see movement. A figure—a man—walking toward the gates of Troy.

I felt a swoop in my stomach, the familiar rolling lurch of insight. I wanted this man to turn around, to walk away, but he kept coming with a confident swing in his stride. My throat burned with the sour foretaste of vomit, and I closed my eyes, but still I saw him, coming toward Troy with disaster at his heels.

I heard the gates rolling back for him, even as I whimpered for them to stop. No one was there to hear me; no one would have listened or cared if they had been. The stone wall dragged roughly against my face as I sagged downward against it, pulling my hands about my head, desperate for it to stop. I could not see the shape of it yet, but I knew this man carried the collapse of the world with him.

Could I run? In front of Troy there was nothing: just the long plains giving way to the beach and the vast seas beyond. Behind us rose the mountains, sparse and scrubby. I saw myself set upon by wild beasts, my bones picked apart by vultures, or suffocated by the heavy water, my carcass gnawed by fish.

And if I ran, who would warn my parents of what had come for them, for us all? This, surely, was why Apollo had given me his insight. A chance to save my city. A chance to earn the gratitude of my people, and a place among them at last.

Nothing burned around me, but I could taste ashes in the air. I put one foot in front of the other, dragged myself toward the palace. I was late. My cheek was torn by scratches where the stones had grazed my face; my white dress was stained with dust. No wonder people looked away from me: the princess of Troy, arriving at a banquet looking ragged and haunted and strange. But I could feel the power thrumming in my body, at last in alignment with my brain. Prophecy, as I had always imagined it would be: a power and a privilege.

Paris, my brother, sat between my mother and father, returned to the bosom of his family. His dark eyes sparkled, his nut-brown skin gleamed with health and vitality, his hair clustered in shining curls about his head. Hecabe's hand lay across his on the table, her goblet of wine pushed aside as she drank in his presence instead. Priam, laughing and carefree as he embraced his son. The sprawling spread of my family filled the hall, the sons and daughters of Priam by my mother in the foremost seats, and the rest thronging on the long wooden benches.

I made my way toward them through the crowded hall. I knew it was all wrong; that I should not approach like this, that I was doing everything badly. But still, my feet moved on. Paris looked up and saw me.

"My sister," he said. "Are you Cassandra? You must be, surely."

I stared at him steadily.

"The rumors of your beauty are true," he said, standing, holding his arms out to me.

He breathed sincerity, this Paris. No flicker of horror as he took in my puffy eyelids and tangled hair. He was not disconcerted by this silent sister, this apparition that loomed before him at his triumphant homecoming. I searched his face and saw his honesty. And yet I could hear the shrieks echoing in his wake, the howls of despair that would ring through the smoking ruins of Troy. I could see the flickers of a fire that would rampage unconstrained behind him when I looked into those warm eyes.

He dropped his arms as I stayed motionless. "You are surprised, of course. I know that everyone believed me dead. When I came to this hall today, everyone was as astonished as you are. You hear this news late and it shocks you, but I will tell you, Cassandra, who I am and where—"

"You are Paris," I said. "My baby brother, cast out to die. Did the herdsman take pity on you, save you from your fate?"

At this, he could not help looking a little taken aback. "Your intellect is sharp," he said, and I could see he had thought me a simple idiot.

Priam took my elbow, gestured for me to sit. I did not move. "Paris has indeed returned to us," he said. "And our joy is complete: to have our son, who we believed dead, restored to our home."

"But he was supposed to die," I said. My words rang more harshly than I intended. "The prophecy said he must die."

Hecabe frowned. "The prophecy told us to leave him on the mountains," she said. "We followed the prophecy, and the gods saved our son in reward for our piety, for our sacrifice."

She was lying to herself; I could see it. She had made a convincing case, but she was wrong. I opened my mouth to tell her so, but I looked at Paris' face again before I spoke. I could see the fine shape of his bones, the exquisite beauty of his features jarring so discordantly with the horror he opened up within me, but the terrible jangle of despair and fear was beginning to separate into distinct notes, and

I was distracted from my words. So much of it was still to come, but one strand of sorrow felt immediate. I saw a woman in my mind's eye, weeping over the baby that gurgled in her arms. Flowers twisted through her hair, a spring bubbled beside her as though in sympathy, and the gnarled branches of an olive tree stretched over her like it wanted to offer her protection. No mortal woman: the spirit of the mountain itself infused her veins. The word for what she was came to me: *Oread. Mountain nymph.* The tears that she sobbed were for her husband, Paris. I knew it, and although I knew that a thousand women would wring their hands and scream in bitter grief because of this man in the years to come, this nymph cried now. Her baby reached up a chubby arm to bat clumsily at his mother's face, and I saw his eyes open big and dark, just like his father's.

Paris' eyes were fixed on me, not the infant's. The vision dissolved, leaving me only with the nymph's name. *Oenone.* I could say it, see if the name of the wife he'd abandoned along with his newborn son brought a jolt of guilt to that calm, handsome face. I could feel the word dripping with poison on my tongue, but it caught in my mouth and I could not force it past my lips.

"Take some wine, Cassandra," Paris said. The solicitude in his voice was real. How could he be so kind and so terrible all at once?

To the palpable relief of my parents, I sat down on a cushioned chair beside them, and I took the goblet that Paris slid toward me. The bronze gleamed, the jewels on its stem glittered, and the sweet scent of honey mingled with the rich aroma of the wine. I let it calm me, and the conversation continued around me as I forced myself to look at nothing but the dark liquid.

"And so, tell me why you are set on Sparta?" my father was saying.

Paris leaned back in his chair. "If I tell you, I must warn you it will be a very strange story." His tone was light. He had no fear of their disbelief. They urged him to speak; my parents and my brothers and sisters all eager to hear him.

I wished him gone, swallowed up by the mountains that should have been his grave years ago. But he was so full of smiles, of joy, a bright beacon, and I, too, was drawn toward him, even as I shuddered at his presence.

"I lived a simple life on the slopes of Mount Ida," he said. "I tended the goats and never dreamed of even entering this great walled city. I believed I was the son of a herdsman and nothing more. Until the day came when, before me on the mountainside, appeared three women— not human women, but goddesses. I knew them to be divine in a moment—they shimmered with radiance and their beauty was beyond compare."

When I had told of my encounter with Apollo, I had been met with scoffing first, anger later. But everyone smiled at Paris' story. I wasn't sure that they believed him either, but they were happy to listen.

"They were Hera, Athena, and Aphrodite, and they told me they had come to me because they had heard of my honesty and my fair judgment. They wanted me to decide which of them was the most beautiful, for all three of them coveted a golden apple that would be awarded as the prize to the goddess I chose." He sighed, a dreamy smile spreading across his face. "They dropped their robes and revealed their nakedness to me so I could better decide."

A flutter went around the table. I could see my brother Hector suppress a laugh, but Paris had sparked their interest surely enough and they all leaned forward to hear the details.

My mind was clearing. There was no fuzz of light at the edges of my vision, no blade of knowledge piercing deep beneath my skull. Paris wove his story, and I weighed his words. I found them light, insubstantial. I thought he spoke sincerely, but I could see he was a man of romance and idealism. Such a man speaks poetry in place of facts and thinks he tells a higher truth when all he spins is fantasy. I did not think he lied exactly, but I remembered the menace and the power of Apollo, and I found that I could not imagine three immortals squabbling before a human man as he described.

"Each of them tried to persuade me," Paris went on. "Hera offered me the kingship of a great city and Athena offered me success in war. But to rule is not my destiny, nor do I seek glory on the battlefield." He tossed back his hair, the firelight from the heaped bronze bowls around us glimmering off its jet-black shine. "I turned to Aphrodite, truly the most beautiful of them all, and I pronounced her the winner."

"And what reward did the goddess of love offer you?" Hector asked. Hector, the protector of our city, swiftly growing to be the finest soldier the world had seen—or so every man, woman, and child of Troy believed. I wondered what he made of his younger brother's disdain for war.

"She told me how to bring harmony to Troy," Paris said, speaking more carefully. "Unity with those who would be our enemies."

Although I had not believed him so far, I had thought that he believed what he was telling us—to some extent at least. Now, though, I was sure I heard his voice rise to a higher pitch, and I was convinced that he moved into absolute untruth.

"It was Aphrodite, then, who advised you to go to Sparta?" Priam asked doubtfully.

"She did! She told me of my birth, the truth of my existence. She told me that Troy stands as a tempting jewel to the Greeks: to Agamemnon, brother of Menelaus, who rules over Sparta; Agamemnon, who gathers the loyalty of all the scattered Greeks to himself. Aphrodite, who brings the peace of love and harmony to all, told me to go to Sparta with a delegation of Trojans to offer them the hand of friendship and avert any battles in the future. We can enrich one another if we cooperate rather than fight."

If he had said it was Athena who advised him thus, perhaps it would have been credible. But everyone knew that Aphrodite had no care for peace or harmony, and it was not love between nations that excited her. I wondered why he strove to conceal the truth. Usually, I shrank from the pain of Apollo's visions, but I yearned for the agony, to know what Paris truly intended and what plans he had formulated in the shade of Mount Ida.

Priam signaled to a waiting slave to pour more wine. "I cannot argue with the wisdom of the goddess," he said expansively. I knew he believed Paris' story no more than I did. But he sat among us, so handsome and charismatic, so welcome after his years of exile, and no one seemed to care whether he spoke the truth or not. I felt the ache of unfairness in my belly. "What do you think, Hector?" Priam asked.

Hector sipped his wine thoughtfully. "It is sensible to go to Sparta as friends. Menelaus is a man of honor, I hear. I can see no harm in such a visit."

I saw Paris' exultant smile. "You should not go," I said. Everyone ignored me, so I said it again.

My mother shook her head at me, a little warning to be quiet. But my words could not puncture her joy in this reunion with her son. They carried on talking of Sparta, speculating on what they knew of the city, of its riches, of the legendary beauty of its queen.

The wine tasted like dirt to me. I could shriek out my warnings, claw at my flesh, hurl my goblet right into Paris' face, but they would still carry on as though I did not exist. No frenzy was upon me; no abyss of truth had been torn open in my mind. I had only the dull certainty of disaster; the presaging of doom that I had carried upon my shoulders since that day in the temple. I felt so very tired, and I wanted so much to sleep.

When the delegation sailed from our shores, I did shriek and howl at the departing ship. I could not stop myself then. I threw myself on to the ground and rolled, the blood from the flesh I clawed at seeping into the sand. Nobody bothered to restrain me. They walked back to the gates of Troy and left me screaming on the beach until the madness dissipated, and I could again see the world as it was instead of what it would be. I lay there, spent and drained, the sand gritty and damp beneath me as the breath shuddered from my body, and I prayed and prayed that the ship would be wrecked before it ever reached Sparta, that my brother's body would sink to the ocean floor and rot.

But no one heard me; that was my curse. Not my family, and certainly not the gods.

⸎

I did not need Apollo to turn my vision white and play the scene out before me to know how it went. Helen, married to Menelaus for fifteen years. So long since a hundred men had bombarded Sparta with desperate entreaties for her hand. No such excitement in her life since. Everyone she saw had seen her before. Would she ever make anyone gasp in wonder again? Would she know what it was to dazzle and to charm and to see grown men stumble and grow red in her glorious presence?

And then Paris, the Trojan prince with an exquisite face and a romantic heart; Paris, who thought himself worthy to judge between Olympian goddesses; Paris, who believed that he was entitled to a love that would be sung of for generations, stepped off his ship onto Spartan shores. The lingering glances, the press of his hand, the stolen whispers in hidden corners. And when foolish Menelaus placed his trust in the sacred tradition of guest-friendship and went on a hunting trip, leaving his lovely wife and the Trojan together in the palace, how could anything else have happened?

When they reached Troy, the adulterous couple talked high-mindedly of Aphrodite's power, of forces beyond their control, of the divine intervention that clouded their minds and made no other course of action possible. They made a great procession through the city gates, as though it was a royal wedding to boast of rather than a shame and a disgrace upon both their families. They seemed oblivious to the stricken faces that watched them waving from their chariot and the hum of nerves that ran through the gathered spectators, who were wondering what this meant for Troy, what it meant for all of us. Helen was veiled, and as they made their approach through the streets of Troy to where I stood with my parents and my siblings, I itched to see her face. Not to see if she was as beautiful as they said. I needed to look at her, to know if I saw the same catastrophe in her features as I had read in Paris' the day he came back.

Her veil was threaded through with shimmering gold, held in place with a delicate circlet of golden vines wreathed atop her shining curls. It was so pretty, and my hands were stained with the slime from the rocks at the shore, from where I had seen their ship on the horizon and dragged myself, heartsick and weary, back to the city to greet them. My fingernails were ragged, bitten and torn, with peeling flesh at every side. It seemed a desecration for them to touch such an exquisite piece of fabric, but I reached out and tore it from her face all the same. I know there were gasps of horror. But I had to see her face.

Maybe another woman would have reared back or even cried. But not Helen. It was not just her loveliness that was inhuman; I was to learn that her self-possession was unrivaled as well. She looked at me, unflinching, and I looked back.

Her eyes were like glass. I waited for the roar of desolation to come, but I saw nothing except a gleam of hazel fringed with thick lashes. Somewhere behind me, my mother was beside herself, but Helen was calm, and I felt her serenity ripple around me. The veil fluttered from my hand onto the dusty ground.

The moment was broken as Paris steered her around me and toward Priam and Hecabe, whose faces were riven with anxiety. What would they do? Even if they returned her to her husband, the insult had been made. I knew that they agonized, that even Paris' easy charm could not overcome their fears as excuses slipped fluently from his tongue in what was no doubt a well-rehearsed speech.

I did not care what he said or what they did. No prophecy of disaster had overcome me when I looked at Helen's face. I had expected a storm to overwhelm my body; to show me in vivid, bloodstained detail what was to rain down on us all thanks to my selfish, arrogant brother, but none had come. For a moment, I felt a rush of delirious joy—perhaps my presentiment of doom had been mistaken after all; perhaps there was no catastrophe to come.

And then I realized. I had seen nothing in Helen's eyes because there was nothing new to see. We had known it all for years, from the moment of my mother's dream. A fire, coming to sweep the city. Troy would fall. And for all that everyone might disbelieve me if I said it aloud, somewhere in their bones, I knew they knew it too.

CHAPTER EIGHT

Elektra

The palace was in chaos. My father was gone for weeks, traveling back and forth across Greece. When he returned, he was constantly receiving visitors in a flurry of activity, gathering as many men as he could. When I asked why so many strangers kept marching into the great throne room, why I would see him standing amid them, his face alight and his fingers jabbing the air as he spoke, my mother only shook her head. It was my sisters who told me.

"It's Helen," Chrysothemis muttered, pulling me from the room. "She was taken away to Troy and they're going to get her back. There might be a war."

War was a frightening word. My father looked full of confidence, laughing and clasping the shoulders of the men thronging the palace, as though they were talking about a great adventure. But I was still weak from illness. I didn't want to come out of my sick chamber into a world turned upside down. I felt tears welling up.

"Don't cry, Elektra," Iphigenia said. "Father doesn't need to see you upset."

I took heart from how jovial he was, how full of purpose. In the early morning, I watched from the courtyard as he and a band of visiting men streamed out over the plains toward the woods, a pack of dogs racing before them, all of them exultant to be hunting. They came back as the sun was sinking, and I raced outside to greet them.

My father strode in front of them all, his face alight with satisfaction. He ruffled my hair when he saw me, and the dog at his heel jumped up in excitement, pressing its heavy paws on my shoulders, its breath hot against my face. I felt my father watching for my reaction, to see if I was scared. I laughed.

"That's my girl," he said, and the approval in his voice warmed my bones.

The dog let go, and, emboldened, I reached out to pat him. He was almost as tall as me, but he dipped his head, and I stroked his thick, dark fur. I was proud of my courage.

"Come, Methepon," my father said to the dog, which at once trotted obediently behind him. As they passed me by on their way inside to feast and drink, one of the men congratulated him on a fine day's hunting, and I heard my father reply, "Even Artemis herself couldn't have done better than me today." There on the palace steps, as the dusk gathered and the breeze carried the scent of jasmine, I swelled with admiration, struck with awe at how impressive a man my father was.

But all the while, the preparations were being made for him to leave. I tried to smile for him, to be brave. I prayed that the gods would bring him a swift victory. My mother found me with an armful of wildflowers I'd gathered from the gardens, and when she asked what I was doing with them, I told her I wanted to take them to the shrine of Athena, the goddess of war.

She knelt down beside me, cupping my chin. "Don't worry about your father," she said. "He will come home safe." She smiled at me, her eyes warm and sparkling, her hair shining in the sunlight. Everyone said how beautiful her sister was, but I couldn't imagine there was anyone prettier than my mother in the world. "Come on, I'll go with you," she told me, and I slipped my hand into hers.

When the day came that we had to wave my father off to Aulis, my sisters cried, but I was determined that I wouldn't. He kissed them, then he stooped to kiss my forehead. "Here," he whispered, and under the folds of his cloak, where no one could see what he was doing, he passed me the lion dagger. "You can keep it, but make sure it stays hidden."

I gripped it tightly at my side, anxious in case my mother saw it and took it away. I knew she'd think it was dangerous, that she'd never let me keep it. She didn't look at me, though; her eyes were fixed on him at the head of the procession, her face strangely tight and cold. Methepon whined as my father walked away, but I stroked the thick fur of his neck and he pressed his nose against my arm, as though he knew I needed the comfort too.

I remembered what my father had told me about my name, that I was the light of our family, and so I tried to shine as brightly as I could for him. I hoped that my face would be the memory he would take with him to war, and that it would draw him home as soon as possible.

CHAPTER NINE

Clytemnestra

M other?"

Her voice was hesitant, uncertain. I looked up, squinting in the sun, thinking for a moment that it was Elektra who spoke, but it was Iphigenia, standing framed between two pillars. The childlike ring to her voice sounded more like it came from her small sister than herself. One hand was twisting at the fine golden chain of her necklace; the other clutched at the smooth stone beside her as though she needed help to stand upright.

"Come to me," I said, patting the cushion of the low couch on which I sat in the courtyard. I had been looking out to the distant sea on the horizon, not such a calming pastime recently. Everything had been thrown into tumult. I did not like to think of the way that Agamemnon had sailed away; of the words between us before he left.

Iphigenia didn't move. I was seized for a moment by the wonder that still made my breath stick in my throat. That glorious maternal sweep of pride and delight that was almost painful in its intensity. I had three daughters now, and another baby kicking in my womb, but motherhood could still swell my heart in these simple moments: my daughter, fourteen years old, standing in the sunshine. Sometimes I saw the woman she so nearly was. The plump little cheeks of childhood, which I had so loved to kiss just to feel their inexpressible softness, had given way to fine cheekbones, and there was a new thoughtfulness in her eyes that replaced the incessant curiosity that had inspired a thousand questions when she was younger. But at other times, when I saw her shriek with laughter alongside her younger sisters, the elegance she tried to assume nowadays shrugged off and forgotten for a moment, I could see the little girl she had been, the infant I had been cradling in my arms when I first felt that fierce, sweet rush of a mother's love.

She seemed just then poised between the two states. There was a keen edge of excitement burning a flush across her face, but I could see a desperation in her eyes as well, a note of fear and confusion, and a longing for my help.

"What is it?" I asked, sitting straighter.

"A herald comes," she answered. She sounded distracted and her fingers knotted her necklace even tighter as she spoke. "You need to come to the throne room to receive him."

"News of your father?" I stood, concern snaking up my spine. I wondered if this was the message to tell us that he had sailed at last. His army was assembled, all the warriors of Greece gathered at Aulis, ready. It had taken weeks to rout them all out—Odysseus in particular had given them some trouble, I knew—but the most recent proclamation had told us they waited only for a fine wind, one that would carry their fleet to Troy. I couldn't imagine it: such a number of ships as had been gathered. More than a thousand, we'd heard: a thousand ships with tall, curved prows, each one crammed with eager young men, armor, and weapons.

So many ships, to carry back my sister. Helen, somewhere across that ocean, behind walls we had never seen. I tried to shake the thought from my head; I could not imagine her there. All of our lives she had been in Sparta, and I had known what she ate, who she talked to, what she wore, and where she was, but now I had no idea what surrounded her, or how she felt.

"I thought that too," Iphigenia said. "That it would be news that they had sailed, and so I said I would come to fetch you myself—I thought you would want me with you." She was always kind, my daughter, and she knew how I had dreaded this moment. I had seen Menelaus when he arrived at Mycenae; the despair that hunched his shoulders, the tears falling loosely down his cheeks. The story spilled out, his chest hitching and sobs gulping in his throat as he told us how the Trojan prince had gone, and Helen was nowhere to be found. His grief embarrassed me. I hated to see a man so shattered, and the words of comfort that I sought wouldn't come. It was my sister who had done this to him, and the memory of her shimmered back to the surface for a moment: her satisfied smile at her own reflection when she wondered aloud what grand destiny the gods might have in store for her. Did she think that she had found it in this Paris?

I left it to my husband to console his wounded brother, and when they returned late that night, reeking of wine, Menelaus was transformed. I don't know what Agamemnon had said to him, but a dreadful frenzy consumed him. His mouth twitched convulsively, flecks of foam scattered in his beard, and fury raged behind his eyes. I could not wish my husband anything other than victory in war, but I feared what punishment awaited my sister at the hands of this man, who seemed suddenly a stranger. Gone was the gentle, worshipful lover who had been so glad to win her; here instead was a vengeful, embittered, humiliated king with all the armies of Greece at his disposal.

I steeled myself. "Thank you," I said, and made to walk with her, but still she stood where she was.

"Only, I heard the women talking as I left the hall," she said. "They didn't know I was there. They said—they said that the army will not sail until a wedding takes place, that Father has promised—"

That look stamped across her face—part excitement, part dread. The way she was unable to take another step, so uncertain and exhilarated all at once. She was luminous with it.

"That Father has promised his daughter to Achilles—that they send for me to come to Aulis to be—to be his wife," she said. A sob of laughter bubbled in her throat, and she shook her head, dazed.

Achilles. So many bargains had been made, so much persuasion deployed across the islands of Greece to bring this mighty force of men together. But of all the great soldiers famed for their skill and strength in battle, no stories paralleled those of Achilles. And it had seemed for some time that he had disappeared from the face of the earth altogether. The scattered fragments of the gossip that had reached us in Mycenae sounded fantastical, absurd: that his sea-nymph mother, Thetis, had disguised him as a girl and hidden him among a troupe of dancers; that somehow he had been tricked (by Odysseus, we had no doubt) and discovered. I had wondered what had changed his mind and made him agree to fight after all—perhaps this was it. Perhaps my husband had offered him our firstborn child in exchange for his loyalty.

I had so many feelings, I didn't know which one took precedence. To me, she still seemed so young, and although she was old enough to marry, I had hoped we might have a little longer before a husband carried her away. And Achilles, a fighter, being the one to take my gentle girl? I knew that Agamemnon would consider him a son-in-law to boast of, but what would it be like for Iphigenia to be his wife? I tried to picture him: brawny and bristling with muscle, a spear clenched in his great fist. It was said that he was handsome, though. And if he had passed unnoticed among the girls that his mother had hidden him with, he could not be the monstrous giant of my imaginings.

Besides, he was to sail to war immediately. And I could not suppress the shameful thought that war was an uncertain thing. For all we knew, he may not come back. At the very least, it could take some time, and my daughter would still be mine for a little longer.

"Mother?" she asked again, tremulously, and I saw that her eyes were swimming with unshed tears.

I did not know how I felt in my heart about this news, but I knew that my child was afraid and unsure, and that it was in my power to ease her worries. How many hours had I spent as a mother soothing away nightmares in the darkness, sponging fever from hot foreheads, singing lullabies, and allaying troubles? My husband sailed soon to slaughter enemies in the pursuit of power and glory, but I had been slaying monsters for years, smoothing the path at my children's feet so that they could step confidently into the future. And if ever there was a time to do that, it was now.

I put my arms around her and drew her close. "It is a great honor," I said, and I felt the shudder of her body against me. Her shoulders felt so fragile, and her heart pounded so fast. She could have been a little songbird in my hand. "The time for marriage has been drawing near; I confess I did not think it would be so soon, but Achilles is a great man. Your husband will be the stuff of legends, I am sure. To be his wife will be a blessing. And—" I drew back, tilted her face to look at me "—his mother loves him dearly. He nearly missed this war for her. He must be kind, to care for her enough to give up his chance at glory."

She nodded. Stepping back, she squared her slender shoulders and blinked hard. The tears that had threatened to fall were gone, and a half smile hovered at her lips. "If you approve, I know it will be well," she said, and my heart twisted again. She was old enough to be married, but still young enough to believe I could solve any problem.

I was grateful to the gossips for letting the secret slip. When the herald delivered the official message—Agamemnon sends for his eldest daughter to give her in marriage to the warrior Achilles before they sail to Troy—both Iphigenia and I were able to smile serenely before the court. We were to leave the very next day, and the great flurry of tasks before us swept us up in what was unmistakably a ripple of excitement. Chrysothemis, at ten years of age, was thrilled by the prospect of a wedding, and woefully disappointed not to be allowed to accompany us, but Agamemnon's message had been unambiguous in its instructions—and besides, the journey would be hot and dusty and arduous. "You must stay to look after Elektra," I told her, and she rolled her eyes.

"Elektra always needs looking after."

I was too busy to reprove her. It was true that my youngest daughter was prone to illness; every malady of childhood seemed to grip her. Many times, I had feared that one of them would take her from us. I had prayed for her survival, called in healers, and nursed her with a fiery determination I would never have known I possessed. I had felt myself close to that abyss more than once in her short life, but always we had pulled her back from the brink and she lived on. A pale and sickly child, without the strength and ebullience of her sisters, but alive. We treated her like a delicate vase; Agamemnon in particular. I was grateful for how, of all our daughters, she had captured his affection.

She worshipped him so, and he couldn't resist her adoration. Even I couldn't deny the sweetness of seeing her shadowed little face light up when her father scooped her onto his lap, and of hearing the thin note of her laughter at his rumbling voice. In those moments, it was easy to dismiss the slave-woman's stories about his family. I kept them buried deep in my mind, never letting them surface. No one had told them for years. We would forget them, I had resolved, and they would have no power over us again.

Elektra was too young, really, to understand why it was that Iphigenia and I were leaving, but she was quite composed as they waved us off in the first rays of dawn the next morning, holding on to Chrysothemis' hand, Agamemnon's dog at her side. She yawned and turned to her big sister to ask if there were fresh figs for breakfast before we had even got beyond the palace gates.

The rising sun was just staining the sky golden over the tops of the mountains as we climbed into the chariot. The journey would be long, and all the cushions heaped upon our seats would not do much to protect us from the bumpy road. I felt I should use the hours that lay before us to impart some useful maternal advice on what was to come for Iphigenia. I wondered what I could really tell her about marriage.

When Helen and I had talked of our husbands back in Sparta, I could see that we were naive, grasping at the prospect of sophistication and womanhood before us without understanding what it would be like. Even at sixteen, neither of us had really mentioned love. The bards would sing of it, but it seemed more the stuff of myth and legend than reality. My youthful heart might have swelled when I heard how Orpheus adored his bride Eurydice so much that, when she stepped upon a venomous snake on their wedding day, he followed her all the way down into the depths of the Underworld and, despite his quaking fear, played his lyre for Hades so beautifully that his wife was released. I might have shed tears when I heard how he walked ahead of her, leading her toward the light of the world above, but could not help glancing back once—just once! Alas, the condition that Hades had set was that Orpheus must not look at her until she was safely restored to the mortal world, and so she crumpled at his feet, her body, which had been gradually transforming back to flesh, becoming insubstantial air once more. Lost to him forever.

Those were the romantic stories of girlhood. They weren't the truth of marriage. So, I could not tell my daughter of love, exactly. I could hope that when she looked at Achilles, she would see enough of a kinship in his eyes to know that they might lead a peaceable, contented life together. I could tell her that the joy of true love would come when she held her first baby in her arms—before then, even, when she felt it roll and squirm within her, when she sang to her growing belly and placed her hands on the warm, taut skin and marveled at the unimaginable miracle that was to be hers. But I could remember the panic I had felt myself at contemplating such a thing: the fear that walked hand in hand with the happiness, the shadow that hung across that joyful prospect. When I looked at my slim, lithe daughter, I could not help feeling the worry stir within me. We would lay down our lives for our children, and every time we faced birth, we stood on the banks of that great river that separated the living from the dead. A massed army of women, facing that perilous passage with no armor to protect us, only our own strength and hope that we would prevail.

It didn't feel like the right conversation to have on the way to her wedding.

Fortunately, she spoke first. "I'm glad we get to see Father again before he sails to war," she said.

"I am, too," I replied. "We didn't part on the happiest of terms; I'm glad of the chance to make peace before he goes."

"Why not?" She was intrigued, and something about the intimacy of the chariot ride made it easy to talk, to say the things that had been turning over in my mind.

"Helen is my sister," I said. "The way the men speak of her . . ."

The chariot jolted harshly beneath us, and the sun was climbing higher in the sky, beginning to beat down on the thin canopy that shaded us. Dust flew from the wheels, and I wondered what state our fine dresses would be in by the time we arrived. Iphigenia shifted a little on her cushions. "I have heard some things," she said, cautiously.

No doubt she had. Hardly anything else had been talked of since we found it out. "Menelaus is angry," I said, "and I don't blame him. But your father should have enough affection for me to think of protecting my sister. He did not, and so I was angry when he left. I didn't bid him a very kind farewell."

"He says the war will be won within days. Even if we were not to see him now, you would have had your chance to reconcile soon."

My kind girl, always seeing the best in everyone. I wasn't so sure. My tongue had been sharp in my last conversation with Agamemnon, and I regretted some of it, though I still felt the injustice of his words.

"Menelaus should have made a wiser choice of bride," he had scoffed. We were in our chamber; his ships were ready in the harbor and already I looked forward to the quiet that would fall once he had sailed. I felt restless and agitated, my mind on fire with questions for my errant sister. How I wished that I could talk to her, that I had been there in Sparta, that I could have seen this Paris for myself, that I had more than wild speculation to fuel my imaginings.

"All the men of Greece wanted Helen," I said. "You should remember that, surely."

He cast me an irritated glance. "If they wanted her that much, why have they all been so reluctant to bring her home?"

Again, this familiar grumble. It had been a constant refrain as he and Menelaus tried to summon the armies.

"War is not an easy thing to contemplate," I said. "They have wives of their own, children to think of . . ."

He scoffed. "Troy is ours for the taking. They will sail home with riches they have never dreamed of, which they can lavish upon those wives and children." He strode to the window and stared through it intently. "But that they dared to shrink back from their duty when *I* called them to arms, the king of them all. Odysseus, feigning madness. Achilles, disguised as a woman. They should have been eager to fight this war when I summoned them."

"You have Odysseus, and Achilles too." I thought of Penelope with a pang of grief. I knew that she and Odysseus must have plotted it together: that he pretended to be mad as he plowed their fields with salt and ranted and raved nonsense. It had taken the shrewd Palamedes,

whom Agamemnon had sent, to pluck their newborn baby Telemachus
from Penelope's arms and lay the infant down before the plow. When
Odysseus swerved away to save the child, the pretense was exposed as
a lie. My heart had leaped into my throat when I heard that particular
story, and my arms had circled my swollen stomach instinctively. The
thought of her baby, exposed and vulnerable on the earth, the sharp
metal teeth only inches away—I felt a shiver of Penelope's fear. And a
strange sensation of jealousy lurking beneath it. She had wanted her
husband to stay at home, wanted it enough to risk his dishonor and
make him break the oath he himself had suggested years before. I
could not quite bring myself to feel the same about my husband's impending absence. His complaining had been driving me to madness
myself as the armies were assembled.

"Achilles, at least, was not bound to protect Menelaus' claim," he
reflected. "The rest of them, though, those who swore at Sparta—they
should have kept their vow and simply been grateful it was not them
who won her in the first place."

I bristled at this. "Perhaps if one of them had won her instead, she
would have kept her own vow and not run away in the first place."

Agamemnon's face darkened.

"If, in fact, she ran away at all," I conceded. I had heard it a hundred
ways already. Helen had shamelessly hurled herself at Paris: how was
he to resist her beauty? Or she had been duped by Aphrodite, lured
away by a glamour cast by the goddess and not returned to her senses
until she was already halfway across the ocean to Troy. Or perhaps
he had seized her, overpowered her, and dragged her to his ship, she
screaming piously for her absent husband all the way. I had noticed a
lot of men liked to dwell on this last one, picturing perhaps how her
dress might have torn beneath his cruel hands, and how she might
have begged. I closed my eyes for a moment, willing the image away.

Mostly though, they talked of her as though the first scenario was
proven. Who cared if it wasn't? She was spoiled goods, anyway, a tar-
nished prize for Menelaus to reclaim—Menelaus, who had thought
himself the luckiest man in Greece and was now the laughingstock of
everyone. Everyone knew she was no better than a whore, a traitor to

all of Greece, a disgrace. They loved that, all of them, as they glugged their wine and boasted of how the walls of Troy would crumble against the might of strong Greek bronze. I stayed silent. I realized that when I had seen all those suitors clamor in the hall for Helen, I had believed they were there because they loved her, but I had been wrong. They hated her. They hated her because she was so beautiful and because she made them want her so much. Nothing brought them more joy than the fall of a lovely woman. They picked over her reputation like vultures, scavenging for every scrap of flesh they could devour.

I shuddered to think what might happen if Troy fell as easily as they all anticipated. Agamemnon made to leave, but I caught at his sleeve before he could go. "What will happen to her?" I asked him. I made him look at me, searched his dark eyes for the compassion I hoped he possessed. "If Troy falls, what will happen to my sister?"

His face gave nothing away. "It is for Menelaus to decide."

"Menelaus is your younger brother. You can convince him."

He shook his head, just a little. "Helen is Menelaus' wife. We go as sworn to bring her back to him. He has the right to do as he sees fit."

"So, you will not intervene?"

He sighed. "Why would I?"

For me, of course. For his wife. I do not know how he did not see that. But since talk of taking Troy had begun, I did not think he had seen anything else but their triumph.

"You don't care for Helen, even though she is my sister and I love her." My voice was low and hard and furious. "You don't even care about the oath you swore. You are glad that this happened! I know you are. You want nothing but your war, to prove that you lead the Greeks."

His eyes were unfathomable. "The greatest of them all," he said quietly.

"I was wrong when I said that," I hissed. "You will never be the greatest of the Greeks. If my sister dies at your brother's hand and you do not lift a finger to stop it, you will be the worst and most cowardly of them all."

And that was how he left to go to war. It didn't seem any better a topic of conversation to share with my daughter than the previous ones I had considered. But perhaps, I reflected, as our royal chariot bumped and jostled its way to Aulis, perhaps he had thought on my words. This marriage of our daughter: no doubt it was to secure his alliances, to fasten Achilles' rather dubious loyalty more firmly to him. But a little of it could be, just maybe, a chance to make peace between us. To honor Iphigenia with a great husband, even if it was a little sooner than I would have wanted. And a way to see us both again.

I sat back and tried to make myself as comfortable as I could. Despite the heat and the dust whipped up from the road that swirled all around us, Iphigenia looked as fresh and beautiful as a newly bloomed flower.

"You are right," I told her. "We will send our men to war with a great celebration, for nothing is happier and more hopeful than a wedding."

And at my reassurance, she smiled.

The sky at Aulis was a solid, cloudless blue. We had grown so hot and tired on the journey that I had been anticipating with some pleasure our arrival at the coast, but not even the whisper of a breeze gave us any respite. My legs felt cramped as I stepped onto the sandy earth, and the taut drum of my stomach ached as though a band were tightening ever more mercilessly around me.

No one was there to greet us. I was surprised at this. All that was before us was a long stretch of tents that spread across the plains as far as I could see. Behind us, the horses snorted and scuffed their hooves in the dust, whickering for water. The herald who had escorted us, he who had brought us Agamemnon's decree, scurried past me, and before I could speak, he was lost among the maze of tents.

The whole of the Greek army was here somewhere, but it was eerily quiet. No shouts or chatter, or any other noise that would have betrayed the presence of thousands of soldiers, broke the stillness. Perhaps it was the heat—the terrible, deadening heat—and the strange flatness of the air that subdued them.

We waited, my daughter and me. At length, I saw a moving shape among the tents, and, as I watched, it resolved itself into a man, short and broad of stature. Recognizable to me in moments.

"Odysseus," I greeted him. I held myself as tall and straight as I could, though I felt rumpled and dirty from traveling. I gave Iphigenia a surreptitious poke to stop her slouching. However thirsty and exhausted we felt, we were royal women, and our dignity was everything.

Odysseus bent his head briefly to us. When I had seen him last, his eyes had danced continually with merriment, with the glee of knowing that he was always several steps ahead of any opponent. His face looked shadowed; gray and grim. I wondered if it was the strain of missing his newborn son and his clever wife. It could be months before he saw them again.

"Clytemnestra," he said. "I hope your journey has been comfortable." He turned to Iphigenia. "And you, my lady," he went on, "we have all eagerly awaited your presence here."

"Where is my husband?" I asked. I could sympathize with his somber mood on the eve of war, but this was the day before my daughter's wedding, and I wanted to feel some cheer, some sense of celebration to lift our spirits.

"King Agamemnon talks of strategy with his advisers," Odysseus said smoothly. "War tactics, and so on. Come, I will show you to your quarters so that you can rest before tomorrow. The ceremony will take place at sunrise," he added, "and we hope to sail shortly afterward."

A jumble of questions jostled in my mind. Why was Odysseus, the wiliest man in Greece, not participating in a meeting of strategy? Why an early morning wedding? If they were to leave so early, having the wedding this evening would make more sense, to allow us all time to celebrate. How odd, to conduct the ceremony and then leave for war immediately afterward. I glanced at Iphigenia. She looked so young, standing in this strange place. Perhaps I should be grateful to Agamemnon that he had arranged it thus, so that her husband would sail to Troy and leave her untouched—for as long as he was away, at least.

"I hope a fair wind blows tomorrow, then," I remarked. "You will not sail far if the day is like this."

"We have had many days of calm," Odysseus answered. He had turned to lead the way, and we started to walk through the rows of tents. It was then that I saw the men, the soldiers taking rest in the shade. Their eyes followed us as we walked. I felt the intensity of their stares boring into us. "But the gods will smile on us after tomorrow morning. I trust our ritual will bring the winds we need to see us swiftly on our way to Troy."

Was this it, then? They hoped the gods would smile upon the marriage and grant them their passage? I did not like the idea of Agamemnon bargaining our daughter to the immortals in this way. I hoped it was not the case.

"Your tent," Odysseus told us. It was set aside from the others, and I hoped for some respite from the heat as we entered. With still no breath of wind to give us even the faintest breeze, however, it was even more stifling within than without. I glanced at Iphigenia. Her cheeks were flushed and her eyes heavy.

"Is there water?" I asked, dizziness seizing me. There was a wide pallet made up with soft fabrics, for us to sleep upon, I presumed, and I sat hurriedly on its side. Our trunks had been unloaded and were already placed in the corner, beneath the billowing sag of the slanted roof.

"The men have drawn it from the spring for you today," Odysseus answered. I saw the jugs set out on a low table, one brimming with water and the other sweet with wine. "You should have all you need for tonight; all you will have to do is rest."

His courtesy was immaculate, but it felt odd, stilted. I could sense his desperation to be away from us, and I could not fathom why that should be. I got the impression that he had not wanted the job of greeting us, that any vestige of friendship from the days we had briefly spent in each other's company in Sparta had dissolved entirely. I could not complain that we were not treated with respect, but I had not expected so muted a welcome as this.

"And my husband?" I asked, my head clouded from the heat, the confusion, the strangeness of it all. "He will be here when he has concluded his business with his advisers?"

Odysseus' words came smoothly, his face still wiped so carefully blank of feeling. "He may be talking late into the night, so do not wait for him. I must withdraw; I am required at his side. But fear not: there are guards all around your tent. You will be safe tonight."

He was gone before I could ask another question. Iphigenia and I shared a look of mutual confusion. "I am sure your father will be here as soon as he can," I offered weakly.

She went to pour some water from the jug into one of the cups, which she handed to me. I took it gratefully, hoping it would clear some of the buzzing in my head.

Where was Achilles? He should have been here to greet us, to lay eyes on his bride. I knew there was a war to fight, but could he not shrug it aside for one night to give us the most meager offering that courtesy demanded?

Iphigenia had crossed the tent to unbuckle the thick leather straps on the wooden trunk we had brought with us from Mycenae. She yanked at the bonds and loosened the lid. As she raised it, the fragrance of crushed petals rose up and suffused the tent with their rich, intoxicating scent. She pulled out the saffron-yellow robe folded carefully within, shaking out its creases. The fine-woven linen was vivid as an egg yolk, slipping through my daughter's hands in rippling folds. Carefully, holding it with reverence, she draped it over the high back of one of the two chairs, and looked it over with a glimmer of pride shining in her eyes. *She will be a thing of beauty tomorrow morning*, I thought. When she stepped out before the soldiers, before her distracted father and mysteriously absent husband, she would take away their breath and make them regret their dismissive treatment of us tonight.

As the sun dipped and the rectangle of sky visible through the entrance to our tent slowly darkened, we could smell the fires burning across the camp, soon followed by the fragrance of roasting meat. The evening air brought no respite from the relentless heat, but I was a little revived by the wine and the water and the chance to rest. I stood up and peered out of the tent.

Ranked around us were indeed the guards that Odysseus had promised. They stood to attention, half a dozen of them flanking our tent. Each held a tall ash spear, its point glimmering sharp in the emerging moonlight. None looked at me.

From what danger did Agamemnon seek to protect us here? Surely, he did not trust his own soldiers so little as to think his wife and daughter at risk from attack in his very camp? But why else would he put an armed guard outside our tent?

"When will we eat?" I asked, directing my question at any of them, since none would catch my eye.

The foremost of them dipped his head. "Your meal will be brought to you," he answered.

"And will your king be joining us?" I asked, irritation fraying my voice.

He did not answer. I fumed for a moment, feeling all at once foolish and impotent as I stood there. At home, I had grown used to giving orders and having them obeyed. Here, in this strange place, with no sight of a familiar face or even one that seemed happy to see us, I felt wrong-footed and uncertain.

I let the tent flap fall, shrouding us again, and sat back. As promised, food did appear, a tray of meat and bread and fruit, brought to us by another silent and anonymous face. No sign of Agamemnon. I bit back my impatience, not wanting to cause Iphigenia any more upset.

"We never eat alone together," she commented. She smiled at me, soothing my annoyance and the faint drumbeat of concern that pulsed away in the back of my mind. "No Chrysothemis, no Elektra, no servants . . ."

"A rare occurrence," I agreed.

"I wonder who will be my dining companions in Phthia," she said.

"There is a war to be fought before that happens," I offered weakly. I did not like to think of her so far away, but when Achilles returned, he would inevitably claim his wife.

"What do you know of him?" she asked me. Her voice was low.

"Just that he is a great soldier," I said. "He will be a great asset to your father in this war." I searched for more. "I know you must be afraid," I began.

She shook her head. "I am not afraid." She looked at me, her face soft and open in the flickering light. "There is an adventure ahead—a new land, new people."

I remembered leaving Sparta, coming to Mycenae as Agamemnon's bride. How frightening it was for everything to change, but that thrill too, of throwing up the dice in the air and seeing how they would land.

"His mother is a sea nymph," Iphigenia went on. "I wonder if I will meet her one day; what would that be like?" Her voice gathered pace, a throb of excitement running through it. "I have heard that when he was a baby, she anointed him with ambrosia and set him on a pyre to burn away what was mortal within him and leave only the immortal. Only his father, Peleus, came in and stopped her, for fear that she would incinerate him whole and entire."

"Or that she dipped him in the River Styx by his heel to give him invulnerability," I suggested dryly. "He is a man about whom many legends abound."

"I wonder what the truth of them might be," Iphigenia said, a little dreamily.

I caught a sigh in my throat. The stories about him made him sound fantastical; I hoped the reality would not be a disappointing one. "You will find out," I told her. "I do not suppose your father is coming to-night after all, so let us sleep. Tomorrow will be quite a day."

I heard the movement outside the tent, waking me from a deep slumber. At my side, the bed was empty and rumpled. I sat up, searching the gray dark for Iphigenia. I could just make out her shape, pulling her dress over her head.

"Can you hear them?" she asked me softly.

Footsteps outside, a host of them, and the soft murmur of male voices. I shook away the fragments of my dream. It still felt like the middle of the night, but Iphigenia had tied back the drapes of the tent, and the darkness was leaching slowly from the sky. The sound of the men was moving away; they must be going to make preparations for the wedding.

I struggled awkwardly to my feet, the bulk of pregnancy making me stiff and slow. "Come, let me help you," I told her.

The yellow fabric draped over her, gathered at the shoulder and falling in folds across her body. I combed my fingers through her hair, letting the curls fall around her neck. "You are beautiful," I said tenderly.

The murky light filtering through the entrance was obscured for a moment. A dark shape hovered just outside. "It is time," came a man's voice.

"Where is Agamemnon?" I demanded. Surely he would at last appear.

"He waits for his daughter at the altar."

I had hoped he would be here before, that I could see him before the wedding took place, but apparently it was not to be. I hurried to dress myself, wishing that we had more time to prepare. This strange, rushed business was not how a wedding ought to be conducted. Still, I held my tongue. Iphigenia seemed to tingle with emotion, and I feared that she might be overcome with the immensity of what awaited.

"Come, I will be with you," I whispered, and took her hand to lead her outside.

The early morning was misty and damp, a welcome respite from the blazing sun of the previous day. Through the haze of drizzle, I saw her eyes burning with fierce emotion, and I drew her close to me and kissed her forehead. No words passed between us.

The guards who encircled our tent now flanked us at either side. We walked across the unfamiliar terrain, past the final set of tents. I strained to see what was ahead in the still silence.

As we passed the edge of the camp, the grasses beneath our feet gave way to sand. Behind us, the tents were a looming mass in the dark. Ahead, the sun had just begun to emerge from beyond the flat mirror of the sea, and there on the beach I could see an altar, temporarily erected on a platform on the sand. The figures that stood there were only dark silhouettes, but one of them must be Agamemnon.

Iphigenia's hand squeezed mine. I looked at her; she smiled at me, though her eyes threatened to fill, and we both breathed a strange, exhilarated laugh.

Just as I opened my mouth to speak, an arm locked about my throat. I thrashed in its iron grip, trying desperately to turn my head, to see who had seized me. At my side, two soldiers took hold of Iphigenia's arms, and her little hand was pulled from mine as they marched her down toward that altar, away from me. Panic gripped me; what was the meaning of this? I pulled at the arm fastened so tightly around me, clawing futilely to escape.

The sun rose higher, orange spilling through the sky, illuminating the figures at the altar. I could see my husband, standing there. He did not move. The baby within me stirred as though it sensed my distress; it rolled and kicked as I wrestled with that solid, immobile bulk that held me fast.

And Iphigenia was marched onward, out of my reach. Agamemnon watched her come. The mist was dissipating in the golden rays of the sun. His face was blank.

I whipped my head from side to side. From every angle, the army watched. Great sullen ranks of men, gathered on this beach in the dawn light, as still and silent as the air.

Odysseus was there, next to my husband; Menelaus on the other side. I did not recognize another face. My breath came in sharp gasps. I searched for Achilles, though I would not know him if I saw him. Against all evidence to the contrary, I searched for signs that this was indeed a wedding, that somehow this could be explained.

At the altar, Agamemnon drew forth a knife. The blade shone in the glow of the sunrise behind him.

I saw the growing realization on my daughter's face in the moment that she saw what he intended, and the fear leaped into her eyes. A shriek tore from my throat and reverberated through the still air.

He had her in a moment, and spun her around to face the army from behind the altar, his arms holding her fast against him. He must have smelled her hair, felt its softness against his chest. She looked at me, my daughter, from her father's grip. In that paralyzed moment where nothing moved, I still thought that it was not real, that this could not happen.

His arm was so fast. It was a blur of movement, a slash through the air against her neck, her soft and precious neck. Before she slumped across the grooved wood of the altar, I saw the blood streaming across that beautiful yellow dress, and for a second I thought how it would be ruined now, how the stain would never fade, no matter how hard it was scrubbed between stones down at the river. The river, back in Mycenae, where Iphigenia would never return after all.

I do not know what noise I made, only that the arm at my neck suddenly loosened. Although my legs gave way beneath my body, I hauled myself across the sand, toward the broken body of my child. I wanted only to hold her, to see life flicker in her eyes, although her blood was spilling down from the altar, across the wooden slats beneath, dripping dark onto the sand. The wood was rough beneath my fingers, splintering the flesh as I gripped it and pulled myself to my feet.

A swirl of wind whipped my hair across my face, plastered it to my streaming eyes. I heard it ripple across the water, the splash of waves all at once against the shore. The rumble through the crowd of realization. Appreciation.

Iphigenia's body slid from the wooden altar, thudding against the platform. I pushed my hair out of my face. The blood, the blood was everywhere, smeared across her drained skin, thickening in her hair, her hair that I had run my fingers through that morning.

He was walking away already. His cloak rippled out behind him in the new-sprung breeze. He had not spoken a word.

⁓⁓⁓

The army sailed almost immediately. Everything was ready; they must have had it all prepared before we even arrived at Aulis. As we had rattled along that hot and dusty track, they would have been loading the ships, anticipating a swift reward from the goddess in the form of a blessing of winds to blow them far away from the bloodstained sand.

A long time later, I would hear the bards sing of my daughter's death, along with all the other stories they told of Troy. Often, they would say that at the very moment Agamemnon raised the knife, Artemis took pity on Iphigenia and swapped her for a deer. In this version of the story, my daughter lives on as a priestess and favorite of the goddess on an island somewhere. Crucially, in this telling, Agamemnon did nothing more than slaughter a simple animal. It's poetic and pretty, and so very clean.

But I saw her body convulse in her father's arms as he drew that blade across her throat. I held her, warm and bleeding and dead on the beach, while the sun climbed higher in the sky and the winds whipped up around us. I remember how the crimson-streaked saffron fabric fluttered around her ankles, and how I stared for so long at her face, not believing that her eyes would not open again and that she would not look at me and call me mother and kiss me.

How long I might have sat there, my child cradled in my lap, I do not know. How many hours had I sat pinned by her soft little weight when she was a baby? On those nights when her eyes had fluttered closed at last and I had not dared to put her down lest she wake, so had stayed there, in my chair, charting the passage of the moon through the sky and listening to her breathe. I felt my own chest rise and fall, here on the bloodied beach, and I wondered how it continued, how my heart still beat in my chest when this had happened.

In a daze, I watched them come. The women. We had seen only men since we had arrived at Aulis, but now the women walked across the beach toward me. Women from the village perhaps, women who had tended to the soldiers while they had camped here. I did not know or ask. Somehow, women always came after a death. In the past, I had been among them myself, tended to a stricken mother, gently loosened her hold on the corpse she cradled. Plagues, poxes, or accident; it was not an uncommon thing to lose a child. I felt the soothing touch of gentle hands, heard the murmurs, the words I had probably said myself to another mother, in another life. When they tried to lift me to my feet, I resisted at first, but they were saying *the baby, the baby*, and at last I realized they were not talking about Iphigenia. They wanted me to come to the shade, to drink some water for the sake of the baby in my womb. Iphigenia's head was resting in my lap, and I laid her down on the rough wood as tenderly as if it had been her crib, as though I feared to wake her. Then I let them pull me up. It seemed impossible that the waves still lapped at the sand, that my feet could take a step and then another. While two of them helped me along, others knelt around my daughter's body. She was so slight, so small, that they could lift her with ease, but I was glad even in my shattered mind that they touched her with such care, as if she was made of glass.

The camp had been left in ruins. Scorched circles of earth where fires had been, abandoned wooden stakes that had held up tents, whatever they considered trash just left upon the scrubby earth. They must have stripped it bare with ruthless efficiency in their eagerness to leave.

The tent in which Iphigenia and I had slept was left untouched. Perhaps no one wanted to go near it. It was there the women guided me now. They pulled out a chair and made me sit, splashed water across my blood-smeared skin and held a cup to my lips so I could drink. The pallet on which we had slept, where she had lain beside me, breathing soft and even through the night—they heaved it out, stripped it of its fabric, and laid her body out upon it. But as they brought water and cloths, I pushed away their ministrations. This I would do myself.

I bathed her body alone. The cloths were soft, the water warm. I pulled away the ruined dress, her wedding dress. I kissed her clean skin. When she was small, she would shriek with laughter when I buried my face in the plump folds of her arms, the dimpled knees. Now her limbs were long and coltish. Now she lay cold and still, and I might as well have kissed the unresponsive earth.

They brought me scented oils to rub into her flesh. They helped me wind clean white linen around her body. They brought me a wreath; a crown of flowers twisted and woven together so that I could rest it on her hair. A coin to place on her mouth. The last things I could do for her. The things I did for my child so she could rest, even while my body felt like it would split apart, that no one could hold this much pain inside them and not shatter.

When I stepped back to see her, stark and beautiful, framed by petals, draped in soft fabric, her hair ruffled gently by that taunting, endless breeze, I could not understand how the sun shone down from the sky, the same sun that had risen over her death.

I wanted to claw my way down into the damp earth and let it suffocate me. I wanted the dark to close over my face forever. But we had not let her go yet; it was not done. In Mycenae, great tombs were cut into the rocks to shelter the remains of the king and his family. Iphigenia would not lie there beside them. Her bones would not molder along with the murderers whose line had led down so inexorably to Agamemnon. In Troy, the Greeks would burn their battle dead atop glorious pyres. My daughter, the first victim of their war, would burn before them.

Later, I would force myself to remember all the details of this day. I would pick them over, grimly intent on knowing it all. But the people of Aulis who came to help me, I never knew their names if they told me. My daughter's body was burned to the songs of strangers; it was their tears that watered the sand, their prayers that accompanied her ashes into the snaking wind and carried them across the ocean.

I remember pouring wine onto the earth, honey and milk and water, too, as the sky darkened. I held a lock of hair in my hand, my hair, and I placed it under her hands, which were folded together over her chest. I know the sunset was magnificent, a burning flame sinking into the sea, setting the clouds on fire with pink and gold. I remember the crackling of the flames as the pyre was lit, and how I dug my fingernails into my palms until the skin bled, to stop myself from plunging into that fire and pulling her body out. I don't know how I let it be consumed, her face that I had kissed, her hair that I had combed, all blackened and charred to crumbled ash.

My children came from my body; their flesh was born of mine. Their arms reached out for me first, they called for me in the night and I scooped them into my embrace and breathed in the sweet scent of their little bald heads. As they grew, I felt the echo always of their infant selves. My body could not know what my mind did; it ached with her absence.

I had feared to send her to wifehood, to become a mother herself one day. That separation was hard enough. I watched the fire spark into the night sky and wondered where she could be. Making her way down that dank, twisting path to the Underworld alone? I had gone everywhere before her; trodden the paths I sent her down to make sure they were safe before I let her go. How could I let her go now, to where I did not know, without me at her side?

But if I followed her there, how could I avenge her? The thought was cold and clear in my mind amid the chaos of grief and pain as I kept my vigil through the night. That pain that clawed me apart from within, tearing away at my flesh and stripping me down to nothing. Nothing but this. The hard certainty at my very core; the cold taste of iron and blood in my center that said: *He will feel this too, and worse.*

It was not the baby I still carried in my body that propelled me from the sand long after the fire consumed my daughter and left nothing but bitter ash behind. In the light of the rising sun, I prayed that my husband would survive this war and come home safe to me. I wanted no Trojan soldier to take what was mine; no glory-seeking warrior to seize his chance of fame by plunging his sword into Agamemnon's heart. *Let him come back*, I hissed into the empty sky. *Let him come back so that I can see his eyes as the light drains from them. Let him come back and die at the hands of his bitterest enemy. Let him come back so that I can watch him suffer. And let me make it slow.*

PART
II

CHAPTER TEN

Elektra

When Clytemnestra came back from Aulis without Iphigenia, her face was streaked and puffy, and her hair hung in tangled ropes. Chrysothemis had brought me out to greet the returning wagon, but when we saw this woman who barely even resembled our mother, I turned and hid my face in the drapes of my sister's skirt. Even her voice was different—hoarse and ragged and guttural as she spat out her words like poison dripping all over us.

Once, Chrysothemis had taken me to the harbor, and I had seen the fishermen hauling great barrels of sea snails, their spined shells rattling together. When I asked her what they were for, she told me how they would be crushed and the purple dye squeezed from the pulpy fragments of their bodies. "It's how we get such pretty clothes," she said teasingly, flicking the deep color that edged my dress. Suddenly, the trimmings I had taken such pride in before struck me as revolting. The deep reddish-purple hue that spoke of luxury and wealth all at once seemed to me to look more like bloodstains, and I could not push away the image of those slimy bodies squashed until the thick, dark mucus spurted from them. Where I had felt beautiful and dainty, I now felt stained and spoiled. That was what my mother's words made me think of then. Like toxic venom, sour bile, heaved from her guts and showered over us.

Iphigenia was dead. I tried to understand it, what it really meant.

She hadn't come back; she was not going to return. I wouldn't hear the light patter of her footsteps; she wouldn't be there to sit and play dolls with me. I would never again be allowed to climb onto a stool so that I could crown her with the flowers I liked to pick from the gardens and twist together.

And Mother was telling us that Father had done it. That made no sense at all.

I looked up at Chrysothemis. Did she know why? Her face was pale, her eyes wide as she listened. I tightened my grip on her hand, trying to make her look at me. No one seemed like themselves and I was scared.

"It was a trick," Mother said. "No wedding. He slit her throat for a fair wind." Her face crumpled as though she was about to cry. I reached my arms out to her, not understanding what she meant, but afraid to see her so broken, so strange. But she just stared for a long moment as though she didn't recognize me. And then she walked away, leaving us there.

It was Chrysothemis who wrapped her arms around me. Even though she was only a few years older than me, she was the one to comfort me, to explain it as best she could. "Artemis demanded it," she told me later, her voice scratchy with sobs. "Father had to give up something he loved, to prove how brave he is."

I nodded slowly. If the gods told you that you must do something, you had no choice. That was something I knew. Something I could understand.

"It had to be him—not another soldier," she went on. "He's the leader of the army, so he had to be the one."

"It isn't his fault," I whispered. Breathing out the words made me feel lighter: the crushing weight our mother had deposited on us lifted all at once with the revelation, with the truth of it. Artemis had spoken and so Iphigenia was dead.

But my mother was not dead, so I didn't understand why she was behaving as though she was. She locked herself away, and even when she came out, she was like a ghost drifting among us. I was scared to look at her blank face, her empty eyes. My legs ached and my head hurt, but no one seemed to notice. Where was our mother? Why didn't she come to bathe my forehead and sit by my bed again?

Out in the courtyard, I stood facing away from the palace, looking out to the rolling mountains, past the domed building that stood farther out on the plain. That was the tomb that was supposed to house the bodies of our family one day. They hadn't brought Iphigenia back, though, and that thought was unsettling: that she'd gone beyond our reach, that we couldn't even say goodbye. I looked up to the wispy clouds wreathing the mountains' summits and I turned my palms up to the sky. "Artemis," I whispered. I tried to think of the priestesses, of how their faces would go slack and their gazes distant when they prayed, as though they were outside themselves. How would I know if she was listening? I stared at the clouds until my vision swam. I didn't know how to address her, how to ask her for what I wanted. All I knew of Artemis was that she hunted, that she ran through the forests, that she was fierce and wild. I didn't know why she'd taken my sister or what she wanted with my family. *Just let it be enough*, was all I could think. "Let my father come home," I said aloud, desperately hoping that she heard me, that she'd listen to a child's bargaining. "Please don't take him too."

Whether the goddess was moved or not, my father was gone, across the sea to somewhere I couldn't even imagine. Iphigenia was in the Underworld, somewhere I couldn't follow. My mother was behind a closed door and somehow farther away from me than either one of them. I couldn't understand why Clytemnestra wouldn't come out, why she wouldn't smile at us like she used to and tell us stories again. But even when I knocked on the solid wood and called to her, she never answered or gave any sign she heard me at all.

If my father came back, he would make her, I was sure of it. Everyone in the palace did as he said. If only he were here, he could tell her. Every evening I took out the dagger he'd left me, which I kept wrapped in cloth and hidden beneath my bed. I cradled it carefully, traced the outline of the lion. I hoped my father would snarl in the face of the Trojan warriors just the same. He'd be unafraid of their spears and their war cries; they would crumple in his path, and he would come home victorious, I knew it. I looked out toward the distant sea every day, searching the empty waves for the approach of his long ships. But day after day passed, every one of them the same, and still he was gone.

CHAPTER ELEVEN

Clytemnestra

I feared the impending birth like I had feared no other. I was not afraid of the pain. I didn't fear for my own life, or even for the baby's. Above all else, I was terrified that I would look into my new baby's face and see Iphigenia. Perhaps it could have been a comfort to me, but all I could feel was an aching dread that yet more untapped grief lay within me, and that the storm of motherhood would wreck me against still more jagged rocks. I cringed away from the prospect, weak and cowardly.

I fought the swelling surge within me when it came. I paced the floor as long as I could, bracing my fists against the wall, swallowing my howls. Sweat bathed my forehead and I whimpered. I could no more stop it than I could go back to that beach, which I saw whenever I closed my eyes, and drag my daughter away.

He was a son. A baby boy, whose arrival I had thought would crumble the cold shell of my existence and leave me squirming in the harsh sunlight, exposed and raw. The truth of it, perhaps, was worse, for while I braced myself against the agony of love and grief renewed, I held my baby and felt nothing at all.

He gave us some version of normality, I suppose. I could not lie, dull with pain, all day any longer. He was only a baby, and I pitied him the lifetime that awaited him. I had not dreamed I would bring my children into a world that could drain their blood in the light of dawn before they'd had a chance to live at all. I felt a swell of sympathy for a blameless infant born to parents such as Agamemnon and me: his father a monster beyond all imagining, and me, his mother, unable to summon a scrap of the devotion I had lavished on my girls. It was a mechanical kind of mothering I brought to Orestes. I cradled him and fed him and kissed his tiny face, but I did not build his future in dreams. I handed him off to the nurses whenever I could. I did not turn to the smoking altars in the city and pray he would be granted a life. I knew those prayers would go unheard. Every mother in Mycenae made these fervent bargains—not just that their babies be spared plague and fever, but that their husbands would sail home from Troy. That latter prayer, I joined. But it was the only entreaty I would make of the gods now. Better for Iphigenia if she had succumbed to sickness before she could talk, before she could dream of her future herself.

So, I tended to the baby when I had to, and left my chamber to resume my other maternal duties, though Chrysothemis and Elektra could see through my tired attempts; the numbing shroud that lay about my heart. To what end did I teach them to weave or dance or sing? How did I know I did not raise another child for slaughter? If the tide turned on the Trojan beaches, if Agamemnon's army was beaten back, would a mob charge the palace for innocent blood to pay the price to the ravenous gods once more? The thought of such pain again was a burning brand to my flesh. Better to protect myself, to hide behind the only armor I could construct. I looked over my children's heads; I stared past them and did not listen when they talked. I wanted no more tender memories to shred my heart when they too were taken from me.

Besides, Agamemnon had left a gulf behind him. Not only was the king gone from Mycenae, but all the men of fighting age. He had taken them with him, determined to have the best and most powerful force among the Achaeans. All that was left in Mycenae were the older men, too frail for war, and boys too young and raw to go. I heard the old men, plaintive and fretting when I walked by. How to run the kingdom, how to arbitrate every dispute, how to manage the stocks and stores for the winter ahead when the men would still be at Troy. How to defend ourselves against marauders, when they saw how unprotected our king had left us in his eagerness to win glory on foreign shores. I paused behind the pillars of the throne room, hearing the anxious whine of the men's voices. Down the corridor, the scatter of my daughters' laughter echoed. I searched for the note of Iphigenia's voice among them before I could stop myself, before I could shield myself. I flinched away from them, turned on my heel, and strode into the great airy chamber of the throne room before I could think.

The men's eyes were upon me; part imploring, part suspicious. I heard the flutter of childish footsteps; the girls had passed by, leaving blessed silence in their wake.

If Agamemnon, despite his fragile ego and fierce vanity, had managed Mycenae, it certainly was not beyond me to do it.

My voice rang out, the echo in the vaulted space making me sound harder and more imperious than I expected. "Mycenae struggles in the absence of the men." Every movement careful and deliberate, I took my place upon the throne beside Agamemnon's empty seat. I smoothed my dress, ran my gaze across each expectant and uncertain face. "It needs a leader." I let my words sink in. "So why don't you bring the most pressing of the problems to me and I will give you my commands."

They might have bristled, might have protested. But their faces betrayed relief instead. No one wanted to be the one to face Agamemnon on his return and explain to our furious king why his riches had been plundered and his power squandered while he was away. They were glad to have someone willing to take the blame. And I was glad, so passionately grateful, to have problems before me that had solutions, to set my mind on something with a purpose and an answer: anything to stop it wandering down dark and winding tunnels to a place I could never reach in search of something I could never have.

Some of the fog that had hung about me since Aulis at last began to lift. But the resolve that had been with me since I stood on that beach beside my daughter's funeral pyre, that did not soften. It burned within me, an inextinguishable flame. I preserved his kingdom, not to present to him upon his return, but to keep as my own.

CHAPTER TWELVE

Cassandra

Paris kept Helen cloistered at first. I didn't know whether it was a glimmering of shame at last, a discomfort when he looked into our father's lined face, creased anew with worry at what this wayward son of Troy had done. Or perhaps my brother just feared that someone else might steal her away, take the opportunity that he had seized in Sparta. But he couldn't resist bringing her out for long. What was the point of having the most beautiful woman in the world as your wife if no one else could see her?

She was charming, too. I watched her in the halls of the palace, observed the ease with which she would talk to everyone. She treated Priam and Hecabe with a deferential respect, and while my mother's eyes stayed shaded with suspicion, I could see my father relax in her presence. I watched her engage Hector in conversation, his smiles genuine as far as I could see. I wondered how many times he had considered bundling her onto a ship laden with gold and sending her back to her husband with our most fervent apologies. It must have crossed his mind. But Priam had accepted her, and he was our king. The days passed and still no sign of Greek vengeance bore down on the horizon.

I stayed away from her. I felt embarrassed that I had torn her veil when she first arrived, ashamed that whatever she had heard of Paris' mad sister was undoubtedly proven true the moment she met me. When I felt the warmth of her gaze upon me and suspected that she was about to speak, I fled. It wasn't until she came to the temple of Apollo that I first spoke to her at all.

She was unmistakable as she made her way across the path toward the entrance. I was in the shadows, half hidden behind a pillar as I watched her come. The breeze stirred her dress, sending it rippling around her legs. She stepped so lightly, like a cloud drifting through our city, sculpted into a perfect human shape, but no more substantial than air. Something we might never take hold of, something that might float away at any moment, beyond our reach. I couldn't take my eyes off her. Her gaze was demurely downcast, her arms heaped with flowers that I supposed she brought to offer the god. It was prudent of her to seek the favor of our patron immortal, to bind herself to Troy and its protectors. The whims of Aphrodite alone wouldn't be enough to keep her and Paris safe.

She didn't look up until she was at the steps. When she did, she smiled as though surprised to see me, but I was sure she had known I was watching her the whole length of the path.

"Cassandra," she greeted me. Her voice was full of sincerity and warmth.

I tried to meet her eyes, but my gaze darted away. A tiny lizard flitted across the warm stone, between the bars of sunlight and shadow that filtered through the columns of the temple. It paused, holding itself in perfect stillness as though it too awaited my response. I didn't know how to speak to her at all.

"I'm sorry if I'm interrupting your duties," she said.

I shook my head. "Come inside," I said, still keeping my face turned away. I had an impression of her hair swinging as she passed me, her smile, the sweet scent of the flowers she carried. Turning inside, I blinked rapidly, trying to shake the burned shapes stamped across my vision by the bright sunshine outside as my eyes adjusted to the dim interior.

"It's beautiful," she said. I wasn't sure if she was talking about the temple as a whole or the statue of Apollo, which she was looking up toward. I thought for a second of his eyes turning toward us, his ivory feet flexing and lifting from his plinth, his carved robe billowing around his shoulders. I wondered if she would still stand there with the same unshakable confidence if he did.

"Are there temples like this in Sparta?" I was startled by the question I hadn't known I was going to ask.

She considered it thoughtfully. "Some things are similar," she said. "But Troy is such a different kind of place." She sighed. "I hadn't left Sparta since I was a child. This is another world."

I wanted to ask where else it was that she had gone, but I hesitated. There was an echo of sadness in her tone when she said it, something I wasn't sure that I could or should probe.

"Did Paris tell you much about it?" I said at last, and then flinched at the image of the two of them on board his ship, sailing away from her home. Was that something she would want to revisit, or was it a painful memory for her? I truly couldn't guess. She didn't seem like the woman I'd pictured, smug and serene in the face of the disaster they had brought with them. Instead, she was quiet and contemplative, quite different to Paris. She wasn't so easy to hate when she was standing right in front of me.

"How do you describe something that someone has never imagined?" She smiled wryly. "Anyway, Paris barely knows Troy himself. He is almost as much a stranger here as I am."

He didn't behave like a stranger, though. He seemed so easy, so familiar in the palace, as though he'd grown up there, sprawling in ornately carved chairs all his life, sipping from jeweled goblets, swathing himself in fine linen, always smiling, always fluent.

"Everyone in Sparta knew me," Helen continued. "Me and my sister, Clytemnestra." A chill draft of air snaked in around the curved columns, prickled the skin of my arms. "And I knew them. Here, everyone knows my name, but I don't know theirs, or anything about them." She looked over her shoulder at me and now our eyes met properly. "Though I know a little about you—that you see things."

"If you've heard that, you know that no one believes it. That they think I'm mad."

She shrugged. "As I said, it's hard to describe something that someone hasn't imagined. For people who haven't been visited by a god, it's easy to disbelieve. My mother—people thought she was lying at first, when she said that Zeus came to her."

"Why did they change their minds?"

"I was born."

Helen's inhuman beauty was the proof; everyone was convinced that she had divine parentage as soon as they saw her. I looked down. Where was my evidence? Even when my warnings came to pass, people seemed to forget what I had told them. My words were insubstantial, lost on the air the moment they were spoken.

"When Paris saw the goddesses, Aphrodite promised him that I would be his wife. And here I am." She smiled and I remembered my irritation with him when he had told us that story—or part of it, at least. He had left out that Helen was to be the prize. "But if Apollo has given you a gift that people can't see, maybe it's easier for them to think it's madness instead."

"A gift," I repeated. The gilded face of the statue stayed impassive. I bit the inside of my cheek, stopped myself from saying any more. Beauty and love were gifts, perhaps—even if I knew that Helen's beauty was a terrible thing, an incitement to war and chaos. But if I told her it was so, for all the kindness she had just spoken, she'd dismiss it like anyone else. I made myself still, my arms locked across my chest. She might seem as though she understood, but I knew that if I told her, if I let her glimpse even a fraction of the insight that shattered my mind, she would find a way to skate over it, to ignore the truth of it, to hear something else in its place. "You have come to make an offering," I said. "Very wise of you, to come to Apollo, new to our city as you are. If you are to be a princess of Troy, you do well to honor him."

"Of course." She tossed her head slightly, her face smooth and friendly as before, but something had closed between us. I was a priestess again, busying myself in the rituals I'd learned, the ones I could repeat and hold on to every day when everything else around me seemed to lurch and twist and change. That was the gift: stability. The solid stone floor that I could press my forehead to, the walls that stood around me, that gave me shelter—at least for now, until the storm I knew was coming swept in.

When Helen left, I didn't watch her go. I knew she would be back, and despite myself, I felt a flicker of curiosity, a pull toward her: the other outsider in my city.

⋯⋯⋯⋯⋯

Although I knew it would come, still I couldn't prepare myself for the moment that the Greek fleet was sighted on the horizon; a vast row of long ships with curved prows that spanned the edge of the world. Never before had anyone seen so many ships.

Even Helen was taken aback; Helen, who visited me at the temple, returning after that first conversation to talk to me as though I were anyone else in the family, a sister of her husband, like Andromache, who had married Hector.

"They must have gathered every man of fighting age from every last island," Helen said, twisting an escaped coil of hair that hung loose by her lovely face.

The twilight air was still, stars glimmering to life in the sky above us. Beyond the city walls, far down on the distant beach, the Greeks were busy setting up their camp. So many of them, it defied belief. In Troy, panic mingled with a strange excitement, a surge of energy as we readied ourselves. The tension was broken at last, the waiting for retribution had come to an end. Priam had received a delegation ahead of the invasion; Troy had held its breath to see if he would give Helen up, but he had not. And so, the army came. Seeing its size, would he falter? Was that what Helen worried about? That he would hand her over to them, back to her husband? Even if he did, surely they wouldn't be content to leave with just her. All those thousands of men who had sailed away from their homes: they must have been promised more than just one woman. I didn't need to see the future to know it wouldn't be enough.

"Why would so many come?" I asked.

She shook her head, her brow creasing faintly. "I don't know."

I wondered if she was scared. I wondered what would happen to her when the army broke down our walls. My fate, like the rest of the women of Troy, seemed clearer. And I found myself terrified by it. I'd suffered everyone's disdain here, everyone's irritation with my curse, but that was nothing compared to what awaited me if the city fell—or *when* the city fell, as I had seen the day that Paris came back to us.

~~~~~~~

The ring of bronze across the plains was all we heard, where once I had been able to step out of the broiling city and feel the sea breeze cool on my face, with the gulls shrieking and wheeling overhead. All of us were imprisoned within Troy's walls, all of us except the men, who hauled on their armor at daybreak and coiled out onto the beach like a swarm of ants. At nightfall they returned, bruised and bloody and broken. The dead lay scattered across the plains, skewered, glassy-eyed, staring while the blood congealed in their wounds and the flies buzzed in thick clouds about them. At intervals there were truces, and Greeks and Trojans alike would gather the corpses. The smoke from the pyres choked the sky, swelling from the sprawling Greek camps at the shore and belching from our besieged city. Only the dead could leave Troy now.

CHAPTER THIRTEEN

Clytemnestra

He said he was a traveler when he came. I barely gave him a moment's notice. "Give him food, a bath, a bed," I said, waving my hand to the slave-girls, whose faces had become indistinguishable to me. At first, I saw the soft curve of Iphigenia's arm or the gleam of her hair in every young woman I encountered, no matter how little they resembled her. Whether they were slaves or the noble daughters of the other wealthy houses of Mycenae, it pained me to see them living while she was dead. It was the hopefulness of youth, maybe, the sweetness of life on its very cusp that I recognized. Not just the girls, either; I saw the woman she could have been in every female figure I encountered: a nervous bride, a transformed mother, even a shuddering crone. All the things she would never be. I tried not to look at them at all.

A passing traveler seeking hospitality was nothing to me. The only visitors I cared about were those messengers who brought us news from Troy. Then I pricked up my ears, listened to what they had to say. I had no system ready at first; I had relied on those heralds who could travel faster than a fleet of ships to give me warning if my husband was to return victorious. Now, I had beacons and watchmen installed, stretching across the islands that stood between us and Troy, ready to send a chain of firelight to carry the news to me as

soon as the city fell. So far, there was little to report. The Greek soldiers camped on the shores of Troy, but the walls stood strong around
the city still.

I had taken to walking about the courtyard at night after spending the day immersed in the kingdom's affairs. Unlike his sisters, the
baby Orestes would sleep contentedly enough in his crib, but I found I
could not tolerate the hours I spent awake listening to his soft breathing. I craved solitude more than I craved anything—almost anything,
at least, not forgetting how my heart quickened at news of the war
and of the countless ways my husband might die, either in it or, most
precious to me, afterward. But most days, what I wanted was to be left
alone. The chattering of other people, be they my own children or
anyone else, was like an unbearable itch. I longed to be lost in my own
thoughts, my own plans, and my one remaining dream. I lived for the
quiet hours of the night, when all I could hear was the soft suck and
hiss of the distant waves, when all that touched me was the cold caress
of the dark breeze.

No one ever disturbed me when I was in the courtyard. I doubt
anyone knew I went there, night after night. It had always been private: back when Agamemnon and I had sat beneath the stars together
when we were newly married; back when I had walked restless babies
up and down; back when I had taken a moment's peace from the bustle
of mothering three lively girls after persuading them to sleep at last.
Now, I spent solitary hours there in the quiet dark, and felt the only
moments of peace I could find in my ravaged soul.

So, the sound of footsteps was so unexpected, so unprecedented,
that at first I don't think I heard them at all. I was not poised or alert
for danger. Before, I had been too complacent. Now, I didn't care what
happened.

"Clytemnestra." His voice was low, soft in the shadows.

I whipped around. For a second, I thought it must be Agamemnon;
that, somehow, he had returned without me even knowing the war
had ended. I was not prepared; no chain of flaming beacons had lit the
darkness to give me warning. I drew back, curled my fingers into my

palm, my breath sharp in my lungs. We stood by a low wall: the palace overlooked a steep drop, and the rocks below would be enough. Fear mingled with exhilaration; I could taste blood, sour and metallic, in my throat.

"Please do not fear me; I mean you no harm."

He spoke at odds; it was not me who had anything to fear, I thought confusedly. But then he stepped forward, and I saw it was not my husband at all. A younger man, lit dimly by the beam of moonlight falling between the pillars. He was thin, taller than Agamemnon, but awkward-looking, as though he had grown too quickly and did not know what to do with his height. That I would fear someone so nervous struck me as absurd, and when the bark of laughter that escaped me made him startle, it was more ludicrous still.

"A palace of guards will run in our direction if I scream," I told him. Defending the palace had been one of my first priorities, and we had recruited men from neighboring provinces to do the job. Men with no loyalty to Agamemnon. Men who had known only me as ruler. "You do not look equal to even one of my men." *You do not look equal to me,* I thought.

"I know that," he answered. He held my eyes steadily, despite the anxiety I could sense rising from him. "Your husband's guards have chased me from this palace before."

"Then you are a fool to return," I said. I was in no mood to entertain whatever entreaty he was ready to make. To scream for the guards, though, seemed a ridiculous idea. He was an irritation, not a threat. I wanted him gone, but could not summon the energy to create a scene.

"Do you see something familiar in me?" he was asking.

I couldn't imagine why he thought I would care enough to look closely. "See what?" I heard myself ask.

He took a step forward and I felt myself stiffen further. It was only that he looked more hunted than hunter that still kept me quiet. I don't think it was pity, though. Maybe a flicker of interest, despite myself.

"I thought my blood would mark me out," he said softly. "As though the curse of Atreus would be emblazoned upon my face like a scar for all to see. But I walked through your palace doors with no notice; your servants gave me sanctuary when I asked with no question."

"What?" The heavy blooms of the flowers that entwined the pillars out here nodded sleepily in the dark air, releasing a sweep of fragrance, and dimly I remembered a conversation with Agamemnon once, in the honeyed air of a Spartan evening so very long ago. At the riverside, we had spoken of the worth of a child's life. At once, the pieces fell into place. "Aegisthus?" I breathed.

I could not see it. No stamp of Agamemnon's heavy features in the narrow, anxious face before me. His hair hung limp, not thickly curled, and his eyes were shadowed and wary.

"I am," he answered. "Your husband—my cousin—he killed my father here, in this palace. He drove me from this city when I was a boy and cast me out alone."

My mouth was dry. Since my return from Aulis, I had thought the world empty of surprise. To be surprised, you had to have a belief that the world would follow its rhythms and patterns as it had always done. I had burned my daughter's body on a strange shore and found the man I had married had a rotten soul. I thought myself immune to any surprise at all. But this revelation took me aback.

"That was my husband, indeed," I said. The words rasped and I was annoyed to sound weaker than I was. I breathed in, stood straighter. "But he is in Troy, fighting his war. If you seek to settle your score with him, you will be disappointed." I eyed him more closely, seeking out any sign of a weapon. "If you plan to avenge yourself on his wife and children in his absence," I went on, my voice hardening, "you will find there is little point in doing so. He is no husband or father; you cannot wound a man by harming what he weighs so lightly as Agamemnon values us."

At this, Aegisthus relaxed a little. "I had hoped you would say as much," he said. He stepped closer, closing the gap between us. I could see the sheen on his forehead, pale and damp in the moonlight. I felt a strange clutching in my chest, an almost protective urge. "There was no one in this world," he continued, "with more reason to hate that man than me—until he committed a more abominable murder than I would have thought him capable, worthless jackal as he is."

A thrill ran through me. Hardly anyone dared to speak of Agamemnon's act. Women I had known my whole time in Mycenae would dart away from me, dissolve into crowds or disappear around corners rather than look into my face and see my pain. But I knew how it was spoken of away from me. A sacrifice, they would call it. An agony beyond imagining, a torturous dilemma: his beloved daughter set against his kingdom and country; one girl's life versus the ambition of all of Greece. Behind my back, they would say his deed was a noble one, that Artemis set her terrible price and of all the men in his army, only Agamemnon had the courage to pay it.

"When I heard that he had murdered Iphigenia . . ." Aegisthus said.

No one said her name anymore. Not the slave-girls of the palace who had loved her; even her own sisters would not say it aloud. To hear it now, in this stranger's mouth, was like the shock of cold water on burning skin. "Go on," I whispered.

"The man who stormed this palace—who killed my father in front of my eyes while I screamed and begged for mercy—I could not believe that even such a beast as that could slaughter his own child for a fair wind," he said.

The tears started coursing down my face before he could finish his sentence. No one said such things. It was as though this young man had emerged from nowhere and begun to articulate the rage and pain that stormed inside me.

"I do not wish to cause you more pain." He stumbled over his words. I shook my head, unable to wrench out any speech, but waving my hand in a way that I hoped conveyed to him that I wanted him to carry on, to please carry on. "Forgive me for speaking of her like this. But when I learned of how depraved this false king truly is . . ." His face transformed from solicitous to seething in a blink. He swallowed hard again, his chest rising and falling as he sought control once more.

"I wondered if there was someone else in the world with even more reason to hate him than me."

He had seemed an unlikely villain, this ungainly, painfully anxious young man, but I understood. The force of his hatred had overcome his fear and brought him I did not know how far, across which ocean or from what place of safety, here to me in the place where his father had died before his helpless eyes; a place that might still cost him his own life. But I knew how easy a decision it must have been; how hatred crystallized the world, how it made everything so simple.

"I don't need your help," I told him.

"But I need yours," he said. That seam of anguish in his voice, the one that threatened to crack and break him apart. I had felt myself a block of stone since I had watched Iphigenia spiral into gray smoke. My living daughters had cried in my arms and my throat had closed around any words of comfort that I might have spoken. My baby was born and all I had known was indifference. But somehow, this stranger's pain made me flinch. Perhaps it was that I could see through to the very center of him, his beating heart exposed to me, mirroring mine. The shriek of agony in our souls, which could only be soothed by one thing. Revenge.

I stared at the quiver in his tender throat. I wanted to touch his skin. I could not bear for anyone else to come close to me. If my daughters flung their arms about my neck, I could only feel their skin cold and lifeless to my touch, could only see their eyes vacant and staring, could only think of their flesh melting on a funeral pyre. Aegisthus, though, seemed like a man already dead. I knew it, because I was as well. What else could I be, when my soul was drifting down the dank and winding path to the Underworld, unable to break that tether between me and my lovely girl, as though the cord between us had never been split at all? Only my body was here, and it lingered for one purpose. Aegisthus and I might have been two ghosts standing there in the courtyard—and, if we were, then who could stand in judgment of us?

I felt the shock ripple through his body as I cupped my hands around his face and drew it close to mine. When I kissed him, he tasted sweet. It was not the sour tang of fear in his mouth or the dry, papery cracks of his lips. It was something else that made it so delicious. My husband's cousin. Son of his rival. An enemy more hate-filled than any massing within the walls of Troy, and more surely set upon his blood than anyone living. Anyone, that is, except for me.

CHAPTER FOURTEEN

Elektra

Maybe in another life, a life in which my father didn't have to go to war and so my family paid attention to what I was doing, maybe I would never have so much as spoken to the son of a farmer. But a deceitful prince of Troy sailed to Sparta and took my mother's faithless sister away with him, and I did not live the life I was supposed to lead. So, I talked to him. No one else wanted anything to do with me, after all. They all thought I stayed inside all day, that I would never dare to sneak away. I held my secret wanderings close to my heart, something that belonged to me alone.

That first day, while I watched the men toiling beneath the scorching sun, the relentless repetitive rhythm of it hypnotizing, I felt a poke on my upper arm and jumped. He had a shock of dark hair, skinny arms. He didn't smile, and I didn't either. Clearly the son of one of the farmers, he was ragged and dirty and not like anyone else I had ever spoken to. His name was Georgios and, quickly, he became my friend. If I didn't steal down to visit him, I seemed to spend days sitting alone. Chrysothemis was always too busy, too distracted to talk to me. She fussed around the baby and looked anxiously after our mother, giving the slaves instructions to bring things to Clytemnestra—broth, wine, platters of fruit—to tempt the queen from her blank despair. I felt the weight of Iphigenia's name unspoken between us. I knew that Chrysothemis wept for our lost sister, for the closeness they had shared. I suppose I was a poor replacement. So, hour piled up on top of hour, a great oppressive weight of time spent in solitude and tedium, with only the faithful Methepon at my side. In those endless days, with just my dog for company, I felt myself begin to grow inward, lost in thoughts that built up inside my head like a twisting maze. I went to the fields, unnoticed by my family, waiting for Georgios to be able to slip away unseen. The vast stones of the fortification wall were warm from the sun, and I felt safe when I leaned against them, tracing the cracks between them with my fingers.

"Cyclopes built these walls," I told Georgios.

His eyes widened, and he reached out to touch the stones too. I looked at his hand, the black dirt under his nails and the gray layer of dust settled into the lines of his knuckles. "Did your father meet them?" he asked.

I laughed. "No. I think it was a long time ago."

"Maybe his father did, then."

"Maybe." It was confusing to try to imagine a time before my father had been king here. I pictured the Cyclopes; great hulking giants, hauling the blocks of stone up the hillsides, making the palace safe from invaders. The thought of their faces, the rough expanse of their vast foreheads punctuated by one staring eye, made me feel queasy. My father wouldn't be scared of them if he had seen them, I was sure. Someone must have commanded them to do it; a king of Mycenae who had been here back then, whose blood must still flow in our veins. I felt a shivery thrill, standing there in the sunlight, thinking of it.

"Can I stroke the dog?" Georgios asked.

I shrugged. "If he'll let you." No one else in the family was interested in Methepon; he'd become my dog alone since Agamemnon had left. Georgios patted his wide head, cautious at first of his powerful jaws and ferocious appearance, but growing bolder as the dog closed his eyes in bliss. I laughed. "I think he likes you."

Another day, Georgios asked me if I knew how long my father would be away. I shook my head. "How long are wars?"

Neither of us knew.

"Why didn't your father go?" I asked him.

"He's a farmer, not a soldier," Georgios answered. That made sense to me. His father always looked weary and stooped; not very impressive compared to my father's bearlike and confident stance. They were nothing alike. I felt sorry for Georgios.

"He says it won't be long, though," Georgios said, and my heart lifted. "He says it's the biggest army that anyone has ever seen, so they will easily win."

I smiled, a rush of exultation washing over me. I was so grateful to him for saying that. No one said Agamemnon's name around my mother. I hadn't dared to ask her how long he would be away, though I hardly thought about anything else.

"My father doesn't know why they went for Helen, though." Georgios looked at me curiously, and I wondered if he knew she was my mother's sister. "He said she's just a whore."

A whore. I frowned, puzzled. "What does that mean?"

He shrugged. "I thought you might know."

I didn't. But there was something in the way he said it, the inflection he must have copied from his father, that I liked. There was a bite to it. It was a word you could spit, with something about it that held frustration, a pent-up anger. I didn't know my aunt, but I hated the sound of her name. If Artemis had demanded her instead of my sister, then my father would never have had to go away. I was glad to have something to call her, in my head at least.

And then one day, Clytemnestra appeared again. Not a shadow of her, drifting down the corridor with her head bowed as though it was she who had died in Aulis. Clytemnestra, looking something like the mother I remembered: her hair shining in the sunlight, a necklace gleaming at her throat, golden threads glimmering through her dress. Her appearance made me jump, jolting me out of the snare of my daydreams. I opened my mouth to speak, but no words came. I darted a look at Chrysothemis, who looked as perplexed as me. An unfamiliar emotion bubbled up inside me at the sight of her, a flash of hope and recognition intermingled, a twist of unanticipated happiness. But before I could find my voice, I saw that there was someone else. A man, mean and scrawny-looking, trailing after my mother as though he had a right. At my side, I felt Methepon sit up, his hackles rising.

She told us his name. *Aegisthus.* I stared at him, unease shifting inside me. I didn't say anything.

Later, I sought out Chrysothemis. She was kneeling in the courtyard, holding Orestes' hands so that he could stand, his chubby fingers wrapped around hers, a look of fierce concentration on his little face as his knees wobbled beneath him.

"You know that man with Mother, the visitor?" I asked her.

She nodded. Her eyes were squinting in the bright glare of the sun, and I couldn't make out her expression.

"How long is he staying?"

"I don't know."

I reached out my hand to Orestes and he loosened his grip on Chrysothemis, clamping on to mine instead. His palms were warm and soft and, unsettled as I felt, I laughed at his gummy smile and plump, rounded cheeks. "Father should see this," I said. "His son trying to walk." Orestes yelped and I realized I'd squeezed my fist around his too tightly. "Sorry!" I soothed him. "Does Aegisthus have news about the war? Is Father coming home?"

Chrysothemis shook her head. "I don't think so. Maybe he's here to help while Father is away, though." She looked dubiously at Methepon. "Should you have that dog here, near Orestes?"

"He's our father's dog," I said. "He'd never hurt Orestes."

I bit my lip, hard. Something didn't feel right about Aegisthus. Maybe it was the way he had been standing, just a bit too close to our mother. Or the nervousness that radiated from him, jangled in the air about him. He didn't look anything like my father. Agamemnon was a big, broad man. His shoulders filled the doorway. His voice rumbled when he spoke. Those things I could remember, those things I would hold on to. He had left before Orestes was born, and now my brother was taking his first steps and my father's face was already hazy in my mind.

I hesitated, wondering if I should mention Georgios. He might know something, or be able to find out from his father. But I wasn't sure that I wanted to share him with my sister. I had a suspicion that she might not approve of our friendship, and besides, I was irritated by her lack of questioning, the way she seemed accepting of this inter-loper, trusting in our mother.

Orestes stumbled and his face twisted, reddening with an oncom-ing storm of tears. I disentangled myself as quickly as I could, peeling his fingers from mine and shoving him toward my sister. "Come on, Methepon." Chrysothemis looked relieved to see us go.

I was right to think that Georgios might have more information about Aegisthus. "He lived here before, when he was a little boy," he told me. "My father remembers him."

"Here? In our palace?"

Georgios nodded. "Before your father came back, Aegisthus lived here with his father." We both paused for a minute, working out the tangle of fathers in the story. "Your father came back to be king." He lowered his voice and looked at me intently. "Your father killed his father."

"Why?"

"Aegisthus' father, that is. He stole the throne. Agamemnon was supposed to be king, so he came and killed him."

I felt a cold slither of fear in my spine. "Has Aegisthus come to kill *us*?" I looked around, starting to panic. "Does my mother know?"

Georgios looked worried. "I didn't think of that."

I looked back at the imposing sweep of the palace behind us. I'd left Chrysothemis and Orestes in the courtyard; what if he came after them? I should have stayed there with Methepon as protection for us all. My legs felt shaky, and I didn't know if I could run if I needed to. I wished so desperately that my father was here. I took a great, judder-ing breath, about to cry—and then I heard it. A sound I hadn't heard since before she went to Aulis, a sound rising up from what felt like the ancient past. The sound of Clytemnestra laughing.

I pressed myself against the wall, close to Georgios. I could feel his breath on my forehead and I held mine, trying not to make a sound. As she got closer, I could hear the soft murmur of her voice, not the forced effort she made when she found it in herself to talk to us, but a rapid and animated flow. I steeled myself to peer around the corner and I saw them, Clytemnestra and Aegisthus, walking together around the palace grounds. He was gesturing toward the dip of the valley and the mountains in the distance, flinging his arm in an expansive arc to take in everything he could see from here. Both of them were smiling. I felt cold, despite the warm sunshine. She hadn't laughed with me for so long. I'd forgotten what it sounded like.

The terror that had seized me was giving way to a steadier feeling of dread. He wasn't running at my mother with a sword; he was walking with her as though they were the best of friends without a care in the world. And my father was on the other side of the ocean, not knowing anything about it. I didn't know how it could be, but somehow, this felt worse.

CHAPTER FIFTEEN

Clytemnestra

How would Helen have done it? That was what I wondered the first time I woke beside Aegisthus. My sister, who had boarded Paris' ship in the dead of night, who now took her place as a princess of Troy. Sometimes I saw her dragged away, other times stepping coolly and with dignity onto the creaking deck, her head held high and a new horizon in her sights. I hoped for the sake of the love we'd had for each other back in Sparta that it was the latter, but when I thought of what it had cost me—my daughter's life spilled across the sand, Helen's daughter whole and living, left behind like the rest of us—then it was harder to endure. Would it be better if she had resisted, if she had been overcome, if it was the fault of Menelaus for leaving her unprotected and defenseless, for having been too dull to notice the covetous gleam in the Trojan prince's eyes? If she had screamed behind the hot press of his fingers clamped over her mouth, if she had sought to tear the flesh from his hands with her teeth in her desperation to get back to Hermione, to hold her daughter in her arms, to stay with her and never bear the blame for this disastrous war?

Whatever the truth of it was, I was certain of one thing. Whether she kicked and clawed and fought as she was taken from Sparta, I was sure that the woman who stepped off Paris' ship onto a distant and unfamiliar harbor was the cool and regal Helen once again. I didn't know what, if anything, might have seethed beneath the surface, but I knew in my bones that she would never betray a whisper of it to the world. She would walk through the streets of Troy as though they had always belonged to her, as though she was the rightful princess of it all, and even if her beauty didn't make them fall at her feet, she would never feel the burn of their smoldering resentment—or if she did, she wouldn't care.

I didn't know if I loved her or hated her, or some curdled mixture of the two, but I needed that poise for myself. I needed her confidence; I needed to move through the world with the placid certainty that everything I did was right, just as she did.

If Helen had sneaked her lover into the palace while her husband was at war, she would not be lying frozen in anxiety with no idea how to proceed. She would stride into the throne room with him at her side, and arch a disdainful eyebrow at anyone who dared to question her.

Aegisthus stirred sleepily and turned his head toward me. I held my breath for a moment, not wanting him to wake. His face was shadowed, the flesh around his eyes dark and hollowed. The image of his skull swam up in my mind unbidden, smashed by Agamemnon's axe, his skin hanging in tatters, the exposed bone crawling with insects.

The light filtering through the window drapes was warming, gray turning to gold. His eyes flickered open. Not Agamemnon's eyes. They might share the burden of their blood, but they were not the same.

He reached his hand toward me. Not Agamemnon, not Iphigenia. I had felt stuck on that desolate beach, her funeral pyre burning beside me, the ships long gone across the empty ocean. Even as I walked the corridors at Mycenae, even when my daughters tried to talk to me, even when my baby son cried, I was still there, powerless and raging, not knowing how to move forward. Now I had an idea.

"What will we do?" he asked. His voice was quiet. Gentle. No kingly timbre.

"Agamemnon took his men with him. He took all the men with him."

Aegisthus' eyes stayed intent on mine. "All of them?"

"He doesn't want the glory to belong to Achilles or Odysseus or any of the rest of them. He wants it to be his. He took every man of fighting age; he only left the old ones and the boys. There is no one to stand against us here."

He frowned. "They can't all be so frail. There must be enough to cause us trouble if they choose. Agamemnon is their king. What if this war is done quickly? They won't want him to return to find them disloyal."

"Is Agamemnon their king?" I asked. "All of them? The men still here are old enough to remember Thyestes, to remember you. Their loyalty turned from one to the other before; it can happen again. I know that there are those here who loved your father. Who pitied you your fate, who would welcome you back. All we need to do is to find out who they are."

"And what about the others?"

"Agamemnon is not well loved," I said. "Even less so now that he has taken the men. Husbands, sons, and fathers, all swept away—and who knows how long this war will last? How many will return? The Trojans have their mighty warriors, just as we do; they have gods who love them too." I hesitated over my next words. "And all for a woman, they will say. A faithless woman who ran away with a foreign prince. Is she worth a thousand of our ships, tens of thousands of our men?"

He wanted to believe me. The sound of my voice was convincing, even to me. I heard it as though it was Helen's, soft but certain, and I felt a giddiness spiraling within me that I had not felt since before the moment Menelaus arrived, gray with shock and despair, with his shattering news of Helen. The looks on everyone's faces would be worth it.

Worth it, yes, but we had to wait for our moment. Aegisthus had slipped unknown into Mycenae, and keeping him hidden was paramount. We needed strength behind us; he had come recklessly, fired with his passion for revenge, intent upon sharing it with me, but I wanted to move carefully. I had my guards already, but we sent for more; men young and strong, but from far enough away that they had not been taken to war.

When I took the slave-woman into my confidence, the woman who had told me early on in my marriage of the curse, her face lit up. "Aegisthus lives?" she asked, and when I told her yes, it was true and he was here, her eyes shone with delight. There was love for the boy who had been chased from the palace, pity for his grief, and anger at his exile. We were not alone in Mycenae, Aegisthus and I. She helped to send our messages, discreet and protective, and when we had quietly gathered enough men, the time came to act.

I was satisfied with the stir it created among the elders of the court, the old men whom Agamemnon had left behind to rule, when I led Aegisthus into the wide chamber, where he had watched his father die. I felt it like the keen edge of a knife blade: not the nerves I had expected, but excitement. Behind us, our guards stood tall.

"Many of you saw Thyestes die; many of you served him as your king before Agamemnon slit his throat here." I paused and let them think of it; the man they had known slaughtered before their eyes as his son looked on. "You saw my daughter grow up here; you waved her away to her new life and husband, and you know what happened instead—the cruel trick Agamemnon played so that he could take our men, your sons and your nephews, to fight his war. I can tell you that he did not flinch, did not waver for one moment when he murdered Iphigenia. Sweet Iphigenia, loved by all of you. He turned his back on Mycenae, killed its loveliest princess, and sailed away." I let my words hang in the air and I settled my gaze on each of them in turn. Some stared back, arms crossed over their sunken chests; others lowered their eyes or looked into the distance as though squinting through heavy fog. Always, our guards loomed, silent and impenetrable. Beside me, I felt Aegisthus standing rigid, but the words rolled from me as smooth as pouring honey. I didn't need to be Helen, I thought.

"I remember," said one. He lifted his rheumy eyes to Aegisthus. "I remember you."

There was a shuffling in the room, sandals shifting on the stone floor, throats clearing and robes rustling as some of the others muttered an assent. Some stayed still and silent. I noticed them. No matter.

Those who resented us did not dare to stand against us at that moment, and it would only become harder for them to do so later.

But if that battle seemed easily won, there was another still to fight.

Chrysothemis regarded Aegisthus with a look of confused suspicion when I brought him to them, but Elektra, small as she was, bristled with outright hostility. She stood stiffly when I said his name, and when my hand brushed his arm, I saw her fist tighten where she clutched her sister's skirt.

Chrysothemis opened her mouth, hesitated, and said nothing. Before I knew I was going to, I knelt down to them both and caught Chrysothemis' hand in mine. I pushed away the image that flashed past my eyes, Iphigenia's hand so pale and cold when I had held it last. "You have heard his name before," I said and she looked back at me, still perplexed, but she nodded.

Elektra's eyes narrowed. Her scowl reminded me of Agamemnon's face, the first time I'd seen him in the hall of suitors. I swallowed hard.

"He is your father's cousin, but your father was cruel to Aegisthus, when he was young—not much older than you are, Chrysothemis," I said. "He was cruel to Aegisthus like he was cruel to your sister. He would have killed him, too, but I had asked him not to."

Elektra said something too low for me to hear.

"What's that?" I asked her, but she shook her head, staring at the ground, refusing to say it again. I sighed. "Agamemnon is a cruel man," I said. "Aegisthus is kind." How much more to explain than that? I wasn't sure there was anything else to say, nothing else that they could understand. Besides, wasn't that enough? "Why don't you play outside?" I asked, standing up again and smoothing the creases from my dress.

Chrysothemis tutted. "The sun is too bright for Elektra; it gives her headaches."

I caught another sigh before it escaped. They were always indoors, their childhood so different from the one Helen and I had shared in Sparta. I thought of the hours my sister and I had spent together by the river, the freedom of sharing our confidences between us, never afraid of being overheard, never afraid of being stopped. My girls had a different experience here, but what frustrated me the most was that they never seemed to miss the liberty they were denied. They seemed content to stay within the palace walls, to learn to weave and to sing. They didn't even seem to wonder what was outside.

Chrysothemis would understand, I decided, and Elektra was so young that she would forget what had gone before. They would never see Agamemnon again; I would make sure of it. This was their life, and it would be better than it had been. They would get used to that soon enough.

That night, I slipped from my bed, as I so often did, and went to the dim courtyard where I passed the hours in which everyone else slept. Only once had I been disturbed there, when Aegisthus had first arrived. Now that his presence was known in the palace, he must have felt emboldened to come out there again for, to my shock, I felt his hands close around my shoulders as I stood, looking out into the darkness. I twisted around, startled. "What are you doing here?" I asked.

"Why do you always come here in the night?"

I stepped away from his touch. "I can't sleep."

"Is it that you're keeping watch?"

I wrapped my arms close around my body. "I do keep watch. I need to know when the beacons will light, when the war is over."

"Slaves can keep watch for you," he said. "They can come to wake you when it happens."

I shook my head. "I wouldn't entrust this task to anyone else."

He didn't answer. I wanted him to go. This was my time: I didn't want to share it with anyone else, not even him.

"Why don't you go back to bed?" I asked him when the silence had stretched on long enough. It was too dark to see his face clearly, but I could feel his hurt.

"Are you thinking about Iphigenia?"

I breathed sharply. "I'm always thinking about her."

"I think about my father, too," he said, and I was glad he couldn't see my expression. I was afraid my disdain would be writ too clearly across my face.

What was the loss of a parent compared to that of a daughter? I didn't want him here, comparing his grief to mine.

"I see it happen over and over," he said.

Her hair whipping to the side as he pulled her against his chest, his arm locked tight around her, and the panic that flared up in her eyes. The knife falling, again and again in my mind, a vision that would never stop.

"But when I think of it, when I think of Agamemnon killing him, I make myself see something else," he went on. "I see myself standing up, I see the axe in my hand. Instead of crying on the floor, I lift it up and aim it at his head."

My irritation with him lessened. "Go on."

"I see him begging for mercy, on his knees on the ground." Aegisthus' breathing was unsteady, his words coming rapidly. "I won't give him any mercy, though; I laugh at him. I make it last, that moment."

I squeezed my eyes closed, felt the grip of the wooden handle in my own hands, the weight of the blade, how it would feel to swing it back in the air, the force and the power of it. When Aegisthus came close to me again, I didn't step away. His hands fastened around my arms.

"Don't think about what he did. Think about how we'll punish him for it."

I reached up, pulled his face closer to mine. "I want to be the one who does it. I swore it at Aulis, after—afterward. It's the reason I didn't throw myself on the pyre with her."

He didn't argue. His breath was hot against my face.

I let my hands drop abruptly to my sides. "You go back to bed. I'll watch out here a little longer."

He wavered for a moment. "Don't be too long."

"Of course," I answered. "You go. I will follow."

I didn't. The darkness belonged to me, the most comforting place

I could find. The closest I could be to Iphigenia as she drifted through the subterranean night. But I forgave Aegisthus his intrusion. I was grateful for the scene he had drawn for me, the taste of his hatred in my mouth. I wasn't so alone in my grief anymore; not so alone in my rage.

CHAPTER SIXTEEN

Elektra

Clytemnestra didn't spend all day in her chamber after Aegisthus came. She was always visible in the throne room, at the long banqueting tables, in the wide and sunny courtyards. Always he hovered there, inches away from her, as though an invisible thread connected them. I was too young at first to understand scandal, to know the meaning of the sideways looks and heavy whispers that followed them. But as time passed, I became increasingly horrified at her brazenness. She could have been stripped naked and dragged through the streets so that the populace could hurl stones at her. I wonder if that would have been enough to jolt her implacable composure. But who would do such a thing? I suppose that was the crux of it. My father was gone, and he had taken the fighters with him. Clytemnestra was allowed to rule until either her husband returned or Orestes grew old enough to take on the mantle himself. It would be left to Agamemnon to deal with his rebellious wife when he returned. If Aegisthus had been strong, I could have understood it more. If he had stormed the palace, taken his place by force, and bent us all to his will, I could have forgiven her. But this craven, hesitant, rat-faced wraith who had all the substance of my mother's shadow—*this* was the man who took the throne beside her, who dared to sit where the mighty Agamemnon had ruled?

The first betrayal, like a shock of icy water, came soon after Aegisthus arrived. Chrysothemis, out in the courtyard, smoothing out a bright rectangle of cloth, holding it for my mother to see. It was easy to impress our mother with our weaving; it wasn't a skill she'd ever taken the time to master particularly well, so the murmurs of admiration I heard drifting over probably weren't false. But it wasn't just the sincerity of my mother's interest that jarred; as I peered around the pillar where I stood concealed, I saw him. Aegisthus, standing by the low wall, nodding along with her praise. My chest tightened. Chrysothemis blinked, unsure of herself for a moment, and then smiled shyly, right at him.

I swallowed back my anger. I didn't dare take a step toward them. I stood rooted to the spot, afraid that one of them would glance in my direction, that they might notice me staring. When I trusted myself to move, I crept as silently as I could. It was something I would become well practiced in later, slipping stealthily through the palace, hanging back in the shadows, pretending that I didn't exist at all.

I was powerless. He was there, always, and so no matter how much more I saw my mother, I never seemed to see her without him. At first, I would wake every morning sitting bolt upright, heart racing from nightmares that I couldn't remember, formless shapes reaching for me from the dark. But every day passed without event, seasons bled into one another, Methepon's legs grew shakier and less steady as Orestes grew taller, walking confidently on his own, and still the war raged on in Troy—and Aegisthus remained in Mycenae, as impossible as it seemed.

It was Georgios who I turned to, of course. Georgios could ask his father for information, and slowly the picture emerged. The palace was more divided than I knew. There were those who had remained silently loyal to the dead Thyestes and his banished son, while there were others fiercely devoted to my father. Georgios' father was one of the latter. I learned from what Georgios heard from him how Thyestes had stolen Mycenae and exiled Agamemnon and Menelaus, and how they had marched back with Spartan armies and the other forces they had gathered in their lonely outcast years to take back what was theirs. I learned how it was my mother's pity that saved the boy Aegisthus from death alongside the scheming Thyestes.

And, most intriguing of all, Georgios told me about the curse.

I listened, enrapt, and when he came to the end of the tales, I looked around at my home as though seeing it through different eyes. Not only were the stones laid by Cyclopes, our palace had been host to Olympian gods, guests of my forefathers. Our ancestors were honored by their company. There truly was greatness in our blood, the blood that came to me through Agamemnon. But like so many great families, there was a diseased branch, deeply rooted and entwined with the nobility. My father was a man loved by the gods; of this I was sure. He had led the greatest army that had ever been seen to war; they must smile fondly upon him. But he bore the taint of those in our family who were not worthy, those who sought things that were beyond them. Tantalus had given way to hubris, but his example had not deterred Pelops nor Thyestes after him. It had been up to Agamemnon to rout out the diseased part, to sever it from the healthy, to leave our family whole and intact, with the greatness of those who had gone before us and none of their foulness. But he had made a mistake. He had left Aegisthus to grow, stunted and misshapen, an insult to our blood. Living in our palace. Lying with the queen.

"Why didn't she ever tell me all of this?"

Georgios looked solemn. "No one in Mycenae is allowed to talk about it."

I sucked in my breath. "So she's kept it secret, hoping people will forget." I shook my head. "The gods were friends to our family once, and they could be again. How could she hide that from me?"

"All I know is that it's forbidden."

As though it were a source of shame. My gratitude to Georgios for giving me this knowledge couldn't assuage the dart of bitterness I felt toward my mother for concealing it. It rankled in my breast, a sharp sting of resentment. She didn't want me to know who my father was, what our family had endured. I wondered what other secrets she might hold close, what else there might be that I didn't know and no one would dare tell me.

"Thank you," I said to Georgios, hoping he would hear the whole-hearted sincerity in my voice, that he would know how much it meant to me.

I could understand that my mother had come back from Aulis swamped in grief. She hadn't been able to see it then the way that I could now: that the gods had a purpose for the House of Atreus. Artemis had made a terrible demand of my father, and of course Clytemnestra had been distraught. I could forgive her that. Looking back, I could see that what had felt like a cold abandonment to me as a child was the pain that shrouded her, a suffering she couldn't break through. Even the arrival of Aegisthus—maybe, if I forced myself, maybe I could make myself believe that she was maddened by her loss and that she was taken in by him while still in its brutal clutches.

But, as the years continued to pass, why had she not come to her senses? And if she hadn't done so yet, would she ever? I had prayed for my father to come home, for the war to end and the victors to return, so that he could put things right. The uncertainty gnawed away at me. What would he do when he came back and found out? Her crime became graver with each passing day.

My frustration boiled inside me all the time, relentless and inescapable. There was nothing I could do. I turned away from Aegisthus whenever I saw him; I never addressed a word to him. At first, I was worried that my mother might reprimand me for my rudeness, but when she never did, I found myself longing for it. Why did she just smile so smoothly and carry on? He gave up on pleasantries soon enough; he eyed me with silent suspicion, and I looked away, full of loathing, as she ignored us both.

He became bolder, walking through our palace as though it was his rightful home. My father's rings glinted golden on his fingers, the luxurious woolen cloaks he draped about his shoulders were paid for with my father's wealth. Now that Methepon was too tired to snarl and snap at him, he didn't edge away from us. One afternoon, while my dog lay sleeping in a patch of sunlight, I saw Aegisthus dart his foot out and kick him in the graying fur over his ribs.

"How dare you?" The words flew from me before I could even think to be circumspect.

In an instant, my mother was there. "What's this, Elektra?"

"He kicked Methepon!" My chest was heaving.

"The dog shouldn't sleep there, right in everyone's way," she said, her hand on Aegisthus' elbow, guiding him away.

I bristled with the injustice. My father's dog, mistreated in my father's home, another insult on top of so many. I knew that, like me, Methepon was holding on for his master's return, but he had grown old over the course of this war, and his good, loyal heart couldn't hold out much longer. When the life slipped away from him, I wept long and painful sobs, soaking his fur until they took his body away from me.

More alone than ever, I tried to avoid them all as much as I could. When I saw my mother and sister talking in the courtyard, just the two of them, I drew to the side, unseen. They looked so alike, the sunlight gleaming from their dark hair, the clean lines of their faces in profile, but while Clytemnestra drew herself up tall, Chrysothemis dipped her head in deference. Clytemnestra gestured, her expression full of animation, one hand tucking back a stray strand of hair as the other swept through the air to emphasize whatever it was she was saying. Chrysothemis stood still, thoughtful, never looking up to meet our mother's eyes.

"What did she want?" I demanded afterward.

"She wanted to talk to me about—my future."

"Your future?"

My sister's face flushed. "Marriage."

How could we move forward, when our father was still at war, when everything was suspended, waiting for his return? It made me nauseous to think of it.

"Who?" I said.

"I don't know, not yet. She was just saying—saying that it's time." Chrysothemis shrugged helplessly.

"How can it be time?" I couldn't stand still, pacing across the court-yard, over to the low wall, looking out toward the mountains. My breath surged in my chest, agitation and anger wrestling together, making it hard for me to speak. "How can she make plans? How could she choose? It's our father's right to do this!"

My sister sighed. "I can't refuse them."

"Them?"

"Mother and Aegisthus."

"What does he have to do with it?"

She laughed at this, exasperated. "He rules Mycenae along with her. I can't go against what they say."

"So you will marry a man of Aegisthus' choosing?" My voice was shrill, and I could see her withdrawing from me, hugging her arms close around her.

"I don't see how I can't."

My teeth ground together. "I would rather die."

She looked at the ground. "I wouldn't."

I turned away from her. So that was how I would lose Chryso-themis. She'd marry an ally of Aegisthus, too obedient to make any protest. All I could hope for was what I'd been hoping for since the day he'd left; for Agamemnon to hurry home. But perhaps Chrysothemis didn't have the faith in him that I did.

Something broke between my sister and me that day. I had no hope anymore that the three of us could be allies: Chrysothemis, Orestes, and me. Orestes was our father's son, a young Agamemnon in our home. But he didn't remember our father; had never even seen him. If Chrysothemis could give up on the man she remembered better than I did, how could I keep Agamemnon alive for Orestes? He was growing up with no father, and our mother had spent less time with him than my sister and I had. It was up to me to make sure that he knew where we came from, what had happened to us, and what we were waiting for. To make sure that when Agamemnon came home, he could be proud of two of his children, at least.

I began to tell my brother stories, recounting the war tales that had been brought home to us, the scraps of information we had received over the years. So much was missing; I had to fill in the blanks. "Our father is the leader of the whole army," I said. "He's so brave and strong that every man across all of Greece wanted to follow him."

Orestes looked at me, his eyes wide and steadfast.

"The gods fight alongside him," I went on. "They've always looked kindly on our family."

"If the gods are fighting too, why hasn't he won yet?" Orestes asked.

I frowned. "I don't know. Sometimes things go wrong. Like here, in Mycenae. The gods want Agamemnon to be king here, but Aegisthus has come. He's stolen from us. It's happened to our family before."

Orestes looked confused.

"Don't worry," I said, squeezing him closer. "I'm here to look after you. Until Father comes back. When Father comes back, he'll get rid of Aegisthus for us. Everything will be better then."

He snuggled into me, leaning his head against my shoulder. "Tell me more about the war," he said. "Tell me about the battles Father has won."

I summoned up all my powers of imagination.

It was the tenth year of fighting, an unimaginable length of time. The boy I had befriended by the farmer's hut now worked the fields himself, a man. Not a man like Agamemnon; not a tall, proud king with flashing eyes and gleaming hair, whose strong embrace I still remembered. Georgios' toil shadowed his eyes; his arms were thin despite their sinewy ropes of muscle, and he stooped from his hours of toiling. Perhaps it was the patience he developed from his grueling hours of labor that made him able to listen to me, over and over again. I was sitting on a stone step at the back of the palace, which overlooked the long sweep of rolling hills beneath us, the palace being built atop the tallest. Scrubby trees dotted the landscape and the late afternoon sun cast a golden glow across it all. I wished its beauty could touch me, rouse some kind of emotion. I felt the absence of the dog at my side. I still reached down sometimes to stroke his head before I remembered that he was gone.

"What are you thinking of?"

I sighed deeply. I didn't turn my head, but I knew what his face would look like as he sat down next to me. His eyes would be squinting against the slanting light, but he wouldn't shade them with his hand. He was no more than a peasant to my mother and her lover, but he was my friend—the only friend I had, the only friend I needed. The only person who had ever told me the truth about my family.

I knew that he wished we would sometimes talk of other things. I wished that I could think about anything other than my anger. Sometimes I could hear myself as though I were outside my body, and I winced at the harsh drone of my own voice. But still the tirades came, strangling in my throat like a knot of vines that twisted and writhed until they were free. I was grateful that Georgios would always be there to listen. "I'm thinking that if my father was here, he would skewer Aegisthus like he should have done twenty-five years ago," I said.

"Your father was kind," Georgios said, echoing again what we had said so many times over. He frowned. "My father always says how much better things were when Agamemnon was king. Aegisthus knows nothing about running a kingdom, and the men he's brought in—they're rough and greedy, or else useless workers. It's not the way it was, not anymore."

If only I'd had the good fortune to be born a son, rather than a daughter. The curse that sank its roots deep within Mycenae; I could slice clean through it myself. Cut out the diseased branch of our family tree, leaving us pure and healthy at last. But I had grown up in the shade; unseen and unnoticed instead of shining brightly the way that he'd hoped I would, and all I could do was wait for my father to come home again.

"Is there any news from Troy?" I asked. We received official messages from heralds of battles fought and men lost, but I knew that among the workers, peasants, and slaves, where tongues were looser, more precious nuggets of information could be found.

Georgios sighed. "None that will please you, Elektra," he said.

"What?" I could feel my mouth drying as I spoke. I couldn't believe that there would ever be the news I dreaded; it could not be that Agamemnon would fail . . . but still, my weak heart feared it.

Georgios' brows drew together as he spoke. "I heard that Achilles doesn't fight for the Greeks anymore," he said.

I breathed a sigh of relief. "Is that all?"

"It is enough."

"Achilles is one man," I answered. "His Myrmidons are a fraction of the army. There are many other fighters." Ajax, a towering mountain of a man. Odysseus, wily and strategic. My father, at the head of them all.

"Troy won't fall while Hector lives," Georgios said. "And no one is a match for Hector except Achilles."

I sucked in my breath; cast him a look of withering reproof. I let a moment pass, bit back my retort. "And why has this great fighter deserted the Greeks?" I asked tightly.

"He quarrels with your father. King Agamemnon has taken his prize, a slave-girl won by Achilles."

I shrugged. "All prizes won in war belong to the king, and he distributes them as he sees fit."

"Well, this girl—Briseis—Achilles didn't want to let her go. He is insulted and will not fight unless she is restored to him." His tone darkened. "The Greeks have suffered a run of defeats. They are struggling, Elektra."

I shook my head. "The tide of war turns often. So many times we have heard that Troy is poised on the brink of falling; then that the Greeks have been driven back and rallied once more. In the end, my father will prevail."

"Should I go?" The sudden intent in his voice surprised me.

"Go where?"

"To Troy. I could go and fight. I'm old enough."

"How would you even get there?" I jumped to my feet. "The journey there would be long and dangerous. Why would you attempt it?"

He stood up too, and put his hand on my shoulder. I didn't want to look at his open, honest face. I'd imagined the Trojan battlefield so many times. It was enough to torture myself every day with the ways in which a Trojan sword or spear could pierce my father's body; I couldn't bear to think of Georgios in the heart of the fray as well. "Your father needs men, Elektra. I'm strong enough. I could be there, helping to win the war. So that he can come home to you."

Tears prickled my eyes. "No."

"Why not?"

I hugged my arms close around myself, looking determinedly away from him. "You aren't a soldier."

"I could learn."

I shook my head. "It's madness."

"Madness to do something to help, instead of staying here, while you suffer every day?"

"You *do* help. You help by being here." I pictured what my days would look like with Georgios gone. The crashing loneliness of it, enduring the sight of Aegisthus in my father's place, with no friend for me to turn to. "You can't leave me."

"I would never want to leave you. But if I can help . . ."

"Then don't suggest it again," I said. "My father will win this war, Achilles or not."

He nodded slowly. "I won't speak of it again, not if it upsets you."

I nodded, blinking away any threat of tears. I hoped it wasn't selfish, to deny my father another willing fighter. But I'd said it already, one man couldn't make much difference in a war. Here in Mycenae, though, Georgios' presence meant more to me than I had known until I thought of him gone. My father's absence had carved a gaping hole right through the center of my life. I didn't think I could face losing my friend as well.

<center>~~~~~~~~</center>

I made my desultory way back to the palace as twilight began to gather. Slipping through the corridors, practiced at going unnoticed in the shadows, I passed my mother's chambers. I could hear the soft hum of her voice, talking to someone—*him*, most likely. I did not care for what she had to say most of the time, but I wondered if she had heard the same reports of the war as Georgios had relayed to me. I wondered if she exulted in the rift within the Greeks.

I drew closer to the door, which stood ajar.

"—cannot surprise me, of course," I heard her say, her tone high and rapid. "And yet—I still wonder how it can be."

Aegisthus' voice, whining and thin, saying something to pacify her.

"He has daughters," she said. A note of despair sounded in her voice. "I know it is the way of war. I know what he has done already. But this girl, this slave, who they argue over like dogs fighting for a bone—does he think of her as a person at all, someone else's daughter, who could be his own?"

I heard Aegisthus more clearly now; I think he had stood and moved nearer to the door where I lurked, maybe to come closer to Clytemnestra. "I have not fought in war, but—"

She cut him off as though he had not spoken at all. "Why would I think for a moment that he would care about a woman's feelings, even if it were his own daughters, even if the Trojans chased him and his armies all the way across the sea to Mycenae itself? All that would matter to him would be his own pride—but the cruelty of this . . ." There was a long silence. When she spoke again, she sounded subdued. "He didn't have the face of a monster. When I married him, I didn't know; I never imagined . . . And now he takes a woman as though she were a thing, he risks his whole war, the war for which he slaughtered his own child like an animal, for the sake of saying this Briseis is his and not Achilles'." Clytemnestra's voice turned cold. "How that poor girl must despise him."

I had heard enough. I turned away, crept on silent feet to my chambers, a ghost in my own home. It wasn't until later, as I turned this snippet of conversation between my mother and the hated Aegisthus over in my head, that I pried out its bitter sting.

My mother felt a kinship with this faraway woman, my father's slave. She imagined her—Briseis—despising Agamemnon, the king who had claimed her as his own. I turned over in my bed, pressed my face into the softness of the blankets. I breathed in, long and slow, and felt the heat of my own exhaled air warm my skin. Muffled deep in my nest, I thought about her. I wondered what she looked like; the woman who had halted the war. I imagined that she must stand tall

and shapely, with rippling hair and wide eyes. Eyes that she could raise
to my father. She could look upon his face, the face I could only see
in the haze of long-distant memory. She must be beautiful. I thought
of how she must have felt; claimed by Achilles, of whom so many stories were told, the young and ferocious warrior who struck fear into
Trojan hearts. And then, the march of Agamemnon's soldiers to the
Myrmidon camp, the crunch of their footsteps in the sandy earth, as
they came to take her away, to bear her to the king.

Clytemnestra pitied her for belonging to Agamemnon. I closed
my eyes tightly. I could almost feel the sand of the Trojan beach trickling between my toes. The orange starbursts that exploded against my
squeezed eyelids could be the flames of Greek torches. The soldiers'
hands would hold her upper arms firmly as they led her toward the
tent. She would look down as they approached, her unbound hair falling across her face until she stood before him.

The scene dissolved in my head. I searched for his features: his
dark beard, his thick curls—would they be streaked with gray from
the years that had passed and the strain of leading the war? I was sure
his eyes would flash dark and warm as ever, but perhaps wearier than
before.

My mother didn't care for how he had suffered, the toll that these
relentless battles must have taken upon him. She would deny him any
comfort, any spoils of war that were rightly his, even as she lolled beside the traitor, the usurper who dared to sleep in Agamemnon's bed.

My lungs about to burst, I pushed aside the blankets, surfacing
from the airless cavern I had made. My hair clung damply to my slick
temples. I felt all at once a great and terrible restlessness, a frustrated
energy in my limbs that made me wish again that the sea did not lie
between here and Troy. If it were the harshest, driest desert that separated us instead, I would walk across it to see my father again.

I was a princess. I slept in a bed draped with the finest fabrics, in
a chamber patterned with frescoes, bedecked with sumptuous hang-
ings, with glittering gems piled up ready to adorn my hair and neck,
and carved shutters at the window to keep out the burning heat of the
daytime sun and to let in a cooling sweep of night air: every comfort

I could imagine was at my fingertips. And yet every fiber of my being ached with longing—every part of my wretched body yearned to be amid the smoke of campfires, beneath the rough canvas of a tent; to change places with a slave who had nothing except the thing I wanted most of all in the world. My father's arms around her.

CHAPTER SEVENTEEN

Cassandra

The war stretched on, unending, through weeks and then months and finally years. How did they have the stomach for the fight still? I wondered. How could it be possible to rise every morning to that same grim, relentless slaughter, and then drink and sleep and wake to do it all again? The Greek army was mighty, despite the bodies that kept the bloated crows squawking greedily overhead, and we watched from atop our city walls as they built their makeshift army camp into something that resembled a civilization.

Still, our walls stood. I could not walk beyond them any longer, but daily I stared down from them across the boiling clash of armies beneath, out toward the placid sea. I would watch until black dots shimmered and swarmed my vision, until my head throbbed and I could see no more. I was searching for the other blindness, the chasm of light, the knowledge of what was to come.

But since the day that Paris had set sail for Sparta, Apollo had not spoken to me. No agony split my skull in two, no searing flash of white dazzled me, and no insight speared me. At times, a truth would come: a child would be skipping in the street, and I would see it feverish and damp, then still as marble in a flash. A day later, the mother would be tearing her hair from the roots and raking her nails down her cheeks as she wailed to Apollo in vain. A grim-faced man, barely more than a boy, whose hands shook almost imperceptibly as he strapped his breastplate to his chest, ready to stride out onto the bloodied earth—I saw him gasping for breath under a hollow sky, his flesh smeared across the sand. These little truths assailed me day by day, but what I searched for when I stared out across the carnage, what I begged for when I prayed at the feet of Apollo's statue every dawn, did not come.

Even I began to wonder about my own foresight; perhaps, I thought, what I had seen in Paris was simply the fact of war? Troy was ruined in many ways, the city held in stasis, all of us trapped behind stone in a siege without end. Despite myself, despite the weight of despair I carried in the pit of my stomach every day, I could not stop that treacherous green shoot of hope from interweaving with my sorrow: perhaps Troy would stand after all.

Apollo's face in the temple was smooth, blank, empty stone. The painted eyes looked sightlessly ahead. He told me nothing.

In the early days of the siege, fear and dread lay thick upon Troy. For once, it was not me alone who saw death and destruction around every corner. Every altar carried savor to the heavens, the air was filled with incense and the lowing of cattle led to sacrifice intermingled with the thin, melodic chanting to the gods. Throughout the city, every face was taut with anguish. Day by day, men died—husbands, brothers, sons, and fathers, mangled and torn, suffocating in their own blood out there. The lands that surrounded the city fell, bit by bit, to the Greeks, taking our harvests and our animals too. The whispering threat of hunger stalked every home. It seemed the burden of it would be too much to bear; every day, the imminent horror loomed, threatening to topple and crush us all at any moment.

But every day, it did not. My brother, Hector, marshaled the forces of Troy. Where the men might have weakened through fear and misery, he revitalized them with his calm command and rallied them with his hope and confidence. We learned to manage with what we had, and slowly we began to forget the fresh sea breeze and lap of the waves at our feet. It was worse for the Greeks, people agreed, away from their homes and their families, living on our beaches, hurling themselves at our steadfast walls and never making any progress. They would not be able to hold on as long as we could. An end would come, if only we could be strong and wait.

Well, we had waited and the tenth year had come, and we waited still. The days had settled into a terrible kind of routine, one that had become so familiar that often I forgot the horror of it all, until it would sweep through my body and I would go rigid with the shock of it all over again. It seemed impossible, but this was normal life to us. So it was that in that tenth year, I woke early one morning to a sky thick with clouds and a metallic taste in the air. The remnants of a dissolved dream clung to me, its fragments tantalizingly out of reach.

Something had changed. I dressed hurriedly and did not linger to drag a comb through my hair or to twist it up, but let it hang loose and tangled as I slipped through the sleeping palace into the city.

He was here. I could feel the raw edge of his menace: the fury of Apollo, as sure and steady as I had long ago felt it in the temple beneath the bruising pressure of his lips. My heart was hammering, at odds with the soft peace of the morning. I wanted to run, but it was as though quicksand sucked me down and I was held fast where I was, helpless and vulnerable. I clutched my arms about my head, felt the scrape of stones tear at my knees as I flung myself to the ground. Panting, I waited for his strike.

The moments passed. I dared to raise my head an inch from the ground as I felt him recede. Crawling to the wall, I heaved myself up against it and looked out across the battle plain, toward the Greek camp.

The pain shattered my head like a bolt of lightning. I pressed my hands hard to my temples, desperate to hold my skull in one piece. My breath left my body as his light sliced through my mind and I reeled against the clammy, fog-drenched stone.

My sight came back, piece by piece. I watched, open-mouthed, as it descended on the Greeks, invisible to anyone but me: the acrid reek of disease, the choking stench of plague, breathed from Apollo's perfect lips, a cloud bulging and distended with every sickness he knew how to heal. A curse of open, rotting sores that would burst their flesh; burning fevers that would ravage their bodies; rattling, wheezing gasps and prayers that would go unanswered. They would beg for his mercy, for his healing powers. He would watch them die.

For ten days, we all watched them. Frantically, the Greek soldiers tried to burn the bodies, but they piled up faster than they could light the pyres. The infection swept the camp, invisible and deadly. I could feel their despair and their terror from the cushioned couches the slaves dragged to the edge of the palace courtyard so that my parents could watch along with me. Andromache, too, cradling her son, her body tensed with hope.

Hector, of course, galloped ahead of the Trojans. Our men were buoyed, giddy with their advantage. There was no one to drive them back. The Greek forces were depleted; so many of their men sickened and dying or dead already from Apollo's plague. They clung on, but only barely, and it seemed impossible that they could hold out against us any longer. The end of the war rose before us; a beautiful vision that seemed so close within our grasp. Only I, alone in my family, alone in the city, did not believe it.

Whether it was the burning altars the Greeks lit in Apollo's honor or some other appeasement, the eleventh day dawned fresh and clear. The vile miasma that had hung across the Greek camp burned away with the sunrise. Undaunted, my brother led his troops once more into battle with their exhausted enemy.

That evening, Hector returned at sunset exultantly, reporting that although sickness no longer ravaged the Greek armies, Achilles refused to fight alongside them. He and his Myrmidons had stayed away from the battle. And true enough, we did not see the unmistakable sight of his chariot flying across the plains after that: the chariot that, every day before, had left our sons and brothers and husbands hacked and mutilated in his wake.

If Achilles had withdrawn from the war, then victory was ours—and everyone in Troy knew it. Weeks passed, but our confidence continued to grow. The Greeks may have survived a plague, but they could never win without Achilles. It was only a matter of time. I saw Andromache's tired eyes aglow, a nervous smile daring to lift her lips. My mother, drinking wine, the tension loosened from her shoulders. And Helen, her face as calm and beautiful as it had ever been.

I chewed on my lip anxiously, the dry skin splitting under my teeth. I did not see our salvation ahead; only the sour dread of disaster unforeseen.

In the ghostly dawn, we ranged again at the city walls, useless spectators gathered atop the ramparts, waiting for our fate to be decided. The monotony of it, day after day for ten years, the helpless despair that pinned us there to watch—could it break at last?

The fog rolled in from the shore with the waves; a drifting tide of white exhaled by the surging sea. It cloaked the enemy encampment, stretched its tendrils out to the Trojan campfires dotted at the base of the walls. We were poised, all of us, a silent city gathered in this endless moment. I think every soul among us held their breath as the warriors massed in their ranks, ready.

Still, the eerie silence reigned, broken only by the hoarse shriek of a solitary bird that swooped low above us, the beat of its wings startlingly loud.

And then, somewhere in the murky gloom, the rumble of chariot wheels sounded. Andromache was at my side, and I felt her body stiffen. We had expected to see a Trojan charge, but before they had taken a step, it seemed that, incredibly, the Greeks approached—the battered, almost beaten Greeks. A vast body of darkness swelled behind the dissipating fog, and, at once, a great whooping cry went up, reverberating against the ancient stones of Troy. A hideously familiar helmet shone in the first weak rays of the sun, the gleaming armor we all recognized.

Andromache clutched convulsively at my hand. "Achilles returns," she gasped.

I shook my head, squinted at the mighty figure spurring on the horses, standing proud upon his chariot, flanked by the Myrmidon army whose absence we had thought would save us all. "No—Achilles sits alone," I breathed. I saw him, solitary and brooding, as sullen as the smoldering embers of the fire beside which he sat. He stared resolutely out to sea; his nymph mother watching him, her black eyes gleaming with satisfaction.

"It is not Achilles," I whispered. It was Apollo's words, burning in my throat.

Andromache, oblivious to my words, went very still beside me, her eyes wide with horror. "Hector."

Of course, my brother charged forward in pursuit of Achilles' chariot; of course he could not watch his men cut down before him. I could feel the sleek silver menace in the air, quivering like the taut string of Apollo's bow poised over the battle, and I felt certain that one of the two men grappling urgently on the sand below would die.

In the distant quiet of the empty Myrmidon camp, I felt Achilles go rigid with sudden tension, and I knew that he whipped his head around in the direction of the faraway battle seething at the base of our city walls. And, in the same moment, I saw the impossible—Achilles' shield dropped into the dirt of the battlefield, his knees buckling underneath him and his great plumed helmet rolling from his head as he tumbled backward.

The blood glittered on Hector's sword, its scarlet shine visible even to us on the battlements.

I paused. Sometimes, in dreams, I knew myself to be asleep, and I would feel trapped in the unfolding events of my slumbering mind, unable to break free. It was like this now, as people turned to one another in dazed disbelief.

Far below, Hector finished stripping away the armor as the Myrmidons swarmed, protective and busy over the tender flesh of the body. The corpse was the seething heart of a newer fight; a raw and desperate skirmish to claim the ragged, blood-streaked remains of whichever man had fought inside the armor of Achilles.

Priam's head dropped, defeated, as he comprehended the message that rang back across the men. "It is not Achilles," he said.

I turned away, sick and weary. I could not watch the slaughter that day. I set my eyes upon the paved streets beneath my feet, searching for the truth lost in the muffling ache that rattled my brain. Somewhere, I knew, it lurked: a shining gem, kept tantalizingly just beyond my reach. If only Apollo would let me see it clearly; if only I could trace out the path to Troy's destruction; if only I could know exactly the shape our doom would take.

In his temple, I prayed again. I did not beg for our salvation. I wanted only to know how long the torment of waiting would last. Wreathed in perfumed smoke, the statue of Apollo stared impassively out above my prostrate body. On the battlefield, the war raged. Every moment that passed stretched out interminably, but, somehow, the hours wore on. Outside the dim interior of the temple, the heavy bank of clouds began to dissipate, and in their wake, pale stars glimmered in the darkening sky. The men would withdraw; those still living would limp back to bathe wounds and grieve their friends and vow vengeance upon their enemies when the sun rose in the morning. And the jackals would slink, keen and hungry, from the shadows.

Hector came. He stepped past me, between the columns, and stood at Apollo's mighty bronze feet. I raised myself to watch him.

My brother's hair hung in damp curls. He must have cleansed himself of the dust and filth of battle before coming before the god. The back of his neck was bare; no vast plumed helmet nodding above his head. The vulnerability of this little patch of exposed flesh twisted my heart. Today, he gleamed with health and vitality, his arms taut and muscular, his chest rising and falling, blood running through his veins. I closed my eyes, tears prickling at my eyelids.

I heard the chink of metal and the pouring of liquid. The sweet aroma of wine mingled with the scent of incense, and I knew that Hector made his libation to Apollo. He would stand before the statue, his arms outstretched, and he would pray.

Through the dim smoke, I felt a steady calm spreading through my body, clearing some of the jangling confusion in my head. I opened my eyes and saw him looking back at me.

"Have you come to ask what tomorrow holds?" I said through dry lips, my voice hoarse from lack of use. I had not spoken since my un-heard proclamation over the battlefield, when I had seen that it was not Achilles falling under Hector's sword.

"Only the gods can know that," he answered.

I wondered how his eyes could be so mellow, so contemplative. He surely came to seek from Apollo the knowledge of Achilles' vengeance. I glanced up at the silent, towering god behind my brother. Finally, I felt the racing blur of my thoughts settle and, piece by piece, they slid together into place. "I can see it," I whispered.

He had never scorned me or scolded me. To the Greeks, he held death in his hands, a formidable warrior with no mercy or weakness. In Troy, he was our protector, as kind to his raving sister as he was to anyone else. "It does not matter what happens to me," he said. He knelt beside me, on the floor. "That is not what I seek to know."

"The man you killed today—" I began.

"I killed many men today," he said. "And every day of this ten-year war. But the man you think of—he who wore Achilles' armor—his name was Patroklos." He glanced at me. "Achilles will want my blood for it, that much I know. Patroklos cursed me as he died, warned me of what will come."

Patroklos. The white was creeping in around the edges of my vision, but I swallowed back the bile that accompanied it and forced my gaze to rest only upon Hector's face.

"But Achilles is one man," Hector continued, his voice quiet. "Before today, we had the Greeks nearly overpowered. We will chase them to their ships, and he can roar and rage against us as he likes. Perhaps his grief will make him careless."

I reached out my hand and wrapped it around his forearm. It was warm, life pulsing under his skin. By sunset tomorrow, it would be limp and dust-streaked, dragged along the earth behind Achilles' chariot. I stared at his wrist, traced the pattern of green veins on the tender inside. I saw the inferno coming for him, ready to consume my patient brother.

"Come," he said, making to stand, gently pulling me with him. "Do not stay here. Come to the palace and be with us tonight."

No one else would want me there. His pity only hurt me more. I followed him as he asked, for there would be no more requests from my brother. I cast my eyes back to Apollo as we left, the wine that Hector had poured in his honor gleaming red in a bowl by his feet. Tomorrow night, Troy would mourn more desperately than it had in ten years of war. I walked behind my brother, already grieving him with every step I took.

CHAPTER EIGHTEEN

Clytemnestra

"Go on," I urged, leaning forward so eagerly that the wine nearly spilled from my goblet.

He eyed me a little apprehensively. He was a wiry youth, tense and uncertain, though he felt that he was bringing me good news. His worried gaze kept flicking to Aegisthus at my side: Aegisthus, whose narrow shoulders did not fill the broad back of his monstrously gilded and towering chair. I surmised it was this which made the messenger so nervous, for he delivered news of Greek triumphs at Troy to a man sitting in Agamemnon's throne.

"They say Achilles fought like a man possessed," he went on, stumbling a little over his words. I nodded encouragingly. "He . . . he tore through the Trojan lines like a fire tearing through a forest in the driest summer."

"Tell me of those he killed," I said.

"He was more lion than man—"

"Yes, yes, he raged like a fire and roared like a lion, but tell me what he *did*."

"Hector wore Achilles' own armor, which he had stolen from Patroklos' body, but Achilles strode forth in armor more magnificent than any that had been seen before—a gift, surely, from his immortal mother and worthy of the craftsmanship of Hephaestus himself."

The young man caught himself as my irritation flashed across my face. "The Trojans were terrified, Queen Clytemnestra, and they fled before his fury. But he pursued them relentlessly."

I savored a long sip of wine.

"Over and over, he hurled his spear, skewering men as they ran. He sprang from his own chariot to drag men from theirs, and if they clasped his knees and begged for their lives, he showed no pity. He hacked apart their bodies, plunged his sword into their livers, severed their heads, and trampled his horses across their bodies until his chariot was decorated with the gore that sprayed up from under the churning wheels and thundering hooves." He was getting into his stride, realizing that this description was just what I desired to hear. "He chased the Trojans to the very banks of the river Xanthus, and there he turned the water red with their blood. Only twelve men did he spare—"

"Why any at all?" Aegisthus asked. I saw that he, too, was gripped by the tale, though I could see him squirming a little on his chair. He did not share my relish.

"He swore to slit their throats at Patroklos' funeral pyre. But he would not burn his beloved's body until he had sated his vengeance and, for this, only the death of Hector would suffice."

"Where was Hector?" I asked.

"Achilles couldn't find him in the great throng of the battle, but he cut down every man in his path in his search. Other sons of Priam died gasping at his feet and the river choked with corpses. Such was his savagery and his reckless lust for blood that he would have fought Apollo himself. Overcome, the Trojans ran to the city, the army desperately seeking the sanctuary of its walls before Achilles could slaughter them all."

I sat back against my cushions, sipping my wine. I had never seen Achilles at Aulis; if he was there, I did not know his face. I had never cared to hear of his feats in battle; none of it concerned me until he turned upon my husband in his pique over a stolen slave-girl. I had worried then that his withdrawal from the war would hand victory to Troy, and that someone else, perhaps the famed Hector, would rob me of the privilege of murdering my husband. Now that I heard of his ferocious return to the fray, however, I felt a kind of affinity with Achilles begin to stir in my breast. I could see him, the grief and rage building in his chest, and I felt the cruel pleasure he must have taken in gripping that spear and striding out across the Trojan earth, ready to vent his passions upon a whole army of men. Envy twisted in my breast. If I could have wielded sword and spear and set out among that Achaean host who had stood and watched my daughter die, I would have taken the same satisfaction—and, like Achilles, I would not have stopped until I found the murderer I sought. I gestured to the messenger to carry on.

"At first, Hector didn't run," he said. "He alone stood before the city gates while his father, King Priam, howled from the walls."

I heard the soft swallow in Aegisthus' throat. I wondered if he imagined it: the father watching his son die, just as Aegisthus had watched his father die. And Priam, this aged king, famed across our lands for his fifty sons—how many of them did he mourn already? For a dizzying second, the bleak truth of it gaped before me: a hideous tangle of children lost and the agony of grief; the violence that reverberated through the legends of Atreus' forefathers, rising like a tidal wave from our past and catching us all in its irresistible surge.

"Hector had fought hundreds of our finest men and lived. But Achilles rose up on the plain with all the might and fury of the sun itself, and, as he made his charge, Hector could not stand so bravely any longer. He fled before Achilles like a man caught in a nightmare, desperately hurtling around the walls of the city, seeking a sanctuary he could not find. He flung his spear at Achilles in vain; it glanced off his great shield and fell uselessly to the ground. And when he summoned his strength and his courage to run at Achilles with his sword, which had dispatched so many Greeks before, Achilles drove his own spear right through Hector's throat."

I breathed out. "I thank you for this news," I said. "With Hector fallen, it cannot be long before we will be welcoming back our men."

Not yet, I knew that at least. Between the pillars around the hall, I could see columns of sky, lit only by the stars. No beacons were yet aflame. Troy clung on still. When it fell, I would be the first in Mycenae to know.

"That is not all," the messenger said. His eyes had flickered to Aegisthus again when I made mention of welcoming the men home. But I knew he would not dare speak whatever thought had crossed his mind at that.

"No? What else?"

"With Hector's dying gasp, he begged Achilles to give his body back to his father. But Achilles' anger was still too great, even with Patroklos' murderer bleeding into the sand at his feet. He stripped away Hector's armor. He slit Hector's feet and forced thongs of ox-hide through the wounds to bind the corpse to the back of his chariot. Then he dragged him through the dust, with his parents watching still from the city walls. They say that the queen's shrieks could be heard all the way back to the Greek ships. He vowed to feed Hector's body to the dogs, but I think he would have feasted on it raw himself if he could have done so."

I kept my face very still. "Well, this is excellent news. You must rest here tonight; we have many comforts at your disposal, and we are grateful indeed for everything you have related to us. I ask for only one more piece of information, if you know it."

He looked at me. I could see the strain carved across his face, that he must address me as queen, that he must do as I asked while Aegisthus sat in his king's seat, while all the while he must be frantically wondering how Agamemnon might punish such disloyalty on his return.

"And tomorrow," I hastened to add, "you may go forth from here with gold to prove our gratitude. A merchant ship sails to Etruria laden with pottery and fine jewelry to sell; I am sure they will have a place for an enterprising young man like yourself on board."

I saw him breathe a fractional sigh of relief at the prospect of escape. "What else do you wish to know?" he asked.

I leaned forward. "Is there news of Helen? My sister—do you know if she lives, if she has been seen?"

"The Greeks have had sight of her, sometimes," he answered. "Atop the city walls, among the Trojans, but unmistakable even from afar. She lives, but that is all we know."

I hadn't expected to hear anything else. Later, as the palace slept and I prowled, I could not keep my mind from going back to her. In Sparta, the daughter Helen had left behind grew into a young woman while my daughter roamed the shadowy Underworld. Did my sister think of Hermione, just a child when she and Paris had crept under the cover of night to his waiting ship? Hermione was older than Iphigenia had become; the younger cousin had overtaken my child, who would be frozen forever at fourteen. And still her mother dallied in a foreign court, the years slipping through her fingers, never to be regained. If my daughter dwelled anywhere in this world, no army or ocean could stop me from reaching her. But Helen stayed away.

I sighed impatiently. And then, from somewhere in the void, I heard the urgent press of whispers. I stiffened, held myself still, and strained to hear.

Deep, gruff male voices. Not quavering with age or high with youth. My breath caught fast in my throat. Alongside the voices, I could hear the muffled thump and drag of an inert object. Some cursing as they shifted it, and then a low snort of suppressed laughter, harsh and mirthless. Somewhere in the darkness, their footsteps faded into nothing. The wind sighed across the sea and silence settled again.

I stayed out there until dawn began to seep into the sky, dull and ghostly on the horizon.

I slept through the early hours of the day. When I rose, the busy hustle of the morning had calmed to a quiet hum as usual. As I made my way down the corridor toward the throne room, I passed Aegisthus' guards in a huddle. Their eyes flickered over me as I walked. The low growl of their voices, the bristle of their hulking posture, served as a reminder to anyone at Mycenae who might have thought to question the presence of my consort. I had been reassured by the promise of their protection while we waited. But we had waited so long. I doubted that it was respect I saw in their ever-lengthening stares, respect for the queen who had made them guards of a king. Was it restlessness I noted?

My certainty never wavered. But my patience was wearing thin. I wondered if theirs was, too; if the stasis in which we perched, awaiting the end of one battle so that we might fight our own, was stretching everyone's tolerance to its limits.

I slipped into the anteroom. Through the columns ahead of me, I could see Aegisthus leaning back against the cushions heaped upon his throne.

"Clytemnestra?" He straightened, squinted through the columns.

I entered the great hall. Between us, the flames flickered in the round hearth in the center of the room. Four pillars stood around it, and the smoke spiraled up to the blue square of open sky directly above it, a break in the ornate painted patterns that repeated across the ceiling. The pillars were painted in a soft gold-tinged cream. Each tile of the floor was edged in warm, fiery orange. And across every wall, wild beasts and monsters cavorted in elaborate frescoes, tossing their heads and stamping their hooves; frozen waves stood poised in painted oceans, while men and gods strode among it all, bordered in vivid, swirling motifs. History swelled and pressed upon me in this room from every angle; the deeds of the past presented as feats and triumphs to proclaim far and wide. The bloodstain had faded on the floor before this very hearth, but we both saw it every day, as bright as if the blood had just been spilled.

"Did our guest board the ship this morning?" I asked. "It is a long voyage to Etruria; he will not return before . . . he will not return soon."

Aegisthus smiled. "He was gone before morning."

I hesitated. Was there an unfamiliar note in his voice? I scrutinized his face. "He brought us welcome news. An end in sight to this war." An end in sight to our waiting. My fists curled at my sides. "I was glad to reward him for that."

"He was well rewarded." It was more of a smirk than a smile.

I was about to speak, but I saw his eyes dart to the entrance from the anteroom. I turned quickly. "Elektra?"

She stood awkwardly, framed between two columns.

"Elektra?" I said again. I heard the sharpness in my tone, the irritation I never managed to suppress. There was nothing but waiting in our lives now; did she have to add to it by lingering in silence before beginning any conversation? It pressed on the raw edge of my nerves and made me harsh, although I had resolved time and time again to be more soft, more patient.

"Is Hector truly dead?" she asked.

"He is," I answered.

"Then the war will end at last." Her voice cracked.

"Troy cannot stand without its greatest warrior," I said.

She lifted her eyes to me. "Then my father will come home."

"He will."

Her gaze slid to Aegisthus, and I felt him tense behind me. The silence stretched taut and quivering in the hall. I could not stand it. "Is that all?" I snapped.

"That's all," she said, a slight smile lifting her mouth as she looked at Aegisthus, and she walked away.

My head ached. I turned back to Aegisthus. I wished I could crawl back into my bed and sleep the day away. The smoke from the fire in the central hearth stung my eyes, and I saw him through a watery haze. "So. No word should reach Agamemnon of—the situation here in Mycenae before he arrives."

The gray wisps spiraled toward the opening in the roof, escaping into the sky.

"No word will reach him. I am sure of that." He shifted his gaze toward the cluster of guards that I had passed at the entrance.

I remembered the whispers outside the palace walls in the depths of night. The shifting sound of something heavy dragged across the ground. Aegisthus' face, different now.

His demeanor, now that the wait was nearly over, was not more anxious, as I had anticipated. He wasn't shrinking away. *He looks ready*, I thought.

And I wondered why that did not bring me any comfort.

CHAPTER NINETEEN

Cassandra

"P aris is wounded! He is wounded!"
The shouting echoed up and down the gathering dusk
through the streets of Troy. In the temple of Apollo, I turned
my head toward the sound, startled.

Paris had been a dead man walking since Hector had fallen. He'd
had his moment of glory on the battlefield the day that one of his
arrows had miraculously lodged itself deep in Achilles' foot. The
poison-coated tip had done its work from there. It was the first time
my sleek, handsome brother had distinguished himself on the battlefield; here, in the dying days of war, when it seemed that barely anyone
cared anymore what happened. Achilles, when his wrath had burned
out, had fought a bleak and desultory fight. His grief shone from him;
the baleful heart of a star collapsing into white ashes. He roamed the
plains in search of his own death; that was why Paris' arrow was at last
able to find its target. Achilles welcomed it. And so, Paris was feted
briefly in our halls; at the meager remnants of the feasts we used to
have that Priam and Hecabe attempted now. Hector's empty chair,
Andromache's blank face, my parents' glazed eyes—it only made the
contrast to those past celebrations more stark.

I had lost track of the days some time ago. Now the shouting resolved itself into clear words and I understood. So, today was Paris'
time to die. Ten years too late.

My parents would grieve. For them, I would go to the palace, even if there were no words of solace left. But when I stepped out from be-tween the pillars, into the soft evening air, it was Helen I saw.

"Where has he fled?" she asked.

I thought for a moment. "When he arrived at Troy, he left a wife behind him," I said. "Oenone, a nymph of the river. They dwelled in the mountains before he left to seek a different prize."

She looked at me steadily. "Will she help him?"

Oenone. I saw her face, ravaged by tears when he left. Twisted with anger when she learned where he had gone and why. I could see Paris, bleeding and limping up the paths they had walked together once, begging for her healing skills, a decade after he had abandoned her.

I shook my head. "She will not."

Helen looked away.

"He should have died on that mountain as a baby," I said. The words jarred in the gentle breeze. They were not what I meant to say.

"He will die there today," she said.

I gave a stiff, jerky nod.

She reached out her hand and touched my shoulder. I looked at her slender fingers, the gleaming pink oval nails. Her touch was warm. Kind. I wondered why she seemed to be comforting me when it was she who was newly widowed, her position in Troy more precarious as she had no husband to claim her, no brother-in-law to protect her. I had heard it said that if Paris fell, she would be given in marriage to Deiphobus, one of Priam's few surviving sons, one of my last remain-ing brothers. How Helen felt about it, I had no idea. But no worry or anxiety creased her forehead, and I could only see sympathy in her eyes.

The names of legend had tussled on the plains before the city for a decade, but now they were all dead. The battles were weary, pain-ful struggles: no glorious fountains of blood churned up in a crimson froth at the wheels of Achilles' chariot; only men exhausted from a war that seemed to run forever, dragging themselves out day by day to fight again.

When it had begun, I had thought the war would end in a mighty conflagration; a huge explosion of violence and savagery, the storming of our gates and the toppling of our towers. But it looked as though it would limp to a close, that the victors would crawl over the heaped-up piles of the dead to extinguish us, that we would close our eyes and bow our heads to the slow and inevitable end.

So, when the Greeks left, it took everyone by surprise. The news reached us across the plains; we gathered at the walls and looked out to a long, empty stretch of sand all the way to the gleaming sea. No ships. The scouts returned, confirming it was true. The army had vanished as abruptly as they had arrived.

My fellow Trojans were dazed, hardly daring to believe it. I watched the incredulous smiles, the gasps of joy pass one to the other, sparking through the crowds. The gates of Troy swung open, and the citizens poured out.

The ground seemed to shift beneath my feet as I followed. I wondered if it would split apart and suck our city down into the bowels of the earth; if we would suffocate in dirt instead of perishing in flames as I had seen, as Hecabe's dream of her cursed baby had foretold.

The coastal breeze whipped up around me, lifted my hair. I breathed the fresh, salty air into my lungs. Tears prickled my eyes. The ripple and shimmer of the water, the damp sand where the foamy waves lapped at the shore, the tangle of seaweed drifting in clumps—it was mesmerizing. I stared and stared until my vision swam with salt water.

When I saw the horse, I felt the sensation of recognition. It was like seeing someone familiar in the distance and then, as they step free of the blinding sunlight, their face becomes clear. *So this is it*, I thought. *A trick. This is how we die at last.*

It was a vast construction, towering above us, with its blank face bowed toward the sea. Great planks of wood were bound together in pillars for the legs and then overlapped in carefully shaped layers for the curving swell of its flanks, the long slope of its back, and its bent neck. How they had done it, down on this beach with only the timber they could gather was one mystery; *why* they had done it was the question gripping the tremulously excited gathering. Although its silhouette was lumpen and ungainly, they had taken the care of plaiting together twists of reeds for its mane, of smoothing its shape and making it a thing of startling beauty.

I watched my father, Priam, stooped with age and ravaged by grief, step closer to it. He studied it, walking back and forth along its length, reaching out a hand as though to touch it, and then drawing back at the last moment, unsure. "Antenor?" he said.

Antenor's counsel was respected in Troy, but I was not the only one to recall how earnestly he had advised my father ten years ago to return Helen to the Greeks with all the gifts we could muster in exchange for peace, and how Priam had turned to Paris and seen the resentment smoldering in his eyes. Antenor had stalked from the palace that day, his cloak flying behind him, his words of wisdom discarded so that Priam's son could keep his stolen wife.

I thought of all the men who had fallen since that day, and shivered as I felt the cold press of that silent, massed throng, their smoke-filled eyes staring at the horse with us.

"A gift to the gods," Antenor said at last. "For their protector, Athena, I wager. They leave it here in her honor to buy her favor for their safe return home."

Relief rippled through the crowd. These words, so sweet and full of comfort: how everyone longed to believe them, how grateful they all were to the wise Antenor for uttering that glorious phrase, for his faith that the Greeks were truly gone.

"Let's take it!" came the shout from somewhere in the gathered spectators, and it began to echo through them, people nodding vigorously and smiling at the prospect. "We will take it into the city; make it our offering to Athena instead, and she will smile on us rather than them."

Black, vertiginous horror drained my vision. Swamped by the rising panic, I began to push my way through the happy groups, groping my way to the front, my breath heaving ever faster, to get to my father.

"Fools!" It was not me who shouted it. At the knotted heart of the crowd, I paused, searching for the voice that spoke up so unexpectedly against this madness. The irritated faces around me, annoyed by my intrusion, melted into surprise and confusion, and then abruptly changed to shock as a heavy spear flashed at once above our heads, slicing through the air so close that I felt the breeze of its flight ruffle my hair.

Not a Greek ambush, as the first horrified screams suggested. I twisted about to see where it had come from, and there, standing apart from the rest of the Trojans, his back to the shore, was the priest Laocoön, his arms still raised above his head, though the spear he had hurled was lodged, quivering, in the wooden flank of the great horse.

Into the shocked silence, he spoke. "Fools!" he said again. "How can you be so blind? How can you not see at once that this is a trick?" His face was contorted with rage, his chest heaving as he spat the words at us all. At his side, his two young sons stared as though they did not recognize him.

Hope splintered in my chest. I was not alone, not the only one to see it, and the delirious relief of it made me laugh aloud: a peal of gratitude that barked far more harshly from my throat than I had thought it would. Those closest to me drew back, a familiar disdain twisting their features as the empty space widened around me. I did not care; Laocoön could see the danger too, and he would be believed. My very bones ached desperately with the fervency of my trust. He had to be believed; surely he would be.

And then the white blade of light flashed through my head, splitting my skull apart. I writhed like a hooked fish as Apollo shattered the interior of my mind again, the crazed and tortured searing rays of the vision slicing through the tender flesh of my brain, and I saw what happened next in a fragmented series of images.

Laocoön's fury. The crowd wavering in doubt. A frozen moment; our future hanging in the balance. Then the screaming, the anguished howl of terror, high and thin, keening from the smaller of Laocoön's sons. His brother thrashed mutely; his cries deadened by the suffocating weight of the scaly coils that already wrapped around his little body.

Sand muffled my cries as I tried to struggle to my feet, blinded again by another piercing flash of light, and I rolled back, my head striking a rock, blood seeping warm and damp down my neck. I could not see through the horrified mass of people, but I knew what was happening as the two giant serpents surged from the waves, twisting around Laocoön's two children. As he flung himself at their gleaming, glistening coils, they entrapped him too. I knew the moment that the little boys' faces went gray and still amid the shifting scales; I knew that Laocoön saw it too, moments before the fangs sank through his neck and venom flooded his veins.

Screaming. Fleeing footsteps. Terror and panic sent the crowd rushing across the sand, away from that frozen tableau of horror. Laocoön, between his boys, desperately reaching across to them still, the mighty snakes looped around them all in an inescapable tangle of death. I could feel the blood pulsing from the gash behind my ear as the blindness started to dissolve.

The hissing died away. The serpents slid back into the sea, their work done. And one by one, the people turned their accusing gaze to Laocoön's spear, still quivering in the horse's flank.

Perhaps it might have been enough: a clear message to the watching Trojans that the gods moved quickly to punish any damage to the horse. But whether they would have dragged it up the plains and through the city gates itself without Sinon, I do not know. He was a Greek, weeping and swearing to us that he had escaped his own army, who wanted to sacrifice him to the gods for a fair wind home. I watched Sinon speak, every word a poisonous lie. They did sacrifice, these Greeks. I knew that was true, for I saw a girl trembling at a makeshift altar, a knife flashing in the light of the rising sun above her bare neck. But they would not have sacrificed this man, whose eyes slid sideways as he spoke, who urged us to take the horse and steal the luck of the departing Greeks, so that their ships would sink and we would prosper.

I clutched at my father's elbow. "Do not believe this man," I implored him.

Priam shook away my hand like it was a fly buzzing about him.

"The Greeks have treated him ill," he said. "See the gashes on his legs where they beat him; the weals in his wrists where the ropes bound him."

"A trick to make us believe him!" I said.

I stilled my panicked breathing, shook back my knotted curls, and tried to square my shoulders, to assume a regal bearing. Andromache wandered the sand with Astyanax toddling at her side, her thoughts awash with sorrow while he squealed with delight at the unfamiliar sensation of sand trickling through his chubby fingers. Helen contemplated the horse. Did she believe that her first husband really sailed back to Sparta, leaving her widowed in this foreign land to which Paris had brought her? Or did she too suspect a grand deception, a final ambush still in store to bring her home at long last? Her beautiful face gave nothing away.

Priam and Hecabe, my mother and father, were shriveled in upon themselves with pain, and I could see that there was nothing they wanted to believe so much as Sinon's story and Antenor's guidance. So many of their sons drifted, pale and wispy, through the Underworld. How bitterly they must have rued the fact that they were left with me, their mad daughter, who tried now to destroy their hopes of claiming some kind of victory at last.

I loosened my grip on my father's frail arm, the marks of my fingers sagging in wrinkled circles. "We could leave the horse here, on the beach," I tried. "Dedicate it to Apollo out here under his gaze in the sunlight, and bolt our gates tonight in case any Greeks remain."

The hammered bronze discs adorning the neck of his tunic glinted in the harsh light. "They buy the goodwill of Athena with this wooden horse," he mused. "But if it is Troy that gives her such a gift, instead of them, then who is to say she will not turn her favor to us at last?"

Tears of frustration burned behind my eyes. My father was staring at the horse so intently, my words were as futile as feathers drifting in the wind.

The crowd hummed with activity, men slinging ropes around the great horse, hauling it with all their strength. The sun shone down on them, their bare arms bathed in a sheen of sweat as they pulled together, grimacing and laughing all at once. A lightness rippled over the Trojans, a sweet breath of joy at being free of fighting and siege, at pressing their toes into sand and talking of freedom again. I stood apart.

If I was going to run, this would be my chance. No one wanted to hear any more of my warnings; they wouldn't care to listen to anything that might puncture this fragile newfound delirium that had overcome them all. In a city succumbed to a credulity that seemed insane, it was only me, the mad prophetess, who had clarity.

A tide of resentment was building in my body, seething into a rage. I had done everything I could to serve Troy. I had tended to Apollo's temple, said the prayers and performed the rituals to keep our patron god happy. I had bitten down on my unwelcome insights as hard as I could manage, all these years. I had fought my best to contain them. Apollo had punished me so cruelly, and I never breathed a word against him, never railed at the injustice, only strove to serve him better so that I could deserve his mercy. And all of them had turned away from me. I had no respect from the people of Troy; I, daughter of Priam and Hecabe, was reviled and ignored no matter how hard I tried to help them. Perhaps I should leave them to their doom, let them happily embrace the devastation of the city.

I opened my eyes. The crowd was farther up the slope, inching toward the city walls. Their shouts drifted over the breeze: the gates were not wide enough, some were calling, they must knock down the wall at the side so that the horse could be taken in without scratching a single panel. The walls that had withstood ten years of the biggest army anyone had ever seen battering against them, now they would fall at Trojan hands, because of Trojan foolishness. I shook my head. Took a step forward, away from them all. And then another. And another.

"Where will you go?"

I bit down on my bottom lip. Keeping my eyes fixed on the sea, I didn't answer her.

"Cassandra?"

Her footsteps, light on the sand as she followed. I shook off the touch of her hand on my shoulder.

"Cassandra, it isn't safe out here."

The ring of panic in her voice gave me pause. I had never heard Helen so rattled. Not even when the army first arrived. Certainly not when Paris died.

"It isn't safe back there," I said.

She gripped my shoulder again. She was so close to me, but I kept my eyes averted from her, refusing to look into her face. "I don't know the meaning of the horse," she said, her words spilling out low and fast. "Why the Greeks left it, if they should take it into the city or not—I don't know." Her fingers dug painfully into my skin. "But you can't stand out here alone, unprotected. If any soldiers remain; if any-one has been left behind . . ."

A sob caught in my throat. Somewhere, in the distance, if only I could walk far enough to find it, there was safety, I was sure. I could see it more clearly than I saw the ocean before me. Soft hills, wooded with welcoming forests. A quiet farmhouse, a spiral of smoke drifting into the air from its chimney. A peaceful solitude, a place where no agony would shatter my skull, a place where nothing of note would ever happen, so there would be nothing to foresee.

"There is nowhere to go," Helen said.

I looked at her. Her free hand rubbed anxiously at the back of her neck, her brows drawn together and her eyes brimming with con-cern. Concern for me, I realized. My parents, my sisters, my surviv-ing brothers, they were all gone far back toward the gates, with the crowd and with the horse. Only Helen stayed here for me. And I could see how much it cost her, how her eyes darted back and forth along the horizon, searching for danger. If any Greeks besides Sinon had stayed on the beach to keep watch, what would they do to Helen if she was out here unprotected? The vision of the farmhouse evaporated, and the world rushed back in around me. My breath wouldn't come. I could feel it, her fear, infecting me: the press of a thousand watchful eyes, the silent masses of an unseen army ranged against us, waiting for their chance.

She was right. I wouldn't make it to the nearest settlement, to any nearby village that hadn't been razed to the ground by the Greeks already. I didn't want to die out here alone. I let her pull me back up the sand, casting one more look back at the empty beach and the silent sea. If there was death in that direction and death in the other, what should I do? Where should I go? Who was left to help us?

My brother, Hector, had been Troy's protector and defender until Achilles cut him down. I stopped for a moment, stood still, ignoring Helen's exasperation as I thought of it.

Hector, prince of Troy, was dead.

Now the city had only me.

I was the only one who could see this threat; I was the only one who knew how and when Troy would fall. Apollo had given me this curse for a reason. Helen had called it a gift once before; what if she was right? I swallowed back the bile, the tears, the pain from the visions that racked my body. Today was the moment that it would have meaning; Apollo had given the knowledge to me alone, and that meant it was I who stood between Troy and the doom I had foreseen when Paris strolled carefree from the mountains, our death in his hands. I, Cassandra of Troy, I could save the city. I could save my family—and I could save myself.

CHAPTER TWENTY

Cassandra

There was a fierce edge to the celebrations across the city. The horse stood garlanded with ribbons in the central square of Troy, and all around, the people danced and cried out their heartfelt joy. They sobbed and howled and shouted at the star-sprinkled sky; the heady blend of disbelief and exhaustion and elation all mingling together in a release of ten years' worth of suffering so suddenly brought to an end. A madness possessed the city, one so seductive that I almost felt as though I could succumb to it myself, as though for once I didn't need to stand apart from my family and my people, that I could lose myself to this gleeful intoxication of the senses alongside them.

But I knew what awaited, and my heart ached with sorrow. Their happiness was an illusion, a deception woven by our enemy, who waited so patiently for their moment.

It was long into the night by the time the revelers gave in to their fatigue and turned toward the waiting comfort of their beds, tear-stained faces shining with relief that tomorrow, for the first time, they would not wake to the hollering of war cries echoing beneath the city walls and the monstrous clashing of bronze ringing in the air.

I had hidden myself in a corner, tucked at the side of the square outside the temple of Athena, to which the horse had been brought. As the last of them left, the fragments of their final songs drifting behind them, I uncoiled my stiff and aching legs and hurried as fast as I could across the square. I held a torch to the sacred flame that burned in perpetuity before the temple entrance, and its resinous head bloomed at once into crackling fire, the long cone of its body slippery in the palm of my free hand. In my other hand, I held the axe I had taken hours before. With this, Hector had held the Greeks at bay until even he had been overwhelmed by the force of Achilles' wrath. He had wielded it as though it were nothing; for me, it was heavy and awkward, but between the flames and its blade, I knew that the hiding Greeks would have no escape.

The horse was built of dry wood; the reeds entwined around the base of its legs to hold them together were perfect kindling. I would need to work fast, build up more parched and thirsty fuel from the fire-bowls in the square around the base of each leg before I set the torch to it. Then, imprisoned within its belly, by the time they smelled the burning, they would face a panicked drop to the ground amid the blinding smoke, to where I would be waiting with the axe.

I must be quick; who knew how long they would linger, giving our people time enough to sink into bleary sleep, their senses deadened to the warning sounds of ambush? And I must ensure the fire would take hold quickly, to give the hidden soldiers no way to climb down through the rampaging flames. I took a deep breath and, torch aloft, made my way hastily toward the towering hulk.

I worked fast, scattering more kindling on the ground, and then knelt at one foreleg. I stared up at the curved wood above me, imagining for a moment that my eyes could penetrate its thickness and see them crouched there, poised to rain down destruction on our sleeping city.

My jaw set with silent satisfaction as I lowered the torch and flames began to lick at the first wooden limb.

"Cassandra! No!"

The shout came a fraction of a second before he barreled into me, the heavy weight of his body crushing the air from my lungs so that I lay dazed for a moment against the stone floor of the square. He was stamping out the fire, and I clawed at his legs, trying to pull him back, but there were more hands on my body, and I screamed and tried to lunge away, but they held me fast. Someone yanked the axe from my clenched fist, the torch was extinguished and kicked away. As they pulled me back, I saw only a pathetic little wisp of smoke rising from the horse's leg.

"What is the meaning of this?" My father's voice.

I struggled against the guards that held me. "Burn it!" I screamed. "Burn it now!"

It was Deiphobus who stamped out the flames, Deiphobus who had knocked me aside. He turned, panting slightly from his exertions, to face Priam. "You were right," he said grimly. "She was waiting in the shadows to harm it."

I twisted and turned, but the hands that clamped my arm held fast in an implacable grip. "It is full of Greeks! You must believe me! Please, burn it—please!"

"And bring down the rage of Athena, right into the heart of Troy!" My father clutched at his head as though he would pull the sparse gray hair right out of it in exasperation at me. "Was it not enough to see what happened to Laocoön and his sons?"

Foam was bubbling at my lips as I screamed, pure fury coursing through my body. My brother's fist struck me, a starburst of pain exploding in my temple, and my shriek subsided to a shocked whimper.

"Do you truly think there are soldiers in there?" Her voice spilled cool from the shadows, taking us all aback.

"Helen?"

She stepped forward, into the square. Her hair was loose around her shoulders, her eyes serious and set upon the great horse. The flames from those torches still burning cast a flickering light across her face as she turned it upward, contemplating.

"We will not damage this horse!" The anger frayed Priam's voice, and I could hear the catch of exhaustion and despair as he spoke, desperate to avert yet another catastrophe from boiling over and engulfing us all. "We brought it here for our protection; we will not tear it apart on the say-so of a dead priest and a madwoman!"

Helen shook her head. "No need to tear it apart to find out what you want to know," she said, softly. Her steps were purposeful and measured as she made her way steadily closer.

My chest heaved as I watched her, the panic still clogging my throat, making it hard to breathe.

She laid a hand on the closest leg of the horse and closed her eyes. "Menelaus?" she breathed. "Menelaus, I am here, alone in the heart of Troy. You have come here for me, Menelaus, my husband. It has been ten years, but I have waited for you to come." She spoke in Greek, the words unused for all this time, but falling smoothly from her lips. "Don't make me wait any longer." She stood, motionless in the gloaming, her profile stark against the dim bulk of the wooden structure. The silence stretched on. All of us were poised for the sound of any movement, any response from within its cavernous bowels.

When she spoke again, her voice changed. Now deeper, a different tang to her words, perhaps accented, certainly with the quaver of a much older woman speaking, not like Helen's mellifluous tones at all. "Diomedes? Diomedes? How I, your mother, long to see you, to behold my son again before I die. Diomedes, make yourself known to Deipyle, your aged mother, once more!"

I saw Deiphobus' hand tighten on his sword as he watched her begin to pace around the horse, calling out to the impassive wooden planks in a cascade of changing tones and voices. "Odysseus," she said, her voice clear and ringing with a note of impatience. "Penelope begs you to be done with this, to end it now and come home to me and to your son, Telemachus, no longer the baby you left behind. Do not linger, waiting in the dark any longer, it's time to strike!" Then in a younger, sweeter voice, she appealed to another. "Anticlus, come to Laodamia, your lonely wife. Do not hide from me, Anticlus."

We watched, transfixed, as she made her way around the silent creature, the eerie harmony of the different voices weaving a spell around us all, a spell that must be so much more powerful to the hidden Greeks. After ten years of fighting so far away from their homes, the tempting sound of her pleas was surely more seductive than any of them could withstand.

But still, nothing moved in the square but Helen; no one made a sound except for her. When at last she had completed her swaying circle, calling every name of every man who could be concealed within that horse, she stopped and turned to us, her eyes shining in the firelight.

I could see that my father was convinced, Deiphobus and the guards as well. "You see, Cassandra?" Priam breathed. "There is no one within; there is no trick here."

I cast my eyes away from him, staring at the ground. Soon, these streets would run with Trojan blood. "Burn it," I said again. "Risk the vengeance of the gods; what the Greeks will do to us is worse."

He sighed, a sad and defeated exhalation, and rubbed his hand across his tired eyes. "The Greeks are far across the sea already," he said. He made a weary gesture to Deiphobus. "Bear her away," he said. "Be sure she cannot escape."

They dragged me from the square, deaf to my pleading. I thrashed my head to the side and saw Helen, framed against the horse, and I cursed her witchcraft, railing against her and the soft light of sympathy in her eyes as my feet scraped across the stones.

I shouted still as they yanked me through the palace entrance, down the winding corridors, to my own chamber. My voice was hoarse, and, as the guards loosened their grip upon my arm, I clutched at my brother's hand before he could turn away. "Deiphobus," I begged, "the only protector left to Troy. Please, you are the prince of this city. Hector is dead and Priam cannot see the truth; it is to you to burn the horse, to stop our doom, to save us, there is only you who can—" But he was shaking his head, his eyes flickering past me in revulsion.

"You should sleep." He caught my wrist in his hand and pushed me away from him, stepping back quickly and slamming the heavy oak door shut between us. I hurled myself against the unforgiving wood even as I heard the key turn in the lock and his footsteps fade away.

I screamed in frustration and clawed at the door, the wood splintering beneath my fingernails, the blood welling from the torn flesh, though I barely felt the pain. Whirling about, I flung myself at the narrow slit window, where the night air spilled through, where I could see a patch of dim sky that I could not reach. I pressed my forehead to the wall and concentrated on the cold, smooth touch of stone. The waiting felt unbearable, each second stretched beyond the limit of imagining, but spilling like sand through my fingers at the same time. The final moments before the end of everything.

Although there was no sound, at once something shifted. The air around me seemed to hum; I felt a prickling on the back of my neck, a visceral shudder rippled through the heavens, and I lifted my eyes to the sky.

It started like a rush of wind, perhaps a crashing wave, and then it roared into a great, rumbling bellow from the fiery maw of a monster as the inferno took hold. The Greeks must have fanned out across our sleeping city and, at some hidden signal, ignited a hundred fires simultaneously.

Through the narrow slit of the window, I could see the tops of the leaping flames as they rose higher and higher, gleefully devouring the wooden rooftops and towers. An orange glow infused the sky as the macabre dance of the fire spread, greedy and rampant, and black smoke hung heavy above.

Now, I could hear the sounds of panic seizing the palace. The pounding of footsteps, the slamming back of doors as people ran and shrieked and urged everyone to flee, as fast as they could. As the breeze turned and a torrent of burning air rushed through the window, choking me for a moment with heat and ash, someone twisted the key to my door and shoved against it. Winded and bent double, I only heard them yell to me to get out as they ran past.

They would storm the palace. In an aching spasm, I thought of my father, my mother, Andromache, and little Astyanax. There would be no sanctuary here.

I squeezed my eyes shut. "Apollo," I muttered fervently. "Apollo, I have been your faithful servant; I have endured my punishment without complaint. Please help, please show mercy to us."

For years, since I had turned from him in his temple and felt his wrath, he had been with me. A taunting, tormenting presence in my head, his brutal attacks coming without warning, his malice permeating every inch of my body, seeping through me like venom while I writhed in agony.

But I was alone. No excruciating twist of prophecy skewered me; no sleek shimmer of menace rippled the air; no mocking trail of laughter followed me.

He was gone. He did not even linger to watch me suffer the last. He had deserted me.

The sound of frantic footsteps had died away. The palace felt empty. A desolate and hollow calm descended in place of chaos.

I could not stand helplessly waiting for the Greeks to find me. Without knowing where I was going, I lurched from the room. Through the pillars flanking the courtyard ahead, I could see the city was on fire, the air choked with ash. Gasping, I ripped at my dress and tore a ragged strip from the skirt, which I clutched over my mouth.

Nightmarish confusion reigned. I could make no sense of anything, straining to see through the smothering veil of fog. Fire bellowed through the chaos, interspersed with screams and yells and mighty crashes as beams gave way and great towers toppled from the sky.

I prayed for one to land on me. To crush me in an instant and spare me what would come otherwise. A quick and merciful death: was that all I could hope for? Somewhere, in the panicked vestiges of my brain, I knew it was not so, that the gods had nothing so kind in store for me. I ran, flinging myself into the melee with no idea where I was going or why.

And then I was back, back at the square where the horse still stood, a gaping hole in its side, from which the Greeks had spilled into the silent, sleeping heart of Troy. The rest of the army must have crept back from the hidden bay to which they had sailed and waited under the cover of darkness at the foot of our walls for the gates to swing open.

Flames licked at the timber shell, too late. Through the fear that swamped me, I felt a rising tingle of rage. I had known, I had known it, and I could not stop it. The anguish twisted through me, an excruciating tide of despair and fury that I had not set it alight while they cowered inside its belly, that they had not burned alive in the dark, every last one of them. That my father and my brother had stopped me, and what would happen to them now? Were they already dead somewhere in the burning city, or did the Greeks hold them, gloating, making them watch the destruction of all we held dear before dispatching them to the Underworld?

The heat was like a solid wall, pressing in upon me from all sides, and if I stood in futile, frustrated rage any longer, then it would consume me too. I don't know why I sought to preserve my life. If Priam and Deiphobus and the men of the city would be slaughtered like sheep led to sacrifice, it was sweet mercy compared to what awaited me, my mother, my sister, and all the women and girls of Troy. The knowledge curdled in my veins, but still I didn't dare to hurl myself into the fire and make it end before what was to come.

The temple. The temple of Athena, no less, protector of the Greeks. Of all the immortals, they honored her the most, their gray-eyed goddess of war who had bestowed her favor upon them so generously in this ten-year battle. If there was anything they might respect, it would be Athena. And it was her temple that stood, untouched by fire, by this very square. It was there that I could find sanctuary; there that I might be spared.

I ran between its columns, turning at the entrance to look back at what lay behind me. Monstrous. Unthinkable. The streets I had walked, the buildings that framed the sky, every familiar sight of my life, melting and collapsing to nothing but rubble and soot. My chest ached, my eyes streamed, and my head reeled from the incomprehensible enormity of it. Despite what I had seen in the bloodless visions Apollo had sent, I had not known the visceral truth of it; I had not felt the heat of it sear my flesh and scorch my hair.

I stumbled through the stone entrance, the cool air of the interior a shock against my raw, burned flesh. The statue of Athena was placed in the center, her features serene, her painted eyes blank and fixed, staring dead ahead. I threw myself at the altar by her feet, pressed my forehead to it, and squeezed my eyes shut. *If the temple caves in above my head, make it happen quickly*, I begged feverishly. *Let me not know about it. This time, please let me not see the disaster before it happens.*

There was nothing in the soldier's eyes when he plunged into the temple and pulled me from the altar. No vestige of humanity to which I could appeal. Beneath the gaze of Athena, I screamed at him to stop, to think where he was, this sacred place in the midst of war, this sanctuary from desecration.

Once before, Apollo had come to me in a temple, and I had known his purpose and turned away from him. His wrath had been terrible; a price I had never dreamed I would have to pay. But this mortal, this Greek, this soldier streaked in blood and filth, did not have Apollo's cold and cruel restraint. The god had not defiled his own sacred place of worship with force; he had taken a different revenge on me, and I had suffered every day since then. Perhaps that was why I did not believe what was about to happen; perhaps that was why my body froze as this man drove me down against the floor, and I thought: *Any moment he will think of where he is, how Athena's sacred image gazes upon him, and this will not be, it cannot be.*

The pounding of the blood inside my head muffled any other sound. Pinned beneath his body, his weight crushing the breath from my lungs, my eyes flickered to Athena's face. I could not speak, but mutely, I implored the goddess to make it stop, to halt him with her divine fury, for she could not let this happen in her temple.

The painted black irises stared back into my own, cold and fathomless as the ocean. I felt her chill contempt, her iron glare, pierce my soul.

Then, as I looked up at her helplessly, her glass eyes rolled to the sky, so she did not have to watch.

⟨⟨⟨⟨⟨

Down at the shoreline, the women were gathered, huddled together in weeping clusters. Just yesterday morning, they had flocked to this beach, full of wonderment and giddy disbelief.

From one knot of women, I heard a hiccuping gasp and my own name croaked out. "Cassandra?"

The men who had led me here shoved me toward her and I stumbled, just managing to catch myself before I fell. It was my mother. Crouched on the sand, hunched in upon herself, looking so much

older, as though the years of war had passed again in one night.
Around her were my sisters. I looked away, blinking back the burn of
tears. Andromache. I had seen her widowed, forced to watch Hector's
corpse dragged through the dirt, and I had thought those were the
depths of despair any woman could plumb. But there was so much
worse than I had known to imagine. The shock pierced me with every
detail I noticed.

The moment I saw that the cradle of her arms was empty.

My sister Polyxena, trembling like a reed, heartbreakingly young.

And Helen, there among us. Her dress was ripped, the fabric frayed
and fluttering across her. When I looked unwillingly toward the
Greeks, I couldn't ignore the way their eyes lingered on her exposed
skin, the gleam of covetousness mingling with something darker, yet
to be unleashed. The waiting was agony, a drawn-out torment while
the soldiers decided our fate.

I realized what it was they were waiting for when I saw the contingent striding toward us from the smoking ruins of the city. Four
of them, purposeful and intent upon us. I glanced back at Helen. The
color drained from her face, and although she drew herself up as tall as
she could, I saw how she trembled. I felt Andromache give way behind
me, her sobs echoing across the eerie silence of the dawn. Where was
Astyanax? I so desperately didn't want to know the answer.

Other Greek soldiers followed these four, fanning out around the
beach. The ocean had spread so vast and empty when we had spilled out
of the city the day before. Now, the long ships filled the shallows, and the
men went back and forth, loading up what they had stolen from Troy. I
wondered how many of them had wives waiting for them, mothers and
daughters perhaps. What would those women think if they could see
their menfolk, as they stood guard over us, the weeping, grieving survivors of Troy? As they waited to discover which among us they could
take as their prizes, just the same as the gold and jewels they piled up?
Would the women of Greece recognize the little boys they had once
cuddled, the tender husbands they had kissed goodbye, the kind fathers
who had cradled them proudly?

I knew that I would never see most of these reunions, would never know whether the monsters who were ransacking my home and murdering the men and boys of my city would walk back into their lives as though this didn't matter. But the Spartan king who had sailed here for his wife stood before us, and this was the moment of Helen's reckoning. A circle widened around her; she stood alone as he advanced.

We were all there because of her. But I remembered the insistent press of her hand on my shoulder when I had thought of running away, how she had tried to save my life. Looking at her, so alone amid the carnage wrought in her name, I wished that I could do the same for her.

Menelaus spoke at last. "I'll take her back. She can face justice in Sparta."

Somebody snorted. The men whipped around, their accusing stares fastening firmly on Hecabe. My mother hauled herself to stand, leaning heavily on the arms of Polyxena on one side and Andromache on the other. "She's going home," my mother spat. "After all of this, she's going home."

Menelaus drew himself up. "Helen will face justice in Sparta," he repeated.

Hecabe laughed, a gritty cackle that made me flinch. "No, she won't."

⁓⁓⁓

On the Trojan shore, where we women waited to be divided up among the Greeks in front of the smoking embers of our city, we thought the worst was done. We could see our lives stretch out ahead of us, captives of those we hated the most, forced to look each day upon the faces of the men who had slaughtered our fathers, brothers, husbands, sons. Our dignity gone, our freedom a long-forgotten dream. But we thought the carnage was over. We didn't think that we would have to watch those we loved be murdered in front of us again.

The youngest man in the Greek contingent was not satisfied. He paced back and forth along the shore, casting a baleful look out toward the sea.

"What troubles you, Neoptolemus?" It was Odysseus who spoke. It was to Neoptolemus, this son of Achilles, that the Greeks addressed their questions, and to Odysseus that they looked for advice. Not to King Agamemnon, who swaggered in his purple cloak, his chest puffed out with his own importance.

"My father gave his life for the glory of this war," Neoptolemus replied. His brooding gaze swept across us, his eyes like the coldest depths of the ocean, black sands that have never known the sun.

"We will honor him always," Odysseus said. He shifted from foot to foot, eager even in his exhaustion to be on his way.

"It is not enough."

Agamemnon huffed, his attention caught by this. "Not enough?" he snapped. "Achilles died with every honor heaped upon him. The greatest warrior of Troy died at his hands before Achilles fell. You have avenged your father over and over. You hurled Hector's son from the city walls." I turned my eyes away from Andromache, too cowardly to see her face at this. "You can have Hector's wife for your own. Troy is conquered. What more honor can Achilles have?"

The young man stared at him; a long, insolent gaze. I saw the heat of anger flush Agamemnon's cheeks, but he didn't speak. Perhaps he didn't dare. The silence extended painfully. At last, Neoptolemus broke it. "I've heard how you sailed to Troy," he said softly. "What you paid for safe passage, how you won a fair wind from the gods. My father must be honored likewise. His shade will not look kindly upon us from Hades' realm if we do not."

Odysseus sighed. "Achilles wouldn't demand—"

"My father slit twelve Trojan throats at Patroklos' tomb. Why shouldn't he have the same?"

"You wish to take twelve of them?"

A ripple of horror shimmered through the women, but I think we all wondered which would truly be worse: to have our throats slit on Trojan land and our bones buried in Trojan soil, or to be led away in chains.

"Just one will do. One will satisfy my father," he answered.

And his eyes landed on Polyxena.

I heard my mother's stifled cry as her youngest daughter stared back at him. The blood drained from her cheeks, but Polyxena tilted up her chin and did not look away.

The soldiers moved quickly, one at each of her elbows in the matter of a moment.

"She's young," Neoptolemus said. "She must be like your daughter was." He smiled at Agamemnon. "I've heard that Iphigenia didn't scream."

They marched my little sister down the beach and Neoptolemus drew his blade: the knife that had torn apart so much Trojan flesh already.

I closed my eyes.

Somehow, even after that, the day wore on. The sun climbed higher in the sky, but the air stayed gray, plumes of smoke still rising from the city. Birds shrieked and wheeled out over the sea. On the sand, we women tended to one another's cuts and bruises, though we had no herbs or ointments to ease the pain. I wondered when any of us would know the touch of a loving hand again after this was done. I held my mother's hand wordlessly.

"She wasn't touched by any of them," I heard Andromache say to her. "She is safe from them all."

At this, Hecabe nodded, a little gasp breaking in her throat. Apollo, a god of the sun, would never show me the dark shadows of Hades' realm, a place where his light could never penetrate. If my visions could show me that, at last I would have some comfort to offer my mother—if she would believe me. If only I could see my little sister in that dim and peaceful land, a world that no invaders would ever shatter, the memory of her pain washed away in the silver-shining waters of the Lethe.

As dusk began to gather, so did the men, a hostile circle closing in around us. They began forcing us into lines. One of them grabbed my elbow, yanking me into place. Hecabe was pulled away from me, down to the other end of the line from where I stood. She didn't look back.

Agamemnon, in his fussy purple cloak, stepped forward and cast an assessing glance across us all. Someone was offering some kind of commentary, telling him who we all were. The fires they had lit around the beach gleamed in the dim evening air, pools of light scattered around. *How do they know?* I wondered dizzily. *Who told them our names? Have they made a list, weighed up our attributes, our status, considered who we belonged to before to help them decide how we are to be most fittingly distributed?* I heard my own name: "Cassandra, daughter of Priam and Hecabe, a priestess. Beautiful, apparently." His tone was dry and matter-of-fact. I was glad of my tangled hair, the streaks of dirt and dried blood, the dust-stained dress that obscured me, but it wasn't enough. Whatever I looked like in that moment, he had heard who I was.

"That one," Agamemnon said, his eyes a void as dark as the painted Athena's had been. "I'll take her."

⟪⟫

We weren't given time for goodbyes. My mother reached out for me, but she was too far down the line, and already there were Greek hands on her shoulders, forcing her back in place. I caught her eyes for the space of one agonizing heartbeat and I saw the same moment flash before us both. Her rising in horror from her bed, transfixed by the swell of her belly, shuddering from the nightmare that told what the baby would be. The same thought hovered between us. If she could have brought herself to hurl him from the highest tower of Troy, it wouldn't be rubble among ashes now. Paris would be as dead as he was today, but the rest of Troy would have lived.

I dug my heels into the sand, but the Greeks who led me off didn't even notice my resistance. I could only turn my head back toward the women for as long as I could bear the sight of my mother's face, the grief that had split her soul apart, the wordless anguish that united all of us in that moment. Whoever we were in Troy, however these women might have turned their heads away from me once, all of us were the same now. They pitied me; I could feel the ragged pulses of their sympathy for me, the first to be borne away after Polyxena, even though all of them would suffer the same. Troy was in ruins, but in these hideous few minutes, I felt more a part of it than ever before. Our city would only exist in our memories; a strange, shared bond that flickered into existence between us all, just as we were torn apart from each other, just as we were about to be scattered across the ocean and separated forever.

And, even in the grip of cold dread that twisted inside me for what was still to come, I felt a spasm of despair for them, too. Every one of them that I would never see again.

It was only Helen who moved, Helen who wasn't held back like Hecabe was, Helen who darted forward and wrapped her arms around me. For all Menelaus' empty threats of justice in Sparta, everyone knew she was going back home, back to a life that still existed. As she embraced me, she whispered into my ear, "My sister, Clytemnestra, she is queen of Mycenae. She will be kind."

I shivered. Helen's words, the last fervent comfort she could give me, rang hollow. I knew already there was no sanctuary for me in My-cenae. As Helen stepped away from me, a desperation engulfed me; if only I were boarding her ship; if only I could go to Sparta with her. The urge to beg flared within me, a howl rising up, but I clamped my lips together. I wouldn't give these men the satisfaction of refusing the pleas of a Trojan princess.

⟪⟪⟪⟫⟫⟫

In Agamemnon's tent, he drank wine and boasted. I stared at a gleaming gold plate, watching how the light slid across its shining surface. I wondered if it came from Troy—if it had been in the palace yesterday, if I had seen it a hundred times in my life and never noticed it.

"She's a priestess of Apollo, you know." It didn't feel like Aga-memnon could be talking about me, but I knew that he was. "Apollo, Troy's protector." He laughed harshly. "He isn't sending a plague for this one, though."

At this, the men stirred uneasily. They were so close to going home, I thought, their victory scraped after ten long years, the dragging war made longer by the foolish pride of Agamemnon and men like him. At the very end of it all, the eve of their homecoming, he dared to talk like this. I felt their eyes flicker nervously to the opening of the tent entrance, to the blank sky beyond, as though the god himself might be roused to anger, might strike them down where they stood.

I knew better, though. The gods had left Troy. They might have stridden across the battlefield once, when the war raged at its most ferocious. Even Aphrodite had sullied her pristine feet on the blood-streaked mud of the Trojan plains for her beloved Paris. Ares had rampaged beside Trojan fighters, his bloodcurdling yell bringing terror to Greek hearts. The great leathery black wings of Eris had rasped in the air just above their heads, carnage unfolding in her wake. And Apollo, sleek and sinuous, along with his wild sister, Artemis, they had stood with us too. It wasn't enough. And, in our defeat, they had deserted us.

All that was left to me of Apollo was the ache in my head, the dull throb of the tender split in my mind. The unpredictable streaking flash, like lightning searing across the sky, leaving its imprint against the back of my eyelids. It flickered when Agamemnon put his clammy hands on me, when I felt the heat of his rancid breath on my face. A strange comfort from the curse that had so blighted my existence, the power that had been my pride and my ruin, as the conviction settled over me like the fine mist of morning, as I thought of Helen's final words to me before I was torn away.

I knew what was waiting for him in Mycenae.

PART

III

CHAPTER TWENTY-ONE

Elektra

As the beacons light in their great chain from Troy to Mycenae, I stay at the window, held rapt by the sight. I have never felt like this before. The flames in the darkness are brighter and more beautiful than any dawn I've known; they herald a new day for Mycenae, washed in light, golden and magnificent. I'm rejuvenated, dizzy with joy: everything is lifted from me all at once, and I feel so weightless I could soar into the sky with no need of Icarus' wings. I've waited for this for so long, I'd stopped believing it would ever truly happen. I've always had faith that my father would win the war, of course. But I have grown so used to a life of listless waiting, I hardly know what to do now it is so nearly over.

And so he will return. I have stood fast, and my faith has been rewarded. I won't think of the sadness that has shaped me. Orestes continuing to grow, a physical reminder of the time passing. Chrysothemis, wrapped in her bridal veil, deserting us for a husband chosen by Aegisthus—that mangy dog sitting in my father's seat, sniffing at my mother's skirts, whining around our palace, making my skin crawl every time I see his narrow, fretful face. In contrast, my mother's serenity, the implacable sheen of her face, which has stayed unlined and unworried, the lightness of her step never weighed down by the guilt she should bear. All of that is past.

I dress quickly and hurry through the quiet palace, outside into the cool air of the morning, swinging around the corners of the twisting path toward the farmer's hut. "Georgios!" I call as I get closer, laughing in delight at the sound of my own voice.

He emerges from the darkness of the hut, his brow creased in confusion, his eyes squinting with sleep. "Elektra?"

"Georgios, he's coming back! The war is over!"

"It is?"

I throw myself against him and he jolts backward, startled. I've never embraced him before. He pushes me away slightly and puts his hands on my shoulders. I can't stop smiling.

"How do you know?" he asks. "What's happened?"

"Beacons," I say. "Beacons lit in a great chain, as far as I could see."

He's shaking his head before I even finish the sentence. "Even if it is the end of the war how can you know the Greeks have won?"

"Of course the Greeks have won," I say slowly. I step backward, out of his grip. I can't look at him.

"Of course," he says quickly. "I didn't mean—of course, the Greeks have won. I only thought—just in case . . ."

"This day has been coming for ten years." My voice is harsher than I mean it to be. "We've always known it would happen, and now it has."

He's nodding hastily, trying to take back his moment of doubt. "Your father is the greatest hero the world has ever known," he says, and the sincerity in his voice mollifies me a little. "Mycenae has suffered while he has been away. Now he's coming back, this is wonderful for us all."

I pause. "Not quite everyone."

Georgios laughs. "You aren't worried for Aegisthus now, are you?"

"Of course not!" I look away. I don't know how to voice the feelings squirming away against my happiness.

I hear his sigh. "She has betrayed him."

She has done a terrible thing; she knows the price as well as Georgios knows it, as well as I know it, as well as everyone in Mycenae knows it. But she is my mother—however passionately I might sometimes wish that she wasn't.

"Perhaps, when he's punished Aegisthus," Georgios says, "he might show mercy to her."

"She doesn't deserve it."

She wasn't forced by Aegisthus. What she's done, she's done of her own free will. She and Helen both, architects of their own disasters. I wonder what Menelaus will do to Helen, what he might have done already. I don't care so much about that. Helen robbed me of my father for ten years. But I can't help feeling a twist of anxiety for Clytemnestra, deserving or not.

"You can ask him to spare her," Georgios suggests. "Maybe for you, he might. If that's what you want."

"Do you think so?"

"Yes, I do. Agamemnon is a good king, a good man. My father always said so."

"I know that's true."

"Mycenae prospered when he reclaimed it," Georgios goes on. "And he united Achaeans from all over to follow him to war. He's a great leader. Whatever he does, it will be the right thing."

These words are a soothing balm. Poised on the edge of a thousand surging emotions, I blink back tears of sudden and unexpected gratitude. Georgios has always been there alongside me, always ready with something kind to say, always constant in his faith in Agamemnon.

I wonder, now that my father is coming home, what will happen to our friendship. When a normal order is restored here, I'm not sure what the leader of all of Greece will think about his daughter sneaking out and talking unsupervised to a humble farmer.

That doesn't matter, though. What matters is that he's coming back.

The palace has come to life while I've been outside. News of the beacons has energized everyone, sent the slaves scurrying and chatter bubbling everywhere. I see the elders of the court, the old men who have submitted to my mother and Aegisthus all this time, hastening to the throne room, their eyes full of confusion.

She's there, of course, calm and composed, holding forth in the center of them all. Aegisthus is nowhere to be seen, and I wonder with a burst of exultation if he might have fled—but then I spot him, lurking beside the farthest wall.

"The war is ended," she is declaring. "But it will take many weeks for the fleet to sail home. We must be prepared. I have watchmen waiting all the way from the palace to the gulf; they will send word as soon as the ships are sighted."

I clutch her words to my chest. The hope is almost painful. We are so close to an end to this.

She's giving directions, telling everyone of the great feast that will be held, of the plans to make in anticipation of the king's arrival. I wonder if anyone will dare to ask her what she intends to do, but no one does.

The beacons stay aflame for days. I stare out at their glow every night until they burn out and there is nothing but the star-strewn darkness to look upon. I imagine his ships sailing closer with the emergence of every dawn, picture Eos trailing her rosy fingers through the sky above us both, every morning another day closer to the day he comes back. Of all the years I've waited, it's these final weeks that are the slowest, these last days when my impatience is ravenous, when it gnaws away at my peace of mind and shreds any semblance of calm I might have.

But however excruciating the wait might be, there is a sweetness in its sting, a euphoria in the anticipation. Day by day, the time passes, and every fresh dawn brings him nearer to me.

And at last, as I lie awake, watching the window from my bed, the darkness of yet another night softens into ghostly gray skies, and a shout echoes from watchman to watchman across the hills. I sit bolt upright, hardly daring to believe I can truly hear it. But it's unmistakable. This is it: the news we've been waiting for. The fleet has landed, safe on our shores. I feel it surging in my chest, the sweet realization, an exquisite moment of pure elation, and then I'm alive with energy, my soul awakened from a long winter. I jump up and dress in the soft light. I'll see my father at last; he's home, really and truly home. I wonder what I'll look like to him. Will he recognize me? My fingers fumble. I yank at the fabric, not caring if I pull the fine wool out of shape. Or perhaps I should care. My appearance hasn't mattered for years, but Agamemnon will see me for the first time since I was a little girl. I want him to be proud of me. I force myself to slow down, to calm my shaking hands. I smooth my hair, taking the longest breaths that I can draw.

It's busier in the palace than the day that the beacons lit. They've been rehearsing for this morning ever since, and the action is smooth and coordinated. Slave-girls hasten to drape magnificent cloths threaded with gold across the walls, encircling the wooden columns in ferns and flowers twisted intricately together, laying gleaming bowls and goblets at the long tables, and piling soft, luxurious cushions on the benches. Fatigue from my sleepless night makes me sway, briefly disoriented by it all. *It's really happening*, I think to myself, and the elation swells again inside me.

I catch a glimpse of Clytemnestra sweeping through the wide entrance to the throne room, tall and straight-backed as ever, no sign of concern or fear. She hasn't fled, she isn't shrinking away. I waver; could the news be bad after all? But then, what is everyone preparing for if not my father's return? *She's brazening it out, like she has done all along*, I think, and in this moment, I admire how fierce she is. Maybe she does have a plan to get through this. Maybe once my father is home, we'll be a family again.

I follow her. "What is this?" I ask her, and we stare at each other. I can feel it, so close to us, opening up before us, something we have never shared before.

But then her eyes darken. Whatever was about to open up closes off, and before I can take it in, arms clamp around me. A hand presses over my mouth and I'm gagging, bile rising up in my throat, as she gives the order.

"Bar her chamber door," she tells them, and I can't scream at her, I can't make any sound at all, and they're pulling me away, their bruising grip suffocating me, until they hurl me into my chamber, the stone floor cracking my knees as I fall. Now I'm gasping the air into my lungs, shrieking at the closed door, throwing myself against it until the sound of my own howls makes me think my head will split apart.

No one comes.

Spent and exhausted, I turn around, my back sliding down the solid door until I'm on the floor again, the taste of blood in my mouth and useless tears spilling down my face.

I know what she must be planning. And there is no way out of my room; no way that I can stop her.

CHAPTER TWENTY-TWO

Clytemnestra

As they bolt the door behind Elektra, her screams muffled by the wood and iron, my breath escapes weak and shaky from my lungs and I pass a hand across my eyes. For a moment, I let myself feel it, the pain that radiated from her, and then I gather myself again and push it down into the rage that ferments in my belly. Something else to fuel me, to stiffen my resolve and strengthen my arm. It may have been me who gave the orders to Aegisthus' guards, but my daughter's suffering is not my fault. I cannot allow Elektra to ruin this. And while she may rage against me, I am protecting her. Iphigenia trusted her father, and look what happened. One day, Elektra will be grateful for what I plan to do, what I have to do for us all.

I am ready. I have rehearsed this so many times in my head, night after night after night. My movements are smooth, calm, streamlined perfection. I feel like a girl again, swimming at Sparta, just my sister and me, kicking through the crystal-clear waters. That silent, solitary marine world beneath the waves was like a secret, a place where I could roll and twist, a place where I was free and utterly myself until my head broke the surface. The sinuous shadows of the palace remind me of it, but this time, when I emerge, it will be into another world entirely. One I shape myself.

One where even a king knows justice.

The years collapse in upon themselves; it could be yesterday that I held her hand in mine and saw her wide eyes luminous with innocence in the dim predawn, moments before we stepped outside and I lost her forever.

And then Iphigenia merges with Elektra in my mind, and I push away the image of my youngest daughter standing before me in the throne room, transformed with a kind of radiance I had not seen in her before, a softness in her stance and a vulnerability so raw in her face that it makes me shudder, as though her fleeting hope pressed hard on a wound that I did not know still hurt. Then the terror in her eyes crystallizing when they seized her, this time at my command; how she held me in her gaze. I still feel myself pinioned by her stare, flayed by her accusation. Not now—I won't think of it.

I won't allow the heightening of my emotions, so close to Agamemnon's return. I can't let them knock me off-balance just as I need all of my poise, all of my calm. I cannot afford to be shaken, not when everything I have dreamed of for a decade stands so close before me, at last within my grasp. Everything is ready. When I go into the bath chamber, the scene is set. Nothing has moved in here, nothing has changed. I breathe in the heady fragrance of the flowers, the heavy perfume spilling from their lolling heads. I cut them myself, I bring them here every day, examining each bloom for any sign of wilting. Every petal is thick and velvety, every flower ripe and bursting with eager longing. Every polished marble surface in the room is crowded with them, a dizzying array set to overwhelm the senses. In dishes interspersed among them, oil gleams, and the crushed petals suspended in the dark golden liquid give off yet more scent, which drifts in unseen clouds throughout the chamber. Only a small bowl of fire burns in one corner, casting a dim light, so the shadows loom large and flickering on the far wall, the only space in here that is not lined with ledges of flowers. It is left clear so that anyone reclining in the low, deep bath set beside it can lie back and appreciate the fresco painted upon it.

The deeds of the House of Atreus are rendered there. The divine Olympians, thronging our hall, ready for the feast of Tantalus. How they honor our palace, never dreaming for one moment what foul depravity festers in that cruel father's heart. Their beautiful golden faces shine from the plaster; the artist I had commanded had given them glorious life. He had the good sense not to question me, either. These stories might never be told, but I wanted them blazoned here, the men whose blood flows in my husband's veins, their deeds immortalized in paint and plaster. Not the slaughter of the infant, nor the revulsion of the gods. It was not needed. Everyone knows the grisly feast that awaited them.

From Tantalus, to Pelops, so the fresco moves on to Atreus and Thyestes, who murdered their own brother Chrysippus in their struggle to rule. The painting shows Atreus taking the crown of Mycenae, but not the children of Thyestes boiled and carved up and fed to their father by their own uncle. It shows Agamemnon rising to the throne, his wife and three daughters about him, but no sunrise slaughter. I had told the painter to only show the victories, the events that elevated my husband's family above all others, knowing all the same that anyone who looked upon it would still think of the darkness and corruption that punctuated these moments, that seeped from the innocent scenes as silently and relentlessly as the fragrance from the flowers permeated the air.

I trace the little painted outline of Iphigenia with my finger. I had thought my heart would be pounding, that the blood would seethe in my veins, that I would tremble with the anticipation of finishing this at last. Instead, I feel a strange calm settle about me, a certainty that holds me fast to my course. I think again of the still underwater world, how it held me buoyant and safe when I kicked through its depths, a carefree girl swimming in the ocean before I ever knew of the House of Atreus at all.

I stroke my daughter's painted hair and the upward curve of her lips. I hope that among the gloomy shadows of the Underworld, she knows what I will do for her, and that, in the dark, she will smile again.

⁓⁓⁓

I sweep through the palace, giving my orders as I go. The confusion is palpable; a bewildered panic sending everyone into a fluster. Everyone except for me. I see myself as though from a distance, gliding

smoothly amid the chaos. I smile into anxious faces, wave away the
stuttering starts of questions that no one really dares to ask. I can hear
it, though, pounding as insistent as a drumbeat. *Where is Aegisthus?*

They do not know—the elderly men who call themselves advisers, whose words I have never heeded and whose tangible disapproval
I have blithely ignored—they cannot understand why I make every
preparation to welcome home my husband. They wonder if I plan to
pretend the last ten years have not happened, if Aegisthus will melt
away as though he was never here. They remember, no doubt, Agamemnon and Menelaus as young men with an army of Spartans behind them, coming to challenge Thyestes in the great throne room I
have had bedecked with fine draperies in honor of the king's return.

I stand and survey the grandeur. I frown. It will not do.

"You there!" I gesture at a slave-girl impatiently and she startles
to attention at once. "These tapestries on the wall, take them down."
She hovers, momentarily confused. "The king has been at war for ten
years; he deserves every honor from the moment he arrives home. Lay
these on the ground outside, let him walk upon them, cushion his
feet from the stony ground with the finest fabrics Mycenae has. He
has known no comfort on the sands of Troy; we will treat him as our
king—as more than our king. We will give him what he deserves."

She knows better than to prevaricate. I can hear the keening edge
in my voice, the hysteria that threatens to break through my composure at any moment. As she hurries to follow my orders, hissing at the
others to help her carry the heavy cloths, I step away from the bustle.

Everything is in place, just as I have planned. Aegisthus hides, his
guards hold Elektra, no one else suspects what I have in my heart, and
all that is required is my calm and my steadfast purpose to carry me
through. I try to slow my racing pulse, to shut out the memory of my
daughter's eyes, to think of nothing but my next step.

In the distance, horns ring out a triumphant blare.

The king returns.

I smooth down my robes, arrange my face into a smile.

Time to welcome him home.

CHAPTER TWENTY-THREE

Cassandra

The palace is a tomb. I see it rearing from the land, this edifice of monstrous stone, and the reek of death that leaches from its foundations overwhelms the salt scent of the wind.

Yesterday, I watched the dawn from the deck of the ship, where the grim and exhausted survivors of the long voyage gathered in its burning light. The waters glowed red behind us, the sky igniting in monstrous flames. I feared to set foot on the land when we docked. I have never stood on earth that isn't Trojan soil before. I never dreamed I would be so far from home. I was sick and sore, and I yearned so desperately for the cool stone of Apollo's temple, its silence and its familiarity.

I don't know how many weeks we had endured at sea before the storm hit. Even the men knew it was a storm summoned by divine wrath; the fury gathering in the skies was unmistakable. Athena's belated outrage at the desecration of her temple.

The shrieking wind had whipped the dark ocean into a seething, roiling frenzy around us, every flash of lightning illuminating more carnage, more ships split upon the treacherous rocks, more men swept away. The wide ocean had rung with the screams of dying men before the goddess's fury was spent. The storm held less terror for me than here; I would rather be at the mercy of the raging waves than standing on Mycenaean earth.

Now, with his palace in sight, Agamemnon once more gathers together his weary survivors and addresses them in a ponderous tone. He speaks of the glory awaiting them here in Greece, the conquering heroes home at last.

They look away as he strides up and down, affecting grandeur. Their eyes rake the land around us hungrily for the comforting spirals of smoke from their homesteads, the hillsides dotted with companionable green trees instead of the bare, sandy plains where they have lived and fought so long for so little reward.

Despite his words of victory, Agamemnon's jaw is set grim and hard. I can see that he is angry, but not at the devastation of the storm that splintered his mighty fleet as they sailed home in glory. He does not rage at the deaths of so many of his men, who followed him to my city and laid siege against us for these past ten years, dreaming always of this day. He doesn't care that they will never again know the embraces of their gray-haired mothers, their long-enduring wives, and their children grown up in their lengthy absence.

It does not anger him, even, that Athena, who has long protected his Greeks, turned against them and wrecked their ships. That the treasures looted from my home now spiral and sink through the waves, their glittering finery doomed to rust and fade on the sand fathoms below. It barely touches him.

He is angry because it is in his bones to be angry. He sees himself slighted again; his authority disrespected. He does not care if his men die, only if they admire him. He hates the way their eyes cut away from him, the sullen curls of their mouths; the way they shrink from me and my madness instead of envying him his captive.

But this man, the king of all the Greeks, he has been angry since long before the war even began. I see the rage simmering in his younger face; I see him slighted in a great hall of men all clamoring for the same prize. I see his arm raised, his sword gleaming as he swings it against the neck of a pleading man whose arms are outstretched for mercy, while a boy weeps and turns his eyes away from his father's bleeding body. The whispers of his rage hiss and tumble in my ears.

I let the breeze lift my hair, its gentle touch soothing on my bruised face. I remember how Polyxena died, her silent refusal to cry out or beg for mercy. Her shade walks free in the Underworld, and for that, she is luckier than us all.

Our long march to the palace is drawing to an end. When the storm blew itself out and Agamemnon saw that he was still alive, and that I, his Trojan prize, was undamaged, he took it as a sign that the gods spared him for a reason. I know that they have—and that the reason is one he cannot imagine. He leads me up the winding path to his palace, eager to display his victory. I know it's been ten years since he saw his wife. I know there is no shred of compassion in his body; I think he strangled the last of it in order to steel himself to cut his own daughter's throat. But still, I am amazed that he shows no deference at all to Clytemnestra in his homecoming, that he marches back up to their home with me at his heels, the woman he's enslaved. His arrogance gives him a blind confidence that everything will be exactly as he expects.

But I cannot hope for the future, for I know what it is to become.

CHAPTER TWENTY-FOUR

Clytemnestra

The clouds are feathery, tinged with fading pink as the gold disc of the sun climbs higher in the sky. The air is warm and filled with promise.

Somewhere, far beyond my reach, wreathed in cold shadows, my daughter waits for this.

He is flanked by guards and followed by soldiers as he marches up to the palace entrance. Behind him, someone stumbles, and I wonder if it is a wounded companion, but then a sharp breeze whips up, and I see the long banner of her dark hair stream out behind her. I feel my jaw clench.

I don't know what I expect to feel when I see the square frame of his shoulders, the imperious jut of his bearded chin, the faint ridiculousness of his cloak fanning out around him as he strides at the head of this weary, battered formation of exhausted men. I had feared that it would all swamp me again, that I would be jerked back to that other dawn and that the tide of grief would overwhelm me. That I would not be able to contain my disgust and my fury. It is not so. His face could be that of a stranger. This is not the young man whose breath caught in his throat when he asked for my hand in Sparta; nor is it the new husband-king, buoyant with the giddiness of victory, who brought me to Mycenae. It is not even the distant figure who stepped forward in the light of the rising sun, knife clasped tightly in his fist, the man I had thought I knew before he destroyed everything I held dear in one strike.

He is older, far grayer and more grizzled than ten years in Mycenae would have rendered him, though the men at his heels are more haggard and worn than their leader. Still, even if he conducted his war from the relative comforts of his tent and rarely graced the battlefield with his presence, the toll is carved on the lines of his face and the graying bristles on his chin. Looking at him does not make it all flood back: I do not feel the sagging weight of her body in my arms; I am not tugged beneath the surface by the memory of her empty gaze as her head rolled back under that pitiless sky.

Rather, I feel the momentum building within me; the surging swell that warms my blood. I had feared the distraction of emotion, but instead it primes me, makes me stand taller, curls my lip into a smile that I hope will pass for one of welcome.

He does not pause at the great square entrance, flanked by thick stone and topped with two carved lionesses, but instead he sweeps through without so much as a glance to either side. And then he is right before me, and his eyes meet mine at last.

"Welcome home," I say. I wonder for a moment if he is going to embrace me, and as I repress a shudder at the thought of being held in his arms, pressed close to his body again, I take a step backward and gesture to the somewhat meager gathering of palace elders and slaves who are lined up outside to greet him. "We thank the gods for your great victory and your safe return." This at least is true.

He inclines his head slightly, an acknowledgment of the gods' benevolence without an outright declaration of gratitude. I can feel his irritation, how it needles him not to receive the praise himself, though he cannot say it out loud. Ten years apart and I still know what will spark his anger, how tender his ego is and how easy it is to bruise.

"We are weary indeed," he says, and I flinch at the sound of his voice again.

"Of course," I say quickly. "The women have prepared baths, wine, food for you all. Please, allow your men to be taken inside."

Agamemnon runs his gaze across those gathered to welcome him home and frowns. "Where are my daughters?" he asks. The unspoken thought flits between us; I know he feels it hum in the air, but the furrows in his brow only deepen, and he tosses his head a little as though batting away a troublesome fly. "And my son, whom I have never met. Why is he not here to greet me?"

I hold my smile. I do not know how this man dares to speak of his children. "It is yet early in the day," I say lightly. "Surely you want to bathe, to eat, and to rest first of all? We have everything prepared for you."

He looks aggrieved, but makes to step forward. I force myself to take his arm.

"You are a king," I breathe. "Do not step where the common soldiers tread." I stand back. "We have laid out our finest tapestries for you to walk upon."

At this, I hear a stifled gasp from the woman who stands a pace behind him, partly hidden by his bulk. I have held my gaze steadfastly away from her. I know what she is, and it is beyond anything I can comprehend that he marches her up to the palace in full view of us all, that he stands in front of his wife with this woman cowering at his back. Now, I let myself look at her. Dark, tangled hair. A bruise blooming at her temple. I don't want to think about how she acquired it. Great dark eyes, cast down to the ground—until now, when she glances up, seemingly unable to stop herself. When I look into the depths of those eyes, I feel something touch me, pressing right into the raw wound of my soul. All at once, I have to blink back tears.

Agamemnon notices me looking at her and smiles briefly. "A princess of Troy," he says. He savors the words slowly. "Cassandra, priestess of Apollo, great protector of the city." His laugh is mirthless, but the woman does not flinch. Her glassy eyes stare blankly at the embroidered cloths on the ground. When my husband follows her gaze, confusion and annoyance mingle across his features, wiping away his smug satisfaction. "What is the meaning of this?" he snaps.

I tear my gaze away from the woman. "Why, a carpet laid out in your honor." The words spill out as smooth as cream.

He huffs, indignant and ridiculous, and I feel my stomach curdle to think this man has ever touched me. "Tapestries, Clytemnestra?" he asks, incredulous. "I hardly dare to think of stepping on such finery; it is what we set out for the gods, and not for any mortal man to desecrate."

A laugh nearly startles from me before I suppress it. What is this—self-awareness? Humility? Perhaps the war has taught him something after all. I shake back my hair, smiling still. "How humble you are, how full of respect for the gods," I soothe. "Be sure of it; they note your modesty. But you are no ordinary man, Agamemnon, you are something other than the rest of them." I pause. "You led your army in the mightiest war that Greece has ever known, and you return victorious. Troy smolders in ruins, the impermeable citadel cracked apart by you and your men, its riches yours. What man has accomplished such a thing before? No one of mere mortal birth, surely." I force myself to step closer to him again, to turn my eyes up to his, clear and steady. "You bring with you a daughter of King Priam himself. Just imagine what he would have done if he had conquered the Greeks. He would not shrink away from stepping upon rich purple cloths. He would take it as his due as the victor of this war. Do the same, Agamemnon. Do not deny yourself this glory."

He looks back at me for the space of one long breath. I can hear my heartbeat thudding in my temples. Then he shrugs. "I will take what I am due," he says at last. "Though not in boots begrimed still with the filth of Trojan earth."

I breathe out, a soft hiss of victory. I catch a slave-girl's eye, incline my head toward his feet, and she hastens forward to loosen the leather thongs and lift the boots from his feet. I watch, exultant, as he steps onto the thick brocade. Beneath him, the intricate stitches tell the story of the pleasures of the immortals. His heels grind into the fine details as he walks, the rich, deep crimson dark like wine flowing beneath him. The elders cast their eyes down, looking away from him as he walks, unable to watch. I drink it in: the sweet scent of the morning air, the sunlight glinting from the buckles at his shoulder, and every slow footstep an insult to the gods. I utter a silent prayer to Zeus, bringer of justice.

The Trojan woman stands, transfixed. I cannot imagine the horrors behind her, the misery she sees ahead, within the grandeur and magnificence of our palace. I do not want to think of the indignity she has suffered, of what my husband has already inflicted upon her, the humiliation of being paraded before me and all who watch here. But I have no time to think of her. I instruct the slave-girl again, to take the woman inside, to treat her with kindness as a guest in our home. Even as my tongue twists around the words, I feel their inadequacy. No kindness can ever make up for what we have done to her, and she is no guest.

As I turn away from her hollow face, they are entangled in my mind, my daughter and this stranger. Iphigenia's face is blurred and faded in my memory, though my body remembers the soft weight of her cradled in my arms, a baby with a future bright and open ahead of her. I think of how this young Trojan woman, this Cassandra, was loved and cherished, and how it has all been torn from her as well. I wonder where her mother is, the proud Queen of Troy who will never see her children again, and I wonder if this mother feels the same as I do—that if we could go back and see our babies' trusting faces lost in sleep against our breasts once more, that we would jump from our highest towers with the child clasped close so that they never knew their terrible fate. So that we could spare them all the suffering to come.

But, inside the palace, the source of all our pain awaits his reward for what he has done. And it is in my hands, and mine alone, to deliver it.

My pounding pulse slows to a steady beat. I do not tremble, and I do not look back as I walk inside.

CHAPTER TWENTY-FIVE

Elektra

I've been staring through the narrow gap of the window, my knuckles white against the stone as though I could push down these walls with the force of my pain. I can picture it, a vast wave surging through me, tearing down everything in its path. But the walls stay strong, and all I can do is stare at this strip of sky.

I hear their approach. By straining up on tiptoes as high as I can, I can see a flash of their heads as they ascend the slope, and my heart pounds painfully in my chest.

Which one is he? Is he leading them all, or do heralds go in front of him, other soldiers clearing his path? I don't know. I've imagined this every day for a lifetime, but I don't know what a returning procession looks like; I don't know what my father would choose. I don't know anything at all.

Useless tears squeeze from my eyes as I twist and crane my neck, desperate to see more. The bobbing heads, flashing helmets, and swaying plumes vanish altogether as they pass through the gate, and I grip even tighter to the edges of the wall, because now they will be making their way along the straight path and turning off toward the entrance to the palace itself, and that's when they'll come more fully into view. I press myself against the stone and stare, not wanting to blink.

They look more tired, more grim, more ragged than I would have expected: not a striding, triumphant army. They pass across the tiny strip that I can see so quickly that I can't make out their faces. My breath is coming fast and uneven, my palms are slick, and the desperate frustration overwhelms me as I search for just a fleeting glimpse of my father.

It's so fast, I don't have time to take it in. A swish of rich, deep purple, a cloak flowing from his shoulders, a cluster of dark curls, and he's gone. I don't know what to do with myself. It must be him, but I didn't even see his face. As I stare at the space where he was, I see her. A woman, I can tell by the loose hair that streams out around her. She's slower than the men, but she's walking right behind my father.

I think of Briseis, the slave-girl that Achilles demanded from him. Not her, though—my father gave her back. Another then, perhaps taken from Troy. I'm motionless as I think about that and then I slam my hands hard against the walls. The shock of it reverberates through my wrists, but I don't care, drawing them back and hitting out again and again. She's walking with him, she's shared his journey home, Clytemnestra will be waiting at the door, and I'm in here, locked away. The lowliest slave in the world has what I can't have, and my mother has penned me in like an animal, like I'm nothing at all. Fury consumes me: rage at my mother, rage at this Trojan woman and everyone who stands between me and my father.

And, in between the pulses of rage, the red raw edge of it, there is panic. Clytemnestra isn't going to go back to being his wife. If she was, I wouldn't be trapped in here. They're going to attack him, she and Aegisthus: that must be what they're planning. And, while I know my father is strong and brave, victor of the Trojan war, I'm afraid of her cunning.

I scrabble under my bed, tugging at the bundle of cloth and pulling out the lion dagger, the last thing he touched before he left me. I remember the last words he spoke to me as I stare at it, the echo of his voice from so many years ago. Its blade is dull: it's no weapon, just an ornament. There is nothing I can do with it, even if I could get out of this chamber.

And then I'm screaming again, choking on the harsh scrape of my own howls, back at the locked door. There's nothing I can do but hope that he hears me, hope she doesn't somehow manage to cut him down outside the palace before he even gets inside. I scream as long and loud as I can, pounding against the door in the desperate hope that he'll hear my warnings, but my voice is swallowed up by the solid oak and no one comes.

CHAPTER TWENTY-SIX

Clytemnestra

He is waiting in the bath chamber. The heavy fragrance hangs in the dim air as he leans closer to the wall, studying the painted figures. Any fear I might have had of rousing his suspicion has dissipated in the warm, stuporous breath wafting from the velvety blooms. He is wearing a silly, complacent little smile that sharpens the edge of my intent. I have thought of little else for ten years, but even so, I'm not sure if I expected to enjoy it like this. It was my duty, what I owed to my daughter. Now, with the image of the Trojan woman's haunted eyes staring sightlessly ahead as she followed my husband, I see it as a service to the world. Something that it will be my pleasure to bring about.

"Let me help you into the bath," I murmur.

Does it even occur to him that the last I saw of him was on the sands of Aulis, our daughter's body broken between us? Is he so stupid, so self-absorbed, that he thinks I could forgive or forget? That I would let it pass unspoken; that I would welcome him back like a wife, even as his prized captive quakes in another room? It seems that he does, for he accepts my ministrations without a word as I help him shrug away his robes. He descends the steps into the warm, scented waters and I lean forward, feeling his eyes on me as I hand him a cup of wine; our finest vintage, into which I have stirred the liquid I crushed from the poppies in our meadows.

"Tell me of the ending," I ask him. "How it all finished at last. What happened when you took the city?"

He lies back, the water rippling about him, petals drifting across the surface. "You want to hear of the sack of Troy?" He takes a long draft of wine.

"Not all of it," I say. "You can spare me the more unpleasant details. But I want to know—" I pause.

"What?"

"I want to know what happened to my sister." I hate to ask him. I hate for him to know that he holds something I want. But I cannot bear it any longer; I have to know. "Did Menelaus . . . ?"

Agamemnon snorts. "For years he talked of nothing else," he says. "What he would do when he took her from Paris; how he would slit her throat before all the army." At this, for a moment at least, he looks temporarily abashed, a flicker of awareness of what he has said crossing his face. But he shakes it away, sending small waves across the bath.

I try to keep my voice low. "And did he?"

"Of course not." He smirks. "Your sister stood up, from among the Trojan women we had gathered outside the city. The moment that he saw her . . ."

"He couldn't do it." I finish his sentence.

He nods.

So, Helen has returned unpunished to Sparta at Menelaus' side. The man she had married could not find it in his heart to murder someone he loved for the sake of his war—unlike his brother. When she steps off the deck of his ship, the daughter she left behind will await her, warm and living. A tingling heat rushes through my body when I think of that, and my jaw clenches tightly.

A long silence stretches between us. For a moment, I wonder whether we ever used to talk. I am sure I remember it, idle conversations and exchanges about the minutiae of our days, an easy companionship that made me believe I would live out a peaceful life in Mycenae. The world is beyond recognition; the landscape of our life torn up, all of it at once familiar and strange, and I have an odd sense that nothing is really there at all, as though I might reach out my hand and find the solid objects before me dissolve into air.

I stand at a crossroads. Beside me, my husband and king luxuriates in a deep bath. Before long, he will rise, and I can take his hand and lead him to the feast being prepared in his honor, or perhaps to his chambers. I could step back into the life set out for me the day I said yes to Agamemnon's proposal, because what else would I do? As careless a way to decide a future as tossing dice across the cobbles. If I abandoned the plan, would Aegisthus slink away into the shadows? Maybe he would raise a stand of his own: my betrayal would be exposed, and my husband would slaughter us both. This does not frighten me. But when I let my thoughts drift further, when I see myself standing amid the dim shadows before Hades, scouring the ghostly throng for my child, it is then that the cold shudder grips my spine. I cannot look into Iphigenia's face without bringing her the news that I have avenged her at last.

"Clytemnestra? Are you asleep?" He sounds peevish even through a slight slur, the poppies in the wine taking effect. I had not even realized that my eyes were closed.

"Of course not," I say. "Are you ready? Allow me to bring you your robe."

He lies back in the water. This is the moment. I lean down to where I have placed it; the thick cloth slides through my hands like the smooth coils of a snake. Beneath it, hidden from Agamemnon's view, I can feel the reassuringly sturdy shape of something else.

I shake out the robe and hold it before him as he stands, steam curling through the low light. He ducks his shaggy head and I settle the heavy brocade about his body. He twists to find the openings, suddenly trapped, stumbling and bewildered by his abrupt blindness in this impermeable net I have cast about him, dizzied by the wine I augmented.

He is disoriented and confused, engaged in a futile search for an escape from the robe, which I had so painstakingly sewn shut so that his hands will scrabble pointlessly for a sleeve. He pulls and yanks to try to free his head from the cloth that hangs heavy over him, the water adding weight to the lower half that is sunk in the bath, pulling

him down still further. Now is the time for me to reach for the other
object hidden at my feet.

The wood is solid in my hand. It fits smoothly against my palms as
I wrap both hands around it and swing with all the strength I can summon, aiming right at the top of the lurching figure that is my husband.

It is darkly comical how ungainly he is, swathed in cloth, his feet
sliding away beneath him as the sharp, gleaming metal edge of the axe
hits him. Somewhere beneath the suffocating weight of the material,
he bellows, but the sound is muffled, and I swing again. The noise it
makes as it hits his skull is a dull, heavy thud. I don't know if I have hit
him hard enough to break through the bone, so I grit my teeth against
the ache in my shoulders as I raise it up once more and bring it down
upon him, again and again and again. His body tumbles beneath the
flurry of blows; he collapses into the water, and I am still bludgeoning
him with all the fury I have burning through me. I can still hear him
spluttering, gasping somewhere under the stitched-up hood, and I aim
there until I feel his head give way beneath the axe with a sickening
collapse, and a splatter of gory liquid sprays from the bath, right across
my face.

He goes limp, and the flurry of water calms around his still form.
The stained petals drift on top of the dark water. I can feel the droplets of his blood sliding down my forehead, and it revives me, like
rainfall on a parched field in the deadening heat of summer. My arms
fall to my sides, and I hear the axe striking the tiles of the floor.

He doesn't move. It strikes me as impossible, just as it did when
I cradled Iphigenia's corpse, that minutes ago he lived and now he is
dead. I had expected a surge of emotion. Whenever I had pictured this
moment, tears had swamped my vision unbidden. I had thought that
exultation would seize me, that I would be flooded with a savage joy. I
had thought it would rush over me and Iphigenia too, that I would feel
her gratitude from across the gulf that divides us and know she had
satisfaction at last.

The silence of the room is as heavy as ever, unstirred by the cold
breath of Hades. Agamemnon is nothing but butchered meat, lying
slumped in the reddened water. No guards have charged in, no one

seeks to drag me away in chains. The palace is mine, and I can walk from here free and unimpeded whenever I want.

Perhaps this is what Agamemnon felt when he walked away from Iphigenia into the light of that terrible dawn. I have murdered him, and there will be no retribution.

The thought of Elektra snakes into my mind, but I shake her away. There is nothing she can do. This is a gift to her, though she does not know it yet.

Agamemnon's men will be grateful to go home, back to wives and children grown older in their long absence, back to their farms, back to aged parents, back to a quiet and comfortable existence. There is no appetite for any more fighting, I am sure of it. In Mycenae, we will forget the war, consign its heartbreaks to our past. The horrors of the line of Atreus can be banished there too, I tell myself. The men who would kill their own to hold their power are all dead, and I will make this city a better place with them gone. The citizens will be as glad to forget Agamemnon as they will be to forget Troy.

Except for one person, it occurs to me as I pull myself to my feet. I turn away from Agamemnon's broken body, from the shattered tiles where the axe fell. There is one person here at Mycenae who cannot put Troy behind her.

CHAPTER TWENTY-SEVEN

Cassandra

A high, narrow window lets a sliver of sunlight into the cell where they brought me. A keening sound slices through the air; a girl is screaming somewhere in the palace. I don't know if I can hear it truly or if it simply echoes inside my head; a gift of Apollo's light. I can summon no howls of my own. Even when I think of Troy, of my sisters scattered on a multitude of Greek ships, those who survived the storm sailing to every corner of our world, I cannot quite believe it. I can't make myself know that Troy is gone, they are gone, and there is nowhere for us to return to.

And what victory do the conquerors enjoy? The vengeance of the gods has been swift and clear. Athena revealed it at the climax of the storm, when the horizon glowed with a vast sheet of lightning, and, in the center of it all, from the deck of the ship, we all saw one man, clinging to a jagged rock amid the churning waters. The man who had raped me in Athena's temple. Drenched in freezing spray, howling defiance at the gods. His crime brought this devastation upon the Greeks, and this was her punishment, saved until the last.

I remember how, for a moment, the storm was suspended: the sky shimmered with a baleful glare and the wind dropped abruptly into an eerie silence. I watched his fingers turn white as they slid away from the slick surface of the rock, his mouth stretched wide in a desperate scream. The lightning struck again, its forked tongue igniting blue

fire above us, illuminating his frantic struggle as he surfaced, gasped
for air, and sank once more. Again and again, the jagged light struck,
and I saw him weakening as he rose, only to be slapped back down,
over and over—until, at last, he rose no more. Here in Mycenae, in
my enemy's palace, I picture that man's bloated body sinking through
the dark, picked apart by fish until his bones lie on the lightless sand.

I watched that man die before my eyes, but I can see flashes of
Agamemnon's fate, too, pulsing stark and white with every sickening
throb of my head. My captor is dead, bludgeoned and battered, his
dignity as shattered as the fragments of his skull. She wields the axe,
triumph gleaming in her face, a savage revenge made manifest at last.
Now I am the prize of a dead man, the property of a corpse. I feel a
shudder of relief that I will never feel his hands upon me again.

Clytemnestra, his wife, Helen's sister, will be coming to me next.
Though she does not dazzle like Helen, I can see a similarity in their
bearing. Two women who seem distant from those around them, as
though they walk on separate ground from the rest of us. I had thought
that Helen seemed far away, even from Paris. Still, perhaps she felt that
distance too. Perhaps she came to me when she did because we were
fellow outcasts in the city.

And here in Mycenae, I have found Helen's twin: the more formidable of the two. With Agamemnon stricken, she will come to me, a
woman with no place here in the palace she rules. No place anywhere.
I know that the girl screaming must be her daughter, a daughter Agamemnon had left living. What would it be like, I wonder, to have a
father like that? I think of Priam, cut down by Neoptolemus. My father did not believe a word I implored him to heed, but he was a kindly
man, full of pity for me, weighed down with regrets that he would
never voice about the baby boy born to him whom he could not bring
himself to kill. A king most unlike Agamemnon.

I would weep for him, for us all, but I am too numb, as though I am
already shrouded in the fog that drifts through the realm of Hades,
that rises in vapor from the great dark rivers that flow under the earth
and drain away the memories of the dead into silt so they can wander
the gray shores never knowing what they have left behind. I imag-

ine the chill, damp peace of it. A place where Apollo's searing light can never reach. A place of quiet and emptiness, where an inhabitant's mind is no more than a flimsy veil fluttering in a breeze. A vast cavern of darkness where the sun-god will never venture.

I know that she is coming, but when the door swings open to reveal her, I am not ready. She stands, tall and composed, and splattered head to foot with her husband's blood. I have seen everything up until this moment, and I have ached so intensely with sorrow that there was no space in my body for fear.

Until now. I feel myself come alive, every inch of my skin prickling with it. The door closes behind her and we are alone. Her eyes are fixed upon me through the wash of blood across her cheeks.

I fling myself at her feet before I know what I am about to do. I am so seized with terror, so afraid at what she has come to offer me. I clasp my arms about her knees and turn my face up toward her.

She flinches at the sight of my tangled hair, my begrimed skin, the desperate light of madness that animates me. She cannot step backward, cannot get away from me.

She speaks, trying at the same time to gently pry my fingers loose, but I lock them more tightly. I cannot make sense of what she is saying, my head too wild to translate the Greek. I shake my head fervently, because I am sure that she means to show me mercy and I cannot bear it.

She looks back into my eyes. I know she is reluctant; that she cringes away from seeing me truly, but I have her now as I hold her gaze, as I try to make her see what I can see.

Emptiness. Nothingness. My home and everything I know annihilated. Dust blowing on the breeze, carried out over the pitiless ocean.

Do not make me live on here, I implore her silently. *Do not condemn me to a life among strangers. I have lived an outcast in my own family; do not make me one here in a place where I am nothing but a conquered enemy, forced to live out years of futile yearning for a world that is lost forever.*

I see comprehension dawning on her face. Through the blood smeared on her cheeks and the dirt and dust that cling to mine, we see into the calm center of each other's souls.

I loosen my hold on her skirt and move my hand to hers. Now it is I who is gently unclasping her fingers, revealing what lies in her palm.

She carries a dagger. Her life is a precarious one; she has murdered the king, and her fate hangs in the balance as much as my own. She will defend it for herself; she has the stomach for battle, she is as ferocious as her lionesses snarling in stone. But it is her compassion I seek, and beneath her monstrous exterior I can see she overflows with pity, and I know that she will help me. It was her pity that I feared; her pity that might have driven her to offer me a future, some attempt at comfort, an exhortation to carry on, to make a life out of any fragments I have left to me. But I know that I can make her understand what it is that I need.

She shakes her head just a little as I guide her hand. As I hold it suspended above my breastbone, the sharp blade poised over the fluttering pulse beneath my skin, my other hand still clutches at her knee in supplication.

"No," she says, and I hear a trembling in her voice. She yanks her hand away.

I twist her skirt in my clenched hand. It is damp from the bathwater; from Agamemnon's final struggles, his flailing desperation. She cut down the king of all the Greeks, the leader of a thousand ships that thronged the Trojan shores for so long. She cannot be afraid to take the life of one woman.

My skull aches with a dreary, familiar pain. It is an injury never allowed to heal; the ragged, gaping edges of the wound from Apollo's relentless violations that rip my mind open again and again. I search for a way to make her see, to make her understand. I only want this pain to stop. Helen promised me that Clytemnestra was kind. I hope with everything I have left within me that it is true.

She takes a step back and I let the twisted fabric fall away from my fist. The soft light of morning falls through the narrow window behind her, and she is a dark shadow, an indistinct silhouette. Then she turns her head and I see her profile; brave and fierce. And then she looks back to me, and I see the white gleam of her eyeballs, and my throat dries up over the words I don't need to say.

CHAPTER TWENTY-EIGHT

Clytemnestra

I pull back from the Trojan woman when she brings my dagger to her breast; an instinctive horror making me look away from her. But even as I stare into the creeping light spilling dimly through the window, I only see the despair in her face. I think of Iphigenia, poised on the threshold of a future that belonged to her; a future that shattered like a vase dropped on stone tiles.

This woman, I think, is dead already. It comes to me in an abstract flash of clarity; a moment of absurd calm. She is a ghost of Troy: a citizen of a world lost in flames and crumbled to ash. Iphigenia roams the dark bowels of the earth, her life stolen from her. Elektra screams with rage and yearning and a pain I do not know how to begin to heal. But here, before me, there is a gift I can bestow. A suffering I can ease.

I touch the woman's face gently. I cradle her trembling jaw. I remember the suddenness of the violence when Agamemnon pulled my daughter against his chest; the spray of blood before I could even scream.

I smooth my thumb against Cassandra's eyelids, closing them gently. I feel her breath, warm against my palm. I keep my hand steady when I draw the blade against her neck. Even when it is done, and my vision swims with tears and her body slumps against me, I hold her like I held my daughters when they slept in my lap. Even though her blood runs warm through my skirt, I hold her there still. I stroke her hair softly, her dark curls spilling through my fingers as if she is lost in no more than a pleasant slumber, the way I last held Iphigenia.

A tumult erupts in the palace: shrieking voices, slamming doors, and clattering footsteps. This is the moment when I should be stepping forth, announcing my triumph. I draw in a long breath and ease Cassandra's head onto the floor so that I can stand, shaking away the wave of sorrow that rears up and threatens to pull me under just as my victory is complete. No longer do I need to sit in shadowy rooms weeping over a dead girl. My daughter is avenged. Somewhere, she is free.

The door crashes open, the heavy wood juddering against the ancient stone wall. Aegisthus' eyes widen as he takes me in: blood-spattered and righteous. The sight of the corpse at my feet stops him in his tracks for a moment and I see he is robbed of words, so I speak instead. "He is discovered?"

Aegisthus nods. He swallows. His eyes flicker over the scene. "Why did you . . . ?" he begins, then shakes his head. "We must go—declare ourselves, quell the panic."

We dreamed of this nearly ten years ago, plotted it out in the hidden darkness together, and we have lingered over the details every night since. Our common purpose, the goal that has united us all this time, our shared grief and rage taking shape at last.

He doesn't touch me. He doesn't draw me into an embrace or take my hand to lead me out into the light as we claim our long-awaited triumph. I see how his gaze slips away from me, how his thin face grimaces with something that looks a little like disgust. I can feel a loose peal of laughter building up within me, and I can only imagine what he would think if I let it escape.

The ominous weight of dread presses in on us as we step out into the corridors; fear and shock thicken the air. I think I am smiling, that bubble of repressed mirth threatening to burst, but it isn't happiness that I feel. The world around me seems muffled and distant. I hear Aegisthus snap at a slave-girl I hadn't even noticed to summon everyone to the throne room, and I hear how she scuttles away from us, but all I am left with is the lingering impression of her eyes rounded in horror.

I think how everyone will shrink from me, and I want to laugh even more. But underneath it all, I feel the hollow void at my core, and how its edges are collapsing in, and I am afraid that I will be lost forever. I keep walking. That is the key. That is what has sustained me since she died; I kept moving forward, intent upon this moment, and now I am here, and I will not let myself think about what happens next.

I didn't see her. I didn't feel her. When his legs gave way beneath my blows, she did not guide my arm.

I shake away the thought. There is no time for it.

It is a wary gathering of old men and slaves in the throne room. I feel the bitterness of their stares when we sweep in, Aegisthus and I, but that is all they have. Although Aegisthus prickles against their animosity, his narrow shoulders raised and his thin chest puffed, I know there is no need. We can afford generosity, he and I. I will bestow certainty upon them, and their loathing will dwindle away, along with their suspicion.

Agamemnon's body has been carried in and it lies in the center of the room, still wrapped in the sewn-up robe. Mangled and bloody; a silent accusation. I suck in my cheeks to stop myself from smiling and take a step further.

"I bring you the truth after ten years of lies." My voice rings out, clear and true. "There is no more deceit in Mycenae, no more hidden secrets. The bloody history of this house stretches back for generations, but I have brought it to an end today. Justice has been done. I have brought down Agamemnon. I have served his sentence upon him." What I am saying is no surprise to them, but the shock in the room is palpable. I feel the flush of pride tingling in my chest, an exhilaration humming in my voice. "He killed our daughter for a fair wind. An innocent girl. He did not stay to face any punishment. I waited for him to return so that I could make him pay for his crime: the old crime of his forefathers—the slaughter of his own defenseless flesh and blood."

I find that I do not care whether they accept my words or not. Their judgment is nothing to me. I look from face to face across the room, slowly and steadily. No one here will challenge us. They are weak and we are strong. The leader of the Greek army lies dead between us at my hand. The pleasure of my words dies away, the thrill subsiding already. I want to be gone from here, to be alone with my thoughts. To find somewhere peaceful, somewhere silent, where I might hear her at last, where the echoes of her gratitude might reach me from a world away.

Into the sullen silence, Aegisthus clears his throat. "It is not just the murder of his own child for which Agamemnon has paid the price today," he says. His voice is scratchy, too quiet to be heard across the cavernous space. "His father's monstrous crimes against my father were a horror I will not speak of, though they were known to you all. Yet instead of atoning for the atrocities of Atreus, Agamemnon came back to drive me out and to murder Thyestes in front of me, here in this very room. I have waited patiently for this day when justice could be delivered."

I think for a moment that someone might speak out at this. I feel the shift in the room when they look at him. He might claim justice now, but he was not the one to swing the axe. That was me and me alone, and everyone in here knows it to be true. But just as I feel the gathered elders teeter on the brink at Aegisthus' words, they see his eyes flicker to the edges of the room. With slow and measured footsteps, his guards step in closer from all sides.

"No one needs to answer us," I say, gesturing at the bloodstained bundle slumped on the floor. "It is done." I turn to Aegisthus. "Come, let us put things in order."

A slave turns to look at me and almost immediately looks away, fearful.

"Yes?" I ask.

She hesitates. "The body . . . ?" she asks, falteringly.

"Take it out for the dogs," Aegisthus sneers. I catch the sleeve of his tunic, shaking my head slightly.

I smile at the girl. "Prepare him for burial," I tell her. Aegisthus follows me, radiating annoyance, but I am not interested in what he feels.

A funeral for her father is the only thing I can give to Elektra.

CHAPTER TWENTY-NINE

Elektra

I scream until my voice is exhausted, until there's nothing left in me at all, until I'm curled into myself on the floor, drained and numb. That's when I hear the shouting, the swell of panicked voices, and, cutting clearly through it all, the words that I dreaded. *The king is dead, the king is dead.* It echoes back and forth along the corridors, hurrying footsteps and slamming doors, and then a terrible quiet. I lie there, unmoving, until long after they're gone, long after he's lost to me forever, and the realization starts to settle into my bones: the single glimpse of him that I got was all that I have, and all that I ever will have.

When they finally come to unbolt the door, the palace is still eerily hushed. The slaves cast their eyes down when I walk past them, and the old men turn away. Only Aegisthus' guards stand tall. Only they look me in the face: insolent, defiant, forgetting that I am a princess, and it is they who are the interlopers.

Shadows flicker on the walls, cast by the fires burning in shallow bowls. The door to Orestes' chamber is open, and as I drift past, I notice it is empty. I know that I need to care about that, but I cannot force it to the forefront of my mind.

There are guards posted everywhere, more than I have ever seen before, but none make a move to stop me from walking out. Has she instructed them to leave me unmolested? I wonder if she would bother, if the thought of me has crossed her mind since she had me locked away.

My steps take me out beyond the walls of the citadel. I have never been out here alone so late before, but no one materializes from the quiet dark to seize me and drag me back. I can hear my footsteps on the path and the distant hooting of an owl. How far could I walk before they found me? A breeze whispers around me, and the thin light of the moon barely illuminates the ground in front. If it were not for the torches burning ahead, I would be swallowed up by blackness, but I keep my eyes on the soft orange glow and do not let the fear skirting at the edges of my mind take hold.

Someone has left these torches burning to light the way to the towering entrance to the tomb, which is cut into the mighty rock of the hillside itself. I know that it is visible from the throne room of the palace, and I cast a glance back toward the citadel. I wonder if she looks out across the plain, watching for me.

The great opening of ornately carved and painted stone dwarfs me. Within, the long tunnel leads to the dim interior, the smooth walls of stone built inside a hill, giving way to a cavernous dome in which I feel so small. This is where they have left him.

I stand back, not wanting to take another step farther into the chamber. Other hands have done this; they have dressed him in finery and assembled riches on the floor all around him: jewels that glitter in the firelight, great vases, a gleaming sword. I turn my head, a wave of dizziness swamping me for a moment. If I drew closer, I would see his face, see if they had laid a gold coin on his mouth, but I am too afraid to look. I do not know what she inflicted upon him. I last saw his face when I was a child, before he left for Aulis, set upon a war that would make him the greatest of all the Greeks. I wish I could muster the courage to look upon his face again, but a crawling dread in my stomach holds me back.

I cannot bring myself to come closer, to lay a lock of my hair beside him, to weep over his corpse. All these years, most of my life that I can remember, I have imagined his homecoming. His face alight with triumph. His arms open to embrace me.

I turn away, abruptly. There is nothing in here for me, no comfort to be found, whatever the misguided fools who brought him here might have thought. The women who dressed his body and laid him here to be mourned must have felt this travesty, that Clytemnestra allows him to be buried with honor as though she is a grieving wife. I wish that he had known what she was, that he could have known to choke the life from her the moment he saw her again. I wish I could tell him to cast her body out into the hills. I wonder if she thought she might buy herself some shred of respectability, too late, in placing him here.

But I will not let her paint her filthy act of cowardice as something grand and heroic. I will not let her fool anyone into thinking her magnanimous by giving him the funeral rites owing to the king as though she could atone for what she has done. What I know is that there is nothing in this great domed tomb for me: nothing but a body, insensible to feeling; a body that strode the Trojan plains and conquered the city, but now lies still and silent; a body that would not stir to my touch if I could bring myself to venture closer. So why would I stay and grieve beside it? This tomb is like everywhere I have known for ten years: devoid of my father, bereft of solace.

Out in the night air again, I look at my home. The moon has slunk out from behind the clouds, casting its silver glow across the acropolis. In the other direction, there is nothing but featureless darkness, stretching on forever. If I had been born a son to my father, I could walk in his footsteps. I could avenge him, as he avenged his father before him. I could give him what he is due. For a moment, I think of taking up the burning torches, tumbling them throughout the palace, letting them swallow up the tapestries and roar through the wood in ravenous flames, closing in on the murderers in a furious inferno.

If I could summon the courage to do it, I would turn away from the burning city and walk into the blackness beyond. Could I scratch out some kind of existence on the mountainside? Eat berries and burn twigs for warmth? I see myself for a moment, walking on until my feet blister and the skin peels away from the bone, until my body wastes away to nothing but the gray wraith I feel I am. But as much as I long to walk away, I fear the teeth and the claws that might be lurking on those hillsides; the ravenous beasts or desperate men who might be waiting for easy prey like me to wander their way. I shudder at the kind of fate I could meet out there, all alone in the void, and I know I cannot do it.

If I could descend to the Underworld swiftly and painlessly, then I would. I would gulp at the waters of the Lethe and let their soporific streams wash away every memory I possess. But I cannot.

I am so absorbed in my thoughts that I don't hear the footsteps until he's almost upon me: a man looming from the shadows. I think it must be one of Aegisthus' men come to seize me, but the terror subsides as I see it's Georgios. And then someone else draws out from the shadows to stand in the light spilling from the tomb. A skinny little figure, hugging his arms tightly about himself.

"Orestes," I whisper.

"Come out of the light," Georgios says, his voice low. A cold fear grips me. Aegisthus' spies might be lurking nearby, hunting for us. So why has Georgios brought my little brother here into danger?

"Orestes," Georgios says. There is urgency in his tone, but my brother's face is turned toward the tomb entrance, and I can see the longing in his gaze. Orestes has never even laid eyes upon our father.

"Come here, Orestes," I say, and he comes toward us, into the protective cover of darkness. I put my arm about his little shoulders. "Why are you here?" I ask Georgios. "Why would you risk this?"

"The palace isn't safe for your brother," Georgios answers. "I took him out of there as soon as I could, before . . ." He does not need to finish the sentence, and I am grateful on Orestes' behalf that he does not. Shame flashes through me. I gave my brother only a brief thought when I stole away, drawn here by the irresistible force of my grief.

Aegisthus knows full well how dangerous it is to leave a son behind when you murder the father. "What will we do?" Although the air is cool, sweat prickles my forehead.

Georgios takes a long breath. "My father has friends not far from here. If I can get him away tonight and take him to them, I can convince them to carry him far from Mycenae. There will be many sympathetic to the son of Agamemnon, many who will recoil from what Clytemnestra has done. We will find him a home, safe from Aegisthus."

As Georgios speaks, I can feel Orestes' shoulders hunch under my arm. He presses his face into me. "I don't want to go," he says, and I think the plaintive note in his voice might break me.

"It's for the best," I say. "I don't want you to go either, but Mycenae is a bad place now. When we thought Father was coming home, we could endure it, but . . ."

A sob breaks out from him, and I hold him close. It tears me in two; the desire to keep him in my arms and the urge to push him away as soon as possible, to get him to safety and as far from Aegisthus and his men as he can be. "Here," I say, and, keeping one hand cradling my brother, I use the other to unfasten my earrings and hand them to Georgios. "You may need them as a bribe—if there was time, I could go back to the palace for more."

He is already shaking his head. The gold circlets that twist into ornate spirals catch the firelight and gleam momentarily before he tucks them into a pouch beneath his cloak. "There is no time," he says. "Come, Orestes."

Somehow it hurts more when the sniffling child at my side steels himself than it did when he collapsed into tears. Orestes has had no father to guide him. The cowardly Aegisthus slinking behind our mother all his life has been no example. Perhaps I have been too soft; perhaps I have made him girlish and younger than his years, but I could not bear to bring any more suffering upon his head. Now, too late, I wish he could be tougher, more of a warrior like Agamemnon. Now I am sending him into an unknown world, and I can only hope the friends he finds there will do a better job than I in raising him for his destiny. That he stands as tall as he can, gulping back his grief, gives me some hope. "Take this, too," I tell him, and I pull out the bronze dagger from my belt. "It was our father's." It's the only thing I have that belonged to Agamemnon. I kiss his forehead, like our father kissed mine. "Make sure you bring it back."

He turns it side to side, captivated by the way the gold embellishments glint in the torchlight. "I will."

The inky darkness where Georgios stands makes it impossible for me to see his face, but there is a moment of stillness and I feel sure his eyes are fixed upon me. For a second, I think he is about to speak, and I have an uncomfortable presentiment about what declaration he could be on the brink of making. I twist away from them both, stepping awkwardly back, closer to where my father lies.

"You won't come with us?" he asks.

I am already shaking my head. "Aegisthus won't harm me," I say. "He won't fear me, or what I might become. In the palace, I will be safe. Out there . . . you can't protect me." Georgios is no warrior; he commands no men and he has never gone into battle. It was me who begged him not to. For Orestes, escape with Georgios is his only chance, and if they travel with a girl, they will attract more attention. I won't risk all our lives just to avoid living with my mother a while longer. "Besides," I add, "if I go, then I won't know what she is doing. Here, I can make our plans for when Orestes returns." Clytemnestra brooded here for ten years, but Orestes will be a man sooner than that.

"How will you get back to the palace?" Georgios is asking, and I shake my head again, cutting him off before he can make any offer.

"The same way that I came here," I answer. "No one will be looking for me. It will be Orestes they seek, so take him before they follow us here."

He knows it's true. "Then, goodbye, Elektra. I will guard your brother's life before my own, I swear—"

"I know you will. Orestes—" I don't know what to say. I hesitate, not wanting to waste this moment. "I will see you again. And when I do, we will both be ready."

My words linger in the night. I hear Orestes' breath catch in his throat before Georgios leads him away, both of them swallowed up by the shadows almost at once.

This morning, I thought I would see my father again at last but instead I stand outside his tomb without the consolation of a single embrace. I have nothing to comfort me, nothing at all except the tiny spark of revenge I must nurture in my breast until the time comes when I can let it rage and burn everything I loathe to ashes.

CHAPTER THIRTY

Elektra

"Where is he?"

I'd prepared myself to see her, but the moment she appears beneath the stone lionesses, I recoil. I didn't know hatred could feel so strong. And, along with the hatred, fear. Something has held us back. The prospect of my father's return was always on the horizon, and, for that, I held my tongue—at least a little. Perhaps she did too. But now she has done the unimaginable. Now there are no boundaries to hold us back.

"Orestes, your brother—where have you taken him?"

I stare at her. I'd thought she'd be smug, smiling in that way that makes me want to rip the serene mask right from her skull and see what she really is underneath. Instead, in the flickering firelight that illuminates the road home, she looks wild. For the first time, I see fear in her eyes. It tugs at my memory, the image of her face ravaged once before. The split in her voice when she told us what had happened in Aulis.

"Why isn't he with you?" Her voice rises.

"I didn't take him with me." This woman murdered my father today. I want to say it to her, scream it in her face and make her crumple, but I'm wrong-footed by the way this has begun.

"Did you kill him?"

I almost laugh. Why would I kill my own brother? It isn't me who is the murderess. Any conversation with her is futile, I can see. There is no point: she has no shame, and, it seems, barely a grasp on reality. I twist away from her, trying to pass her without touching her, but she blocks my way.

"Did you? Did you take him to the tomb and—?"

I am sure she will grab at me, and I can't bear the thought of her seizing my arm, the same hands that killed my father on my skin. "Don't be ridiculous." I try to infuse every syllable with the contempt I feel for her, but three words cannot contain the limitless oceans of it.

"Then where is he?"

I shake my head. "Why are you pretending that you care? When did you last even look in his direction? I'm amazed that you remember he exists—as though you've noticed any living children of yours."

She flinches, as though I'd slapped her. I wish that I had. I wish I could steel myself to do it. "She was your sister." Her voice is low. "And he killed her."

I snort. I try again to contort myself to get around her, but she steps in front of me.

"Children die every day," I say. "How many grieving mothers did the war create? They don't all rise up and take revenge. What makes your grief so special? What difference does it make?"

"What difference? What difference does it make that your father slit his own daughter's throat?" Her words spill out too fast. She really is rattled, maybe for the first time I've ever known.

"Iphigenia was a sacrifice. The gods demand a heavy price sometimes, and it is an honor to pay it. I wonder what they will ask of you, to atone for what you've done. If that could even be possible."

"Don't you care? Can you really not care? That your sister was slaughtered, that your brother is missing?"

"The only danger to Orestes shares your bed. You invited him into our home. You brought him here." I watch her eyes widen in shock. "Are you really so stupid that you can't see it? Do you think for one moment that Aegisthus, cowardly as he is, would let the son of Agamemnon live?"

She knows. I can see, through her defensiveness and her worry, that the truth of what I'm saying is not new to her. Perhaps that's why she panicked upon finding Orestes already missing. She didn't think Aegisthus would strike quite so soon. Maybe she even planned to send Orestes away herself, and she fears her lover has second-guessed her. That she's been outmaneuvered after all. Well, she has, but not by the dull-witted Aegisthus.

I can't resist pressing my advantage further. "You brooded so much on Iphigenia's death that you opened the door to a man who would kill your son." I laugh. "Isn't it a little late to play the loving mother? To pretend that you care what happens to Orestes . . . or me?"

She's confused. She didn't expect this. I don't know what lurid scenario she concocted in her mind; some twisted idea of the kind of revenge I might take upon her by murdering the brother I've just sent to safety. How she could think me capable of such a thing, I don't know. She doesn't know me at all—and no surprise, since she's spent most of my life staring into the distance, as though she could conjure my sister back from the Underworld.

I'd love to find the words that could wound her even more deeply. But I know her far better than she knows me. She will rally in a moment, gain control of herself again. This sudden vulnerability is temporary, and if I linger to luxuriate in her pain, she'll be Clytemnestra again, cold and unreachable, and hurling more words at her will be like hammering at these thick stone walls with my bare fists.

I shove past her. I shudder at the feel of her body as I knock her aside, but it's so brief I can tolerate it. And then I'm free of her, running up the path toward the home I hate almost as much as I hate her.

꧁꧂

I stay in my chambers as much as I can. Life in Mycenae has always been a tedious thing, but now I have nothing to look forward to—and, without Orestes, I am more alone than I have ever been. I can sit for an hour doing nothing more than staring at the patterns on the floor, letting my eyes blur so that the lines run together, wondering when I will summon the energy to stand. But why bother? There is nothing to get up or, no one to go outside to see. No point in leaning out over the courtyard walls to scan the distant sea for the sight of sails returning victorious against the blue sky. I wonder if Georgios has managed to deliver Orestes to his friends, if his friends will hide him away and if I will ever see my brother again, but the thoughts meander without urgency. Maybe I will and maybe I won't, but even though I know I should be consumed with my revenge and my fury, instead a heavy listlessness has settled upon me. When each day dawns, all I want is for it be over.

Through the palace, the atmosphere has changed. Aegisthus no longer skulks and trails behind my mother. I watch him daring to stride ahead of her. I hear his voice, louder these days, ringing through the halls. And I see her face, smooth and inscrutable, watching him. Whatever she thinks of her newly emboldened lover is well concealed behind her smiles. I can't begin to guess at it.

For me, for the most part, I cannot bear to witness him wrapped in purple cloaks and laden with the gleaming jewels that belong to a man he did not even dare to kill himself. He was no match for Agamemnon, and he must know it, but the knowledge doesn't choke him, and he carries on stuffing roast meat into his mouth at my father's table and lounging back in my father's seat, his face alight with self-satisfaction.

Meanwhile, food curdles in my stomach. I thought that grief would be like a sea of suffering within me, that it would rack me with its storms and endlessly replenish my tears, but instead it lodges like a heavy stone in my throat. I don't want to eat; I can barely swallow. The effort of talking overwhelms me, so I fall silent. Besides, with Georgios and Orestes gone, there is no one here to talk to anyway. I can't even summon the energy to cry, beyond a few trickling tears that I let roll down my cheeks. I think of the dagger, always glinting at Aegisthus' waist—a man can't be too careful when he's married to a woman who thinks nothing of killing a husband, after all—and I wonder dully what the blade would feel like if it pierced my skin. I wonder if my blood would swell out in a river of crimson. I can't imagine it flowing in my body; I feel like such a shriveled and dried-up thing. I think of Iphigenia, and how she died pressed against my father's broad chest, and I burn with the slow smoldering of envy.

They buried the woman, the one I saw walking behind him. No one has told me how she died. I wish that I could have talked to her: perhaps she could have told me stories about my father. The slaves say she was a princess of Troy. She was so lucky to be chosen by a king, the greatest king in Greece, to be brought here to a palace that must be as fine as the one she left. Finer, I'm sure. Whatever wealth Troy possessed, Mycenae had Agamemnon. And she did too, for a little while.

But she's dead, as so many who knew him are. The war took a heavy toll. Even I, his daughter, have so few memories of him to cherish. Agamemnon, descendant of the House of Atreus: a mighty family that should know such greatness, but, time after time, has been struck down by the curse upon us. It can't burn out with his murder. I am left living and so is Orestes. But I'm so tired, so weighed down with my despair, and Orestes is a boy, and so far away that I wonder how we can hold up the weight of our destiny on just our shoulders.

I don't take note of how the days pass from one to the next, but there comes the afternoon when I am watching the blistering glare of the sun fall across the sweep of the valley, its heat pressing down, and I notice through the narrow slit of my window a spiral of smoke rising from the farmer's hut in the distance. Georgios has returned.

There is no one in the palace who cares what I do or where I am. I know that Aegisthus has sent men out to search for my brother. It is the only time when Clytemnestra's facade cracks; the anxiety flaring briefly in her eyes when they return empty-handed. I wonder if she is more afraid that they will find him or that he will remain missing. I think I see relief on her face when they report again no news. But while they may fear what Agamemnon's son might do, I think everyone has forgotten that I am here at all. Still, I look up and down the corridors as I slink out of the palace and make my way toward the farm.

The familiar sight of his narrow frame is a surprising comfort to me, a balm I hadn't expected. When he sees me, I see the rush of warmth in his face, and I'm glad of the first flicker of happiness I've felt since the morning of my father's return.

"Elektra!" he says, hurrying toward me.

"Orestes?" I ask, casting a glance behind me to make sure no one has followed.

Georgios nods. "I delivered him to my friends. They will take him on to Phocis. The king there, Strophius, is married to the sister of your father. It's likely that Orestes will be received kindly there."

I feel a pang at this. Orestes will be with my father's sister, among our blood. I wonder if she resembles him. What stories she might be able to share. My thoughts must be writ clearly upon my face, because I can see the sympathy brimming in Georgios' eyes. If he speaks too kindly to me, I am afraid of how I might respond. "So I'll wait."

"For Orestes to return?"

"What else can I do?"

Georgios sighs. "Orestes is a boy," he says. "It will be years before he can come back here, before he can challenge Aegisthus. Do you think you can stay here, in this palace, living alongside him and the queen?"

I look away from him, stare steadily out across the scorched hill-sides, bare and brown from the relentless summer heat. "There is nowhere else for me to go."

I hear him swallow. "Do you truly believe that you will be safe? As Aegisthus becomes more accustomed to his power, do you think he will tolerate your presence?"

Despite the hot glare of the sun, I wrap my arms around myself. "He won't kill me."

"He doesn't have to. If he wants to get rid of you, he can marry you to any man of his choosing. He can send you to the farthest reaches of Greece, or worse, if he wants you gone."

I imagine not being here to watch justice being done, living across a wide ocean when my father is avenged, with no way of coming back. "I won't go," I say. But I know it means nothing.

"Do you think you will have a choice?"

I still won't turn my eyes back toward him. I stare steadfastly ahead, but I don't see the sparse hillsides. I see my father's tomb, dark and silent.

"Elektra?"

I know that I can't ignore the heavy note of meaning in his voice. I think I know what he will say, and I wish that I could stop him.

"Aegisthus will only grow bolder the more time that passes. Right now, his power is new. If you are to escape whatever he has planned, this is the time."

"How will I escape?" My voice is flat.

I hear him take a breath. His hand is on my shoulder. All at once, he is so much closer to me. "Choose your own husband, Elektra. Announce it to your mother. If her heart is not made entirely of stone, she may take pity on you, knowing how you grieve your father. If you tell her, if you are resolute, then you can stay here in Mycenae, waiting for Orestes to come back."

I shrink back from the touch of his hand. "And who will that husband be?"

"I know I am only a humble farmer. I know that you should marry a king. I would never dare to offer, except that I can keep you safe in Mycenae until your brother comes back. I would not—I would never—"

As his words stumble into confusion, I finally look at him. His face is stiff, and a faint flush over his sun-roughened cheeks hints at his embarrassment; I feel suffused with it myself. Everything that he says is true. And I know that this offer is meant with kindness.

But I have never imagined that I would marry, and if I did, it would never be to a man like Georgios. Is this my mother's victory? The anger flares back up inside me. That she takes my father from me, that I need to seek protection in a marriage he would never have chosen for me. Marriage to a man who is nothing like Agamemnon. My body revolts against the thought.

And yet . . . if I say no, it could be so much worse. I feel Georgios' nerves thrumming in the air around us. There is no breeze; the heat presses down upon me. I have to give him an answer. I know if I say yes, I can leave this palace, I can get away from Clytemnestra, but still stay close enough to watch her, close enough to count down the years until Orestes returns. Perhaps this is the only way I can truly honor my father.

"Yes," I say. "We will marry. It will thwart any plans Aegisthus might have."

It's a strange acceptance of a marriage proposal. It weighs heavy in my heart; another sorrow heaped upon my others, dragging me down beneath the surface, farther away from the light than ever. Although he offers me escape, I feel another door slamming shut upon my future.

I force myself to go on, to say more, even though I know the words are wounding. "But that is the only reason why. I would not give this answer otherwise."

"Of course. I understand." He nods. "We'll wait together, until Orestes returns."

I take his hand. My friend, the only friend I've ever had. I wish I had more in my weary soul to offer him in return for his kindness, but this is all I can muster.

CHAPTER THIRTY-ONE

Clytemnestra

Everything is at odds in Mycenae and nothing is as it should be. I felt my life spin into a tumult when I took my eldest daughter to be married and she was slaughtered like an animal before my eyes instead. Everything I knew veered suddenly off course at that moment, like horses startled on an empty road that bolt at once and drag your chariot across bumpy, uneven dirt. The path I had seen ahead of me—the calm and comfortable life I had envisaged—disappeared, and I learned to navigate the unknown terrain of grief and rage until I became familiar with every boulder and ditch that could have tripped me up again.

But now I have killed the king, and no one can punish me. My clandestine lover is out of the shadows, parading before the world. And I feel again that the world has tilted, that my grip upon the reins could falter, that perhaps I do not know what lies ahead. Because, yet again, my daughter stands before me, telling me of her impending marriage: one I had not foreseen, and one that has thrown everything into a new confusion.

There is no happiness in Elektra's face when she tells me. No softness in her voice, no dreamy cast to her gaze. She looks at me, cold and sullen as always, and the only emotion I can detect in her is bitter triumph.

"A farmer?" I repeat. She is bristling for a confrontation; I can see it. I keep my voice deliberately neutral. "What a surprise."

She scowls at me. Hardly a joyful bride. But then nothing about this is as it should be. We have become a family who flout the rules, and I can hardly begin to question the absurdity of this—that she should choose her own husband, that he should be so humble—when I think of what I have done. Will I forbid this? I married a king, and look what happened to me. The nobility of his blood did not temper the stain of the curse that ran through it. His riches did not buy him honor or kindness. Why would I want my daughter to follow in any of my footsteps? If Elektra has made her choice for love, I don't care who she marries. I am fodder enough for the gossips of Mycenae; I hardly fear their judgment of my child.

She is waiting for my condemnation. I think the idea of it excites her far more than the prospect of her wedding. *I am so tired*, I think, *of pitting myself against her*. Besides, I have thought of what she said to me beneath the stone lionesses, when the panic of seeing Orestes' empty chamber had made me think for a moment that she had taken the most terrible revenge she could conceive. It never crossed her mind to harm her brother. But Aegisthus . . . I have turned what she said about him over and over in my mind. I cannot dismiss it. Any threat to my son most certainly comes from Agamemnon's usurper. And so once again, I find myself bound to a man who would kill my child.

Murdering Agamemnon had been my obsession for ten years; the whole of my son's life. It was as though I walked in my sleep, dreaming of my husband's death tangling together with Iphigenia's. Now, I am awake and what I can see disturbs me. My son is gone, far beyond my reach. I am sure that Elektra knows where, but she hates me too much to tell me. If I am ever to see him again, I must soften her. I must make her see that what I have done, I did for her.

And if she marries a farmer in Mycenae, I will still have one child remaining here. Even though she despises me, she will be close at hand. It must mean she does not plan to run away.

"Do you have nothing to say?"

I realize how long the silence has stretched between us. "It is an unusual choice," I say. "People will talk."

She flashes me a look of deepest contempt. "About me?"

"If you don't mind, then neither do I."

My mildness infuriates her. "I don't believe you."

"You can marry him, if that's what you want. I hope it will make you happy."

"I can never be happy." She stares past me, simmering with resentment. I wonder who Georgios even is. I have never cared to look closely at the people working around the palace, have never noticed Elektra stealing away to the fields or talking to anyone. I didn't know she had a friend, much less a lover. I wonder what he finds charming about my brooding, angry daughter. "And Aegisthus?" she asks, her tone lifting a little. Clearly, she hopes that he might give her the reaction she seems to seek. "What will he say?"

"Why would you care?" I think she's surprised at my directness. For years, we have skirted around one another. But since she let out her fury beneath the stone lionesses, I think we have both let go of our caution. It feels reckless, bold, to speak so frankly, but I can't see the point in any more deception.

"I suppose he'll do what you say." She sweeps her eyes across me, scathing and quick, but then she smiles a little. "Or will he? Does he still do everything you tell him, now that he thinks he rules Mycenae himself?"

"Aegisthus is the king," I say placidly. "But I am sure that he will hear my plea on your behalf, and he will have compassion for your grief. If you find comfort in your chosen husband, we will not deny you."

It looks as though a thousand replies are boiling in her throat, but she doesn't speak. Instead, she wheels around and stalks away from me. With her gone, I let the calm smile drop from my face. I don't have the confidence in Aegisthus' reaction that I have just claimed. I have started to wonder about my accomplice in murder, the man I have plotted with all these years. He is so unlike the brutish, burly husband I dispatched. I saw in him a quiet cunning, not a showy authority. I did not think him a king likely to assert himself too strongly. If I am honest, I thought I had him where I wanted him. It was always me who drove the planning, me who calculated what to do and how. I never dreamed I would bring a man into the palace who could threaten my children. On his own, Aegisthus would never have taken revenge on Agamemnon. He needed me to do it. So, I can't think that he would take the initiative, that he would have the stomach to make a plan himself. But I cannot shake what Elektra said to me. I am glad Orestes is gone. He would not be safe in Mycenae. I have walked into a trap of my own making: in order to avenge one child's death, I have enlisted the help of a frightened man and given him power. And his fear might drive him to lash out, like a cornered animal.

I will need to tell Aegisthus of the marriage in a way that makes it seem to his advantage. I'm turning it over in my head as I go to find him. The afternoon is hot, so I expect he will be sprawled upon a couch in the courtyard. As usual, my instincts are correct. I smile at his ever-present guards as I pass them and receive nothing back. Much like Elektra's reception of me. It seems no one in my home is ever very pleased to see me. I perch on the edge of Aegisthus' couch.

"I have good news." I smile at him, willing him to be swept along with my cheerful demeanor.

"Has Orestes been found?" he asks, propping himself up on his elbow.

I suppress a shudder. "No, it's Elektra. She has found a husband."

"What?" Aegisthus' face creases.

"She has chosen a farmer by the name of Georgios. She came to tell me today."

"Is this some kind of joke?"

"Why would it be?" I keep my smile steady, as though what I'm saying isn't utterly preposterous, as though my breezy tone might be enough to convince him.

He pulls himself to sit fully upright, his hands clenched together. "How could she choose a husband? What nonsense is this?"

"I know—" I begin, but to my amazement, he cuts me off.

"A girl can't choose a husband! And she can't marry a farmer! Have the gods driven the wits clean out of your mind?" He stares at me, his color rising. "I know that your father gave Helen a choice of suitors, but this isn't how it is done—and your sister is no good example for anyone."

"It isn't how things are done," I agree. "But if I did what I was expected to do, I would have handed you over to my guards the night you stole into this palace. I would have waited dutifully for my husband's return and never breathed a word of recrimination for what he did." I draw a long breath. "I made no protest when I was told that Iphigenia was to be given to Achilles. It wasn't my place. And look where my obedience led."

He starts to speak, then stops, confused.

"Her marriage could be arranged; an advantageous one to someone suitable—a wealthy king, far away perhaps," I continue, and he nods vehemently. "I'm sure we could find someone who is undeterred by our own . . . unorthodox situation." *Someone prepared to make an alliance with Agamemnon's murderers*, I think. Perhaps they wouldn't be too hard to find; the more I hear of my husband's behavior at Troy, the more I realize how widely shared my loathing of him must be. "But then Elektra would be far beyond our surveillance, somewhere with money and power at her disposal." I don't want to mention Orestes, to remind Aegisthus of any threat he could pose. I need to tread so delicately. "She could make friends there, sympathetic to what she would tell them. What if she were able to persuade her husband to bring war to Mycenae, to avenge her father on her behalf?" I reach out and place my hand on his. "This marriage she suggests is perfect for us. She will have no army, no resources. She will be close at hand, where we know what she is doing. She thinks that she insults us by doing this, but it is a gift to us that she does not recognize."

"I hadn't considered that," he says slowly.

"Of course not. You were shocked, and rightly so. But when you take the time to think of all the implications . . ." I leave the sentence hanging.

"I can see how this would be of benefit." He twists his fingers together.

I don't push him to say more. Instead, I just watch him for a moment. Agamemnon is newly dead; Aegisthus has yet to become accustomed to his power. Neither of us forgets that it was I who wielded
the axe, while he sat hidden in a far corner of the palace. But in time,
I wonder if his recollection of events might shift; if he might begin to
imagine a more central role for himself. It will not befit his image as
King of Mycenae to think of how he trailed at my skirts for a decade,
or to remember where he cowered when Agamemnon's skull was shattered into fragments. At the moment, my children are a threat to him,
but he knows he must be cautious. When he becomes more confident
in his new position, that might change. I feel a headache starting to
press on my temples. He wants Elektra out of the way. I want to keep
her safe. She wants to punish me. Can this strange marriage be the
only way for all of us?

"Agamemnon's daughter should not marry a king," Aegisthus
muses. "It is better that she is bound to a commoner." His face lights up.
"Of course, it should be so; I wonder that I didn't see it myself before."

I call upon my patience. "Then it will be done." I rise, anxious that
if I stay longer, I may give away my anger at hearing him speak of my
daughter like this. He exults in her degradation; sees it as fitting for
the child of his enemy. But she is my child too.

He waves his hand to dismiss me, even though I am already leaving. Beyond the courtyard, I pace the length of the long wall that
overlooks the valley, that ridiculous tomb central in the landscape,
dominating everything around it. I feel that hollowness inside me
again. I had four children, I think. I am grateful for Chrysothemis'
quiet submission, her easy marriage that has taken her out of danger.
Aegisthus has no fear of her gentle spirit. She will be left alone. But
Elektra is too fiery, too full of anger. I had thought that once Agamemnon was dead, I could make her understand, but it has driven her
further from me, made her reckless, and so she condemns herself to
a life so far beneath her—to escape from me? Or does she despise me
so much that she will humiliate herself for the rich pleasure of humil-
iating me by association? And Orestes . . . Orestes, whose whole life
has been subsumed by my grief over Iphigenia. Orestes, whom I have

never really learned to know. He is cast out somewhere in the world, and I fear that Aegisthus will not be willing to forget him.

For Elektra, I can't think of the answer. I don't know where to begin. But my son—the only way I can make sure he is safe is to find him first.

I look out at Agamemnon's tomb, grotesque in its opulence. He deserved to die, a hundred times over. But Iphigenia is still dead. And the thought torments me that, in avenging her death, I have brought only more suffering down upon my living children's heads. In all my years lost to sorrow, I am coming to realize how much of their lives I lost as well.

Somehow, I have to make preparations for Elektra's wedding. I don't know how. Will we celebrate it? Feast in honor of such an odd match? Iphigenia's saffron dress flutters in my memory. Her eyes, wide and serious in the dim light before dawn.

I shake my head to clear the vision away. Elektra will want nothing from me anyway. I feel quite certain she will exult in the most meager wedding imaginable. But after it is done, however it is done, I must seek out Orestes. I cannot leave this in the hands of watchmen, of anyone whose loyalty could be bribed or beaten from them. I will have to go in search of him myself—and the first place I can think he might be is my childhood home, where Agamemnon's brother has returned so triumphantly with his recaptured bride. I will have to go to Sparta.

PART

IV

CHAPTER THIRTY-TWO

Elektra

I don't think about Georgios on our wedding day. When I walk toward him, it's my mother's face that I can see in front of me, even if I studiously look away from her. I want her to be so very disappointed. I hope the humiliation of it burns her from within. My own humiliation never occurs to me. Georgios is a better man than Aegisthus; however lowly and poor he might be, I have chosen a husband superior to hers in every way that matters.

With Georgios, I will appear powerless and weak, unable to gather allies to take my revenge, and so Aegisthus will let me live within sight of the palace, where I can watch them every day. Where we'll be ready when the time comes.

And he's my friend. He's loyal to my father. With Georgios, I can keep Agamemnon's memory alive, and one day I'll bring our family back to greatness.

But I don't know if there is any capacity for love in me anymore. I feel so much older than my years, hollowed out by loss. I don't think I could put one foot in front of the other if it wasn't for my hatred. It fuels me, it drives me forward, it roars inside me, obliterating anything else that ever was or could be.

After the wedding, we go to Agamemnon's tomb together. We stand outside, underneath the stars.

"He was the bravest of all the fighters," Georgios says solemnly.

"Aegisthus can spread all the lies about him that he likes, but in Mycenae we know. We remember."

Georgios doesn't remember him, though, not any better than I do. He barely ever saw my father. He's parroting the kind of thing his own father used to say. Still, I'm grateful for it. I hunger for any words of praise for Agamemnon, from anyone who dares to remember the true king fondly. There are many of them, Georgios assures me; they lie low while Aegisthus reigns, but all of them long for Agamemnon's son on the throne. I make him tell me it, over and over again.

At Chrysothemis' wedding, there was feasting and celebration. Every smile, every note of music, and every happy word grated on me then, made me flinch. How could our family pretend at happiness, at joy or love? I prefer this silence and solitude. Iphigenia's supposed wedding day flickers in my mind. My sister, just a blurry recollection to me, a hazy impression of dark swinging hair and a dimpled smile. She ended that day in the dark, in a quiet and empty place. In peace. I think she might have been the most fortunate of us all.

I shiver slightly in the cold air and Georgios moves to put his arm around me. I stare at the entrance to my father's tomb.

In the months after my marriage, I do try. I'm grateful not to have to set foot inside my old bedchamber, never to have to look out again on the place where my father walked to his death. When I wake up, screaming for him to stop, to turn away, not to step across those tapestries she laid out, Georgios is there to offer what comfort he can.

We can see the palace from our home. It gleams and shimmers in the sunlight. To my shame, there are days when I can't stop myself from remembering the cool shade of the courtyard in summer, the vivid painted walls, the fragrance of roasting meat and the sweetness of honey dissolving into wine.

When I thought of poverty before, I thought it was preferable to the sight of Clytemnestra and Aegisthus. I thought that not seeing their smug and smirking faces would make living here a luxurious delight in comparison. I thought that leaving would buy me my dignity. But there is no dignity in being poor. It is a grinding, exhausting existence, and every morning I wake and stare at the dry, plain walls, which seem to shrink closer around me.

Of course, I am hopelessly incompetent at everything I attempt, and Georgios' indulgent smiles have given way to quiet dismay as I burn bread, forget to fetch water, and let families of spiders festoon every corner of our home with cobwebs. He works endless, exhausting days out in the fields, and when he comes home so tired and finds me still mired in my despair, the easy conversations of our past friendship seem impossibly out of reach. I worry that he regrets tying himself to me and my misery, though he tells me it isn't so.

She doesn't come here anymore. She tried, a few times, ridiculous in her sleek finery, with her unshakable composure, in the doorway of my hovel. She tried to give me things—jewels, gold, precious trinkets. All belonging to her. Nothing of my father's.

"I don't want it." I tired of telling her. I never mentioned her visits to Georgios, much less her gifts. "I don't want you here."

Her frown on her final attempt, her perfect forehead creased with confusion. "What can I do?"

My arms were locked around my body. I fixed my eyes on the square of sky behind her. "Leave. Don't come back."

I heard the quiver on her inhale. A long silence. When she spoke, her voice was cold. "He would have killed you. Chrysothemis. Orestes. Any of you. All of you, if it bought him his war."

I shook my head. She had nothing new to say, only the same arguments over and over. I was too exhausted to tell her again. "I wish he had."

"I thought you'd see it too. When he was gone. When I'd made you safe."

"Safe? Like Orestes is safe?"

"Is he?" she whispered. "Do you know?"

At this, I looked at her. I'd learned enough from these exchanges to know what would twist the knife, what would give her a taste of the pain I'd endured in those years spent waiting for news of my father while she looked the other way. "No. He might be dead—and if I knew, I'd never tell you."

Her face hardened. "You didn't need to choose this, Elektra," she snapped. "You still don't."

She turned on her heel and was gone.

"You're wrong," I told the empty space where she'd been standing. I had no choice at all.

CHAPTER THIRTY-THREE

Clytemnestra

Menelaus will kill you the moment you set foot in Sparta."
Aegisthus shakes his head in disbelief.

"I will take guards to protect me. I will approach Helen
in secret. Menelaus need never know I am there at all," I insist.

"If he is harboring Orestes—"

"It's the only place he could be," I say. "My sister is queen there; I
will be safe. I know it well; I can avoid being seen. But Orestes must
be there." And if he is, I am sure that Helen will help me to find somewhere safer for him. Together, we can spirit him far from the reach of
Aegisthus' men.

"And you will bring him back to Mycenae?"

"Of course." I wonder if he believes me; if he thinks I trust him
enough that I would bring my son back here. If he takes what I did to
Agamemnon as a lesson, perhaps he would not dare to harm a child of
mine. Am I absurd to even think he might? To let the poisoned seed
that Elektra planted in my mind take root inside my head? She spoke
from spite, but still, I can't dismiss it out of hand. This isn't something
I can leave to chance. Aegisthus might think that I will bring Orestes
home as I promise, or he might know I plan to hide him all the better.
He might think this is his opportunity to double-cross me, to use
me to find my son and end it all. I don't know. I never dreamed that
Agamemnon could kill our daughter—how could I know if Aegisthus,

too, harbors the same terrible violence? He wanted to kill my husband badly enough, so why not my son as well? I know that the years I spent with him are no defense; Agamemnon had no pity, no respect for me as his wife, nothing to stay his hand upon that knife. Do I think Aegisthus so much better than him? I must have done, but I am afraid I was wrong again. My fingers curl tightly into my palms.

"If you think he is really there—"

"Where else would he go?"

Aegisthus shrugs. "And you can speak to Helen in secret? You are sure you won't be seen?"

I laugh. "Menelaus will never know I am there."

"Then it's worth finding out," he says.

And so, I find myself setting out in a chariot once more, this time wrapped in a plain cloak, on the road to Tiryns. I travel flanked by guards, Aegisthus' men, who for all I know could have been instructed to murder Orestes the moment they see him. I need them to ensure my safe passage on the road; to pass a heavy bag of coins to the captain of the trading ship at the port of Tiryns in payment for my discreet place on the voyage to Gytheio, hidden from the notice of the crew. When I sailed from Sparta as a royal bride all those years ago, it was a different thing altogether. This time, I am smuggled on board like a sack of grain, the rough shouts of the men mingling with the slap of the waves against the wooden sides until my head aches. I am relieved when the ship docks, and we wait until it empties before the captain comes to release us. The fresh salt breeze is a blessing when I dare to raise my face to the sky and look out from under the heavy hood of my cloak. The wooden planks creak with the motion of the water beneath us, and the captain stands respectfully while I look out at the horizon for a moment, grateful to be free of my claustrophobic disguise.

"The island just there," he says, nodding to a tiny spit of land, clustered with trees, just a little way across the sea from where we are, "that's Kranai. It's where the Trojan took the queen when he stole her from Menelaus. Before they sailed to Troy." His voice is laden with meaning.

So, that's how they are telling it here. Since Menelaus has chosen to forgive my sister her adultery, it must be the official story, at least, that she was taken by force. I wonder how she felt; what choice, if any, she had. My own twin sister, but I can't imagine it at all. All the death and destruction that would chase them across the ocean; the years of relentless war that bought them their escape. Did she have any inkling of it? Of just how far the suffering would spread, how the tendrils of it would twist out to ensnare so many others? My own daughter's blood exchanged for the wind to blow an army over the sea toward them.

On the road, as we draw ever closer to Sparta, I start to think about what I will say to Helen when I see her. I have thought only of Orestes. Now a hundred other questions are mounting in my mind. I have not even resolved on how to begin when the wagon rolls to a stop. I know that we are still some distance from the palace of Sparta, so that no one will be alerted to our arrival. I will steal in on foot, just like Aegisthus at Mycenae when all this began. I step out into the gathering twilight, beside the bank of the wide Eurotas River. The air is still and quiet, a fragrance in it that takes me back so many years, and I am swamped at once by a wave of longing. A longing that is not just nostalgia for my childhood home, but for the time before war tore our lives apart; a time before suitors thronged our halls clamoring for Helen; a time when everything was inconsequential, and an afternoon could slip away unnoticed; when I could lie beside the river with my sister and talk of nothing that mattered at all.

⚜

When we reach the palace, I tell the guards to wait, concealed beyond its entrance while I go ahead. They shift uncomfortably, but I insist. I know this place; it was my home for many years. It is fortified well against invaders, but as an anonymous woman I can slip inside unnoticed, through the secret passages only someone who lived in the palace would know.

Night has fallen, but the palace is alive; torches burn and slaves bustle back and forth across the grounds. I can hear the distant whickering of horses in the stables, and from the heart of the palace, sounds of song and laughter drift across the breeze. I watch carefully, hidden within the folds of my cloak, and judge the moment when I can flit through the secret gap in the wall that I remember from our mischievous childhood excursions, which I'm so relieved to find is still here. Keeping my eyes lowered, looking like any slave, raising no one's attention, I move swiftly across the courtyard and in through an open door. I have not set foot here in more than twenty years, but it feels as familiar as if it were only yesterday that Helen and I whispered our secrets in these corridors. I try to push down the rush of emotion I feel.

While it is busy in the center of the palace and slaves swarm between the kitchens and the great hall, I stay where it is quiet and still. I know the way to the queen's chambers; if I can make it there without being noticed, I can await my sister. Even if she stays up feasting and drinking until the early hours, I can wait. But, when I press my hand against the heavy wood of the door that once led to my mother's private rooms, I hear that there is someone within.

I don't feel afraid. I don't stop to think it might be anyone other than Helen, and so when I push the door, I am entirely unsurprised to see her standing there, turned toward me. The same cannot be said of her; her face is bright with shock and disbelief.

"Don't call out," I say.

Her eyes dart across me, taking me in. "Of course I won't." She still stands frozen where she is. A low fire burns in the shallow bowl on the table beside her, and I see a bundle of herbs tied together and a small paring knife in her hand. "What—what are you doing here?" she asks.

"What do you think?"

She seems to shake herself out of a trance. "A visit—now? You risk your life to come and see me?"

My heart pounds. "Why not? Are you horrified? Do you want to turn me in to your husband?"

She laughs, a dazed kind of sound. "Of course not! I cannot believe it, though; I wonder if you are a dream! Come." And she drops the little knife and steps toward me, her arms open.

I don't stop her from embracing me. Her hair is soft against my cheek. Menelaus lived in a humble tent on a foreign shore for ten years to have her in his arms again: men beyond number died for it; my husband murdered his own daughter for the privilege of winning Helen back. In these long years, she has become something other than herself, more than one woman could be. I can't reconcile all that bloodshed with my sister.

"But what are you doing here, really?" she asks, stepping back. She looks intently into my face. "It is a dangerous place for you to come, so soon after . . ."

"Wasn't it dangerous for you, too?" I ask. "To come back here? I didn't know if Menelaus would bring you home, if he would even let you live. Where is he?"

"He feasts in the great hall," she answers. "They are sharing stories again of Troy, becoming maudlin as ever. It's why I stole away."

"Won't you be missed?"

She shrugs, languid and graceful. "I only intended to be gone a matter of moments." Her eyes flick to the table, the scatter of dried leaves there. "But Menelaus won't question me if I am longer. And if you are discovered, I'm sure I can plead on your behalf." She smiles, and in the soft firelight she could be sixteen again, so confident and sure of herself. Helen of Sparta; a vast crowd of men jostling in our halls, ready to offer anything to have her. Marriage, motherhood, ten years of bitter siege and bloody battle and its aftermath—and still, nothing has changed for her. "Sit," she urges me. "I will send for wine."

I sit on the soft couch while she pads to the door, and I hear her murmured instructions to a passing slave. I feel a twist of irritation, even when she comes back with a jug of wine, its rich sweetness fragrant in the air. I need her help, I remind myself. My son is what matters. The slave has brought bread too, the sight of it reminding me that I am hungry. I tear a piece off, wishing I had the strength of will to refuse her hospitality. As I eat, she picks up her knife again, chopping the herbs on her table swiftly and neatly, sweeping them into a little pouch that she ties onto her belt. Then she draws a stool closer and sits, facing me expectantly. The weight of everything I have to say feels at once overwhelming, and I cast about for something to delay. "The herbs?" I ask.

"A soothing blend," she says. "Dissolved in wine, they lift the spirits, help the drinker to forget his sadness."

I imagine Menelaus, weeping at the feast for all he lost at Troy. I look at the pouch dangling at Helen's waist and suck in my breath. "Why did you go?" I blurt out. I wasn't sure I ever intended to ask the question, to show my weakness by asking what everyone must long to ask her, but I am just as desperate to know.

"Why do you ask?" Her eyes are steady on me. "Do you think our armies would never have sailed to Troy if I hadn't?"

I don't answer.

"Those who came home returned on ships laden with spoils and women. The bards sing each night of their bravery, their glories, the fame they won there. And Troy, the city everyone thought impermeable, is razed to nothing. Do you really believe that those thousand ships carried men who wanted only to restore one wife to her husband?" She laughs. "I watched from Troy's towers every day. The battlefield was full of mighty warriors. Everyone said that the gods strode alongside their chosen heroes."

"The bards sing of you too." One woman, daughter of Zeus, at the heart of their story. Troy was about one woman, for me at least. My daughter, the first of them all to die. I don't want to say her name, not here in this room, where my mother used to dress, and Helen and I would play together, what seems like a dozen lifetimes ago or more.

"I'm sure they do. But did you come here just to ask me that?"

I sigh. Plenty of sons of Zeus fought on that battlefield, earning their place in the legends. What was his daughter supposed to do? If it had been my choice, I would have left her there. If it were up to me, no mother would have lost her children. Helen could have stayed across the ocean forever. "My son, Orestes, he was born just after—just after the Greeks left for Troy. Now he has vanished. I hoped he had come here."

She is already shaking her head. "We have had no word of Orestes."

My stomach drops. "Nothing at all?"

"No." She pauses. "We heard of what happened to Agamemnon, of course. But your son has sought no sanctuary with us. I would not hide it from you if he did, not for a single heartbeat."

I look away from her. Tears are burning in my eyes, and I am determined not to let them fall. Could he have died on the journey here? Of course he could. Brigands, beasts, anyone loyal to Aegisthus, any opportunistic thief or false friends ready to betray him for gold or favor. He could have been buried hastily at the roadside, flung into the sea, or left on the ground for the crows, anywhere between Mycenae and Sparta.

Or he could have been spirited away elsewhere, anywhere in the vast world beyond here. He could be hidden on the smallest island or tucked away in the most sprawling city. Where will I find one child in the whole of Greece?

"Wherever he has gone, we will hear of it," Helen is saying. "Take heart; we will find out in time."

I nod dully. "If he comes here, he will not want you to tell me."

"I won't let him know about this. But I will get a message to you the moment I hear anything of your son, I promise." She takes my hand. "It is likely he will come here, to seek his father's brother. But I can tell you, Menelaus has no appetite for fighting anymore. Not to avenge Agamemnon. I can speak for you, if Orestes arrives here: he will hear your cause." She hesitates. "When I heard you had borne a son, I thought of my daughter—that the two of them could marry one day, join our houses closer again."

I try to imagine that. Helen can so easily sketch out a future, seeing years ahead how things might fall to our advantage. Since Aulis, I have only made one plan, and that is done. I do not have the heart to look to what might come; I do not have the faith to envision that it will be in my favor.

"My guards are waiting, outside the palace walls," I say. I pull my hand from hers and stand. "I have what I came for—I must return before they come to find me."

"I'm glad you came," she says softly. "It was brave of you to risk it."

I bite my tongue. "You go back to the feast," I say. "I will slip out, the same way I came in."

She stands. "I will seek news of Orestes. I will tell you anything I discover."

I let her embrace me. I needed to come here, to see for myself. I am sure she isn't lying, that she knows nothing of my son, but the urgency that brought me here has all drained away, and I feel nothing but a great weary disappointment.

"Farewell," she whispers in my ear, and then she slips out of the room.

I watch from her door to make sure there is no one around. I jump at the sound of a voice, but it isn't the booming sound of Menelaus; it is a soft and girlish tone.

"Mother," she says, and I see a young woman step out and catch Helen's arm at the end of the corridor.

"Hermione, have you come to find me?" I watch as she slips her arm through her daughter's, pulling her close as they walk on together, their chatter dying away as they disappear.

Hermione, the daughter Helen left behind. Still here in Sparta, waiting for her mother all those years since Helen walked away from her. Fury blooms inside me, though I know rage will do me no good. Why rail against my sister's good fortune? It will not bring any of my children home to me.

CHAPTER THIRTY-FOUR

Elektra

E lektra! We have news."

Georgios is standing in our doorway with another figure, someone I don't recognize from this distance. We never have visitors. I nearly drop the jar of water I'm carrying. I set it down carefully on the ground, trying to calm the pounding of my heart. I don't want to have to walk all the way back to collect more if I spill it all. I won't let myself hope that this could be Orestes. I walk over to them as steadily as I can, my eyes raking the stranger for details. He's roughly dressed, a peasant like Georgios—like me, now. There's nothing familiar about him, and no light of recognition in his eyes either.

"Word has come of Odysseus." Georgios looks more concerned about it than I would expect. I can't see why it matters so much.

"Odysseus?" I shake my head, confused. "Isn't he dead?"

"He's alive, all these years after the war," Georgios says. "Everyone's talking about it, what they've heard."

"What does it have to do with us?" *How lucky for Odysseus' wife and son*, I think, *to have him back even so many years after the war has ended*. I would have waited so gladly, for twice as long, if it meant my father could come home alive.

The stranger clears his throat. "He's been to all kinds of places. There are many stories, but no one in Mycenae is allowed to talk about it."

"Why not?"

He lowers his voice, even though there is no one visible anywhere near our deserted shack. "The queen and Aegisthus have spies, constantly searching for information about your brother. But they aren't always so discreet, especially when their lips are loosened by wine. One of them recently returned from Sparta, where they are always monitoring in case King Menelaus takes Orestes in, and he overheard the whole tale recounted to the king by a herald."

I can hardly breathe. "Did Odysseus find Orestes? Is that it?"

He shakes his head. "Not Orestes, no. It's said that Odysseus went to far stranger places; that Poseidon wanted him dead and wrecked his ships; that he had to battle monsters and seek refuge with nymphs; and that it was Athena who guided him home at last."

Georgios interrupts. "Odysseus claims he's been to the Underworld. That he spoke to the dead."

I feel a cold thrill. "How can that be?"

"I don't know. But they're saying he spoke to Agamemnon."

It's like a blow, his words striking me with so much force I think my legs will give way. "He saw my father." I won't believe it; it can't be true. If it is true, then I can't bear it. Why would Odysseus, a man we all thought dead years ago, get to see my father and come home alive and triumphant? Rage crackles in my chest.

Georgios steps toward me, concerned, reaching out to steady me. "I thought you'd want to know."

"I do! Please, tell me the rest of it," I say to the other man. He has all my attention. I need to know what they're saying about my father, true or not.

"He sailed across the ocean to find the place, a stream that runs underground all the way to the house of Hades. He poured libations there and sacrificed a ram, to lure out the dead. The ghosts rose up to drink its blood, and Agamemnon was among them."

I close my eyes, overwhelmed for a moment by the thought of it. My father, the king, the leader of the greatest army the world had ever known, reduced to a wraith tussling over sheep's blood. "Go on."

"He told Odysseus how he died, how shameful it was to be killed by a treacherous wife. He begged for news of his son, but Odysseus knew nothing of Orestes, or anything that had happened here. They wept together over it all."

"Elektra?" Georgios' voice is solicitous.

"Everyone knows." I can imagine them all talking, the gossip igniting again, the burn of their words. My father was murdered so long ago, but still his death goes unavenged, still Orestes is gone and no one dares breathe a whisper about him. And now this. A rumor of Agamemnon of the House of Atreus, the head of our family, mourning the loss of his reputation, which tarnishes more every day that his son does not come back to bring retribution to his killers. "Everyone knows what a disappointment we are to him."

Georgios is shaking his head vehemently. "You are no disappointment. Not you, not Orestes either. That's not what this means. It is Clytemnestra who betrayed him, it is only her that people will condemn for his suffering."

"How can they not condemn us too?" I can hear how shrill I sound. "My father is languishing in the Underworld, desperate for justice, and it still hasn't been done!"

"That's not your fault."

"He can't find peace," I whisper, and Georgios takes me in his arms. I wish that he wouldn't. I don't want comfort. There is no comfort for my father; nothing but a bitter thirst for revenge, a worse suffering than Tantalus in his desolate lake.

···

I rise early and stand in the doorway, watching the stars fade from the dim sky. He comes up behind me, places his hands upon my shoulders, and when I stay still and unresponsive, I hear him sigh as he retreats. Always, my thoughts return to that pit where my father's ghost broods. Wearily, I turn back inside and search within the shadows for the little knife I have just for this purpose. I feel Georgios' eyes following me as I pull a lock of my hair forward and slice it free with the blade. The ends of it are jagged and uneven, and I feel a fierce pleasure imagining my wild appearance. It is years since a handmaid combed my hair and fussed at my clothes, trying to transform me into something other than what I am. I revel in my unadorned clothes and my knotted hair: *Clytemnestra's daughter*, they whisper when they see me, noting my degradation, how she lets me live. I scorn the pity I get from the other women; I never speak of my sufferings, and so they believe I have been cast out from the palace, that she married me to a commoner to exile me from the family. No one would ever believe I walked away willingly.

"Are you taking another offering to the tomb?" Georgios asks. His tone is quiet and measured.

"My father is dead," I answer. "This is all I can do for him."

"And when you've hacked off every hair from your head?"

"Do you think I shouldn't honor him anymore?"

"Of course you should honor him. I honor him too."

"Then why do you disapprove?"

He looks so tired. "I'm sorry that I let you hear about Agamemnon in the Underworld. It hurts me too, to think about it."

I sink onto the stool opposite him. "It was you who told me who my family really are. How we've suffered, how we're cursed. The gods can't forgive us until we put it right. We have to make the murderers pay."

He drops his gaze, stares at the table. "I don't know if that's true anymore."

My breath hisses out of me. "What do you mean?"

"Is that what the gods want?" he asks. "If we do it, will they be satisfied?"

"I don't understand."

"You've lived under the shadow of this curse all your life. You've learned from your family's history that blood must be repaid in blood. But I've been farming, working on your father's lands for all of mine. I learned it from my father, how everything dies away and comes back again, how we sow and reap the harvest every year. I've learned the rhythms of the seasons, and how even the harshest of winters is always followed by spring." He straightens his shoulders, sits up taller. "It's a cycle constantly changing, but always the same. And your family's curse, it's like that too. All the way back to Tantalus, your ancestors have done the same thing to one another. There's a terrible crime, unbearable pain and then the lashing out of vengeance, and then it all begins again. I know it's hard for you to see it, when the storms are raging and it's impossible to imagine the dead earth will ever bring forth crops again. But it does—it always does."

"But if we don't take vengeance, if my brother lets our father's killers go unpunished, what will the gods do then? It's our duty." I clutch at the lock of hair in my hand, the only thing I have to give my father until Orestes comes back. "A woman can't kill her husband, a usurper can't steal a throne, and neither of them pay. It's an insult to the gods, to my family, to everything."

"But where does it stop?" His vehemence startles me. I've never known Georgios like this before. "Can't you see that it just goes on, over and over? The gods demand their justice, but we suffer for it, every time."

"Well, what else should we do?"

"You could be happy." He reaches across the table for my hand. "You escaped your mother and Aegisthus. They have nothing to do with your life anymore."

I snatch my hand away. "My father is dead because of them."

"Many people have dead fathers, Elektra."

The same words I flung at Clytemnestra once, more or less. I had spat my recriminations at her: many mothers lost daughters, it happens every day, why did she have to spend her life planning revenge? I shift uncomfortably. I hate to remember that I am her daughter; hate to think that what I know, I learned from her. "Perhaps those people have other family," I say at last. "But I lost my brother too. I lost everything."

"We sent Orestes to live with his uncle, a king," Georgios says. "We sent him to a safe and happy life."

Impatience consumes me. "How can we know that? If he lives as a prince, it's no guarantee of safety. He could be thrown from his horse while hunting, gored by a wild boar, hurtled from his chariot in a race and mangled beneath its wheels. Disease could take him; no wealth in the world can cure a plague. He could be in the earth, buried without the touch of his sister's hand." *And if he isn't dead*, I don't add, *perhaps he enjoys the luxury of his life too much to jeopardize it*. Like Chrysothemis, who never spoke a word against our mother, who hid away in the comforts of her rich marriage, who would never have dared to endure as I have done. I haven't seen her since her wedding day, since her husband took her away to another palace, far from here, away from me and any chance I might have had to convince her to be my ally, my sister once again. She might as well be dead too; all of them rotting in the ground while Clytemnestra sips wine and laughs with a man wearing Agamemnon's robes, sitting on Agamemnon's throne, wielding Agamemnon's scepter.

"You're right, we don't know," Georgios says. "But you are alive, and your life is passing you by. Like Atlas, holding up the weight of the sky, never able to move beneath its terrible weight, you are stuck, waiting for Orestes to lift it from you." His sadness is palpable. "But I've always been here at your side, and I can bear it with you, if you'll let me. If you can let it go."

I can't hear this. It's the difference between me and Georgios, the ever-widening gulf that divides us from each other. He isn't blood of the House of Atreus. His father died peacefully, slipping from the mortal world as though he fell asleep. Georgios doesn't have to imagine his father's shade weeping in the Underworld, begging for justice, or he'd know it's worth a lifetime of suffering. Clutching my shorn lock, I stride back to the door. "I won't give up, even if you're tired of waiting," I say.

Outside, the air is still and dark, the world not yet stirring. The only sound I can hear is the plaintive chirrup of the nightingale, a soft and lonely note in the silence. Her song is so sad. I wonder, does she remember when she was a human girl? Philomela, seized by her own sister's husband, who tore out her tongue when he was done with her so that she could never speak of it. She wove her testimony into a tapestry instead, and when her sister saw it, she slaughtered her own son and fed him to his father in punishment. Now Philomela has a voice again, transformed by the gods into this sad and solitary bird whose lament rings out alone in the darkness before the first light of day. Her family's legend is so like the stories they tell of my own ancestors, but no gods have taken pity on me, given me feathers and wings to fly away from this place. I'm condemned as much as she to only give voice to sorrow, but I must bear it in this body.

Again and again, I am drawn to the tomb. Over and over, I leave offerings: a twist of hair, a cup of wine poured onto the ground, the first fruits of spring, which I leave to molder until they collapse in upon their own spongy rot. I don't know why I still do it. I ache to believe that my father is there, somewhere in the caverns of the earth; that he knows how I honor him; that it brings him some solace in the grim shadows beneath. But my piety and devotion go unrewarded.

I have wept long and loud at the silent stone entrance countless times, scratched my nails through the flesh of my cheeks and ground my teeth in despair. But today, the tears that well up in my eyes are effortless; they fall gently and spatter on the ground with no anguish and no rage. My father is not here. If he had lived, I would be some-where else. I would have children of my own; I would not be trapped in this humble marriage. My brother would be here, not raised by strangers in some distant land. I've lived with this for too long, and the weight of my misery is crushing me.

Dawn is beginning to creep into the dim sky. I can't bring myself to enter the tomb today. I turn away from the arched gateway, into the glow of the rising sun. The sliver of gleaming orange climbing above the horizon blinds me for a moment, and I squint into the glare of fiery light. A dark shape looms from the dazzle of dawn. The shape of a man. For a moment, I think it is my father, risen and returned to me, whole and entire.

As he steps forward, though, my whole body shakes. Another fig-ure draws beside him.

"Are you here to mourn the king?" the first figure asks. His eyes roam intently over me, pausing on the lock of hair I still hold.

I nod, not trusting myself to speak.

"Are you a loyal serf of the palace, perhaps?" He sounds dubious.

I stare at his face. It's rude of me, but I am so very far past caring about that. In my mind's eye, I see a frightened little boy, and I will my memory to show me him, so that I can compare his face to the stranger standing in front of me. How could it be anyone else? But he does not recognize me. Am I really so changed by the passing of years? They certainly haven't been kind to me. The same is not true for him. The man standing before me, strong and vital, is no longer a boy, but I think I can see in the shape of his face and the set of his features, the child I knew.

"I am no serf," I answer. "I look like one, I'm sure." I take a deep breath. "I am here to grieve my father, Agamemnon, who lies in this tomb behind."

His eyes widen. "You are Elektra?"

I have hardly been able to tear my eyes away from him, but I glance at the figure who accompanies him. It's enough for me to see how handsome he is, standing so confident and sure. I feel a flush of shame heat my cheeks, at once embarrassed by how unkempt and disheveled I have allowed myself to become; how much I have reveled in my own disgrace. "I am." I square my shoulders, tilt my head up in defiance.

"Then take this as evidence; you are my sister, and I have come back as promised!" His face shines with excitement and he thrusts his hand forward.

A bronze dagger lies across his palm, a tiny golden lion snarling at its tip. The hunters, just as I remember, pressing forward with spears and shields.

"Orestes," I whisper.

He is nodding, his eyes aglow. "We've come back to Mycenae, Pylades and I." He gestures to the other man, who dips his head respectfully toward me.

I feel a panicky kind of excitement. It's all I've dreamed of, the only thing that has sustained me since my father died—and at last it's happening.

"Come, sit before you fall," he says, taking my elbow and guiding me to the low wall at the side of the pathway. I sit gratefully on the stone. "I must make my offerings at my father's grave; it's why we came here first."

"I come here every morning," I answer dazedly.

I wait for them as the warm light of day spills across the ground, the song of other birds joining the lonely nightingale. A laugh bubbles absurdly from my throat, and I clamp my hand over my mouth. I raise my face to the sun's spreading rays and try to compose it into an expression of serious reflection.

"Elektra? Are you well?"

I press my lips together, not trusting myself to speak at all.

"She must be overcome," I hear Pylades murmur. "This is all unexpected to her."

Orestes hovers for a moment before sitting beside me. I feel the tug between solicitousness and uncertainty within him; so long has passed since we were together.

"Why now?" I choke out at last. "I had given up hope, I had thought . . . why are you here?"

"I'm ready," he says. He glances toward his friend. "Is there somewhere we can go, somewhere safe that you know? Somewhere we can talk?"

"You can come to my home," I tell him. "But—"

He looks questioningly at me. "Yes?"

I straighten my shoulders, willing my body not to betray my embarrassment. "It's not the kind of place you're used to. It's no palace."

"It's where my sister lives." His voice is soft. "There's nowhere I would rather visit."

Still, I feel as though my body will cave in on itself when I bring them back to our miserable little dwelling. There is nothing in here to make it a home. It's dark and shadowed, an unloved and unlovely thing. I'd thought myself past such worldly considerations, but when I look at it, I see it through their eyes. Georgios appears, and I want to shrivel even further into myself.

"Elektra?"

"It's my brother," I announce. "Orestes has returned—at last."

A shock of joy fills his face, his smile so genuine. It's a long time since I've seen him look this way.

Orestes steps forward, almost shyly. I wonder if he's trying to conceal his disgust for our home. But, just as Georgios seems truly happy to see him, Orestes looks sincerely pleased as well. "Do you remember me?" he asks.

Georgios laughs, opening his arms wide. "Of course I do!"

And they're clapping each other on the back, both of them beaming.

I hug my arms around myself. "Let's go outside." I don't want any of them to see how rattled I feel.

"Of course," says Georgios. "Go and sit outside; it's so dark in here. I'll bring you food and drink, you must be tired from your journey." He ushers us all through the door, back into the sunshine, and he disappears. It's my role, of course, to do this, to welcome the guests and feed them, but it's just another thing I've got wrong, another courtesy I've forgotten.

"I'm sorry I can't welcome you in a better way," I say, as we find a shaded patch beneath the spreading branches of a great tree.

Orestes shakes his head. "I'm sorry that this is what's happened to you."

The blood rises in my cheeks and he catches himself, realizing how it sounds.

"I mean, I'm sorry that you were driven out of your home," he says. "I'm sure you're far happier here, with Georgios, than there with—with them, but it shouldn't be this way. It shouldn't be them, living in our father's palace and us both exiled from it."

I swallow. I'm not so much an exile as a runaway. She didn't make me leave. But then, she made it impossible for me to stay—and for Orestes too. I watch him, casting his gaze all around, taking it in. I feel almost shy of him, the man he's become and all the experiences he's had without me. For the first ten years of his life, I shaped his world. Now I don't know him at all.

Georgios comes out, and I wince at the sight of the bitter black bread he's brought for them. Orestes, though, takes it as if he's truly grateful. I wave it away, squirming a little. Everything is wrong. I'm sitting with them, my husband is serving us, I'm horribly aware of how unevenly I have hacked away at my hair. I wish I had been prepared. I wish I'd known the day he was coming. I wish I'd made myself hold on to my faith that he would.

Georgios, apparently far more at ease with my brother than I am, starts asking the questions I can't manage. "Why have you come now? What prompted your journey?"

Orestes' forehead creases. "I've lived comfortably in Phocis," he says. "The king was always kind to me, he treated me like his own son—like Pylades—so we have lived like brothers." He glances at his friend and takes a long breath. "But however welcoming and loving my home there was, I knew it was not my true home. It burned at me always, to think of Mycenae."

My shoulders relax a little at this. "You didn't forget us."

His eyes widen. "How could I? Elektra, I thought about you every day, about what might be happening to you here. You were so brave, smuggling me away, saving me from what Aegisthus would have done. I knew I had to come back, that I had to repay you."

I can feel tears brimming in my eyes. I lock my hands together, pressing my fingernails into the back of each hand. The sharp pain holds me fast to the moment, keeps me from crumbling.

Orestes shifts uncomfortably. "Still, I wrestled with the thought of coming back and what that would mean—what it would require of me."

What they're here to do is no easy task. Though, in this moment, I wonder if perhaps it could be. If I imagine channeling all my pain into the fall of an axe, if I think of Aegisthus beneath it, and Clytemnestra too . . . I pause, horrified for a second to think perhaps this is what my mother felt when she saw her beacons blazing. Revolted by the thought of sharing any communion with her, however brief, I shake my head vehemently. "She drugged our father and imprisoned him in a net she wove." The words are bitter in my mouth. "Then she cut him down with an axe. Her own husband. The gods cannot tolerate a woman who does such a thing." I don't add that she has lived a peaceful life since that day. Zeus didn't hurl his thunderbolt at her; no god intervened. I have heard of them striding out into the fray and heat of battle in Troy to save the mortals that they loved and to take vengeance on those who offended them. I can't understand how Clytemnestra has lived on unmolested so many years since her crime.

"I know," Orestes answers. "Every night when I lay down and

closed my eyes, I saw our father. His shade, weeping in the Underworld at his dishonor." He swallows. "So I visited the oracle of Apollo and begged for answers."

"What did the oracle say?" I'm intent on my brother.

Orestes' eyes meet mine. "I told the priests what I sought to ask. They gave me instructions, what I needed to do and how I should approach the Pythia. I was purified there; I made my offerings and bore laurel wreaths to the temple. She sat in shadows, wreathed in smoke. I thought the words would desert me altogether, but I found them somehow. I needed to know. Her eyes rolled back in her head while the god spoke to her. And at last, she told me the answer." The world falls still and silent around us before he speaks again. "Our father will not rest while his killers live. If I turn away from my duty, if I fail to avenge him through my own cowardice, Apollo's priestess warned me that the god will punish me. It's his command." His head drops forward into his hands. "There is no choice."

He has returned a fully grown man, but seeing him here, sitting on the ground, his knees drawn up in this attitude of despair, I see the boy I sent away, and my heart twists. I don't doubt the words of the oracle. Even as I pity him, I can feel a swell building up within me, something akin to excitement. "She has been no mother to you," I tell him quietly. "You recoil from it because it is a dreadful deed, I know, and you are a good man. But only you can let our father rest. Only you can bring justice to the house of Atreus."

He lifts his head. "Can I?"

Before I can answer, Pylades reaches out and grips Orestes' shoulder. "You aren't alone," he says.

I stare at the two of them. The weight of their duty hanging so heavy above them, their courage in the face of it. It sends a strange thrill through my body, a feeling of roots uncoiling, branches stretching out toward the light. I don't turn my eyes away from Pylades this time, I look him full in the face—and he looks back at me.

He is like a soldier, I think. His shoulders are broad, his dark beard and heavy brows making him look so much older and more serious than Orestes. I wonder if this is how my father looked when he marched back to Mycenae, a Spartan army at his back, to reclaim the palace as his own. This brave hero, accompanying his friend on his righteous quest—this is the kind of man I know my father would have chosen for me, if I had lived the life I was born to live.

"Have courage, Orestes," I whisper. "You are Agamemnon's son." I feel it, humming through the three of us, binding us together, too terrible to speak aloud, but too vital for us to shrink from.

"How will you do it?" Georgios' voice breaks the moment, making me jump.

For a moment, I can see the moisture gleaming in Orestes' eyes, the tiny quiver of his lip, but then a determined blankness sweeps his face. It's so like Clytemnestra that nausea swirls in my stomach. "We've come back in stealth," he says. "We didn't want more blood-shed than—than is necessary." He gulps a little, looking down.

"We planned to arrive as strangers to Mycenae," Pylades inter-jects. "Strangers bringing news of the death of Orestes, looking for a reward for bringing such good tidings to Aegisthus. That way, we'll get an audience with him. He'll want to hear all about it. He'll think the threat to him is gone—if Agamemnon's son is dead, he will believe himself secure at last. That's when we'll have our chance."

I'm nodding along to every word he says.

"Could that be enough?" Orestes bursts out. "If we cut Aegisthus down there and then, is that enough?" He looks ashamed as soon as he's said it, but there is a defiance in the jut of his chin. *Clytemnestra's son*, I think again. I'm horrified to see so much of her in his features, instead of my father.

There is a long silence. "The oracle said to avenge our father's killers," I say. "You know that she was the one with the axe. More than that! You remember, don't you, how she was in front of Aegisthus al-ways, how it was her making the plans?"

"What if it was him who told her to do it?" Orestes suggests. His eyes are hopeful, turning to me, seeking out his big sister to help him again.

"You know the truth," I tell him softly.

"Elektra," Georgios says, and I flinch. He catches my expression and hesitates before he goes on. "She is your mother." His earlier words hang between us: when he told me revenge was futile, that it would only lead to more misery. He's wrong though, I know it. We can end it, but only if we're brave enough.

"It's the command of Apollo," I say. "Our family has ignored the words of the gods before, and all of us suffer for it. How can we risk it?"

"She's right," says Pylades and relief bolsters me.

"I don't want to disobey the oracle," Orestes says slowly.

I hardly dare to breathe as he considers what we've said. The threat he heard at Delphi, that Apollo will punish him if he leaves his father's murderers untouched, it tells me that we're right, even if what we're talking about is a horrifying thing. But what I don't say out loud is that, if he kills her, it will be the Erinyes who come for him instead. The snake-haired Erinyes with their baleful eyes and their unquenchable desire for revenge on those who kill their own parent. Apollo might punish a son who doesn't avenge his father, but they will chase down a son who kills his mother. My brother will be pursued to the very ends of the earth, their wings beating through the sky and blocking out the light of the sun. Their barking cries will ring in his ears day and night, their thirst for torment unabated.

But at least then she will be dead, along with her lover. It's easy for Orestes to prevaricate. He's lived in comfort since I sent him away, while I've been here, living in disgrace and squalor. I've borne the burden of suffering for what she's done, and no one else has had to. Not yet.

"Do you think it's the only way to fulfill Apollo's instruction?" he asks me.

I'm sitting here, rank and disheveled, a peasant on the ground, but these three men are turning to me, waiting to hear what I will say. I am Agamemnon's daughter. I feel the truth of it, and that my future is unfolding before me, this life I've found myself in feels only temporary. I can see a chance ahead, something different at last. I turn my face up to the sun, like a flower ready to bloom.

Orestes has always trusted me. I told him what the world was years ago, and he's never had reason to doubt me. If I tell him, if I set this in motion, it will happen.

For the first time, the power is mine.

"It's the only way, Orestes." I lean forward and rest my hand on his. His eyes meet mine and I feel a shudder, as though I'm looking right into the cracks of his soul. "You have to kill her."

It's agreed that Orestes and Pylades will spend the night hidden in our hut. I watch them talking, making their preparations, praying to the gods for success. I know it's ours. We won't fail.

Georgios is busy all day, working as always, and I make more than my usual half-hearted attempt to prepare food and impose some sense of order upon our home. I sweep the floor, startling the spiders, who scuttle frantically away from the brush I've barely ever wielded. I grind up barley for the dense, tasteless bread I bake, and slice wrinkled vegetables for broth. Chores that I despise, carried out today with a willingness that surprises me as much as the poor spiders. I'm jerky, restless, full of agitation as I work. The smell and the smoke churn together nauseatingly, and my head pounds in time with my throbbing pulse. All the while, I keep glancing out to Orestes and Pylades, pacing up and down outside or coming in to sit across from one another in exactly the same attitude, leaning forward with their elbows on their knees, intent in conversation. But for all their preoccupation, I feel Pylades' eyes rest on me when I look away from them. I even steal away when I can and drag a comb through my uneven hair, twisting it back neatly into a coiled braid, my fingers remembering the steps from years ago, when I last cared. I smooth down my tattered skirt. I wish for a moment I'd accepted some of the fine linens Clytemnestra had tried to bring me, some of the gems. But why would I think that? How could I sit with my brother, wearing clothes that she had given me? However self-conscious I feel before them both, I have my dignity. I'm not besmirched by anything she's touched. I drum my fingers impatiently.

Georgios returns with the sunset. He takes in the scene: a fire burning in the hearth, the smell of simmering broth, my brother and Pylades seated at our table, where the ripe fruit I've gathered lies on a plate at the center, beside a jug of wine. His mouth twists in a half smile that tugs at my heart for a moment, and unexpected tears rise up, blurring my vision.

I curse as the broth I'm stirring splashes up over the side of the pot, droplets scalding my arm.

"Are you alright?" he asks.

"Fine," I snap. "It was just clumsiness."

"Come with me." He takes my unburned arm and steers me away from the other men. I follow him outside into the darkening air. The breeze stirs, the scent of jasmine heavy and sweet, the stars glimmering to life above the red-streaked horizon. I wish that he wouldn't speak at all, that we could leave it all unsaid.

"After tomorrow," he says. He clears his throat, looking down, not meeting my eyes. I fasten my gaze on the sinking sun. Everything is infected by its crimson glow; the whole world inflamed and seething. "After it's done—" He stops.

I won't make him be the one to say it. I think I owe him that much, at least, not to draw it out any longer. "I won't come back here."

I can hear the splintering of his heart in the silence. My old friend, Georgios. The only person who understood, who remembered the Agamemnon that I did. We'd constructed him together, the king whose absence has carved the shape of our lives.

"I knew when I married you that you deserve more in life than I could ever give you," he says quietly.

I wish I could have been happy in poverty, happy with Georgios: a good man with an honest heart. But I'm a daughter of the House of Atreus. If Orestes must take responsibility for bringing justice to our father's killers, I can't turn away from my duty to live the life that Agamemnon wanted for me. He hoped I'd bring our family honor with a glorious marriage, a great alliance. "I'm sorry," I tell Georgios, and although the words are inadequate, I mean them.

I leave him, standing alone in the gathering darkness. I go back into the house, where my brother is; a house that has been empty of feeling for so long. Now it is alive and vital. At last, it is our time, and though the magnitude of it makes me unsteady, grasping the doorway for support as I walk inside, I won't let sympathy pull me back. There's no place for weakness, not anymore.

CHAPTER THIRTY-FIVE

Clytemnestra

Sleep comes easily to me now, every night. I don't roam the palace in darkness anymore, don't stare out across the black void searching for distant flames. My slumber isn't restful, though; it drops over me, heavy as a cloak, trapping me in its folds. I feel my dead limbs, inert and useless while my mind races frantically like the thrumming wings of a hummingbird. I lie paralyzed as the nightmares come.

I'm back in the torchlit chamber with the old slave-woman telling me of the curse that creeps throughout our home, twisting around our family, ensnaring us all. My belly rises in front of me, taut and round, but when I see the baby stirring restlessly beneath the thin fabric of my dress, I can't make out the shape of a foot kicking from inside my womb. It looks like the heavy roll of coiled flesh, something snakelike and inhuman slithering in my body. Then I'm in my chamber, a swaddled bundle in the crib, but it writhes, a mass of scuttling creatures wrapped in its folds, and when they swarm out, I cannot scream, cannot see, cannot move, as they tear at my flesh, as they gnaw down to my bones. The dream tilts dizzyingly; I am outside on a vast plain, rubble smoking in the distance, the ground sticky under my feet, and it oozes up between my toes, a glistening crimson. There is a river, but its waters run red and dark; the earth is choked with the dead and the blood spills out to the ocean itself, staining its vast waters.

When I wake, gasping, in the early light, the horror clings to me like a vapor.

CHAPTER THIRTY-SIX

Elektra

There is no possibility of sleep tonight. Orestes and Pylades spread their cloaks on the floor in the center of our home in hope of some kind of rest. Georgios, when he comes back inside, studiously avoiding my eye, lies down near to them. I perch anxiously on our hard, narrow bed, listening to the sound of their breathing. The restlessness surging inside me won't let me relax for a single moment. When I can't bear to even sit any longer, I rise noiselessly and creep past them, outside to the garden. Liquid shadows ooze pitch black from every direction. The tormented screech of an owl makes me freeze, the flesh of my arms prickling into goose bumps. This is the ancient, primordial night that could have given rise to the vengeful Erinyes. It was from such a depth of darkness that they first stepped, from the formless oceans of Chaos, coursing with insatiable fury. Or else, they rose up from the blood-clotted earth, baying in vengeance when the titan Kronos sliced his own father open with the blade of his sickle. Whichever story is true, I can feel their presence, the stench of them carried on the breeze, the serpent-slithering sound of them, the cold hiss of their breath at my ear.

Let them come for me if they will. Whatever torment they devise, it cannot be worse than what I've lived already.

However brave my thoughts, I still yelp when I feel a hand closing around my elbow, and I spin around in the darkness, my chest heaving.

"Sorry," he says. It isn't Georgios' voice, nor is it Orestes'.

"Pylades?"

"I heard you get up," he says. "I can't sleep either."

I should go back inside at once. But a recklessness has taken hold of me. This man is my brother's trusted friend, I'm safe with him, and I can't deny my curiosity about him any longer. "Why did you come to Mycenae?" I need to know.

"Orestes is my friend." His voice is calm and measured, soothing in the black void. "I saw how distraught he was at the oracle's word. I wouldn't let him do this alone."

I try to discern his face through the gloom. The shroud of night makes me feel freer, bolder. "Did you ever know our father?"

"No. I was an infant when the forces sailed to Troy. Even though my mother is a daughter of Atreus, she never knew him either."

So Pylades doesn't bring me any new stories of my father. I'm not as disappointed as I might have been. Tonight, when everything in me shifts with unease and anticipation, all at once I don't want to immerse myself in the past. Tomorrow is the day that we move into the future.

"Are you afraid?" he asks me.

I laugh. "Why would I be afraid? You can only fear if you have something to lose, and I have nothing."

He doesn't answer, and the silence between us is taut, crackling with an edge I don't recognize.

"If I was afraid, I would think of the shade of our father, begging us to take revenge," I say at last. "The image of his ghost, not able to rest. That's the only thing that could make me afraid."

"Agamemnon will rest tomorrow," Pylades says. "Orestes, though—"

"We will be here for Orestes." I'm firm and decisive, on steady ground. "Whatever happens after—we can care for him."

"What about your husband?"

"He married me to help me escape Aegisthus," I say. "It is no true marriage."

I don't want to think about Georgios; I want only to think of Agamemnon. But then, I'm standing here with the son of Agamemnon's sister—this is the closest I could be to my father in the living world, besides Orestes. The thought of it rears hungrily inside me for an instant, a sweep of flame, searing and sweet at once.

"We should go back inside," he says.

For the first time since the night I knew my father was coming home, I am impatient for the dawn. The world sings with promise again, my hope as fragile but tangible as glass, and this time our mother won't shatter it. This time, we are the strong ones, and there is nothing that she can do. I follow him back inside, and, although I thought it impossible, when I lie back on the lumpy bed, my eyes flicker closed and I sleep.

CHAPTER THIRTY-SEVEN

Clytemnestra

As I dress in the amber silence of dawn, I marvel that I have stayed here so long. What holds me to Mycenae? The comfort and luxuries of this palace are rotten illusions, its grandeur decaying from within. I'm not afraid to walk away from it all, alone. I have never cared what anyone else might think, and I have wits enough to live on my own, as far away from here as I can get.

I used to think incessantly of Iphigenia, lost in the realm of the dead, roaming that shadowy kingdom, unable to find peace. Now, instead, I find memories gushing forth: a child shrieking with laughter, running through the pillars of the courtyard, her hair streaming behind her. Her face, creased in concentration as she learned to master the loom; her beaming pride in the tapestries she wove. I think of all the mothers of Troy. Hecabe watching her sons slaughtered on its battlefield, her daughters dragged away onto Greek ships. Andromache's infant torn from her arms and hurled from a Trojan tower onto the unforgiving rocks beneath. I hope they heard of Agamemnon's death. I hope it brought them some comfort to know the commander who brought the armies to their shore met such a brutal end. At least I can give them that, if nothing else. But since I did it, I don't know what there is to propel me on anymore. Now that my thoughts are unclouded by anger, the desire for revenge no longer burns through my veins; I can feel my sadness in its cold and crystal purity.

And with the ebbing away of my rage, I look at the sleeping Aegisthus and wonder what ever bound me to him at all. Did we ever speak of anything except retribution? If we did, I can't recall it, can't summon any intimacy or find any common ground between us. When I look at him, I only think of my missing children. It's their absence, rather than Iphigenia's, that causes the aching in my heart.

And if I leave, will Elektra find some peace at last? I wonder if all I can offer to my embittered daughter is my absence.

Noiselessly, I gather my jewelry: thick gold bracelets and earrings that glint in the dim room, shining necklaces of carnelian and lapis lazuli, wealth to buy me safe passage anywhere I want in the world. Elektra disdained it all when she married, but if I'm gone and she realizes she only degrades herself and not me by association, maybe she'll tire of flaunting her poverty.

The sun climbs higher in the sky, light washes through the room, and I am ready to go, to leave all this behind me. But before I can take a step, a great clamor shatters the quiet—men's voices, shouting outside the palace. And, to my horror, the din resolves itself into the words I dread the most to hear.

CHAPTER THIRTY-EIGHT

Elektra

"E lektra, wake up." Orestes' voice is soft as I swim back into consciousness, bewildered for a second until it floods back to me, and I sit bolt upright.

"Is it time?" I ask. "Is it nearly morning?"

"It is. We must go now—but Elektra, you don't have to come with us. We can come back for you, when it's over."

I push the threadbare coverlet away from me and rise to my feet. "I'm coming with you." I look around the room. "Where's Pylades?"

"Waiting outside."

Georgios is sitting at the table, watching us. When I look toward him, he darts his gaze away. Orestes makes as though to step outside, but I clutch at his cloak. "I'm ready," I say. Orestes looks between Georgios and me, a question on his face, but I shake my head determinedly. The last thing I want is a goodbye, anything that might cloud my head. I did wonder, briefly, if Georgios would speak anyway, but he just looks down at the worn wood. I feel a spasm of pity for him, but I shove it down, far inside, and follow Orestes through the door for the very last time.

I'm taking nothing with me. There is nothing there that I want.

We walk in silence along the winding path toward the palace. The sky is beginning to lighten, feathers of pink and gold spiraling upward. Pylades keeps a watchful gaze on Orestes, his eyes thoughtful and solicitous. Orestes' face is grim, carved into something that sets a tiny quaking in my stomach. As we get closer, my head swirls and my eyes roll up, toward the roof of the palace.

They're up there. Hunched black figures, crouching atop the sprawling edifice. Three of them, silhouetted against the sky, monstrous blots on the rose light of dawn. I dart a panicked glance at Orestes, but his face is still granite, staring straight ahead. I wonder if Pylades would be able to see them, even if he looked up.

"Come," I whisper through my clenched teeth. "Come for us, then."

I think I see one of them twist her head around, extend her neck. A flurry of hissing coils stir up around her, weaving their blunt heads in and out. I see myself, pinioned by her glare, spread and flayed on the earth under the pitiless blaze of it, my soul bare and cringing. But we keep on walking, those cold eyes following our every step.

It isn't real, I think, a kind of hysteria bubbling up in my throat, though I know it is. We reach the gates, and Pylades and Orestes look at each other and nod. I grab hold of a pillar, my knees buckling, and they start shouting, hollering the words over and over, the words they know will draw Aegisthus out. I want to stand up tall and brave; I want him to see my face, too, before he dies, but I can't make myself step forward. I can see him, running toward my brother, that hated face alight with hope, and there is no hesitation from Orestes. His legs don't give way, he doesn't cling to a stone column for strength. I don't think he hears the scrape of snake-flesh against the unfurling wings, don't think he catches the reek of their breath as they poise, ready, high above us. I can taste their eagerness for it, the satisfaction rippling through the air—and then, all at once, my vision clears, the scarlet tint to everything drains away and I can stand alone. Their hunger is mine.

CHAPTER THIRTY-NINE

Clytemnestra

"Orestes is dead!" they are calling, over and over again, hammering on the palace doors.

I'm frozen in shock, but Aegisthus moves like lightning. He leaps from the bed, dragging a cloak around his shoulders as he runs to the door. In his feverish excitement, he doesn't wait for his guards, his usual escorts everywhere he goes.

I race after him, pulling on my own cloak over my dress, my hair streaming loose behind me as I run through the palace, silent except for the relentless din of these terrible voices, through the great doors at the front. And in that moment, I know it all.

My son is alive. He stands before Aegisthus, his sword raised, his face contorted in a snarl of fury. Aegisthus is frozen, his arms outstretched, a tableau of confusion. The world falls still and quiet, the menace palpable in the air.

Orestes strikes.

His blade sinks into Aegisthus' neck. I watch, mute, as he staggers backward, his face bright with astonishment, his desperate eyes meeting mine one last time, and then he falls.

I stare at the blood blooming across the ground. I can hear the sharp scrape of Orestes' breath. Footsteps frantic within the palace, the guards coming too late.

I drag my eyes away from the scene in front, holding my hand to stay the advancing guards. "Your master is dead," I say. My voice is so steady. "You will not harm my son."

I can feel their resentment and panic. The usurper is defeated, and they know how he and I are hated in Mycenae. Agamemnon may not be mourned by many, but his conquering son returned from exile will find far more sympathy and loyalty here than they will. I see them weighing it up: to run or to fight.

With a look of loathing, the foremost of them turns away. I watch as, one by one, the others follow.

So, it is me, alone in front of my children. I sense the watching eyes of the household staff, the slaves gathered breathlessly in the halls, peering out to see the outcome, but when I turn back to face Orestes, Elektra, and their companion, I am entirely alone. No one else steps forward to speak in my defense; I have no friend to plead for me or stand between me and their justice. I am glad of it. I want nobody else in the living world at my side.

Orestes is not looking back at me. His hands are tightly clenched around his sword, his knuckles white, but he gazes resolutely away. I take a step closer to him, and then another. I can see a sheen of sweat break out across his forehead.

If I beg him for my life, I think, *he will grant it.* I could plead that I am his mother; that what I did was simple justice; that he has taken his revenge on the man who took his father's throne, and must not commit a monstrous crime before the gods, here in the newly risen light of day. I know that I could break his already wavering resolve. It's what everyone expects me to do. It's why he won't look into my face.

Elektra must know it too, because she says his name. Her tone is one of warning, a rebuke to his hesitation. When I glance at her, she is alight with righteous hatred.

No jewels would ever buy a softening of her fervor, I realize. There truly is nothing I can give Elektra that would ease one tiny part of her suffering. As long as I am alive, it devours her from within. I shudder at the memory of the swarming creatures of my dream, the teeth against my bone, and everything slides sideways in my vision. And, swimming back up from the past, there is Cassandra, holding my gaze, asking me silently to be released in death.

I wanted nothing but peace for Iphigenia for ten years. Elektra has known nothing but seething, relentless disquiet for twice that long. The same torment rends my son in two. I thought this morning when I rose, intent upon escape, that the only gift I could give my children was for me to be gone from them forever.

I hope it eases their pain, I think, as I close my eyes.

CHAPTER FORTY

Elektra

I'm still staring, mesmerized by the sight of the life draining from Aegisthus in crimson rivulets, when she orders the guards away. I lift my head. What does she have planned? Is she about to beg for her life? Does she not want them to bear witness to her weakness? Does she think she can negotiate with us, that anything she says will move us?

I'm as motionless as the night-black hags above us, the monstrous crones leaning over to watch.

Do it, I urge him silently. *What are you waiting for? Just do it.*

But he doesn't move. He's looking into her face and, against my will, my eyes are dragged toward it too. Her true face. No smirk, no smooth mask of indifference, no cold complacency. The years have fallen away from her, and I can see the mother I remember, from before Iphigenia died, from before any of this happened. The mother who bathed my forehead when I was ill, who prayed to the gods for her children's health, who sang and told us stories. Her love for us, a love I thought had burned away on my sister's funeral pyre.

A mother that Orestes doesn't remember, one he never had a chance to know, because of what she did. I'm back there, imprisoned behind a locked door, and my father is marching home, but I'll never see him, never feel his arms around me again. He won't know what kind of woman I've grown into; that I'm not the kind of woman I should have been. She stole it from us all. I remember the elation I felt when I thought he was returning and then the shock of her guards' hands on my body, dragging me away at her command.

"Orestes," I say. I don't need to say any more. He can hear everything we've already gone over, everything I've told him. He stiffens, stands taller, ready.

I don't look away, not once. I scrape my fist against the stone wall beside me so the blood trickles through my fingers, but I don't take my eyes from my brother. I thought he would crumple; that he didn't have it in him. But then I think perhaps he hears it too—the unfurling of leathery wings, the malevolent hiss of the serpents seeping down from the palace roof. My pulse beats deafeningly in my skull, a relentless drumbeat. He cannot fail me, I want to scream at him that he mustn't, but I don't have to say anything else at all.

I watch her fall. I hear the clatter of Orestes' sword as he drops it to the floor beside her body.

I hear them take flight. Their heavy, ungainly bodies swooping from on high. The shrill bark as they circle overhead, their furious gaze centered on the killer in the courtyard. I hear my brother cry out to Apollo as they dive, and I flinch away as they sweep so close to me that my hair flies back in their wake and my ears ring with their howls. I duck down, but they pass me by, intent upon Orestes alone.

My eyes are screwed tightly shut, but I know it's Pylades who's standing at my side. The warmth of his hand on my shoulder brings me back, steadies my racing heart and heaving breath. "It's done, Elektra," he is saying, and I'm crying. It's over, at last, it is over.

I straighten myself up and Pylades' hand clasps mine. The scene in the courtyard shudders and then resolves itself. The bodies, there in the center. Orestes, kneeling, his hands clamped to his head, his eyes desperate, his mouth stretched into a grimace as though he endures the most unthinkable torment. The creatures are gone to our eyes, they are beyond what Pylades and I can see. It's Orestes' burden to bear, but we will be with him. Together, we draw him to his feet and although he whimpers, he acquiesces.

Pylades makes as if to lead us out, but I hesitate and shake him off.

Orestes is hunched, his shoulders shaking, his face buried in his cloak, but I can't look away. Her cloak, only loosely held around her shoulders before, lies on the floor where it fell beside her, a bright pool of fine cloth. I'm hypnotized by it: the intricate stitching, the rich purple hues of its folds. Orestes is muttering, a low, intense stream of indecipherable words that rises to panic as I take a step, and then another, toward her.

Everything around me is so vivid and clear, the earth so steady beneath my feet as I move closer. I pick up the cloak and the scent of her perfume drifts out on the warm air. I close my eyes and breathe it in. Then I lay the cloak over her body, smoothing it out so that it lies straight, and I stand back.

After a few moments, I feel the gentle touch of Pylades' hand on my back and I turn away. I don't need to look any longer. The sun is a bright gold disc, climbing in the blue sky. Our arms around my brother, we walk away together, into its light.

EPILOGUE

There's a chill in the air today, a bitter edge to the wind that whips up froth on the tips of the waves. The water surges around my ankles and retreats, leaving the sand slick and dark gold beneath my feet. Out on the horizon, clouds and sea merge into one another in a gray haze.

These are the easiest days. In the silent, barren months when the earth yields nothing, when Demeter wanders in grief for her daughter, this is when I feel a communion with the world. I spent so much of my life in a dreary vigil; the stillness and the sorrow will always feel comfortingly familiar.

But as Georgios told me once, it doesn't last forever. I thought it would, when we were driven from Mycenae, helpless against the wrathful Erinyes. Pylades and I could do nothing but wipe the spittle and foam from Orestes' chin, bathe his fevered brow and murmur soothing words as he writhed and screamed, his terrified eyes fixed on a vision we could never see. He couldn't take the throne in his madness. The kingdom was in disarray, and when we fled to Phocis to ask for help from Pylades' father, he cast us out, horrified by our crime.

If I thought I'd known what scorn and censure were before, I was wrong. No friends would take us, polluted as we were by matricide. I was grieved to find there was so little loyalty to my father, that no one wanted to help his children. Even Menelaus condemned us, his love for Helen greater than for his long-dead brother. I felt as though we were turned away from every home in Greece.

How long the journey to Delphi took us, I don't like to think. Every step of the way, Pylades and I held Orestes up between us. Every night was shattered by the sound of his shrieks and his whimpering pleas for them to leave him at last. I had time enough to think of Georgios' words, how he had seen the curse plague each generation of our family, how the merciless gods demanded more and more from us. In those dark days, I truly thought it would be unending.

And then, at the oracle, respite at last. It's murky in my memory: a cave wreathed in smoke; the whites of the priestess's eyes gleaming; a stream of incantations I couldn't understand. Fire and blood; bones wrapped in fat burning on the altar, flames roaring and sparks streaming all the way up to Mount Olympus. Cool water on my face. Petals crushed into oil, the sweet fragrance perfuming the air. A quiet dawn, Orestes' face calm, upturned to the rising sun.

After the purification was done, our crime atoned for, still I couldn't go back to Mycenae. All I'd ever known there was pain and yearning. There was nothing there for me. Orestes, free of his pursuers, went alone. And Pylades brought me here, to make our home, a remote settlement far away from anywhere that we might be recognized.

The calm gray mist on the horizon makes me think of my father's shade, somewhere beneath the earth. No longer tormented by his thwarted vengeance. We gave him peace, and knowing that brings me solace. The ache in my chest is still there, but it only hurts with the memory of the wound. It's healed enough that I can think of her as well, if I make myself. Drifting along in a dim and shadowy cavern, silver ripples darting across the surface of the dark river, the shadow of a girl at her side. They walk together in my mind, the girl's laughter as sweet as I remember. Our mother smiling back.

The baby swaddled at my chest stirs and her eyelids flutter. She sighs and snuggles closer, lulled by my movement. She sleeps most soundly here, close to me, unburdened by any knowledge of what I've done. And who will tell her now? Orestes' rule of Mycenae is just and fair. He gave Georgios a place in his court, a voice of reason and mercy to help him unite the shattered kingdom, to build it up stronger than ever before. My once-humble friend, raised up from his lowly station to power and influence, an adviser to the king. Meanwhile, I, my father's hope for our family, live an unobtrusive life here, happy to be forgotten by the rest of the world.

Rain begins to fall, softly at first, but quickly gathering pace. I pull my cloak around my daughter, sheltering her little head from the wind coming up from the east, and, holding her close to my heart, I turn back home.

ACKNOWLEDGMENTS

I knew that writing a second novel is often notoriously difficult, but *Elektra* was also written throughout a global pandemic and repeated lockdowns, which added an extra level of challenge. It really wouldn't have happened without the support I had from so many people.

Firstly, my agent, Juliet Mushens, who loved the novel from the first draft and made me believe in it too. Thank you for suggesting the title as well! Also, thank you to the whole Mushens Entertainment team, who are a glorious, leopard-print dream of brilliant women.

To my editors, Kate Stephenson and Caroline Bleeke: you understood exactly what this book needed to be before I did, and I'm so deeply grateful for all of your insight and perception. You make the editing process so rewarding and completely transformative.

Thank you to everyone at Wildfire and Flatiron for your faith, encouragement, and tireless work. I'm so proud to be published by you!

An enormous thank you to the designers of my book covers, Joanne O'Neill and Micaela Alcaino, who have created such incredibly beautiful artwork. I am so in awe of your talent.

I was staggered by the energy and enthusiasm of everyone working on the publicity and marketing for *Ariadne*—thank you so much to Amelia Possanza, Caitlin Raynor, Lucie Sharpe, and Vicky Beddow for making it so exciting to launch a novel in a pandemic!

Thank you to the classics community online and all of the authors and readers who have been so supportive. Thank you, Elodie Harper, for your friendship and all the events we have done together, which have been such a joy.

My Northern women writers' group has been the best support in this very strange year. Bee Barker Horton and Steph Pomfrett—the yoga, the letters, the socks, the Zoom calls, and the cheerleading have been the brightest light, and I can't wait for the world to find out how incredibly talented you both are.

Jo Murricane, superstar photographer and friend, thank you for all the website help, drinking gin and champagne together, and sharing all the many homeschool woes.

Thank you to all of my family, my lovely nephews and niece in particular! Evan, Luke, Thomas, Eoin, and Thea—thanks for being excited for me, for all the quizzes, and for being so brilliant. Thanks, Sally, Gabriel, Catherine, Alan, Lucy, Tim, Gemma, Steve, and Lynne, for everything.

To my parents, Tom and Angela, words will never express all of my gratitude and my love.

Alex, Ted, and Joseph, you make anything possible, and everything I write is for you, always.

Read on for a bonus scene from

ELEKTRA

Clytemnestra

Ten years after the start of the Trojan War . . .

The darkness stretches on, unbroken by even the faintest pinprick of light. When I close my eyes, it makes no difference except that I feel hemmed in, so I open them and search the blackness before me. I know the shape of the mountains rising in the distance, although their bulk is indistinguishable in the night.

I could be in the still black depths of the ocean. I could be in the cavernous belly of a beast. I could be in the loneliest corner of the Underworld, unable to see my own hand reaching through the chill, dank emptiness.

I am not in any of those places. I let them flit across my mind, wondering idly if any of them will spark fear. It has been so long since I felt afraid. I wonder if I am still capable of it.

Not that the dark has ever held any terrors for me, I suppose. We would always sit out here when we were first married, he and I, and let the night sink in around us. Behind us, a distant torch might flicker in the palace, but we would watch as the dying rays of the sun were swallowed up by the black. Sipping wine on cushioned couches, comfortable in our youthful arrogance, we would look unflinchingly into the abyss that loomed as unknowable as our future.

He was giddy then, uncertain and eager. He would reach out in the dark, let my hair fall through his fingers like water and cup my cheek in his palm like something precious. I can still hear the catch of his breath in his throat, the tentative, disbelieving wonder of it.

I have walked here so many nights both before and since he was gone. I know every flagstone, the shape of the walls, where each column looms and the spaces between them. I walked here night after night with her, soothing her and singing to her. I can see her now, caught in my memory so clearly, standing just between these two pillars with that luminous blend of excitement and fear stamped across her face as she looked to me for an answer, for approval, for the reassurance I was foolish enough to give so freely.

When I press my hand to that cold stone, I wonder if my fingers rest just where hers did. If I could find the exact place, if I press my palm to that very spot, I wonder if somewhere in this endless night that envelops us both she will feel the touch of my hand against hers and her eyes will spring open.

I let my forehead rest against the cool marble. That the pain can still overwhelm me like this, that it can still steal my breath in the same shock as the first time, that the wrongness of it still racks my bones—I suppose it surprises me. I feel nothing else with the same intensity now. Even the sting of the cruel words spat at me earlier this evening has faded away. I heard nothing that I didn't already know anyway.

I have become the master of my passions, and I know now that however strong the grip of this agony, however fiercely it squeezes me in its terrible embrace, it can never break me. I turn my head away, back to the lost horizon, and in the murk and enclosing gloom, I see what I have been looking for.

A flicker of orange, glinting on the farthest hill. A flame in the darkness. A beacon.

And then its twin on the neighboring peak and then another and another and another springing to life in reply. A chain of light, dazzling fire burning through the night, getting ever closer.

I have waited ten years to see this. I am poised, alert, so very alive as I watch the sequence. One beacon lighting after another. Now I hear the distant cries of the watchmen, scrambling to their stations at the signal.

Ten years. Ten years have passed since I gave the command. The words scraped harshly against my throat then, rasping out through raw skin, inflamed by the sobs that racked my body. Every night since then I have waited here for this moment. My tears dried long ago, and I thought that all of my emotions save the grief had shriveled away with them. But now I watch the fire leap toward me and something within me answers it. A kindling among dry leaves, a spark catching on dusty ground. A flame dancing into life.

ABOUT THE AUTHOR

Due to a lifelong fascination with ancient Greek mythology, Jennifer Saint studied classics at King's College London. She spent the next thirteen years as an English teacher, sharing a love of literature and creative writing with her students. She is the internationally bestselling author of *Elektra* and *Ariadne*.